THE BIG DISRUPTER

A THRILLER

Paul Markun

P

PORTFOLIO

MILL VALLEY, CALIFORNIA

This book is a work of fiction. Names, characters, businesses, organizations, places, events, and incidents are the product of the author's imagination and are used fictitiously. Any resemblance to actual persons, living or dead, events, or locales is entirely coincidental.

Copyright © 2014 by Paul Markun

All rights reserved.
Published in the United States by PORTFOLIO, Mill Valley, California.

www.paulmarkun.com

Cover Design by theBookDesigners
Photo of Paul Markun by Teal Thomsen Photography

Cataloging-in-Publication Data is on file with the Library of Congress.

ISBN: 099148620X
ISBN: 978-0-9914862-0-5

V9.0

DEDICATION

FOR MY WIFE, RACHEL, MY INSPIRATION . . . .

ACKNOWLEDGEMENTS

My sincere thanks to:

Developmental and content editor Caroline Tolley, whose talent turned random lightning into electricity

My technology advisors, especially Dr. Woody Weaver for his security and cyber crime advice

Copy editor Nancy Russell for her mastery of detail

William Hauser, founder and president of Two Degrees, the first one-for-one food company, for his insight into young social entrepreneurial success

Beta reader Neal Marlens for his keen writer's eye and encouragement

A lifetime of mountain town and off-the-grid ski friends, especially Jim Hughes for backcountry and avalanche advice

Colleagues and friends in the venture capital community, in particular Scott Halsted and his creative insight

Natalia Boyadjiev and Yana Kopilevich for their business and cultural knowledge of all things Ukrainian and beta reading feedback

Debbie Newmyer of Outlaw Productions for unfailing beta reader candor and enthusiasm

Police Chief Jim Wickham for sharing his vast experience at the field level in law enforcement

My young energy drink experts and advisors and, in addition, Bob Biggart for his lifetime of insight into the beverage industry landscape

Entrepreneur and visionary Joel Schatz for painting a rich canvas of global characters and experiences

My wife Rachel (beta reader extraordinaire), children Peter, Leslie, and David, and my family and friends who encouraged or otherwise motivated me with threats and ridicule

And finally, my Starting Five, Gordon Rich, Bobby Newmyer, Wayne Robertson, Jerry McIntosh, and Stuart Hollander, gone before 50 but still living in our minds.

CONTENTS

Title Page	I
Copyright	II
Dedication	III
Acknowledgements	V

CONTENTS

Chapter 1 - Saturday, March 15th	1
Chapter 2 - Wednesday, September 25th — Six Months Earlier	5
Chapter 3 - Thursday morning, September 26th	20
Chapter 4 - Thursday afternoon, September 26th	31
Chapter 5 - Friday, September 27th Telluride, Colorado	46
Chapter 6 - Friday, September 27th	58
Chapter 7 - Friday afternoon, September 27th	69
Chapter 8 - Monday, September 30th	74
Chapter 9 - Wednesday, October 2nd	88
Chapter 10 - Thursday, October 3rd	103
Chapter 11 - Tuesday, October 8th — Wednesday, October 9th	107
Chapter 12 - Thursday, October 24th	118
Chapter 13 - Monday, October 28th — Tuesday October 29th	124
Chapter 14 - Friday, November 8th	130
Chapter 15 - Tuesday, November 12th	139
Chapter 16 - Thursday, November 14th	148
Chapter 17 - Friday, November 29th	157
Chapter 18 - Tuesday December 10th — Wednesday, December 11th	166
Chapter 19 - Thursday, December 12th	174

Chapter 20 - Wednesday, December 18th	178
Chapter 21 - Thursday, December 19th	184
Chapter 22 - Monday, December 23rd	192
Chapter 23 - Tuesday, December 24th	196
Chapter 24 - Saturday, January 4th	201
Chapter 25 - Thursday, January 9th —Friday, January 10th	205
Chapter 26 - Friday, mid morning, January 10th	217
Chapter 27 - Friday, late morning, January 10th	222
Chapter 28 - Saturday, January 11th	235
Chapter 29 - Sunday, January 12th	249
Chapter 30 - Monday, January 13th —Tuesday, January 14th	253
Chapter 31 - Tuesday, January 21st	260
Chapter 32 - Wednesday, February 12th	270
Chapter 33 - Friday, February 21st	278
Chapter 34 - Saturday, February 22nd —Sunday, February 23rd	286
Chapter 35 - Wednesday, February 26th	289
Chapter 36 - Monday, March 3rd	300
Chapter 37 - Tuesday, March 4th	312
Chapter 38 - Friday March 14th	320
Chapter 39 - Saturday, March 15th —Present Time	329
Chapter 40 - Sunday, March 16th	332
Chapter 41 - Sunday night, March 16th — Monday morning, March 17th	342
Chapter 42 - Monday, March 17th	357
Chapter 43 - Tuesday, March 18th	363
Chapter 44 - Wednesday, March 19th	369
Chapter 45 - Thursday, March 20th	374
Chapter 46 - Thursday evening, March 20th	381
Chapter 47 - Thursday night, March 20th	393
Chapter 48 - Friday, March 21st	402
Chapter 49 - Friday morning, March 28th — Final Day of the Big Disrupter	412
Chapter 50 - Friday afternoon, March 28th	415

Chapter 51 - Early Saturday morning, March 29th	419
Chapter 52 - Late Saturday morning, March 29th	421
Chapter 53 - Saturday noon, March 29th	428
Chapter 54 - Friday, April 4th	436
Connect with the Author	447
About the Author	449

1

SATURDAY, MARCH 15TH

The rapping broke the quiet. His eyes scraped open and stung in the bright light. As he blinked, grit etched his eyelids. The rapping became pounding. Then the shriek of wood ripping apart signaled an invasion. He jerked up.

Full daylight flooded the room. *What? Where was he?*

A woman groaned. *She was right next to him.*

He turned to see a tussle of brown wavy hair and creamy skin. Pinched and puffy eyes looked back at him.

Who was she?

Smooth contours wiggled under the sheet. *She's naked! What is going on here?* He rose unsteadily. His temples buzzed like bees. His head felt like a thick hive of angry blood.

BevGlobe. Crowds. Party.

With a crash the door swung, jamming against a liquor cabinet lying on its side.

He staggered toward a pile of clothing.

Beyond a sliding glass door palm trees swayed outside. Or was the apartment building swaying? *Whose apartment?* His head was killing him.

"Open the door. Open or we'll shoot through it."

He had a gun? He felt his heart trying to escape from his body. He turned to the woman. "Come with me." The sheet dropped as he grabbed her hand. In the other she held a cell phone.

"I can't," she moaned, pulling back.

"You have to! We can get out this way." He tugged her over to the sliding glass door, yanking it aside.

The cool wind rushed across his face and body. He eyed the fire escape ladder, dropping to somewhere he couldn't see.

She jerked free, recoiling.

"We need to leave!" He didn't wait for a reply. He swung his arm low and heaved her on his shoulder.

"Dammit, put me down!" He winced as her fingers tore at his hair, bucking on his shoulder.

"This is the only way." He clamped his arm tighter around her taut torso.

"Stop blocking the door!" The voice yelled, angrier.

Her nails dug into his back and her legs pumped. "Leave me alone. Just go." He stooped down, scraping through the sliding door.

They teetered at the top of the rusty fire escape ladder, the breeze blowing his on nakedness.

A loud snap signaled the collapse of the cabinet. Footsteps approached.

He started down the metal steps, swaying. They pitched forward and she screamed.

Toppling, he thrust her onto the landing before dropping. He flailed in mid-air. It seemed like forever. Then his hand caught the railing. He jerked like a flag on a pole. He hung by one hand, forearm burning. Four stories below the trash-covered alley waved.

With a kick his foot curled around a rusting tread. He rolled his shoulder to grasp the other rail and pulled himself back on the ladder. He looked up, chest heaving and adrenaline flowing like rocket fuel.

The brunette was crouched on the landing above him, her eyes huge.

"Take my hand—we'll climb down together."

She grabbed the railing of the fire escape with both hands in a wide defiant stance. Her cell phone went tumbling.

He stared at her as the phone dropped away. She had a wild attractiveness. A curvy dancer's body and blown hair. Tough. And soft. Her head shook angrily following the distant smack of her cell phone. She swore.

"Come on! The guy has a gun."

"I can't go."

"Why? You're safe with me."

She glanced back inside. "I'm with them." Her mouth curled, like she spat out a bad taste. "I'm sorry. Go before they hear me. Take the video." She nodded toward the smashed cell phone.

She was playing him? A vague memory of her flashed from last night. *What did we do?* He felt betrayed.

She looked back as someone rushed onto the balcony. He turned and leaped down the stairs, five at a time, hands sliding along the side rails.

The landing rattled as he pounded onto it. His feet went numb. He forced himself forward. Crossing the grates, he glanced up to see a bald head and something shiny pointed at him.

He jumped down the next flight of stairs, his hands chafing and burning as they slid on the metal. He hit the next landing so hard it rang like a gong. He rolled, then raced down another flight. He'd dropped three stories, one to go. The final landing was spring loaded, swinging down under his weight. It clanged as he jumped off and skidded across the alley's loose gravel.

Directly across the hot blacktop was a graffiti-covered cinderblock wall. Along its top, razor wire spiraled in both directions. Something industrial loomed behind. Overflowing dumpsters, rusty shopping carts, and garbage cans were scattered everywhere.

He picked up the smashed cell phone. The screen was a dense white spider web of cracks, shattered but still stuck together. *What was on this?*

He noticed blood on the ground and he realized his feet were cut. Suddenly he felt exposed, standing in the alley, naked. *He needed clothes. And shoes.*

He looked up to the apartment, spotting the bald head on the fire escape aiming a long lens at him. He whirled and ran down the alley. His arms and legs felt alien, like disjointed puppet parts. He struggled, mystified at how slowly he gained speed. Trash, chain link, and dumpsters floated by, like streaming visions. Industrial buildings and more razor wire loomed above. Loud gasps echoed strangely in his head. Suddenly he wondered, *Where are my friends?* Then he thought he heard her voice.

He twisted his head back, legs still pumping forward. Something flashed. Was it her or someone gaining on him? He surged forward as he strained his neck rearward, eyes searching. He heard a truck motor and the fast scraping of metal. He spun forward and saw an orange dumpster sliding at him like a steel wall.

2

WEDNESDAY, SEPTEMBER 25TH — SIX MONTHS EARLIER

The grassy park was a small oasis on San Francisco's Nob Hill, surrounded by ornate historic buildings and hotels. A few smokers in tuxedos fidgeted on a nearby bench. Lionel Lane was pacing. As he circled the gingko tree his hand gripped and scraped the rough bark, tingling his skin. His ear was numb from jamming the phone in concentration with his CPA, Harding Liu.

"Give it to me straight, Harding. Net out the annual numbers."

"We got killed on unsold inventory. Five million. We'll lose money this quarter and probably for the year."

"Five million, that's painful. And what's our cash situation?"

"Not good."

That's what accountants say when it's a disaster, he thought. "Not good, meaning stretch out receivables and renegotiate our leases?" Lionel asked hopefully.

"Not good, meaning we need ten million dollars cash in thirty days." He heard Harding sigh. This guy took the numbers to heart.

Lionel's tuxedo tightened. He put a raw finger under his collar and tugged at it, trying to get more air.

A couple, also in their twenties and dressed for a black tie event, approached on the sidewalk. As they walked the evening light was fading around them.

"Maui is awesome, but everyone goes there," she complained, shaking her styled blond tresses.

"Kauai has unbelievable natural beauty," he enthused, waving a tan hand across an imaginary sunset, his heavy watch glittering.

"Too boring." She smoothed her long silk sleeves.

"We don't want you bored. How about the Big Island? And we helicopter to private beaches and the parties?" He offered his elbow with a confident smile, jutting his jaw. His short dark hair was gelled and immaculately parted. Lionel wondered if the guy thought he was a modern day Don Draper.

She squeezed his arm. "Could we take the firm's Gulfstream?" she gushed. "God, it'd be so great not to have to fly commercial."

A yellow, black, and white striped caterpillar, days away from being a monarch butterfly, dropped from the gingko tree. It inched across the sidewalk. Lionel stared while his accountant rattled off more numbers.

As he committed to the Gulfstream a loud splat spurted from under the young man's Gucci loafer.

"Gross," she cried, pulling away from him. He danced on one foot, as though he'd been shot. He toppled awkwardly, catching himself on a bench.

"It's a stupid . . . I don't know, insect thing." He scraped his foot on the grass.

"You must get your shoes cleaned before the dinner. That's disgusting." She pinched her face and her nose rose up, pig-like.

"The concierge can take care of it. After we make our entrance, honey." They hurried across the street toward the Fairmont Hotel. Approaching the red carpet they slowed, then went arm-in-arm and smiled as if sharing a joke.

"Lionel. Lionel, are you listening?"

"I am, Harding. We've burned through all our cash and need a new investor pronto."

"Exactly."

"Kind of ironic. I'm invited to this entrepreneur beauty contest tonight, told to prepare to be an award finalist, yet we're about to go bankrupt." Lionel moved over to a bench and dropped heavily, shoving hard against the back as though he could shape it into something comfortable. He ran his fingers through his long, golden brown hair, massaging his temples.

"You're better at doing good than being cautious, Lionel. Your business model requires deeper pockets than we have right now."

Lionel didn't reply. Harding continued. "Anyway, isn't that event you're attending tonight swarming with investor types?"

"Yeah, some just walked by. Real nature lovers." His stomach rumbled and he realized he hadn't eaten all day. *No wonder he felt light headed.*

Harding paused. "Well, you are great at schmoozing when you want to. And it's time to land some other people's money. You're tapped—the seven million you invested from your Rock Rags sale to Consolidated Clothing is used up."

Consolidated. Staying with that corporate giant would have been much safer. Ugh. But emotionally impossible.

Lionel considered Harding's advice as he stared at the long line of Teslas, BMWs, and black limos carrying attendees to the event. Beautifully coiffed women in colorful silk gowns draped with glittering jewels were escorted from the cars. *Did they earn it like me, or inherit it?* He sighed. Either way, a wealthy investor could save them. But self-promoting and parading like a best-in-show trained poodle? It made him sick.

"How long, Harding?"

"We've got thirty days, tops. And then it's bankruptcy." Harding's voice hesitated, thinning. "And layoffs."

Lionel heard the pain in Harding's voice. He was so different from the controller of Consolidated. That guy looked like a vulture. Huge watery pools behind bifocal goggles that wrapped a wrinkly head, with an annoying metallic voice. His job was to rape your company, rip it apart, and screw down operations for the convenience of HQ. Not like Harding. Harding cared about the company culture.

"I hear you, Harding. A lot of people are counting on us."

"You're a lot more savvy now, Lionel. This isn't like Consolidated. I know you hate losing any control, but an outside investment is our only hope."

He was right. His due diligence with Consolidated was naïve. The CEOs of companies they had previously acquired lied to him. They sold out. He had been shocked when he arrived. But not as surprised as they were, when he walked out of Consolidated at the end of the first week, with half his cash left on the table.

Lionel sighed. "Okay, Harding, the event is starting. I have to go." Lionel hung up and hunched over. The hotel tower loomed overhead.

The bow tie, the cummerbund, and the tuxedo felt like phony packaging. He fought the urge to rip them off. He sat stewing in a funk for several minutes.

Suddenly Lionel smelled something. He raised his face, sniffing and recognizing the scent of an alluring perfume, a familiar mixture, wafting across from the cars. It was getting darker and he scanned the fading figures as they paraded to the entrance, now illuminated by twinkling lights.

She was here? His curiosity excited him. Energy flowed. *Come on Lionel, go big or go home.* He jumped to his feet, pounding his fist into his palm. He threw back his shoulders and headed toward the bright lights of the Fairmont Hotel ballroom, to the Social Entrepreneur of the Year banquet.

***

Leah Barko's jeweled glasses sparkled in the chandelier light. Her torrent of black hair formed endless tight curls well beyond her shoulders. She stood close to Lionel, rocking toward his face with a voice that boomed from her short and heavy frame. Bright and sharp-witted, passionately devoted to her work, she was a star reporter for the *National Times Journal*. Lionel knew her intensity often intimidated others. He drank it in.

"Lionel, I don't think I've seen you in a tuxedo before. It's always the outdoorsy clothing or some crazy wingsuit or ski gear."

"That's exactly what I'd rather be wearing. I think clothes should be functional, not for show. God, I sound like my dad. If the plain-speaking cabinetmaker were still alive he'd have hated this event. Ah, Leah, please don't quote me on that."

"Your dad sounds wise. But I'll protect his legacy. So, what's the latest on Double Vision? How many free nutritional meals have you given out now?" Leah's face got even closer.

"We've donated over fifty million meals. You and I need to get your editor to spring for a trip to Africa or Haiti and see our work in action—I'd get you up-front access. You'd win a Pulitzer and we'd help feed kids."

Leah reached out and gave Lionel's arm a squeeze. "Let's keep working on that."

He could talk to Leah forever. With her intellect and the amazing people she interviewed, she was like a Wikipedia hologram. But right now he needed to follow up with investors.

Lionel started scanning the room, momentarily forgetting about Leah. He spotted several familiar VCs mingling nearby.

"Lionel, it looks like you have a lot on your mind. But I've got some news you might want to hear."

Lionel looked back at her flashing glasses. "Sorry, Leah. I'd much rather talk with you than schmooze with VCs, but . . ."

"I understand," she interrupted, brushing his arm. "Listen." She lowered her voice. "Your company, Double Vision, is going to be one of the five finalists selected to present tonight."

"Really?" *Leah was like a big sister who always looked out for him.* He cupped her elbow. "How do you know?"

"I got a quick look at the list."

"Seriously? Winning would skyrocket exposure and validation." *We'd definitely get the financing we need.*

"Yes. So be ready to present and rock them."

Lionel broke into a wide grin. "Well, I'm glad that presentation I had to submit wasn't a waste of time. Tell me, anyone else I know?"

"SocialLending. They got new funding from Hank Welcher of Falconvest. You know Hank, of course."

"He's on my radar." Hank Welcher funded SocialLending? He wondered if that meant Hank was passing on him. *He needed to find Hank.* Lionel dropped his hand.

"One other thing."

"What's that?"

"The press is supposed to be ready for a surprise announcement tonight. Something big."

"I could use something big."

A familiar throaty voice distracted Lionel. And then he smelled the perfume. He turned as an attractive African American woman with a rapid-fire delivery played to the throng following her. He recognized several VCs, including some from Axlewright Capital. Her eyes met his briefly. She arched a distinctive eyebrow before continuing by in conversation.

Maxine. He *had* recognized that scent. His thoughts rushed back to the last time he saw her. The closing dinner on the San Francisco waterfront. The deal that made his first millions. And she had helped, although on the opposite side, consulting the buyer, Consolidated Clothing. She finally agreed to a secret rendezvous once the business of the deal was done. At her hotel room he was sensitive about being too aggressive. She took the lead and nearly swallowed his tongue. They romped in her hotel bed peeling away inhibitions, then talked until dawn watching the sunrise over the bay. Their passion peaked so high he wondered if they could ever recreate it. And then they didn't. "Lionel. Who is that?" Leah persisted.

He shook his head slightly, finally breathing. "Maxine Gold."

"So that's Maxine Gold," said Leah, her voice rising. She leaned even closer. "I hear she's brilliant. Do you know her?"

"The last time I saw her in San Francisco she still worked for McKinsey, as one of the advisers to Consolidated on the Rock Rags deal. We negotiated on opposite sides for months. A few years before that we went to college together."

"Oh, fellow Harvard connection. Tell me, is she everything I've heard?"

He hadn't expected to see her here. Or maybe he didn't want to see her under these circumstances.

"And more. She is such a committed capitalist, she'd make Adam Smith blush. I'm surprised to see her at a social entrepreneurship event." He remembered their last conversation, when he told her he had quit Consolidated. She told him he was foolish to leave cash on the table. He replied that he hadn't expected the purchase price to include his soul. She never understood.

"She recently joined the board of CBO, the Community Bootstrap Organization," Leah informed him.

"She must be advising them on the financial side, not the humanitarian aspects."

"I sense a little competition, Lionel. Can I quote you?"

He looked back at her. "It's not a competition, Leah. We are just so different."

Leah tilted her head, curls bunching against her glasses. She brushed them back then whispered, "Her company is also on that list of five finalists."

Oh, no. Maxine always got what she pursued. He tried to remain nonchalant with Leah. "I'm not surprised."

"Keep that confidential. Good luck tonight."

"You're the best, Leah." He kissed her cheek as they parted.

Lionel sought out several VCs. He flashed a confident smile as he pumped hands and projected success, pulling several aside for brief conversations. Then he found Hank Welcher, founder and senior partner at Falconvest. They moved to a quiet corner and Lionel pitched him on a new round of funding. Hank listened passively.

"So, what do you think, Hank?"

Hank rocked on his heels as if in deep thought. Short, with a shaved and shiny pale dome, his squinting gray eyes radiated intensity. Then he leaned forward, his mouth in a permanent grin as he spoke. It made his upper teeth stick out as though poised to bite.

"Lionel, we already like everything about Double Vision. You and the product. But nutritional drinks are growing slowly. Lots of competition. So your valuation still comes in much lower than you'd like. I can't make an investment but I could offer a bridge loan, backed by your equity." He shrugged and his hands extended upward, his face an expression of sympathy.

"Meaning?"

"I could lend you ten million for your cash flow issues. If you turn things around in six months, good for you. If not, my loan converts to equity in Double Vision." The face was neutral now, hands at his side.

This was the moment of truth. *Be nonchalant.* Lionel sipped his drink. "How much equity are you asking for?"

"Ninety percent." Hank's expression didn't waver.

Lionel jolted, nearly spilling his drink. "Ouch. I want to invite you in, not hand you the keys."

Hank reached out and pressed Lionel's arm. "It's not a lack of trust in you. It's the way the numbers work. We need most of the stock to justify the risk. You hit your numbers in six months and you keep your company." His tone softened. "If you believe in your projections, then it's a good deal for you."

Lionel braved a smile. "Thanks Hank, I appreciate your perspective. But it's contrary to my instincts." *I'd do better in a bankruptcy workout.*

Before they could continue, the lights flickered.

"If you're confident, it's the best way. Think about it."

"Appreciate your thinking of me, Hank."

As the wealthy attendees moved toward their seats, Lionel moved closer to bankruptcy.

***

The lights in the Grand Ballroom were dimmed. Three spotlights cut a sparkling swath over the tables and lit the stage. Champagne glasses bubbled on white tablecloths. The room was buzzing as the president of Schwab and Young, Jules Longsworth, announced the five finalists for the Social Entrepreneur of the Year award. Longsworth had a short wave of white hair combed straight back and scholar-like glasses. His large handlebar mustache, brilliant white under the gleaming lights, distinguished him.

All five finalists were seated together near the front. Several ladies wore bright party dresses with plunging necklines. One young rebel anchored his tuxedo with neon statement sneakers and jeans, fidgeting and constantly texting. Lionel and Maxine were placed together, as the only finalists without companions.

Maxine had been distant and cool to Lionel when they were initially seated. "Hello Lionel," she said, extending a hand. She then immediately turned in the opposite direction. "Jan Swenson, tell me how Sweet Boomerang is taking the Midwest by storm." *Okay,* he thought, *was it because we're competing, or choosing to forget the past?*

Lionel glanced sideways and watched Maxine's intent focus on the speaker. Her ivory dress glistened against her raven black hair and dark brown skin. The short sleeves exposed strong but graceful shoulders and arms. A zipper made a dramatic angle from her throat to her right breast, suggestive but not revealing.

She is such a class act. Yes, but an act. There really is such a thing as trying too hard to be perfect, he thought.

"But first, before we hear from our finalists, I have a very special announcement." Jules Longsworth waited for the crowd to quiet down.

"The Entrepreneur of the Year organization has attracted an extremely magnanimous donor, who would like to remain anonymous. Even though the donor prefers to be behind the scenes, they have imagined and enabled an award that will have a major impact. The donor personally named this social entrepreneurship award the Big Disrupter."

The crowd grew quiet as Longsworth paused. He smoothed his white handlebar mustache.

"Six months from tonight, the judges, which include the Schwab and Young committee and myself, will announce the winner. The purpose of the Big Disrupter is to significantly advance social entrepreneurship and cause disruption in the market, for the betterment of mankind. And here is the difference." He paused, putting one finger high in the air.

"This award is for one billion dollars."

Someone screamed. Another shouted, "A billion!" Longsworth's sincere expression, constant under the bright lights, made it clear he wasn't joking. Several people stood up and started applauding. Then one thousand people came to their feet in a thunderous ovation.

The buzz was unstoppable. Eventually Longsworth's numerous motions for quiet were honored. "Thank you, thank you one and all." He withdrew a card from his breast pocket. "Allow me to read a brief statement from our benefactor." He cleared his throat.

"To all you brilliant social entrepreneurs out there, continue your magic to make the world better. Your vision of helping others far exceeds the narcissism of conventional entrepreneurs who believe that more eyeballs and clicks and revenue change the world for good." Longsworth looked up from the card from which he was reading. "Technology alone doesn't. But you do. In this next six months continue to do your best. No matter what, you and others will win. And you may also win this new prize, the Big Disrupter. It's a big Nobel Prize for social entrepreneurs."

The crowd started cheering again, interrupting Longsworth. He waited and then continued.

"And the reason it is so large . . ." Hoots interrupted again.

"The reason it is so large is because we believe the winner will serve as a catalyst to change both their respective industry and the world for the better. You will be one of, if not *the,* dominant leader in your industry with enormous influence. The influence a market leader exerts cannot be underestimated. We've heard about Big Brother and Big Data. Now let's make the world better with the Big Disrupter. Go forth and disrupt *Big.*"

Longsworth strode offstage as the audience roared.

A billion dollars, thought Lionel. *Unfreakingbelievable! This literally was the chance of a lifetime.*

***

It took five minutes for Jules Longsworth to restore order once he returned to the stage.

"First I want to thank all of you, the many generous attendees who support the Social Entrepreneur of the Year award. While the Big Disrupter Award is six months away, certainly the honor bestowed tonight is splendid recognition. This year our five finalists will each provide a brief presentation."

Jules Longsworth called up the first CEO finalist. Jan Swenson popped up from the seat across from Lionel like a rising firework. Her shock of blond hair topped a five-foot-two effervescent sparkler. She presented with infectious enthusiasm about Sweet Boomerang, which made and sold chocolates and candies in Minneapolis, Chicago, and other Midwestern cities, hiring employees with developmental disabilities. Heartwarming pictures showed employees intent with purpose. Jan pirouetted on stage in a glittering short skirt and athletic legs, with a girl-next-door charm, highlighting the use of local ingredients, without preservatives, and a free sample policy. She summarized Sweet Boomerang customers as fiercely loyal, propelling a solid growth rate in their small stores strategically located in airports and shopping malls. Lionel stood in enthusiastic applause as she returned, beaming.

Raj Singh bumped the table and rattled the glasses as he rose, his tall, rangy frame swaying like a giraffe. Lionel caught a glass as it tumbled off the table. Raj whispered, "Thanks." A brilliant white smile then emerged, surrounded by dark skin, jet-black hair and a close-cropped beard. Onstage his soothing, melodic voice had a hypnotic effect, and his charm won over the audience as he described the clothing and shoes Step-by-Step made from recycled tires and plastics. Thousands of jobs were created and attractive products were crafted and sold in the U.S. and Western Europe, with matching clothing articles donated for every one purchased. His Step-by-Step clothing brand was gaining a significant following on social media among affluent shoppers. His supporters whistled and cheered as he made his way back to the table.

The third presenter, Larry Furtig, rose like a man on a mission. Shoulders erect, head high, he walked like someone with a lot to say. Thick sandy hair swept aggressively from a large forehead, and while not tall, his stout frame suggested a quiet power. He punctuated his delivery with crisp sound bytes. His microfinance company, SocialLending, serviced rural communities by providing peer-to-peer lending, creating opportunities ignored or denied by traditional lenders. SocialLending was still relatively small, but he proudly emphasized their high profits and rapid growth. The impressive results prompted loud applause from the crowd. Maxine turned and glanced at Lionel, her eyebrows raised slightly. *She recognizes him as a serious contender*, Lionel thought.

The announcer called for the fourth presenter. "And now, Maxine Gold, a board member for the Community Bootstrap Organization. She is presenting for their CEO who unfortunately was taken ill tonight." Maxine stood up and walked to the stage with purpose.

She was striking in her ivory dress, a narrow sheath encasing her curves. It was the perfect contrast to the dark glow of her African American and eastern European heritage. Onstage, she stood behind the podium.

Her presentation began with colorful slides. "Please review the charts here, as I'd like to impress upon you the importance of the analysis behind the planning. Using statistically significant results for all our projections . . ." After two minutes Lionel was concerned. *This is a crowd drinking champagne at an awards banquet, not a classroom.* Ten more slides and Lionel could see the audience was turned off. It was a sophisticated hour-long oral argument crammed into five minutes. Maxine's voice became monotone as she rushed, then hollowed as the audience fell silent and unresponsive.

The moderator, Jules Longsworth, mercifully called time after five minutes and she returned to the table to polite but subdued applause.

Lionel stood and gave her a brief hug as she approached the table. He smiled and said, "Brilliant as always, Maxine."

Her glance showed pain, but she held her composure. "That's irrelevant if they aren't listening." She pursed her lips as she sat down.

"And now, I'd like to introduce the CEO of Double Vision, Lionel Lane."

Lionel burst to the spotlights with enthusiasm, ignoring the podium and taking the wireless microphone to the center of the stage. The glare made it nearly impossible to see the faces in the audience, but he began with a surge of energy.

"I'd like to start with a song written specifically for all of us doing innovative social work around the world. Let's give it up for *Thinkaboutit*, by the Rock Strings."

The rhythm and vocals of the hit song quickly ramped up. At full volume the song rocked through dozens of high definition speakers surrounding the audience. Lionel started dancing and the popularity of the Rock Strings' hit song did the rest. Lionel could see the swaying shoulders, bobbing heads, and clapping hands moving with the feel-good beat.

The music softened to a background level and several people cheered and whistled. Lionel waved and then started projecting slides. The first close-up image was of a dark woman in a soiled and worn dress, with dry cracked skin, feeding a food package to her thin child. "One of you bought our nutritional drink here in the States, which paid for this food packet in Malawi."

The picture transitioned to a little boy, dominated by a large brown skull and a twig-sized arm. "Here is starvation in Haiti. Then a customer, maybe one of you, indirectly fed him a food pouch." The images continued, interspersed with some pictures of Double Vision juice drinks. "When we make a choice to enjoy a Double Vision beverage, to sustain ourselves with its good nutrition, the customer is providing a meal to a hungry child. Directly from you to them. That is the power of our one-for-one offer. Buy one and give one. And we, via our customers, have provided over fifty million meals so far. Double Vision, here and around the world." He concluded with a world map of their donation locations as the music wound down.

The audience stood clapping and buzzing until he reached his seat. Some wiped away tears. His fellow CEOs welcomed him back, led by Jan's outstretched hug and kiss. Raj enthusiastically wrapped a long arm around him.

Lionel felt supercharged. The pressure of public speaking, then the success of the music and presentation, the cheering, all worked like a powerful drug. He chattered nervously. Then Maxine leaned over and put her mouth near his ear. "You certainly win for drama, Lionel."

He looked at her and crossed his fingers. Was that a compliment or not? *All he knew was he really needed this. And it's not about beating her.*

President Longsworth retook the stage. After a few attempts it became quiet enough for him to be heard.

Lionel stopped breathing. He could hear his heart banging.

"In what was an extremely close vote in a very impressive field of entrepreneurs, the Schwab and Young committee would like to present this year's Social Entrepreneur of the Year award to . . . Larry Furtig and his microfinance company, SocialLending."

Lionel's chest ratcheted inward. He felt the audience's focus pass right by him. All the attention turned toward Larry Furtig at the end of the table.

His hands moved mechanically, joining the applause. He became a bystander.

Suddenly Raj was whispering in his ear. "I would have voted for you." Lionel felt Raj's arm around his shoulder.

"Raj, my man," Lionel croaked. He managed a smile. Then they both continued applauding until the room returned to the buzz of goodbyes and departure. They turned to the other contestants. Lionel hugged Jan and wished her well with Sweet Boomerang. They agreed to stay in touch. Quickly their table became a magnet for VCs and well-wishers swarming the winner, holding the shiny plaque. Lionel couldn't stop thinking about bankruptcy and his stomach churned.

Leah Barko circled the table and approached Lionel. "Off the record, you should be holding that plaque." Then she turned on her recorder.

"Lionel, based on the crowd's response to your presentation, it appeared you might win. What is your reaction now?"

He had to rally. He tightened his core and breathed in, catching sight of Maxine behind Leah, watching him. "Absolutely proud of Larry and the company he built, SocialLending. Congratulations to them."

"How do you think this shapes up the race for the billion dollar Big Disrupter Award in six months?"

"There are some brilliant people here tonight, like Maxine Gold." He nodded toward her, and she furrowed her eyebrows defensively. "Jan Swenson's candy company and Raj Singh's clothing company are doing great work with killer business models. I wouldn't count any of them out."

Leah asked a few more questions and he did his best to be upbeat. Finally she concluded and Lionel moved away from the victor's table.

He hoped to talk with Maxine alone. He saw her across the thinning crowd, but she was absorbed in conversation with an older couple. The woman had long hair and an artistic look. The man waved his arms animatedly, shaking a full beard and gray ponytail. Maxine nodded at them, giving her full attention.

He sighed and decided to retreat. His feet grew heavier as he walked toward the exit, dragging in defeat. The judges had spoken. Loser. Double Vision was in serious trouble.

3

THURSDAY MORNING, SEPTEMBER 26TH

The early morning bike ride along the waterfront normally invigorated Lionel—the refreshing mist of the fog on his face, the salt like a spice in the air. The flat commute was a glide, a game of playing cat and mouse as he passed through backed-up traffic. But today each pedal rotation seemed like pointless monotony. Every vehicle left him a smelly noseful of exhaust. Even his feet and legs complained as the ride dragged on.

His destination was South Beach, near San Francisco's downtown. Double Vision's office was in a trendy neighborhood of restored brick warehouses featuring hot start-ups, live/work lofts for lottery winners, and hip restaurants for people on expense accounts.

At Brannan Street he clattered over a brick courtyard toward the front of a four-story building. He swiped his smart phone to get into the elevator and punched the third floor. The elevator climbed the building's exterior, and he scanned the piers on the bay and the brick surrounds of the San Francisco Giants baseball park. Piercing the fog he saw the oversized old-school glove and eighty-foot Coke bottle above the left-field stands. That should be a Double Vision bottle, he groused.

The elevator dinged. With a deep breath he rolled his bike through the entrance. Colorful pictures of kids around the globe helped by Double Vision's nutritional outreach lined the walls. He forced a cheery hello to the handful of early employees scattered at desks in the open bullpen. Hellos and waves responded. Lionel paused to chat briefly, then made his way to the far end of the building, pushing into his office. He leaned his red and black bike against the wall below his windows, which looked toward buildings that actually had views of the waterfront. Peeling off his backpack and riding gear he produced his laptop and powered it on. He dropped heavily into his desk chair. Mournful foghorns bellowed. *You're singing my song,* he thought.

The first thing to review was the latest online cash management report. Grudgingly he created a spreadsheet of recommended budget and personnel cuts. He kept going off track with new inspirations on how to turn things around.

A call on his cell interrupted him. Unknown caller. He wasn't in the mood and he silenced it. Three minutes later his desk phone rang.

"I'm sorry, Lionel, but this guy is very insistent. He says you won't know what his call is regarding. But he says he saw you at the Schwab and Young awards banquet."

"Huh? What's his name?"

"He was talking really fast. Jacob . . . Jacob Havermorgan?"

Wait, could it possibly be . . . "Jacob Havermyer?"

"That must be it."

"Thanks, I've got it, Sam."

Lionel took a deep breath. "Hello, this is Lionel Lane."

"So good to speak directly with you, Lionel, since I wasn't able to meet you in person last night at the S and Y awards. This is Jacob Havermyer, and I am hoping we can get a chance to meet." He spoke quickly with passion in his voice and Lionel felt pulled into his pace.

"That would be a pleasure, of course. Honestly, getting this call is a surprise. May I ask what you'd like to discuss?"

"I'd like to review that in person. I wouldn't normally be so rude as to ask to meet today, but I am scheduled to fly out of the country tomorrow. Is there any chance today would work?"

"I'll make it work, no problem."

"Great. I have a little office in my home. Broadway and Broderick in Pacific Heights. See you at ten?"

"Of course. Should I prepare anything?"

"No, let's just brainstorm, okay?"

After they hung up, Lionel immediately started researching Jacob Havermyer online. Escaped from the Nazis as a young boy, he made his way to the U.S., learned the language, and worked his way through college. Fought prejudice on Wall Street because of his religion and class, and in spite of that made billions in international currency trading. He was a legend in the financial community.

Lionel launched another search. A *National Business Journal* article highlighted a quote, attributed to Havermyer. 'With the deregulated international currency markets that were unfamiliar to U.S. centric investors at the time, I was a one-eyed gambler in a world of blind men.' The author concluded: 'Jacob Havermyer single-handedly makes or breaks small empires around the world.'

Holy shit. Why did Havermyer want to meet?

***

The man wanted to appear to have it all. He sat at a desk meant to intimidate, in an office designed to impress and in front of a view to inspire envy. Several large flat screens shimmered with multiple open windows.

A short article had his attention, in the online edition of the *San Francisco News*.

Road bicyclist killed off Highway 1 near Carmel. The rider and bicycle plunged over a protective guardrail, down a rock-faced cliff over one hundred feet, landing on the rocks below. The body was discovered by a fisherman. The sheriff reported the body appeared to have been exposed for several days.

What they weren't saying, he thought, is that the crabs and birds had picked his flesh clean. A suitable ending.

He continued reading.

The victim was identified as Aaron Budd of Palo Alto. His shocked colleagues at Arrowrock Capital, the Silicon Valley venture capital firm, described him as a brilliant businessperson, struck down in his prime. The police suspect a hit and run, but have no witnesses or leads on the accident.

That was the best part, he thought. *No witnesses or leads.* He smiled and looked out at the view. Contracting Fanachi's muscle was quite expedient. He reflected back on his bold move.

Months earlier he had spoken to his lawyer. In very general terms. Who referred him to another lawyer, a criminal trial lawyer. They spoke, again in very broad terms, trying to help a friend, he said. And he referred him to someone he defended, a guy popped on a gun charge. That introduction led to another. The calls were vague. The last conversation ended with instructions to go to the Junipero Serra rest stop, off Highway 280 near Silicon Valley. At exactly two p.m. He picked up a padded envelope taped to the underside of a picnic table. Inside the unmarked package was the encrypted phone. On the back outside wall of the men's restroom was a number written in chalk. The number he was to call.

He thought of sitting in his car at the rest stop, about to call Fanachi for the first time. The encrypted phone in his hand seemed ordinary, yet it represented a completely different capability. He had reminded himself the result he wanted wasn't unthinkable or even regrettable. It simply required money and courage. He felt powerful with the phone.

He shook his head. But why shouldn't it work like that? Relationships, money, and the balls to have an outrageous plan. That's what made him millions and millions of dollars. Their conversation that day was just another deal, actually.

"Fanachi, here. Who am I speaking with?"

"This is Alpha."

"Alpha, we are using a sophisticated phone system based in Canada to avoid U.S. government eavesdropping. It automatically scrubs all the call data from these encrypted phones, when we conclude. So far so good?"

"Yes, very good."

"Here is my service. You identify a target. Remarkably, the target meets with an accidental death, one so plausible that few, if any, ever raise questions. Are we still having a conversation here?"

Alpha responded, "Yes."

"Good. My requirement is that you identify the target but not the means to accomplish the ends. That is why you hired us. Am I understood?"

"I understand."

"One other point. My price is my price, no negotiation. When you identify the target, I tell you the amount. Take it or leave it. But save your negotiation for whatever you do in your life to make money. I'm sure you are very good at that. But this is different. Do we understand each other?"

"You name the price. And I take it or leave it. I understand."

"Okay, last rule. Payment. You will pay an account in the Cayman Islands via wire transfer. Is that a problem?"

"No. No problem at all. I am quite familiar with Cayman Island accounts and procedures. However, I will pay only after the job is complete, not before. That's the way I do business."

"Of course. You pay when we are done. And if you don't pay, then when we find you, you pay me double. That is the price of your life." Fanachi paused. Alpha bristled. "But you come referred to me as a gentleman. I'm sure that won't be necessary. So Alpha, tell me what I can do for you."

Alpha had decided right then that Fanachi was tough but reasonable. What more could he expect? And now his adversary was a statistic, a short article in the paper. Yes, there was a family with a missing space in its Christmas photo. But his problem was solved. Aaron, the Arrowrock guy, had learned way more than he should have, and was so self-righteous he was planning to go to the authorities. No one was going to do that to him.

He took a deep breath. The Arrowrock situation was under control. Complete. But, goddamn it, he couldn't have anyone in the way of his new plan. He thought about the hundreds of millions he could pocket. But he needed to protect that path to liquidity.

The caffeine was kicking in. He struck the large ironwood desk with his palm. He had to speak with Fanachi again.

Suddenly his phone rang. He reached across the large desk, tilted the iPhone, and saw the Facebook executive's name displayed. He answered immediately.

***

The huge elaborately carved teak door swung open. "Hello and welcome. I'm Jacob Havermyer." A full white beard, combed out beyond the width of his face, gave him a sphinxlike mien. His hair was pulled back in a gray ponytail that disappeared down the middle of his back.

"Thank you for the invitation," Lionel said, shaking hands and stepping through the doorway.

Jacob, full of enthusiasm, gave Lionel a tour. With a lively gleam behind thick glasses, he explained. "My wife, Deborah, is fascinated by different cultures. So we visit countries, support the local artists, and bring back loads of art work."

They walked past a colorful ten-foot high Ganesh from Bali, overlooking the front entrance hall. The Hindu deity's elephant head and multiple arms were carved from deep red mahogany and stone. He smelled incense and spice wafting in the air. World music, exotically unidentifiable but full of drums, strings, and varying languages, floated around him.

Lionel felt privileged to be walking with one of the world's leading philanthropists, in his inner sanctum. They entered the studio gallery where huge canvases of native art in earth tones from Indonesia and Africa made a primal impression. They passed through a three-story domed foyer, their footsteps echoing off the marble walls. They approached the white granite back terrace. Three eighteen-foot arched windows streamed sunlight inward, while golden islands floated in the blue waters of the San Francisco Bay far below. He was on a cloud of beauty.

At the table on the stone terrace sat a woman in a flowing Indonesian print dress, long gray hair down her back. He'd seen her before, somewhere. She was leaning in toward another woman . . . What? No. Maxine Gold. *Why was she here?*

Maxine turned, appearing as surprised as Lionel. Her eyes widened and she immediately stood up.

"Jacob, I'm confused. Did I come at the wrong time?"

He smiled. "Not at all. I wanted you two to get to know each other. Maxine Gold, please meet Lionel Lane."

Maxine and Lionel stood awkwardly staring at each other. "We know each other already," said Maxine.

"Good morning, Maxine," said Lionel.

Maxine ignored him. "Jacob, I thought you wanted to hear about my idea."

"I most definitely do."

"So why is he here?"

The woman in the batik dress stood up, looking at Lionel. Jacob put his hand on Lionel's back. "Lionel, allow me to introduce my wife, Deborah. Without her, I am completely lost."

As Lionel took her hand, she said, "Welcome, Lionel. I've heard about your company, and I like the one-for-one offer." Her voice had the softness of the wind. He was immediately taken by her kindness, and he expressed his thanks. Her eyes sparkled like water, the crinkles around them suggesting wisdom.

"You know, Maxine," Deborah said, a knowing smile on her lined face, "you remind me of a young Jacob."

Lionel looked at Maxine.

"I can think of no higher compliment," she answered. "But I've done so little to earn it."

"Oh, you will, young woman, you will." She patted Maxine's hand. "Now, I have a charity event to attend to, so please excuse me. Wonderful meeting you, Lionel, and seeing you again, Maxine."

As Deborah left the terrace, Jacob came closer. Maxine crossed her arms.

"Let's address your question, Maxine," Jacob began. "You have a business plan for an energy drink company. And Lionel here is running what appears to me to be a kick-ass nutritional beverage company, with a very cool one-for-one offer and a social conscience. I thought there might be synergy."

"He is a competitor. I can't tell him my business plan." Her dark eyebrows furrowed.

"I see two driven and wonderful people who can perhaps make more of a difference working together than competing. Perhaps. Can we spend a few minutes considering the possibilities?"

Work with Maxine again? He wasn't sure she had an operations personality. Her complicated strategies might not stand up to the rough and tumble world of beverages.

Havermyer took Lionel by the elbow and walked him over to the side table. "Please, there is fresh organic tea, coffee, and some fruit. Plus killer chocolate croissants that I really shouldn't have. Help yourselves, let's sit, and at least chat a bit."

Lionel poured some juice while Maxine got coffee.

"Let me start," said Jacob. "I met Maxine's grandparents in the Civil Rights days, when they were both liberal activists in the 1960's. They not only wrote and protested about racial inequality, but participated in desegregation efforts when it took a lot of courage to face the abuse and danger." His eyes stared intently at Lionel. "Can you believe the first time they met was at a staged lunch-counter date, in a segregated restaurant in Washington, D.C.? She is black and he's white. They were actively fighting for desegregation. They got married and continue as vocal civil and consumer rights advocates to this day."

"You never told me that, Maxine."

"You never asked."

"So you two met at school?" Jacob asked.

"Yes, Harvard classmates," Lionel answered. "But Jacob, it sounds like you are a family friend, especially with her incredible grandparents. I can see why Maxine would be hesitant of my intruding on that relationship."

"I said no such thing. I said you are a potential competitor to my business plan," Maxine interjected.

"I thought you were part of that Community Bootstrap Organization?"

"I'm on the board and presented last night as a favor. Their CEO became ill. I don't work there."

That helped explain the poor presentation, he thought. "Good luck with starting an energy drink company. All due respect, have you ever been in this business?"

"I advised leading brands when I was at McKinsey."

"Competing with the Big Four in beverages is nearly impossible. And it takes a lot of money."

"What I like about Maxine's description of the energy drink market is that it is growing very quickly," Jacob intervened. "The leader,

Red Bull, has grown to over five billion dollars in annual sales. And is very profitable."

"I'd be lying if I didn't admit I've considered making energy drinks," said Lionel. "But caffeine, sugar, herbal ingredients like Taurine or Ginseng—that is a far cry from our nutritional drinks. Frankly, I don't think energy drinks are that great for you."

"You'd rather struggle with products of limited appeal?" Maxine challenged.

What a smart ass. He wished his balance sheet would let him shut her up, but it couldn't anymore. He rolled his eyes and said nothing.

"What if we think bigger?" offered Jacob. "What if you challenge the Red Bulls, the Monsters, the 5 Hour Energy types? You broaden Double Vision's product and marketing strategy to accelerate into higher-growth-rate areas. Lionel, you already have the infrastructure of a nimble and youth-centric beverage company. And isn't that who drinks this stuff?"

"It's definitely a youth market," Maxine said with authority.

Lionel clenched his jaw at her assumed expertise. Then he looked at Jacob and Maxine. "I'd never abandon the one-for-one offer."

Maxine shot back, "That's expensive. And I don't know if people really care. It may be better to simply donate a percentage to charity."

"Fine, that may be the consultant's view. But I have real-world competitive information that shows one-for-one makes a difference with consumers. And, most importantly, with the right in-country partners, we cost-effectively combat hunger. But I'm sure that isn't your primary concern anyway."

"It does no good if your company goes bankrupt," retorted Maxine.

Jesus, did she have access to his internal information? Or was she that good at reading him? "Well, if you are going to be the same as the other guys, making high margins off sugar and caffeine, then why bother? You're making a living but not improving anything."

Jacob interrupted again. "Let's assume you can offer both nutritional and energy drinks, grow rapidly and profitably, and provide a one-for-one nutrition supplement for the poor. Is that a meaningful endeavor?"

Neither said anything. "Maxine?"

"Yes, conceptually."

"Lionel?"

"Agreed."

"What do we know about valuations and the industry multiples? Considering events such as Coca-Cola buying Glaceau, makers of Vitaminwater, for four billion dollars, and Monster going public?"

"Valuations for established players are in the six to eleven times revenue range," Lionel answered.

"Okay. I accept that," said Jacob. "What is your best valuation estimate for Double Vision today, Lionel?"

Lionel wondered how he could possibly out-negotiate a legend. He glanced at Maxine. She had a poker face. Then he looked straight at Jacob, deciding his best course was a valuation multiple he'd be happy with, neither greedy nor desperate. "Our revenue is at a sixty million dollar run rate, but we are having profitability challenges, mostly due to limited distribution. With the cash to fix that, and assuming we had an energy drink line, Double Vision is worth two times revenue."

"So you'd have a one hundred twenty million dollar valuation?"

"Right."

"There were several 'ifs' in there," pointed out Maxine.

"I understand," said Jacob, sitting back. "The word is you're facing a cash squeeze right now. Is that correct, Lionel?"

"Yes. Admittedly, it's very bad."

Jacob stroked his long beard. "What have the VCs said?"

"I've had extensive negotiations with a dozen. It comes down to three things. They want a faster growth market, they want better distribution, and each wants someone else as lead investor."

Jacob adjusted his glasses. Then he leaned forward. "Here is what I propose. I'll support a thirty-million-dollar investment in Double Vision, for twenty-five percent of the company. That matches the one hundred twenty million dollar valuation."

Lionel repeated what Jacob said to himself, to make sure he had heard right. *Incredible! A thirty-million-dollar infusion would save everything. And he'd still have control.*

"You'd invest thirty million?" Lionel said, as calmly as he could manage.

"We're talking about getting Double Vision thirty million, yes." Jacob smiled mischievously, his eyes darting about.

Wait. That sounded different. Then suddenly Lionel realized there was a bigger problem. Memories of being manipulated by the Consolidated CEO flashed back.

"I'm sorry, Jacob. It won't work." Lionel caught Maxine's look of surprise.

Havermyer asked calmly, "Why is that?"

"I can't work for Maxine."

"I can't work for him either," she replied quickly.

Havermyer looked at each of them. He tugged his beard. "How about this? Co-CEOs. Numerous companies have Co-CEOs, or Co-heads of divisions."

Co-CEO. He'd still have the majority control, not Havermyer or Maxine. His natural optimism made him excited. He and Maxine looked at each other, searching. Finally Lionel said, "I think we'd need to discuss this."

"I agree," Maxine added.

"There is one catch to my offer."

Of course, thought Lionel. *How bad would this be?*

"Of the thirty million dollars, I'll supply fifteen million cash. But within twenty-four hours, let's call it by noon tomorrow, you have to find one of those VCs to match my fifteen million dollars, or the entire deal is off the table."

4

THURSDAY AFTERNOON, SEPTEMBER 26TH

The cab pulled up to Havermyer's mansion. Lionel and Maxine entered on opposite sides and slammed their doors nearly in unison.

The cab driver's hat was Rastafarian green, gold, and red, and dreads flowed down his back. Reggae music was playing.

"Allo."

"Hi, there. Townsend and Fourth please," said Lionel. He sunk back into the worn seat.

"Make that Market and Montgomery," countered Maxine. "Take the Broadway Tunnel and cut over on Columbus to Montgomery. Got it?"

The driver's dark eyes appeared in the mirror. "Excuse me, people. Which one?"

"Townsend and Fourth," answered Lionel.

"Market and Montgomery. Lionel, my office is closer and there will be fewer distractions with your employees. If we are going to work together, you need to be logical."

The cabbie's eyes rocked between Lionel and Maxine, getting larger.

"We'll need some key team members to help pull the deal together. My office is the headquarters—our headquarters, as Co-CEOs, if we can raise the cash. Together."

"Fine. Since you put it that way. Cabbie, Townsend and Fourth. And take Ellis Street across town."

"No worries. Glad we have a destination." Then the driver chuckled. "And instructions too. Lucky day." He cranked up the reggae and closed the sliding window between them.

"Lionel, we have exactly twenty-four hours to raise the matching fifteen million. Let's start comparing who we can contact and how we develop an investment package." Maxine unzipped her tablet's leather case and started typing.

"Why didn't you tell me that story about your grandparents and Jacob? That's amazing." Lionel wondered why that topic hadn't come up during their few romantic getaways in New England, their senior year, in springtime. Although he remembered concentrating more on her on the blanket than talking.

"Ancient history. Let's focus on the narrative and projections we need to put together. I've got the competitive intel and energy-drink research I assembled for Havermyer. Lionel, Lionel, are you listening?"

Lionel turned to Maxine but his thoughts were still far away. That night after the Rock Rags closing dinner. The last time they saw each other, they shared so much. Dreams. The future. Even fears. "Why didn't you ever call me back?" he asked quietly. "I left messages."

"Yes, usually from the edge of the wilderness. Just like you did in college—you always had another place to be, or were consumed by another adventure with a new group of friends. And there always was some other girl. You've got commitment issues, Lionel."

"Commitment issues?" Lionel's voice rose. "You're the one who was the workaholic. When you were at McKinsey I only saw you when you worked on my deal with Consolidated. After that you took their offer in London. I was starting a company in California, and you were all over Europe working 24/7. Talk about commitment issues." The sunken seat made her skirt slide far up her thigh, distracting him more than he cared to admit.

"I was focused on success at McKinsey. That's what it takes. Now let's focus on the task at hand."

"Okay, you were being independent. But what about romance? Did you find someone else?"

"I was working." She stared ahead, ignoring him.

"Weren't you lonely?" Lionel looked at her, searching for eye contact.

"I was surrounded by more than enough people, thank you." She kept looking away.

"No romance at all? Then why didn't you respond to me?"

Maxine pounded on the sliding glass window in front. "Driver, stop the cab. That's it." She turned to Lionel. "You can't think about anything but, but, personal relationships and sex."

The cab stopped suddenly and they lurched forward, falling together against the front divider. After a moment the driver slid the glass open. The reggae music and mellow smells of Jamaica wafted in. "You two wan' to stop?"

Lionel sat back up and answered. "No, keep driving please. We're talking. Catching up." Out of the corner of his eye, Lionel saw Maxine tug her skirt down with a frown. Then she checked her watch.

"Lionel, in twenty-three hours and fifty minutes we need to have a matching fifteen million. How exactly do you propose to do that?"

The glass slid closed and the cab began rolling. "Honestly, our best shot is two words," replied Lionel. "Jacob Havermyer."

"That's it?" she said, her eyebrows arching.

"There are a dozen VCs that already are very familiar with Double Vision. They represent our only hope in this tight time frame. We need to quickly present the news of Havermyer's backing and this new energy drink approach. Hopefully several will want to dance, despite the time pressure."

"We can certainly put together a deal package. I have the energy drink plan already written. With operational details and budgets."

Lionel looked into Maxine's light brown eyes. Her liveliness excited him—like before. There's was something special about her, along with being brilliant. She was wilder than people realized. Memories of their last marathon night together came back so vividly he could hear the groans. He felt like burying his fingers in the thick hair cascading over her shoulders. It was so close. "So how about now?" Lionel asked.

"You mean in terms of next steps for the deal package?" Maxine responded.

"No. I mean now, right now, do you have a boyfriend?"

Her eyebrows arched and she sighed. "That is none of your business."

"Okay, I'll take that as a no."

"Assumptions are dangerous."

"So you are in a relationship but you don't want to be honest with me?"

"Stop the cab, driver!" She pounded on the glass again, then braced herself.

The cabbie hit the brakes. As they came to a sudden stop the cars behind them honked. He slid the glass. "Dis is da way you told me to go."

"Don't worry driver, it's me, not you," apologized Lionel.

"Will you stop acting like a juvenile?"

"Sorry." *Something is bothering her—she can't loosen up.*

He saw the driver's puzzled look in the mirror.

"Okay, good luck, mon. I go now." He slid the glass closed. The honking got louder. As the cab pulled forward the driver waved out his window and chuckled, "Doan worry, be happy." He started rocking his head to the music.

"Lionel, can you please try to act professionally?"

"I thought I was. I'm sorry, but I thought professionals ask hard questions and analyze the answers honestly."

She turned, her face inches away. "About relevant topics."

"I'm trying to figure out how we're going to be Co-CEOs. We have history, Maxine."

"It's not going to include my sleeping with the ... other ... CEO."

"I didn't ask that. But since you brought it up, our relationship was really special until ... until we took a break. And please don't yell at the driver."

"That aspect is over. Do we really need to go there?"

"Look, I realize we went apart. But can you at least admit that when we were together it was special? It seems weird to reboot as business partners, without recognizing we've been close." He smiled as he opened his palms toward her.

"Why would I admit that?" She held up her tablet like a shield.

"I care about you. I want you to have affection in your life. I'm sorry our romance didn't ultimately work out."

Maxine put the tablet down on the seat. Her hair brushed Lionel as she turned her face closer, electrifying him. "Look, Lionel, I know you care what people think of you. You love being outrageously frank and genuine."

"Who doesn't?"

"A lot of us. You're an idealist. You want to save the world. You want people to know you are caring and generous. No BS."

"So that's bad?" He looked at her, baffled.

She thought for a moment, her lips drawn together. She locked eyes. "No, that's fine, for you. But you want to know what I care about? I want a stellar career. I want to make big money. At the top, running something huge. Okay? And do you know what will screw that up? If people think Havermyer is my sugar daddy. Or worse, if they think it's because you're my old boyfriend and you brought me in as a plaything and figurehead."

He saw the fear of vulnerability flicker in her eyes. How could anyone not realize she was destined to create her own success, no matter what? She was so committed to her aspirations. And driven.

"I want to be successful. I don't mind being a Co-CEO. But I don't want a bunch of rumors about my private life ruining this opportunity. I want to be judged on my mind, my strategy, and decisions."

Of course. As brilliant as she was, the McKinsey background was purely consulting. She'd never run or started a company. She needed to prove her operational abilities. Not to mention overcoming skepticism or worse by being a female African-American leader. But she'd never admit that. Lionel slowly nodded his head. He suddenly felt like a jerk. "I get it."

"Do you?" Her voice had softened a notch.

"Done. No one needs to know about our history. Co-CEOs. We're lucky to have you. We went to the same college. We met our senior year. That's it. Period."

"The Havermyer background?"

"Forget about the personal side. We don't need that to be public. He's a high profile investor who believes in us and our company."

The glass divider slid open. "Allo back there. We stopped now."

"Why?" Lionel said, absently.

"We der, Fourth and Townsend."

He glanced out the window. "Oh, yes. Thanks."

Lionel realized his hands were clenched. He turned back to Maxine. "Okay, the personal aspect is behind us. We're Co-CEOs and friends. That's it."

"Good. We agree then." She smiled. They climbed out of the cab and stood on the sidewalk facing each other.

"To settle it, goodbye to the past and hello to the future. Co-CEO." He opened his arms wide for a hug.

Maxine breathed in. With a look of genuine relief she put out her arms. Lionel strode toward her just as she took a step toward him. They collided, snugly together. Memories rushed to Lionel. It felt like zipless sex. As he pulled back, Lionel saw the same confused look in her eyes that he felt. Then she turned away.

***

Five minutes after the cab arrived at Double Vision, Maxine was on the phone. "Walter Proudstone, Maxine Gold here."

"Maxine, a pleasure to hear your lovely voice."

"Am I interrupting?"

"Not at all. I'm at Brooks Brothers waiting for the tailor. By the way, congratulations on being a finalist for the Schwab and Young social entrepreneurship award."

"Why, thank you, Walter. You are always on top of what's going on."

Walter responded with a satisfied chuckle. "That's one of the traits that has helped me succeed over the years, paying close attention to the rising stars." She heard the murmur of a low voice in the background. She imagined Walter with his bushy eyebrows staring intently in the mirror as tailors knelt and hovered, fitting him with imported bespoke fabrics. "I saw your email. You're now Co-CEO of Double Vision?"

"Exactly. In fact, that is why I am calling." Maxine paused for emphasis. "You already have background on the company from Lionel. And since you and I know each other from the Harvard student-alumni committee, would it be presumptive of me to get directly to the point?"

"What a pity. You know, you are one of the few young people with whom I genuinely enjoy conversing." Maxine heard Walter shoo away the tailor. "But I sense you have a deadline. We'll catch up in future conversations. What can I do for a young and brilliant fellow alum today?"

Thank goodness for the Harvard connection. "Thank you. Jacob Havermyer has committed to a thirty million dollar package investment for twenty-five percent of Double Vision. That's a 2 X revenue multiple. He wants to share that with one other investor that we select; meaning he'll do fifteen million, and the other investor fifteen million, each getting twelve and a half percent."

"Jacob Havermyer is in for fifteen million?" Maxine heard the surprise in his voice. "I thought he was busy with his global arbitrage, making billions."

"He likes what we're doing."

"Interesting. Well, Jacob certainly travels in the right circles."

She could hear the wheels turning. He was imagining impressing potential clients and egotistical competitors with the prestige of having personally worked with Jacob Havermyer—the man global rulers want to meet.

"Walter, I know Deepwater considered working with Double Vision a year ago, but passed. Now, with Havermyer in, our planned expansion into energy drinks and my leadership, do you think you could reconsider?"

"That certainly changes things. I am open to discussion, Maxine."

"Forgive me, but we have a very tight timetable."

"Deepwater is proud of its quick entrepreneurial reflexes." He paused, adding dramatically, "We're built from decision-making DNA."

"Excellent, because here is what Havermyer wants. We have twenty-three hours to make the choice and close the deal. Jacob doesn't want to waste a lot of time, pardon me, screwing around."

She could hear the sputtering before he caught himself. "Twenty-three hours to commit fifteen million? Uh, Maxine, that's very unusual."

"Sorry, Jacob insists."

"I . . . I have to socialize the idea, and get some buy-in from my partners. We like Double Vision, but that is an extraordinarily short time period. Why does he . . . oh, never mind. Let me get back to you."

***

Lionel was in his office, across the hallway from the conference room where Maxine was working. "Roger, Lionel Lane here, Co-CEO, Double Vision."

"Lionel, good to hear your voice. Didn't I see something on Twitter about you?"

"Was it the social entrepreneur award?"

"That was it. Congratulations. But you deserved to win it all."

"Appreciate that, thank you. Still, it was an honor. Can you talk? Sounds a bit windy where you are."

Roger Scalton of VentureEast Partners was on his sailboat, *Eagle Wave* on the Chesapeake Bay. He described the preparations for the upcoming Defender's Cup race as the crew scurried about. Lionel pictured him sitting at the stern of the fabulously expensive high-modulus carbon fiber catamaran, as strong westerly winds piled up waves across the water.

"It's blowing like snot, we're still tied off near the dock and rolling about, but we're planning to find a window here and go out soon. You love extreme skiing, I love extreme sailing. What the hell. So, how is business?"

"Fantastic, sales are up, and we have a great expansion opportunity. That's why I am calling. Here is the deal . . . ."

"Twenty-three hours, fifteen million! Hell, Jacob may have that kind of money sitting around in his wallet, but I have to get a lot of approvals to fund that level of investment."

"Your firm and my company have been dancing around for over a year. You know us. Now, the deal just got better for you."

"Good points. Let me ask you, how long has Jacob been studying this?"

"Oh, we must have met for an hour at his house in Pacific Heights, and half of that was walking around and looking at his incredible art collection."

"Holy shit, he's such a frigging stud. I'd love to be in with him. All right, I'm off the grid for about ninety minutes after we shove off. This is a Cat, not some fudgy deck rider, so soon we'll be leaning off the edge doing thirty knots. Let me launch some calls and get back to you by tonight."

***

Maxine saw Lionel slip into the conference room, flop into one of the beanbag chairs, and stare at the ceiling. He looked wrung out.

Immediately after arriving at the Double Vision offices, Maxine and Lionel had drawn up their "A" list of venture capitalists and private equity firms. These were all people Lionel had pitched before. Maxine knew several from her Harvard connections and McKinsey days. They agreed on a short script to follow for consistency, split it up based on relationships, and started dialing and pinging like crazy.

Meanwhile Harding was working his CPA magic on the marketing and operational numbers with the team, to ensure they would support the investor package the lawyers were drawing up. Lionel and Maxine had left Havermyer's mansion five hours ago. The deadline was nineteen hours away.

"How are you doing?" asked Lionel.

"I've called my entire list and actually got hold of five decision-makers so far, which is pretty amazing. Jacob's name definitely gets their attention. But they all want more time. They tout their speed of execution, when actually everybody wants to sniff and approve in some slow dance ritual."

"Same thing for me. Fifteen million in twenty-four hours is killing us." Lionel stared at the ceiling. "Well, I'm moving my calls more to the West Coast now that it's getting late. Let's regroup when it's time to review the deal package?"

"Right. And we'll need your ops, marketing, and finance guys to work on the business plan tonight. Can you let them know it'll be an all-nighter?"

"You don't think a short overview and the financing agreement is enough?"

"Absolutely not. I've got people on the East Coast counting on the whole package first thing in the morning—their time."

Maxine's phone rang. "Great, Blaine Latrell is calling back. Axlewright Capital."

Lionel jerked himself out of the beanbag and went back to his calls.

Blaine's voice thundered with excitement. "Maxine, I can't believe you've got Havermyer in on this deal. How'd you do that?"

"Come up with fifteen million and you'll hear all about it."

"I hear that's the price of admission. But seriously, what is with the twenty-four hours?"

"Blaine," she said, drawing his name out like old times. "This is the big leagues, where Havermyer plays."

Maxine knew Blaine from McKinsey, and understood his fascination with wealthy personalities. Blaine didn't just want to be rich, he wanted to show off and be recognized as wealthy. He had an almost Gatsby-like fascination with the lifestyle and personalities of the wealthy. True to form, he asked, "Come on Maxine, what is Jacob Havermyer really like?"

"Here is an example. I asked Jacob how long it took him to decide to do this with Lionel and me, after he met Lionel for the first time. You know what he said?"

"What?"

"I made up my mind in the first ten seconds. The rest of the conversation was background."

Maxine could picture him shaking his head in awe, then straightening his shoulders in his blazer as if to measure up. Blaine always wore dark blazers with colorful accessories. He wanted to look the part.

"Impressive. Those are billionaire instincts. Has he put up his fifteen million yet?"

"Jacob is committed. He's waiting for the match."

"When is the deal package ready?"

"Tomorrow morning, first thing."

Blaine paused. Then, with a dramatic flourish, added, "I'd very much like to see it."

"Good." She bent over in concentration. "Blaine, we've known each other a while, and worked together, so let's skip the BS. Okay?"

"Of course. Maxine, I value our relationship more than purely for the business, you know that."

"Thank you, Blaine." She moved on quickly. "So would you be in a position to act on the deal within twenty hours? Literally noon tomorrow."

She waited as he processed this. "I assume you need the signed financing agreement and proof of funds, correct? Or do you need the funds wired?" Suddenly his voice grew concerned. "Double Vision isn't about to be insolvent, is it?"

Maxine's voice raised a notch. "You don't think Havermyer would invest that way, do you?"

"I needed to ask, that's all."

"I understand." She softened. "It's a solid deal, especially with Havermyer. The signed financing agreement and proof of funds is all we're asking for."

"What about the price? What kind of room is there?"

"Jacob set the price, based on comparable multiples. He's committed. No strung out haggling."

"That's unusual."

"What Jacob wants is another investor who is nimble and decisive about the fifteen million. Not a partner trying to prove they can shave ten percent off the asking price by dragging their heels and wasting everyone's time. Frankly, his time is worth more than that."

"I guess that's the cost of investing with Havermyer," Blaine agreed.

"Wouldn't you want to be his wing man? Come on."

"You're killing me. Who wouldn't?"

"Precisely." She smiled inwardly in satisfaction.

"What's the competition, Maxine, or is there any?"

Maxine's voice rose. "Oh yeah, are you kidding me?" Then she proceeded in a lower confidential tone. "Lionel had tons of people tracking Double Vision. The real players recognize this as a doorway deal, to do more with Havermyer. The only hindrance is the time window. It's a fantastic opportunity for a quick mover."

"I understand. All right, consider me very interested."

"Smart man." She clenched her fist in satisfaction.

"I'll look for the deal package tomorrow morning. We can be in a position to move, if the deal is right."

"Ping me with any issues anytime. Can we conference with Lionel at eleven?"

"That works."

"You are on, my friend. Talk soon. But I can't guarantee Lionel doesn't already have some heavy competition ready to pull the trigger. I'd really like you to have a shot. But don't be upset with me if someone else beats you to it."

"I'll do everything I can to get a piece of this, Maxine. Trust me."

***

After they signed off, Blaine stared at his phone. He was worried. His boss at Axlewright had been pressuring him to bring in deals that would explode with 10 X returns. *But he was so picky and political. And he was going to hate the time frame of this deal.* It would take a lot to convince him. He sighed, and placed a call to his admin to schedule an emergency meeting with John Anderson.

***

"You're Kate Zell, correct?" Maxine had interrupted Kate's discussion and was standing right next to her desk in the open bullpen.

"Yes." Rising, with a smile she said, "Aren't you . . ."

"Maxine Gold. I need this plan updated with the Double Vision logo and name everywhere. Add some boilerplate about the company too." She extended a memory stick in her hand.

Kate ignored it. "Nice to meet you. I'm sure we can arrange for someone to help you with your word-processing needs. I am the Director of Marketing."

"I am aware of that. No disrespect, but I don't want some secretary determining whether the lights are on or off in a month."

"Excuse me?"

"I don't have time. Talk to Lionel. But Double Vision's only hope is getting into the energy drink business and we have twenty hours to fund it." Looking at her phone she continued, "No, make that nineteen hours."

The heads at the adjacent desks immediately spun around.

Kate practically sputtered. "What in the world? Lionel hasn't discussed this with us. Energy drinks?"

"And in the management overview, put me down as Co-CEO. It's Maxine with an 'i', Gold as in Fort Knox." Her phone started to ring. She dropped the memory stick on Kate's desk and strode away, hard on her heels. Her voice suddenly gained an expansive enthusiasm. "Vaughn, great to hear back. Hope you aren't too late . . . ."

Maxine turned into the conference room and closed the door. Through the glass partition she saw Kate rushing over to Lionel's office, her blond hair snapping as it swung.

***

Lionel looked up as Kate barged into his office. He motioned to his earpiece. Kate clamped her mouth in a hard line, closed the door, and sat down with a thud.

"Randy, I apologize for the tight time frame. But that's Havermyer. It's how he earned his billions."

"Send me the new deal package right way, Lionel. But I can't promise anything."

"Great, thanks Randy." Lionel ended the call, and immediately started typing an email.

"Lionel, what is going on?"

He glanced at Kate as he pushed his hair back behind an ear. "Kate, sorry, but I'm absolutely jammed." He returned to typing.

"Evidently. You and this Maxine Gold are selling the company and turning it into Red Bull?"

He stopped typing. "What? No way." Oh shit, he hadn't announced the Maxine thing. Probably because he was still adjusting to it himself and freaking out over this insane deadline.

"What is going on then? This Maxine person says we're about to go bankrupt unless we become an energy drink company in nineteen hours. Plus she is now Co-CEO?"

Damn, damn, dammit. "What? Uh no, and yes. Look, we have a ridiculously short time fuse to raise fifteen million dollars. If we do—when we do—we'll have lots of time to discuss this and plan it out. As Marketing Director, you'll be front and center."

"Why am I hearing this now?"

"This unfolded today at Havermyer's."

Kate looked at him blankly. "Havermyer's?"

Oh man, too much to explain. Lionel jumped up, scrambled around the desk and dropped in a chair next to her. "Look, I am so sorry, but can you trust me on this?"

"It's all over the office, thanks to Maxine dropping the bomb."

"Oh, shit. Shoot. I understand." Maybe he could get Kate to help diffuse questions from the rest of the staff, until they had the time to explain. But he wasn't going to discuss bankruptcy. Not yet. "Look Kate, I promise we'll all talk about this soon. But can I ask you to help me here, please?"

Lionel saw the hurt in her eyes. For a communicator like Kate, being out of the loop was more deadly than a cash flow shortage, for sure. He gently put his hands on her shoulders.

"Look, confidentially, we're working with Jacob Havermyer, a renowned billionaire, to raise more money to expand. That's between you and me. Okay?"

"And Maxine," she corrected him.

"Right." He nodded and put his hands down. "If people ask, let them know we are working on raising a pile of money, and the rest is confidential for now, okay? And give Maxine what she needs?"

Kate's eyebrows furrowed. Her hands gripped the arms of the chair like she was strangling it.

"Please? I promise I'll fill you in soon and you'll have tons of input. We need your marketing expertise." Their faces were feet apart. "I'm sorry, it wouldn't be happening this way if . . . if the circumstances were different."

"You built this entire company based upon openness." She leaned forward and put her hand on his. "And trust."

Kate's words stung. She was right. Where was that line drawn? He exhaled quietly. "You, and the rest of the team, deserve a thorough discussion. But we don't have that time right now. Help us get through noon tomorrow."

Rapid knocking rattled the door. Maxine's face appeared through the glass side panel, giving Kate an impatient look. She pushed the door open and walked in. Behind her came Hugo Shannon, head of production, and Harding Liu, the finance chief.

"Kate, perfect," said Maxine. "We're about to assign responsibilities for tonight. We have to finish and email this investor package by three a.m. our time for the East Coast."

Then she strode up to Lionel's whiteboard and started dividing assignments.

5

FRIDAY, SEPTEMBER 27TH
TELLURIDE, COLORADO

Reddi Christiansen's work clothing was in a heap at her feet. She peeled off her bra and underpants and threw them on top with relish. A breeze came through the open windows and she shivered, her long red ponytail shaking down her back. *Crap, she forgot to close the curtains.*

"Wolfie, scare them away," Reddi whispered. Wolfie stretched her long frame, pushing her huge chest and front paws forward, extending like a telescope. Her deep howl rumbled the old glass panes in the one-room house.

Reddi laughed and rubbed her fingers through Wolfie's fur. Turning her back to the windows facing the quiet street, she pulled on her stretch shorts, hopping from one foot to the other. She tugged her sports bra and tank top over her broad freckled shoulders.

"Fine, we're respectable now. You ready to run to the top of the pass?"

Wolfie jumped up. The fur covering her one-hundred-twenty pound frame was snow white. She sat and cocked her head to the side, tuning her vertical ears toward Reddi. The black markings around her curious blue eyes created a theatrical mask on her white face. She was a wolfdog. Part Arctic wolf, part Siberian husky, and every bit Reddi's best friend.

"Okay, get your leash." Wolfie sprung over and picked up her leash, swinging it like a lasso. Then she pranced and juked side to side, with motion as fluid as mercury.

"Save some for 13,000 feet, darling," laughed Reddi. The old door creaked as it opened. Wolfie rushed onto the weathered front porch, leaping over a hand-drawn railing. As she landed she spun about, kicking up a dusty cloud in the dirt street.

Reddi rolled her mountain bike into the bright sun, the warmth feeling glorious on her skin. She slipped on her riding shades and pulled her ponytail out the back of her helmet. She glanced down the row of cribs along her street. Each was small with simple wood framing, former bordellos where madams entertained during the town's boomtown mining era.

A mahogany-tanned guy with a shock of curly black hair was loading a hang glider on his truck. She waved. "Hey, Crazy Jack."

He paused, balancing the kite with one hand on the rack. "Heading up, Reddi?"

"Yeah, me and Wolfie. To Imogene Pass."

He shoved the kite on the rack and walked toward her, thick calves below his baggy shorts. "Good news. The new demo skis from Volkl came in. Your comps. Maybe come by the ski shop after your ride?"

"Whoohoo! For me? Really?" With a quick crank she glided over, standing on one pedal. Wolfie playfully circled them.

"I promised. No way a skier like you should have to buy skis. This winter fifty people will come buy a pair from me, because they saw you on them." His face crinkled in a smile around his mountaineering sunglasses, which made him appear a decade younger.

"You're the best." She threw her arms around his shoulders and squeezed, her six-foot frame a half-foot taller than his.

Reddi knew Jack often had free deals for her. But she didn't realize how special he believed her to be. He had watched her outcompete the boys in adventure sports since she was eight. Then she blossomed. With the face of an unaware movie star, from the cliff-launch cheekbones and perfect complexion to waves of red hair. He smiled at her like a proud uncle.

She shook her bike handlebars, like Wolfie wagging her head. "When should I come by your shop?"

"Whenever. After your ride or after work. I'll be there."

"See you then. So excited, Jack!" Reddi beamed a megawatt smile, feeling like a kid at Christmas. She launched up the dusty street with a hard push and a wheelie, whistling at Wolfie.

Crazy Jack couldn't help but admire the muscular arms pulling on the handlebars and the sculpted hips and calves cranking effortlessly. "One hell of an athlete," he muttered, shaking his head.

In six blocks Reddi and Wolfie had passed through town and reached the former mining road that would lead them to the top. She called, Wolfie ran closer, and she grabbed the leash and stuffed it into her Camelback. She started the timer on her sport watch and immediately increased her pedal speed. The air smelled like spruce trees. She breathed deeply and pushed herself to break her personal best. As she rode she dreamed of being an Olympian.

The rocky road climbed above Telluride's horseshoe canyon toward a mining ghost town called Tomboy. Wolfie loped ahead, darted around outcrops and scampered over scree slopes. It was a long continuous climb. She quickly passed 9,000 feet, then wound her way beyond 10,000 feet. Above 11,000 Reddi was breathing more heavily. It became rugged and isolated as they climbed high above the tree line into Savage Basin. A panorama of colorful rock cliffs surrounded her, squeezing closer. Reddi grunted as she wrestled the handlebars and pumped, her wheels slipping in the deep, sharp-edged hardscrabble. Sweat streaked her face and back, then quickly evaporated in the dry air. They never stopped during the hour and a half ride. As the agony of each revolution became unbearable and she sucked air like a vacuum, she and Wolfie reached the summit. With a huge gulp she yelled, "Imogene Pass, baby, 13,000 feet!"

She dropped her bike on the knife-edge pass, hooting in excitement between breaths. Reddi looked out over the expanse of the Rockies. Dozens of peaks shouldered together nearby. "Let's climb all of these, Wolfie," she yelled, throwing her arms up high above her. Then she sat and hugged her dog, rubbing behind the ears, her fingers digging into the thick and warm coat.

"It's a lot of hard work for a few moments up here on Imogene. But we're in training, right?" She looked into shining eyes. Wolfie nosed her and licked the salt on her face.

"Oh, lovely kisses." She rubbed her muzzle affectionately. The breeze blew over the surrounding snow glacier. Reddi quickly chilled. She zipped on a windbreaker. After a long Wolfie hug, she pulled on her pack and got ready to go.

Her bike felt like it had wings on the descent. Reddi crouched and hopped over dips and rises, her full suspension absorbing the impact. Dropping down 5,000 vertical feet around twists and turns felt weightless and free. It was forty-five minutes of dancing through a kaleidoscope of colors, textures and geologic beauty. She braked occasionally for Wolfie. The wolfdog's feet were conditioned to the rocks, but Reddi kept an eye on them, worried about cuts.

The transition back to town always struck her. The severe peaks and remote basins had a rugged beauty with cliffs glowing red, orange and blue. Below the surrounding mountains, the town looked like a board game, with quaint Victorian houses and small buildings sitting like little pieces on the flat valley floor. A former mining town going back to the 1870's, it had been a hideout of outlaws—the devil's den of whiskey, dance halls, bordellos, and anything else that could attract a miner's hard-earned pay. As a school kid, she was captivated by the edgy history. Today, what Reddi loved was the skiing, mountain and adventure sports, and dozens of music, film, and food festivals that attracted and supported the extreme zealots.

As they entered Telluride, Reddi put Wolfie on her leash. They leisurely walked down Main Street, which was lined with trucks, SUVs, and bikes. Most of them were covered in red dust. The UPS driver called out and waved to Reddi. They bantered as his truck slowly rolled by. She paused in the shade of the awning outside the former bank building famous for being robbed by Butch Cassidy and the Sundance Kid.

Wolfie tugged the leash, pulling Reddi over to The Roast Cafe. A huge metal water bowl sat in front. As Wolfie lapped like a gurgling stream, the door swung open.

A woman wearing a gold scarf, blond bangs peeking from underneath on her forehead, came rushing outside. "Good afternoon, Reddi." She spoke as though every word mattered, with clear vigor.

Reddi loved Helga's charming German accent. She had run The Roast for as long as Reddi could remember. "Hi Helga. Wolfie couldn't pass your cafe without stopping."

"Ja, Wolfie. You should always stop for a treat." Helga extended a hand with a dog biscuit. Wolfie's long pink tongue eagerly wrapped around it.

"How was the ride today?" Helga crouched next to Wolfie, rubbing her white fur as she happily crunched on the biscuit. Her glasses slid on her nose. She looked up at Reddi, pushing them back.

"New record. So I'm psyched." Reddi took off her helmet and shook her hair in the warm sun.

"You see, you will be an Olympic champion. No one can keep up with you except for my Wolfie."

"Helga, you have to be the world's most enthusiastic person."

"I know what I am talking about. You will be a champion."

"I hope so."

"But me, I must get back to my work." She took Wolfie's head in her hands and kissed her black markings. "My snow white beauty with the black mask." Then she kissed Reddi on the cheek and slipped her more biscuits for Wolfie.

"You are too good."

With a wink, Helga hurried back inside to her customers. Reddi did a sweeping wave with her helmet, then headed toward her house for a shower.

"This time we're remembering to close the curtains, Wolfie."

After her shower, she slowly pulled on her work clothes. Hard toed boots, a worn leather jacket, and spatter-stained blue jeans.

She walked three blocks to a dusty alley and faded red metal building.

A sliding door, with the same dull paint, was wide open. Hanging on a huge corner timber was a sign on which Reddi's little sister had proudly drawn, 'Larry's Welding Shop' in multi-colored chalk.

"Hey, I wonder where my favorite pack of fun is?" Reddi shouted, peering inside. Her eyes adjusted to the dark as she looked across the collection of welding projects, half-completed inventions, and rusting antiques. The shop felt cool. The aroma reminded her of the inside of an old car—the cracked leather and oil and weathered wood.

She walked further inside and passed the welding table, covered with spatters of flux and chop saw grit, with the sharp smell of exploded fireworks.

Reddi found her sister Hannah far in the back, curled up in an old broken-down couch, reading a book. Her long brown hair was a piled-up mop on her head, brown rim glasses on a button of a nose, long pre-teen pony legs in shorts.

"Hello, hello, earth to Hannah."

Hannah's glasses peered over the top of the book. "Hi Reddi. Sorry, it is a very absorbing story," she said, with the drama of a twelve-year old. Getting lost in reading was Hannah's secret getaway, thought Reddi. Not unlike her own bike rides.

Reddi moved behind her and wrapped her arms around her shoulders, tickling her sides.

"Stop," she whined, but Reddi knew she loved the attention.

"Are you going to stay inside all day?"

"I'm reading."

"So?" Reddi responded.

"Don't you remember the quote from the famous bank robber, Willie Sutton?"

Sometimes Hannah sounded like a schoolteacher. "Who? Huh? Where do you get this stuff?"

"Willie Sutton, who robbed many prominent banks for millions of dollars, was asked why he robbed them. Do you know what he said?" Hannah adjusted her glasses as she looked up at Reddi.

"Nope. But I do know who I'm going to tickle even more."

"No!" she squealed. "Willie Sutton answered, 'Because that's where the money is.'"

"That's funny. Do you have a point, bookworm?" Reddi's fingers massaged Hannah's shoulders.

"The point is, inside is where the books are. That's why I am on this couch."

Reddi got one more squeal as she hugged Hannah. "Okay, I give up. Time for me to get back to work."

"Okay, flamethrower."

"See you later, bookworm." She kissed her on the head and walked out the front door, Wolfie prancing alongside.

Outside, she waved to her dad, who was bent over a metal piece clamped to a jig. A large gray welding helmet was perched on his head above an enormous set of shoulders. He nodded and then his helmet flipped down. His welding gun spattered brightly, like a big sparkler.

Reddi donned her protective welding helmet. It was like being a deep-sea diver, she thought, plunging into her work. She pulled on her heavy leather gloves and concentrated on fabricating a set of brackets for a new spec house. She cut out patterns in one-half-inch steel plate, the oxy-acetylene torch burning white hot at six thousand degrees. Sparks flew. Hot steel dripped to the ground, the edges still glowing orange. Occasionally she stamped out little smoking fires started by the molten metal.

As the hours passed her hands ached. Summer days were long, as the rush of construction work kept them busy. She pushed ahead, knowing winters in the Rockies could slow the pace to a frozen crawl.

Late in the afternoon, as the sun was falling behind the mountains, she saw her father pause in his work. He pushed his helmet back. A giant of a man, his block-like head was anchored by a red beard.

"Can we talk a bit?" He asked in his gentle voice.

Reddi worried about disappointing him. As she took off her helmet, she wondered, *Hell, did I do something stupid again?*

They went over to the doorway of the shop and sat down on the cutting table. Her dad clearly had something on his mind. She watched him take a deep breath, like he was winding up.

"As much as I love this town and the people, I keep seeing your Mom, Anna, everywhere. It's been three years since she died. I thought this sadness would pass. But everything about the building, the town, the old friends, all remind me of our time with her. And it makes me so sad." He paused, his shoulders rising and falling as he took mountain-sized chests of air. Reddi was hardly breathing. Her dad had never admitted this pain.

"You know, we were wandering the West, and drove our VW van up this valley. You were in the back seat asleep, just eight years old. We stopped in the middle of Main Street, got out, Anna twirled in her Gypsy shawl, looking around at the town and the mountains, and said, this is it. We looked into each other's eyes and knew. We didn't need to go any farther. We woke you up and you spun around, arms outreached, eyes sparking at the mountains in awe, just like your mother."

She'd heard this story a dozen times before, but each time it was magical.

"Life is different now. Hannah needs a mother's advice and attention, as she becomes a young woman. And I need to find someone. Someone to fill this hole in my life."

"Dad, no one expects you to remain single." Her chest felt tight as she breathed. "I'm sure Mom would feel that way too."

He nodded his huge head. "You are like your mother. Not only the tall and beautiful part. You are kind." He paused again, gulping a breath.

Reddi felt the back of her throat starting to choke up.

Her dad continued. "But, this is a small place. Especially for someone my age, with two, well really one kid. You, you are a young woman." He smiled proudly at her. "But me, there aren't a lot of eligible candidates here for my dance."

"Dad, it takes time to meet the right woman."

He nodded and then squared his shoulders.

"Anyway, my mind is made up. I'm leaving Telluride with Hannah. And I'd like to offer you all my tools and the lease on the building, to take over the business."

The words sounded foreign. Like someone else had said them.

"What!? You're leaving?" How could he leave? Without her?

"I'm serious."

Reddi was stunned.

"With five more years on the lease your costs are locked in. You'll generate more than enough to make a good living."

Five years? Stuck here by myself running a welding shop? She understood why this might be better for him. But being left behind hurt. And the shop—that could tie her down forever! *What about skiing competitively, traveling the world, winning the X Games or even the Olympics?*

"I don't know what to say, Dad."

"I want you to have the business. All of it. The shop, the customers. Tools. Everything."

He had no idea this sounded like a life sentence to her. "Dad, where would you go?"

"Santa Cruz, in California. I have some friends there who have offered to help get us started in the community. I want to go soon so Hannah can get setup in the school year."

Wow, he had thought about this. "Have you told Hannah?"

"No. I'll tell Hannah tonight. I wanted to talk to you first about taking the shop. So that you are comfortable with the transition."

"Comfortable? It's not only about the business, Dad. She's going to miss me more than the stupid shop." Reddi couldn't help the tears that started. She angrily wiped them away.

"I'm sorry. I will miss you, we both will miss you, Reddi." Her dad stood and held out his massive arms.

Reddi swung off the cutting table and threw herself into him. She squeezed until her arms hurt. But it was nothing like the pain she felt in her heart.

"See you at dinner," she said. She let go of him, then quickly walked out before he could see the tears streaming down her face.

She kicked rocks all the way back to her place. She threw off her jacket and hugged Wolfie. Wolfie leaned forward, her pink tongue licking Reddi's tears. It felt rough and warm. But her father's plan brought back the ache of losing her mother.

She grabbed her laptop and curled up under a blanket on the couch, clicking through pictures of her mom and family. Of their early times together before she got sick. Pictures at Christmas, fishing in alpine lakes, and skiing together. Then a picture of Reddi and Trig Garcia popped up, when he first visited Telluride three years ago, just after her mom got the cancer diagnosis.

Trig. He was so solid. Like the big brother she never had, growing up next door in Austin, Texas. She had loved to bother him, following him around and asking questions, but he didn't seem to mind. He was seven years older than Reddi, a quiet electronics and computer geek. After her family moved to Telluride they had fallen out of touch. When he showed up to visit, she learned he'd joined the Navy and became a SEAL. Over the past three years he'd been kind of a part-time town resident. Maybe she'd call him.

She launched Skype. Then she realized he could be anywhere in the world. It might be the middle of the night. He had such crazy assignments, working for Ancill Corp, the military security contractor. Maybe she shouldn't bother him.

Suddenly it was ringing. Oh, heck. Well, if he didn't answer right away, she'd hang up. After the fourth ring she started to disconnect.

"Hi Reddi."

"Oh, hey Trig," she said, quietly. "Sorry, I'm probably waking you up."

"No, it's fine. We're good." The video screen came to life and she saw his dark eyes above a square, shadowed jaw.

She sniffled.

"What's wrong, Reddi?"

"Is it that obvious? Oh, I probably look a mess."

"No, never. With you, if you aren't ecstatic, I know something is wrong. Take it as a compliment."

She blurted out the news. "Dad's moving to California with Hannah and leaving me behind. He wants to find a new wife and Telluride's too small. And he wants me to stay with the shop and spend the rest of my life welding."

"Whoa, hang on. Your dad loves you."

"He thinks giving me the shop is perfect for me. But that isn't all that I want to do with my life." She looked at Trig, miserable.

"He's probably feeling a little guilty and trying to set you up financially. He knows the customers love your work. You do all the billing and accounting now anyway. From that standpoint it's pretty sweet."

"God, I wish Mom were alive. It was easier to tell her my dreams. My dad is always so damned practical."

"I'm sorry. But he doesn't think like a twenty-one-year old. He's thinks like, you know, an older dad."

"That's the problem."

"You're afraid running the shop will mean you won't be able to competitively ski or travel?"

"Yes. What if I want to compete in New Zealand in the summer? Or train all winter? But if I tell this to Dad he'll think I'm ungrateful. Or irresponsible. Or both. Oh shit. Am I a terrible person?" Reddi looked away from the screen, afraid of the answer.

"No, not at all. You're actually trying to be obliging to your dad. But that's crimping your dreams."

She looked back and smiled at Trig's image. "Thank you for not thinking I'm selfish."

"You aren't. I mean that."

She rubbed her eyes and took a breath. "So how are you? Are you coming back soon?"

"I'm good. But I'm not sure about timing." He gave her an expression she always thought was cute, when he raised his bushy eyebrows, in a "who knows?" look.

"Can you say what you're doing?"

"International project. Can't really say. You know this crazy life."

He was such a mystery man. "I understand, Big Trig. Remember when I used to call you Big Trig all the time, to drive you crazy?"

"You used to do a lot of things to try to get me to pay attention. Pretty funny."

"Sorry. I was such a brat. Anyway, Trig, what do you think I should do?" She rubbed her head, looking for an answer.

"You don't have to decide today. Or even before your dad leaves with Hannah. They are making the change, not you. You can let things evolve. Keep your dreams and the shop. Then see."

"Oh. Jeez. That's logical." She thought for a moment. "But what if something comes up . . . an amazing opportunity, that is completely out of this world?"

"Then take it. And deal with the shop then."

She thought about that. "Oh, okay. Like always, you can figure anything out. Thanks, Trig."

"You're the one who is dealing with all this. I'm just suggesting patience. Let it evolve."

"I will. But I have a weird feeling. Changes are coming in my life. Big time."

6

FRIDAY, SEPTEMBER 27TH

The curved clock on the dashboard of Maxine's Mini Cooper said eight a.m. Four more hours to meet Havermyer's deadline. Her chest tightened, which annoyed her. She normally thrived under pressure. Was it that she wanted to prove herself to Havermyer? *Damn it, or was it Lionel?* He was the one truly impressive guy whose ego had room for her career. But he was always chasing a new dream. With a deep breath she took a last look at her apartment. *Focus Maxine, separate business from personal.* She started the Mini.

She navigated through her neighborhood in the Mission District of San Francisco, a diverse and vibrant area. Traffic was hectic and loud, horns blaring, buses growling, scooters and bikes weaving in and out. Maxine passed by mural-covered buildings, small ethnic markets, and taquerias with security gates.

As she drove she thought about last night. The team had gotten a solid investor package out by four-thirty a.m. The production guy Hugo was an irreverent wiseass, although extremely smart. Harding the financial guy was passable but somewhat unimaginative. And Kate the marketer was a prima donna who didn't believe a frigging thing she said. Everything had to be approved by Lionel. Maxine wondered if they were sexually involved. Kate would probably do anything to get ahead.

Gradually the neighborhood gentrified. Expensive European cars were parked in front of remodeled Victorian and Edwardian homes. Trendy restaurants appeared with clever names and wordy menus posted in the windows.

A huge Google bus pulled right in front of Maxine. She slammed on the brakes and honked. Oblivious, it continued its trip to the Googleplex in Silicon Valley, full of young city dwellers already logged on, sipping cappuccinos on the ride. As she picked up speed she gave wide berth to the shiny white Facebook shuttle bus. It was at the curb loading up for the trip to Menlo Park, casually dressed people hunched over smart phones, stumbling onboard. The thought of Double Vision having its own buses one day made her smile.

Her phone rang. She glanced and answered. "Morning, Lionel."

"Just making sure you didn't sleepin after that long night. How are you doing?"

"It's a big day. I feel great."

"A shower, a change of clothes, and good to go, right?"

She had always liked his early morning enthusiasm. "Sure isn't the first time, Sparky."

She heard him laugh at the name. "Where are you?"

"In SoMa. I'll be five minutes." She turned to business. "Any interest yet?"

"Some. I've got two conference calls in the next hour. And then another at ten. So three possibilities so far."

Her stomach tensed. "I've got three calls as well. Two back east, one here in the city. Can you make an eleven-thirty with me?"

"Sure, but that's tight with the twelve o'clock deadline. Who's it with?"

"Blaine Latrell, with Axlewright. He had to push it back."

"Right, the guy you know from McKinsey. Will do. We've got to land at least one of these, Maxine."

She sucked her breath in. "Today is the day. Let me get another call in before I hit the office." She hung up and kept dialing for dollars.

***

Maxine walked into the office glued to her mobile. With a quick wave to the bullpen, she disappeared into the conference room. She camped out there, on calls and online. The foghorns periodically moaned, marking time she wished was not passing. She kept dialing, texting, and emailing.

"Admittedly it is quick, but you have been tracking Double Vision for a year now." The rapping at her window jerked her head from her screen, and she waved Lionel in, distractedly.

"I understand. Well, if the opportunity to co-invest with Havermyer changes his mind in the next few hours, let me know. But I'm afraid I need to take this other call. Thank you. Bye." She stood up and met Lionel's eyes, shaking her head. She slipped out of her teal blazer, put it around the back of her chair, and tugged at her cowl neckline. Her insides churned.

"I've had my share of those too," Lionel said, exhaling. "Quick update?"

"Please."

"Roger Scalton from VentureEast Partners looked at the package and claims their interest is incredibly high. He knows our deadline is in three hours. I think he is at least an eighty percent possibility. The second is Hank Welcher of Falconvest. He's cooled since Havermyer's offer, which surprises me considering he offered me a bridge loan backed by equity."

"Isn't he backing SocialLending, the micro finance company that won Entrepreneur of the Year?"

"Yes. Anyway, he committed to respond by ten a.m. our time. But realistically, just those two for me."

Maxine nodded. "Blaine Latrell from Axlewright Capital pinged me last night with a few questions their attorney forwarded him, so we know they are looking at the package seriously. When I talked to him earlier this morning, he was very positive, but it sounds like their managing director is a bit of a stumbling block. But Blaine is over the moon with Jacob's involvement. I think he expects the relationship would be a huge career advancement."

"He was lukewarm with me a year ago. He seemed exclusively focused on whether we had home-run potential."

"Blaine and I overlapped at McKinsey for a little while, so we have some history."

"Ah, so he is strongly in our corner?"

Maxine paused, then decided to keep it simple. "Yes, but he isn't a partner at Axlewright, yet." She moved on quickly to the next one. "Walter Proudstone of Deepwater Investments is very senior, but he's concerned about their being East Coast and our being out here. You know how they hate to travel. Could be a handy excuse—I'll know more in an hour."

"So we have four strong candidates and barely three hours."

Maxine managed a brave smile. "It's the final four for the big dance, and we only need one."

Both of their phones started vibrating. Lionel walked out, phone to his ear.

By nine-thirty a.m., Lionel let Maxine know Falconvest was passing. "Hank Welcher told me his appetite in the social entrepreneur category is filled with his SocialLending investment. Down to three."

Maxine's next call was with Deepwater at ten a.m. Double Vision's attorney, Greta Dahlstrom, joined in the conference room with Maxine and Harding, the CPA.

The Deepwater call quickly grew to fifteen participants. Then it became a free-for-all, voices cutting in and out, with confusion over who was asking what questions. Some partners had dialed in from cell phones and weren't muted, so loud background noise was drowning out the conversation. *This is hellish,* Maxine thought.

She scrambled into an empty office, calling Walter Proudstone of Deepwater directly on his cell. "Walter, all due respect, this call is a runaway train."

She heard him whisper into the phone. "Maxine, this has devolved into typical playground behavior. Younger partners are trying to muscle in to rub shoulders with Havermyer."

"Is there any reasonable compromise? We could offer them observer seats, nonvoting, of course."

"I thought of that option as well, but dismissed it as not being in either your or my best interests."

"I see." Maxine tugged at her hair, her mind racing.

"So you see my dear, I don't want this sort of dissension, perhaps better described as a lack of unanimity at Deepwater, to surface."

Maxine glanced at her watch. The next conference call was in exactly one minute.

"Walter, is this essentially a 'no' by indecision?"

"I'm afraid so."

"Thank you, Walter. I apologize. I have another investor call literally in sixty seconds. I do appreciate your efforts."

"Let's stay in touch, my young protégé. Good luck, Maxine."

Maxine crossed off Deepwater as she punched her cell, threw open the door, then started running down the hallway to the conference room and the VentureEast call. Damn, only two chances left.

She was breathing hard as she burst into the room. Lionel was seated at the scuffed wooden conference table, engaged in preliminary chatter, buying time until Maxine arrived. Their attorney and CPA sat ready.

Maxine gulped for air as she wrestled a chair. Her stomach growled as she slid down next to Lionel. Somehow she smoothly announced, "Good morning everyone, this is Maxine Gold joining. I've been looking forward to this meeting. Lionel has thoroughly briefed me, so please consider me up to speed on VentureEast. That is, with the exception of your decision today, of course."

"Welcome, Maxine, this is Roger Scalton." For the next twenty minutes Roger proceeded to compliment all the parties, especially Jacob Havermyer. He described the rigor and depth of their research and analysis. Then he raised issues, which Lionel and Maxine handled easily. Maxine sat motionless and focused. Lionel twisted like a caged animal. Then the VC finally got to the "however" sentence.

"However, although Jacob Havermyer has the money and reputation to support a social entrepreneur experiment, the VentureEast investors expect a focus on high returns, without consideration of social impact."

Lionel hit the mute button and turned to Maxine. "That's it, that's the problem."

She looked at him, perplexed. "They are afraid Jacob is throwing us a bone. That he isn't worried if he loses his fifteen million, or more, in a social cause. And these guys don't want to have to argue with Jacob about profitability."

"Jacob's treating this like a serious investment," Maxine said, defensively. "And so are we."

"I agree. But they are worried it's only a charity. Maybe if we let them talk directly to Havermyer they'd change their mind?"

She shook her head. "It may be ego, but I want to bring him a done deal, not a deal he has to close for us."

Lionel sucked in his breath. "Are we willing to walk? Then everything rests on closing Axlewright."

Maxine looked at the blinking mute button, knowing the other side was waiting. Time was running out. "I have a good feeling about Blaine and Axlewright."

"Hello, Maxine and Lionel? Can you all hear us? Hello?" The mute light blinked faster on the speakerphone. Greta and Harding looked across the table anxiously.

Lionel frowned. "Let's challenge them."

"Pretty aggressive."

"Go big or go home," said Lionel.

"Big is good," replied Maxine, showing confidence in his strategy.

Lionel hit the mute button. "Pardon us, Roger. My apologies."

"There you are. We thought we lost you."

"Roger, the time is here for us to select a partner. Frankly, we are concerned VentureEast doesn't seem to value the social entrepreneurship model. And we need a partner with no equivocation on that point."

There was complete silence on the line. Ten seconds went by.

"Hello. Roger?" Another five seconds ticked off.

"Lionel, thank you for your consideration. I believe we agree with you."

"You agree with the terms of the deal?" Lionel responded.

"No sir, I'm sorry. We agree that we do not share your unequivocal belief in this model. We are passing on your opportunity. Thank you and good-day."

The lights went out on the phone. Lionel looked up at the ceiling.

"Damn. I screwed that up." He slammed back, exhaling.

"No, it was inevitable," replied Maxine.

He kicked the table edge and his chair rolled backward.

"So now we're down to our last shot."

Lionel pulled himself back to the table. He gripped the old speakerphone, flexing the black plastic triangular shape. Maxine saw the frustration in his face as he twisted the plastic like a Mobius strip. Suddenly the speakerphone snapped with a loud crack, as plastic shards exploded on the table. Lionel's hands started to bleed.

"Oh shit."

"My God, are you all right?" exclaimed Greta.

"That was so stupid." Lionel shook his head as his hands dripped red.

"You're bleeding, let me get something," said Harding.

"I'm fine." He wiped his hands on some papers on the table, creating a mess. Lionel crumpled up several stained balls.

"You are not fine. Where are the bandages kept?" asked Maxine.

Just then her cell phone started ringing.

"Damn, it's Blaine."

"We've got ten minutes. Let's use every one of them," said Lionel. He motioned for Harding to sit. He wrapped more papers around his hands. He buried them in two piles, the document a smeared mess.

"Your hands." The phone kept ringing.

"The papers are stopping the bleeding, seriously. Please, put it on speaker."

Maxine cocked her head toward him. "Okay superman, let's turn that power into closing our last hope."

Maxine's phone was vibrating, dancing across the conference table. She answered. "Blaine, good to hear from you."

"Please don't tell me I'm too late. I've been moving heaven and earth over here."

"You aren't too late. We're in final discussions. It's hard to decide which is the right firm."

"You haven't chosen someone else have you?"

"No, not yet. Should we be considering Axlewright as well?"

"Not only considering us, but selecting us. We've got history together Maxine, I think we'd make a great team. The other firms don't have that."

"That's a good point, Blaine. Would you mind holding for one minute, to get Lionel?"

She placed the call on hold. Lionel started whooping and jumping around the conference table, dancing on one foot and the other like a medicine man in a peyote dance. Bloody papers scattered everywhere.

"Let's save the dance until we have a deal." But she shook with excitement. Lionel sat back down and they all leaned toward the cell phone on the table. Lionel nodded.

Maxine pressed the speakerphone button.

"Blaine, I pulled Lionel off a call with another investor group. You two met before, during your earlier discussions, right?"

"Yes, Lionel, hello again."

"Hello, Blaine. Maxine mentioned you two worked together at McKinsey."

"Oh yes, we go way back. A lot of experience together."

"Indeed. And beyond that, we're impressed with Axlewright's success with companies in the food and beverage vertical," Maxine complimented smoothly.

Lionel looked at his watch. It was eleven-fifty three. Seven minutes to the deadline.

"Thank you. Well, I think that is a strong reason why we are a great fit. The companies we invest in draw a lot from our expertise, not solely our money and contacts, but our strategy for operations, marketing, and sales. Our insight produces meaningful outcomes."

"Blaine, this is Lionel. Here is how I see it. You've got experience with Maxine, you're local, and focused on our vertical. Plus you appreciate the upside of working with Jacob Havermyer. All told, I think Axlewright is the ideal fit."

"I'm glad you see it that way."

"But of course, you can't be in the game without a letter of intent and the proof of funds transfer. With the deadline nearing, I have to ask, are you prepared to move forward?"

"How do we stand in comparison to the others? Do you have other commitments at these terms?"

"Blaine, this is Maxine. I can assure you we have not altered the terms for anyone. Jacob was adamant about that. And we maintain confidentiality among all investors. However, I can say you are one of four finalists."

"Very well. Then, here is my one caveat to the deal."

"Oh, and what is that?" Maxine looked quizzically at the phone.

"I'll email you my scanned LOI and funds proof right now, if you accept it on the spot and we have a conference call with Jacob Havermyer to introduce us as partners."

The table was silent. Then Maxine suddenly answered without looking at Lionel. "I'm sorry, Blaine, but we committed to Jacob no negotiation or interviews by the other investors prior to closing. You know me, I'd do it for you if I could."

Maxine looked up to see Lionel's surprised expression. He whispered in her ear, "Let's close him. We can control the phone call with Havermyer." She shrugged and then nodded.

"I understand, Maxine. The point isn't to bring up deal terms with him. The introduction is a way of letting my managing director and the other senior partners know I have been in communication with Jacob, that he knows me, and we see eye to eye."

Lionel was bobbing his head up and down. It was eleven fifty-seven.

"Blaine, can you give us a moment to confer?"

"Yes, of course."

She put Blaine on hold.

"Lionel, it's interesting he is doing this solo, without his boss on the call."

"Who cares? This is great news. The larger groups introduce more objections."

"Good point. Seems unusual, however."

"At this point he is our only shot. Let's do it." He pounded the table and then winced.

Lionel used his other hand to take the phone off hold. "Excellent news, Blaine. Maxine and I have discussed your offer. If I get your signed copies right away, we have a deal."

"Terrific. I just sent them to Maxine."

Maxine saw Lionel pause, as though he was still getting used to sharing the top role. He continued: "We'll countersign right away. Welcome to Double Vision."

"Excellent, pleased to be an investor. Thank you, Maxine, and you too of course, Lionel."

"Welcome, Blaine," chimed in Maxine. It was eleven fifty-eight. She tried to sound calm while her stomach ached in a tight knot.

"Should we get Jacob on the line?" asked Blaine.

"Certainly," said Maxine. "I'll get Jacob and conference you in. Hold on please." Almost there, she thought. Her fingers were vibrating as she dialed Jacob's line.

Maxine looked at Lionel and they exchanged an exhausted look.

"Havermyer."

"Jacob. It's Maxine and Lionel."

"Maxine, so good to hear your voice. I'm glad you called, in a minute I'd be unavailable." Havermyer's distinctive high and fast-paced voice rang out.

"Perfect timing then. We are pleased to say Lionel and I have a signed commitment for the matching fifteen million, from Axlewright Capital in the city. We're working with their vice president, Blaine Latrell. I have him on the other line and he is dying to say hello in person. May I trouble you for that?"

"I see. No problem, put him on, Maxine." She suddenly realized she had been holding her breath.

As Maxine conferenced them in she imagined Blaine squirming with excitement as he cleared his throat, squared the shoulders of his blazer, and prepared to meet the renowned billionaire.

"Hello again everyone, Maxine and Lionel here. Jacob, may I introduce Blaine Latrell. Blaine, Jacob Havermyer.

"Hello Jacob, this is Blaine. Pleased to meet you, sir."

"Welcome to Double Vision, Blaine, nice to meet you too. Maxine and Lionel, I'm wiring over my fifteen million right away. Make sure you have an account where you can make some money on it until you spend it. I'm sorry, I have another commitment so I need to go, but I do have one quick question."

"Yes?"

"Let's see. It's been twenty-three hours and fifty-nine minutes. What took you all so long?" A booming laugh followed. Maxine pictured him with his long gray ponytail and white beard, his eyes glowing like a mad scientist.

Then the line went dead.

7

FRIDAY AFTERNOON, SEPTEMBER 27TH

Antonio Fanachi took his usual spot in the quiet Italian restaurant in North Beach. The table was in the rear of a roped off private dining room, with views out to Saints Peter and Paul Cathedral. The windowpanes were rippled with age, twisting the light that glowed on the weathered oak floors. The dark wood furniture had seen years of baptisms, first communion, and other celebrations. Paintings and black and white pictures from the old country hung on walls of faded gold and aqua.

Fanachi sat upright against the back wall, like he held it in place. His starched white collar stood out against his tan skin and olive sportcoat. A Sig Sauer 9 mm pistol rested comfortably in his shoulder holster. Two broad-shouldered guys with squashed noses and gruff demeanors sat near the entrance, popping out of triple X suits. In the front room the bartender kept a double-barreled shotgun under the counter.

He focused on the steaming plate of pasta with red sauce in front of him.

The entrance to the private dining room was through a set of double doors, presently swung open. At exactly twelve o'clock Fanachi looked up to see Igor Vasilchenko unhook the soft braided rope hung across the opening and walk in. He was slender with short blond hair and blue eyes. Fanachi watched him stride carefully but confidently toward him, with a nod to the big guys as they eyed him.

"Hook it behind you."

Igor stopped abruptly. "Yes." With a brief frown he turned to the task, his smooth entrance undone.

Nicco, the darker of the two hulks, let out a grunt. Fanachi turned his head toward him and caught his own reflection in the gold-leaf mirror on the wall. His dark hair, edged with silver, was combed straight back. He was broad across the forehead. His eyes were black and deep set. Carved furrows intersected with his large Roman nose, creating flat chiseled planes for cheeks. His thin lips ended their straight line in downturns. *Jesus, the older I get the more I look like an ancient stone statue. What the hell,* he thought.

Fanachi motioned for Igor to sit.

"Do you remember when we brought you from Russia?" He spoke slowly and deliberately.

"Yes. October of last year." Igor sat straight and attentive. His legs jiggled under the table.

"And you had been smuggling Afghani junk, through Turkey and then by ship on the Black Sea to Odessa, for sale in Europe?"

"Yes."

"Your Russian friends, the gang you were with, they are being eaten by fish right now. Chained together at the bottom of the Black Sea." Fanachi forked several pasta shells and stirred them in his red sauce.

"What?!" Igor's leather jacket pulled tight as he leaned forward and slapped his hands on his knees. "Who?"

"A rival gang, from Moscow. Sevskaya Bratva. They had some fun first, with ice picks and axes. Once they finished hacking them up they dropped them overboard, all wrapped up in fish nets and heavy weights." The sauce-covered pasta disappeared into Fanachi's mouth. He followed it with red wine.

Igor hunched over like he was about to throw up on the floor. His face twitched and he sucked in his breath. "Everyone? Alexander Bubka, Ivan Shevchenko, Dmitri Kovalenko . . . ." His voice drifted off. "How many?"

Fanachi dipped a slice of juicy tomato into olive oil and stuffed it in his mouth before answering. "I don't have the names. There were twelve people. Afterward the Sevskaya Bratva called me as a courtesy. So I wouldn't retaliate because of our relationship." He wiped his mouth with a napkin as he motioned between himself and Igor. With a shrug he added, "They said they had no choice. It was business."

Igor slumped lower over the floor. His torso convulsed. Fanachi saw his lips pull back as if bile had surged up into his mouth. Finally, Igor said, "Dangerous business."

"Yes, it is."

Eventually Igor looked up at Fanachi, elbows still on his knees. "You know this for sure?"

"Would you like a one-way ticket back to look for them?" He drilled his black eyes into Igor.

"No." He shook his head slowly.

"It's good to be here in San Francisco and not with your old friends, right?"

Igor nodded at Fanachi.

Fanachi softened his tone. "If you do what I say, follow instructions, then one day your sister and her kid can join you here, understand?"

Igor slowly sat back up, stretching his hands out in front of him. He cracked his knuckles. "Yes. They are eager to come to States."

"Good. And in case you are planning revenge for your friends, my contact with the Sevskaya Bratva mentioned your sister by name. He said they know her address in Moscow."

Igor gripped the edge of the table, rattling the glasses. The two huge guards leaned forward, like chained bulldogs. Fanachi waved a hand.

"Why would those pigs hurt my sister?" Igor whispered.

"They won't as long as you don't do anything stupid. And you keep me happy."

Igor withdrew his hands. His face returned to a smooth mask and he rocked back and forth slowly. "Of course."

Fanachi wiped his mouth and hands. He dropped the napkin on the plate and pushed it away. Then he placed his hands in front of him on the table, as though playing cards, and the shoulders of his coat flared out.

"Igor, you are a very smart guy. I don't know why you got mixed up with that gang. Much safer using computers than smuggling junk and competing with the Russian Bratva."

"A mistake. I met them in Russian Army. Because I know electronics and explosives they talked me into helping them." He shook his head. One of his cheeks kept twitching. "Now they are gone."

The kitchen door swung open, followed by a staccato of high heels across the hardwood floor. A middle-aged waitress wearing a tight red skirt and low cut blouse arrived with a bottle of Chianti Classico. She smiled at Fanachi. As he nodded, she leaned forward gracefully and poured him more wine.

She turned to Igor, arching a painted eyebrow. "Vino? Or something to eat?"

He shook his head. "No, grazie."

Fanachi slowly sipped his wine as she cleared. Then she left in a swivel of motion and pronouncement of heels. Igor waited, staring at the floor.

Fanachi put the wine glass down. "I have a new assignment for you."

Igor looked up and nodded.

"This is your top priority. Understand?" He slid the wine glass to the side and tapped a finger on the table in front of him.

"Of course."

"Finish the other stuff later." Like a priest giving a benediction Fanachi waved his open hand at Igor. "Okay? Am I clear?"

"This is top priority. Right now," Igor repeated.

"Good. There are several groups I want you to track. Get into their email and have copies sent to the server so our people can look, okay?"

Igor perked up. "Of course."

"But don't disable anything. And we can't have this tracked back to us, understand? Use the standard protocol. But this one is special."

"I understand."

Fanachi stared at him, using his stone-like face and the silence for emphasis.

"Now this part I want to be clear on. Are you listening?"

"Of course. Always."

Fanachi drew closer and spoke in a low voice. Igor was about to begin paying the price of admission to the U.S.

***

That evening, Igor designed the spear phishing attack. He would target Kate Zell, since she was Double Vision's active online marketer. She would think the file was one of her regular marketing newsletters and click on it, but it would time-out before opening. Meanwhile his malicious link would give him access to her browser and ultimately her entire machine. He grinned, rubbing his hands together. Fanachi would be pleased. Then he would exploit vulnerabilities in the operating system and expand his control to all the company servers. From there, it would be trivial to regularly download all the key company intellectual property, such as their surveys, contracts, business plans, financials, emails, and schedules. The proxy servers and spoofed IP addresses would make this anonymous, just as Fanachi wanted. Igor loved America, the land of opportunity.

8

MONDAY, SEPTEMBER 30TH

The Double Vision leadership team crowded around the battered conference table. Lionel could see faces were tight. The usual banter was gone. Change was hard, especially when you weren't controlling it, thought Lionel. He sat in the middle, his laptop open to a spreadsheet. As usual, he'd dressed casually. A colorful woven shirt worn untucked, canvas rivet-reinforced pants, all terrain slip-ons.

Maxine walked into the room and found a spot opposite Lionel. "It's ten. Should we start?" she said. Her tablet was cradled in her arms. It was white, like her cashmere sweater and jeans.

"We should. We've got great news and a lot of planning ahead."

He brushed the long strands of hair from his eyes and smiled reassuringly. "Let's start with the great news. It's official, we raised thirty million dollars on Friday."

He saw the team exchanging glances. An awkward pause followed.

"Congratulations, this is good for Double Vision." It was Harding Liu, the young financial chief. He looked earnest in his crisp button-down as he applauded, his gold wire-rimmed-glasses bouncing as he bobbed. Scattered applause followed.

Damn, thought Lionel, *we're disconnected*. They should be elated. They had no idea how close they were to bankruptcy, so they can't appreciate this saved their jobs and the company.

Lionel jumped up out of his seat and started pacing around the room. He struck one hand down on top of the other, like a piston going up and down. "Okay, restart. Here is the deal." He marched to the whiteboard.

"Together we're going to review the high points of the new Double Vision plan, then divide up and conquer the details. But first, hit me with your deepest, darkest concerns or questions." He looked around the table. "Anything. Anyone."

Dasha Romanyuk, the head of IT, shot her hand up. "Why do we need thirty million dollars?"

Lionel decided to be very direct, like her question. "Candidly, because otherwise we would have been bankrupt in thirty days."

Dasha looked shocked. Murmurs and whispers ping-ponged around the room.

Harding jumped in. "Now I don't want people to panic or start spreading rumors. We have our financial reputation to consider."

Lionel waited for quiet. "Look, every company starts in the red, then hopes to move to profitability. Double Vision, we, us—have always been ambitious. Bottling our own products isn't easy. We give away one-for-one. We have taken the time to work with efficient partner companies around the world, that provide the local meals that fulfill our one-for-one commitment to the poor. Granted, our revenue has grown nicely—and you all deserve credit for that. But we aren't profitable. Essentially we ran out of investment cash. That's why we needed to make these changes." He walked around the room, getting close to people, making eye contact.

"What else?" he called out, his hands held open and wide. He could tell the faces were still absorbing the shock and fear of bankruptcy.

Hugo Shannon, the team-anointed Juice Genius, cocked a thick eyebrow upward. "Perhaps you can elaborate on our new planned foray into energy drinks, the questionable upstart of the beverage business."

"Great question. With that, allow me to personally introduce Maxine Gold. You all got the email last night announcing her as our new Co-CEO. Many of you have met her. She was critical in our raising the thirty million dollars and developed the business plan for the energy drink expansion. Welcome Maxine."

Polite applause followed. Maxine nodded her head curtly as she walked to the whiteboard and grabbed a marker.

"We're competing in a twenty-five-billion-dollar market. The analysts define it as functional and natural beverages, comprised of three big segments. The first segment is energy drinks/shots, sport drinks, and nutrient-enhanced waters—which are over sixteen billion dollars." She wrote in bold strokes as she spoke.

"Second is ready-to-drink coffee and tea. And third is the category we are currently in, nutritional beverages, which includes juices, fruit smoothies, yogurt drinks, and more."

She pointed back at the board.

"The first category is bigger and growing far faster than the third, where Double Vision has been stuck."

She looked around. "And the energy drinks are where smaller independents have exploded. You know the success stories of Red Bull, growing from nothing to over five billion dollars in sales currently. Monster is now a billion-dollar public company and 5 Hour Energy and Rockstar are in the hundreds of millions."

"So essentially people are stupid and love to drink crap that is bad for them?" Hugo asked, laughing. "Lots of caffeine, sugar, taurine, guanine, plus other questionable supplements and stimulants?"

"Juice Genius, you are our mastermind product guy. But most consumers don't have your PhD in microbiology from Stanford or experience as a nutritionist at Odwalla and Jamba Juice."

"Lucky for them, a lot of student loans followed by marginal pay," he quipped.

Maxine gave him a cool smile then looked around the room. "We want to be successful, right?" She extended her hand toward Lionel. "We heard about how close to failure we were, even when growing." She paced around the crowded room.

"In the past ten years in the U.S., energy drinks have grown from eight million dollars per year to over nine billion dollars. That's one thousand times bigger in ten years. Imagine doing that worldwide."

Kate spoke up. "One of the reasons we are all here is the one-for-one offer, our social commitment to donating a meal to a starving person for every drink we sell. How would that work?"

"Even better. The margins in energy drinks compared to nutritional drinks are far higher." Maxine motioned toward Hugo. "Our Juice Genius pointed out the basic ingredients in energy drinks. Frankly, they aren't nearly as expensive as the organic fruits that go into the nutritional drinks. So plenty of margin to donate."

"But isn't it a different market segment? Do they care?"

"Look at TOMS Shoes, Two Degrees Food, and Warby Parker. They each have the one-for-one offer, and they reach a young audience, like we want. They are making a difference in health and nutrition globally."

"We'd have to test," responded Kate, looking skeptical.

"That's what marketing does. There will be a lot of work and new initiatives to explore, no doubt." She looked around the room. "That's true for everyone. Frankly, your workload probably will double."

Lionel heard a collective groan. Team members whispered. Others fretted and shuffled.

Lionel jumped in. "Look, I know how hard everyone works already. You crank it out." He studied their faces, smiling appreciatively. "What Maxine is pointing out is there will be synergies by having a parallel product line. Our productivity and output will double, not necessarily our hours." He noticed a few nods.

Glancing at Maxine, Lionel saw her matter-of-fact expression remained. He decided to change the topic.

"Most impressively, imagine Double Vision as a five-billion-dollar company, one of the leaders in energy drinks. We'd be selling approximately four billion cans per year, and donating a nutrition pack per can. Four billion meals. Talk about making a difference in the world." Lionel waved his hands, trying to stir up some enthusiasm. More heads nodded.

"That would be awesome, Lionel. We're behind that." It was Kate. She started clapping, her hair swinging as she nodded.

"Hey yea, go DV." Call-outs and applause joined her.

That's the spirit I'm used to, Lionel thought.

But then Maxine interrupted. "One last thing. And it may be the most important point." The enthusiastic outburst skidded to a halt.

"One week ago we lost the Schwab and Young social entrepreneur award."

Ouch, Maxine. How about a little positive spin? "We *were* one of the top five," reminded Lionel.

"Second through fifth won't matter six months from now. Because that is when the Big Disrupter Award is presented."

Lionel shrugged in agreement.

"Only first place gets the one billion dollars. And there are fifty social companies like ours vying for that award. So if we're excited about billions of meals that accompany billions of dollars in revenue, we need to win."

The room was quiet.

"We need to achieve specific goals every day. Each of us. If you want to make a difference in the world, then make each and every day in the next six months incredibly effective."

Scanning the faces, Lionel sensed a mixture of guilt and resentment. It was different when a new person presented advice. It sounded like criticism, not motivation. *Rally time.*

"We all know this a defining moment." He drew near Dasha, looked Hugo in the eye, then worked his way around the room of senior talent, getting close to each of them. His spoke with passion. "I realize my eyes may look tired from a lack of sleep, but I have never felt more excited." A few chuckles rolled out. He hit his chest with his hand and spun around. "To have more capital than we've ever had. A booming market in energy to go after. A brilliant strategist like Maxine to help us. And a billion dollar upside. Fellow entrepreneurs, I realize we are young, with long lives ahead of us. But I don't think it is any exaggeration to say . . . this next six months is the ultimate opportunity in each of our lives. I don't think any of us will ever have a chance to accomplish something as insanely great in our business careers."

Lionel held up a finger. "It's a quest of a lifetime." Twenty expectant faces were turned to him. "One billion dollars. Let's do it together, people."

Kate and Dasha and Hugo and Harding looked at one another. "We're in," someone shouted. "We're all in."

Lionel clapped, yelling, "Six months, team, six months to make it happen."

***

As the meeting broke up, Lionel approached Hugo. "Can you join Maxine and me in my office?"

In a mock whisper Hugo replied, "Is this the secret meeting after the meeting?" His quick wit thrived on mischief. Combined with his boyish looks, constant fluid movements, and rumpled clothes, the Juice Genius seemed elf-like to Lionel.

"I'll be sure to label it that way on the public calendar," Lionel cracked.

As the door closed in Lionel's office, Hugo commented. "Well, the money announcement went well, eventually. A bit sugar-coated for my taste, but effective. Then again, you probably didn't ask me here for management advice," he laughed.

"That rah-rah isn't my style, either," said Maxine.

"Okay. Let's be very clear and direct among the three of us, then," said Lionel.

"I may surprise you," Hugo said with a grin. "But I'm up for it."

"Hugo—in the interests of time, we need you to be more of a dictator."

Hugo cocked his head. "A dictator. Interesting. In what ways?"

Maxine responded. "We want several products to launch right away. A healthy energy drink, without caffeine. Also, the polar opposite—heavily caffeinated shots. And chilled flavored varieties in the middle."

"But that's the extent of our input," said Lionel. "You're the Juice Genius. Forget the damn taste testing. Forget the focus groups. You choose—it's your expertise."

"Ho-ho," Hugo said, cracking his knuckles.

"Carte blanche. You brew it." Maxine raised a finger. "But, we need to be able to stand in front of a hostile televised Senate Committee and explain why we made our choices. Everything—from formulation to packaging to appropriate targeted audiences, needs to ring pro-consumer and pro-environment."

"That's why even though we have juices without caffeine, we need at least one energy drink formulated as non-caffeinated. We need the right packaging—glass, plastic, or aluminum. Have a low carbon footprint and reduce that as we grow. We should probably be FDA approved versus skirting regulation by being a supplement."

"I like this," said Hugo, rubbing his hands together.

Let's see how he responds to this, thought Lionel. "And Hugo, we want the new products—packaging and all—to be beautiful. Even beyond what you and Kate did with our nutritional juice line."

Hugo nodded.

"Look, I realize each of these new products usually requires at least a six-month product cycle, considering the new branding and packaging. Plus we need a year to buy land and build a plant—all this could easily total well over two years."

"Here is what we have." Maxine pulled up her tablet and showed a Gantt chart. "In order to have a prayer at the success we need to win the Big, you need to come up with all the flavors and packaging specs in one month. And one month later, have a plant online."

"What! In two months you want to be manufacturing and shipping five new products?"

"Ask me or Lionel for anything you need. But this is the time frame, starting right this minute." She glanced at her phone. "I have a meeting, please keep me updated." Then Maxine walked out.

Hugo stared at the empty doorway. "Holy shit, Lionel."

"I know. She's intense. Just like this contest."

Hugo turned toward Lionel as if numb. His eyes were far away, like he was doing calculations. "That's an insane time frame."

"That's the Big Disrupter. Sorry, man. We're all hustling like lunatics."

"Hustling is good. But this means absolutely no life. The research... testing... and the plant... so many variables...."

"Can you do this?"

Hugo ignored the question. "What about ingredients? We don't want any BS fictional ingredients like bull semen or phony supplements."

"Agreed. But we do want something different."

"In our nutritional drinks, it's been the wholesome organic fruits and vegetables. Here, it's sugar, caffeine, stevia or sucralose, taurine, a few fillers, and water. All common commodities. How do we make that special?"

"That's why you're the Juice Genius, my friend."

***

Leah Barko's cab stopped in front of the tallest building in the heart of San Francisco. Schwab and Young's name shone in huge chrome letters against the dark granite. In smaller letters the sign read, Global Corporate Accounting and Consulting. *They're definitely projecting the image of a powerhouse,* she thought.

After ten minutes of security checks, Leah pressed a green fingernail against the elevator button. Top floor, she noted. Typical corporate excess. She wasn't going to compliment Jules Longsworth on his Master of the Universe view. It was corporate bragging rights. What kind of view did billionaire Warren Buffet have in Omaha, Nebraska? Maybe that's how Warren saved up thirty billion to donate to charity.

A chime interrupted her. The elevator stopped, then three dark suits entered. As they whisked upward in silence she thought more about her research. She was surprised to learn Longsworth was the former head of an Ivy League college and author of books on Plato, Nietzsche, and Heidegger. A philosopher who left academia to join Schwab and Young. Why?

The elevator glided to a stop at the top floor and she presented her credentials to the receptionist, who led her down the hallway. Leah marched into the office quickly, coming down hard on her heels, bouncing her long curly black ringlets. Her exaggerated cat-eye glasses shined. Today's pair had bright green graphics along the temples.

She ignored the wall of glass presenting commanding views of the waterfront.

Instead, she peered into Jules Longsworth's eyes as she leaned close to him, pumping his hand. His white handlebar mustache dominated his face. He was casually dressed in a V-neck sweater without a tie. *Is this for show, or does he march to a different beat?*

"President Longsworth, thank you for the time today. When I called, I was so impressed you remembered me from the awards banquet."

"Please, it's Jules. And I've been a fan of your reporting long before I had the pleasure of meeting you in person that evening."

She smiled at the compliment. Then she placed a recorder on the desk and opened her thin laptop. "I hope recording isn't a problem?"

"No, of course not. *The National Times Journal* is noted for its ethical and in-depth reporting. I'm sure being accurate is part of that."

"I'd like to think there is some good writing and analytic insight as well."

"Touché." His hand swept toward her deferentially as a smile creased his tan face.

Leah began with the highest priority of her forty questions, knowing she had way overprepared. She couldn't help it.

"Jules, a number of wealthy individuals have been creating prizes for scientists and visionaries recently. But at one billion dollars, the Big Disrupter Award is far larger. For example, an individual Nobel Prize is only about one million dollars. So, who could have afforded to donate this?"

"There actually are a surprising number of people with that financial wherewithal. But I must respect the donor's privacy. And frankly, it doesn't really matter."

"It doesn't? The world, my readers anyway, would like to know."

"The curiosity is normal, I suppose, but the real heart of the matter, the real story, is encouraging great initiatives that help mankind."

"Then why a single billion-dollar prize for one company? Why not spread it around? Is it for dramatic effect? Or ego?" Her words hung like a challenge.

Jules responded with a smile that suggested he enjoyed her candor. "I think the anonymity answers the ego question."

He doesn't take offense easily.

"Furthermore, spreading investments makes sense for risk mitigation, if one is saving for retirement, for example. The old adage of not too many eggs in one basket. Fair enough?"

"To my point," Leah responded.

"But here we have a different situation. We're trying to make a big change, not balance risk. Our benefactor is willing to take a risk to achieve enormous returns for mankind."

Leah nodded but pressed on. "So this could end up being a waste of a billion dollars if you make the wrong choice?" She looked across her keyboard, the ten painted nails ready to pounce.

"Potentially. But consider this. We know a brilliant programmer can be more effective than ten very good ones. Mark Zuckerberg of Facebook and Marc Andreessen, the famous developer turned VC, have said this repeatedly. It's also true for many other creative and analytical pursuits as well. However, we believe the same is true for great organizations."

"Organizations?"

"Consider a venture capitalist's portfolio of companies. Or the consumer options in music, the movies, or the arts. In each case, a few are outstanding, the runaway hits, and the rest add up to a mere fraction of success."

"So the philosophy is survival of the very fittest. Nothing less," she interrupted, short-circuiting his Socratic reasoning.

"Right to the point, you are." He brought his hands together. "We don't see how else an organization can make a big disruption, especially given large competitors."

Leah quickly scanned her questions. "This begs the question, how will you select that winner?"

"A combination of metrics. First, as social entrepreneurs, are they creating tangible benefits for society? Just as important, are they successful in the marketplace with demonstrable customer acceptance and sales? The market, not us, will ultimately measure their ability to have sustained impact. And third, the problems being solved should be of a critical nature. Health or shelter or hunger trump convenience or comfort, for example." He stroked his mustache as he studied Leah's reaction.

"Many contestants donate to social causes but provide products or services that satisfy typical consumer desires. For example, snacks, energy drinks, fashion clothing, or general financing. Those products aren't necessarily socially redeeming themselves. Do you factor that in?"

"It is a factor, but we look at it holistically. How do the companies compare to the major competitors in that industry? What social commitment do they make with each sale? And does that impact lives?"

"So it isn't strictly a measure of who has the most socially responsible product or service?"

"Correct. That is a factor, but if the product isn't accepted by the market, it isn't disruptive. We'd rather select a company that has the potential to be a highly successful company as well as socially conscientious."

I wonder how he'll handle this one? Leah looked up from her laptop, her glasses perched on the end of her nose.

"As president you are balancing the demands and influence of your corporate clients as well as the social entrepreneur decision. Candidly, how can this award be judged fairly?"

"Another excellent question. A panel of five, all senior partners here at Schwab and Young, have been carefully selected for objectivity. In fact, the benefactor of the Big award does no business with us, so we have eliminated the possibility that we would steer things in any direction other than the most beneficial."

That's the answer I expected. Now for a curve ball, she thought. "President—I mean Jules, how does heading up the Big Disrupter relate to your leaving academia? You were all set. Dean of a very prestigious college, tenured, a successful author. Then this dramatic change to Schwab and Young."

"Leah, I promise a forthright answer, but allow me to ask you this first. Why did you choose journalism?"

"Fine. I'll go first. The simple answer? I found academia a lonely life and considered my PhD a hollow accomplishment. I was afraid I'd feel the same way in thirty years if I'd stayed in academia, so here I am."

"Really?" Jules leaned forward. "You have a PhD? That's impressive. Where did you attend?"

"Oh, it wasn't Ivy League, you wouldn't be impressed."

"Humor me."

"The University of Chicago, Graduate School of Anthropology."

"Leah, you've been holding out on me. That's one of the very best programs in the world."

"So they say. Still, it wasn't for me. I want to research and write things that people read, on topics that matter today, taking pride in the publication of which I'm a part."

"Perhaps I'm just a slower learner than you. I loved academic life. Then I lost someone very close to me, to cancer. Call it a midlife or existential crisis, but suddenly the many layers of abstraction between my work and actually making a difference in the day of a fellow human, were simply too numerous."

"I'm sorry, I didn't know," she said, embarrassed. *How did I miss that in my research?*

"Very few people do. Don't feel bad. And thank you for your candid answer. It seems we share more than we realized."

Leah leaned forward. "So Schwab and Young engages your brain and the Big Disrupter your soul?"

Jules Longsworth laughed. "That's the best succinct description I've heard."

She saw her opportunity. He was impressive. Forthright and brilliant. This could become the mother of all awards. Leah reached over and turned off the recorder.

"Jules, would you consider partnering on this? You and your fellow judges do your analysis and rankings, while I do associated stories? Instead of waiting until the announcement at the end, we provide interim status. Background, human interest, the Technicolor, as it were."

Jules sat back and studied her. "I suppose it would help the entrepreneurs and the program gain awareness."

"Absolutely. And everyone loves a hotly contested race."

***

A couple of Chinese take-out containers sat off to the side of Lionel's desk.

The evening had descended like a dark curtain over the windows, a few glimmers of light peeking through. Quiet time, off stage and able to concentrate. He cherished that. He looked through his open door toward the bullpen.

The sales team had left around six p.m., wrung out from a day on the phones and online, although that never stopped really. Most of the operations team had left for workouts or meals. Others were taking night classes. The team was young and energetic, and although they were very dedicated to DV, they had many life passions. Their hours were largely flexible, so it was not unusual to see people at the office on any day, at any time. As Lionel ran his eyes over the cubes and small desks in the open office he wondered how the announcements in the morning meeting were sitting with the team.

Maxine's face appeared in his doorway. "All done. Want to see?"

"I was wondering what you were doing, banging on the walls," he said.

Outside in the corridor a huge new whiteboard was mounted. "Each week is a vertical column, while horizontally we list products and revenue," Maxine pointed out proudly.

"You have revenue goals already drawn in for energy drinks that haven't even been created yet."

"I guess we'll have to get cracking. And this entire board, plus other reports, are going to be on our intranet website. Dasha, in IT, said she'd do it for me. That woman has the right answers."

"What do you mean?"

"Everything I ask for, she says, 'No problem.' Do you think she'll deliver?"

"No question. Make your requirements clear and she'll knock them out. She has our entire IT operations on her plate, which is enormous. From applications to infrastructure. But she handles it."

"Russian?"

"Ukrainian. Dasha Romanyuk."

"I like her style."

"The best. And this looks very organized," he added, waving at the whiteboard. "But right now, I'm toast. I'm heading home. It's nearly ten p.m."

"Good. See you tomorrow." Maxine headed back to her desk.

Lionel packed up and rolled his bike out of the office. His mind was still racing but numb from the day.

The elevator hit the ground floor with a thud, interrupting his thoughts. Outside he stepped over the top tube then pushed off. He had a bright handlebar-mounted halogen light and a red xenon strobe that flashed from his seat post.

A car started up in the alley, with an eager turbocharged pitch. He barely heard it over his tunes.

Lionel looked into the darkness. Fog had covered the stars and the moon. Washed by his narrow beam of brightness, the surrounding warehouse district seemed squat, newer brick buildings interspersed with old lumpy ones, like weathered sand castles.

He leaned into the pedals, heading down the alley. He cranked through the cover of night, lost in thought. Then, above his music, a high whine emerged. He couldn't tell which direction it came from. He entered the next intersection scanning both directions. Darkness. Was it the music player? Definitely louder. He yanked off an earpiece. A shiver went down his back. It was close. He reached for his brakes. *Weird, no lights.*

Suddenly a dark blur was on him.

He jammed his brakes hard. Chrome flashed by taking his front wheel. He was flying in a somersault before he realized his hands were wrenched from the handlebars. His shoulder slammed into the rear of the speeding car, then his neck snapped back and his head pounded off the side. He fell face down to the gritty blacktop.

9

WEDNESDAY, OCTOBER 2ND

Lionel opened his eyes. The hospital room came into fuzzy focus. Was someone knocking somewhere? A TV, mounted high, ran a daytime show. Glad that was muted. Who turned it on? He noticed the bandages on his chest and arms. His neck and back were still numb. The floating feeling reminded him of being prepped at the dentist. The painkillers were doing their job.

He heard the knock again. Then he saw a man in the doorway, scanning the room. His scattered head of hair tapered sharply near his ears. A mustache curved around his mouth. His eyes roamed upward. Lionel couldn't tell if he was thinking or looking at something.

"Inspector Winston Chang, San Francisco Police Department. Any chance you can talk now?" Suddenly he was looking straight at Lionel.

"Hi there."

"Lionel Lane, correct?"

"Yes."

Inspector Chang came closer and held out his badge. Lionel nodded and motioned to the chair next to the bed.

"Do you mind if I stand? Hospitals make me nervous. I don't like to touch too many surfaces here."

That's a candid admission, especially for a cop. "Want to roll me out into the street?" Lionel joked. "I'd welcome the fresh air."

Chang's shoulders shook with his quick laugh. His eyes squinted cheerfully above flat cheeks. But then Lionel realized the inspector was carefully sizing him up, head to toe.

"The accident hasn't affected your sense of humor."

"That's a rule for me. Can't lose your sense of humor."

"I like that." He got out a small recorder and looked at Lionel. "Okay?"

"Of course."

"So can you tell me about the accident?" His smile became more serious. "It happened two nights ago, correct?"

"Yes. I was riding home from work."

"Do you remember what time?"

"Right after ten."

"Pretty late. Is that customary for you?"

"It can be. Order in dinner, then work through it."

"Did you notice anyone around you when you left the building?"

"Nope."

The inspector nodded his head. "Your bike is in pretty bad shape. Was the light working at the time of the accident?"

"Absolutely. A 600 watt halogen in the front and a red xenon strobe in the back. Impossible to miss in the dark."

"What do you remember of the actual accident?"

Lionel's first thought was hitting the car with his helmet. A thunderclap inside his head. Then the silence, followed by the annoying ringing in his ears, like a tire leaking air through a pinhole. But he realized the inspector needed tangibles. "Well, I was crossing an alley. Fast. In case you're wondering I didn't have a stop sign."

"I saw that. No stop sign in either direction," Inspector Chang replied.

"Still, you don't frigging run into well-lit bicycles."

Inspector Chang nodded sympathetically.

"Anyway, approaching the intersection, I heard an engine whine, but didn't see anything. Then, I braked and bam—he nailed me. Directly into my front wheel from the side—with no lights on. What idiot does that?"

"You didn't see any lights at all?"

"None. No running lights, no headlights."

Chang looked away. "I was given a report from the ambulance driver. May I ask, were you wearing headphones in both ears?"

"It was late at night, hardly any traffic. But yes, I had earbuds, not full headphones."

Chang grimaced, shaking his head. "Not legal in both ears in San Francisco."

"All due respect, I heard him anyway. It was a high-pitched engine, revving way up."

Chang looked at him. "What kind of car?"

The rushing dark wave played through his mind again, like it had a hundred times before. It always ended with a resounding pop. He shuddered. "I have no idea. It was black. There was some chrome."

"Did you see a license plate or a brand?"

"Honestly, I don't remember. I heard this screaming engine, my head explodes off the side of the car, then the next thing I know I'm in an ambulance."

"You don't remember calling Maxine Gold?" Chang shook his head with a curious look.

"No. She was here at the hospital earlier today. Told me I crawled across the street onto the sidewalk. I must have looked like a lurching drunk, staggering out of the road, and collapsing. I was wedged against the wall, my backpack still on, face down on the concrete when the ambulance arrived. Totally blanked."

"How'd they find you?"

"She figured out my general direction and stayed on her cell with the ambulance until they found me. She's pretty smart."

Chang rubbed his mustache, nodding his head. "Back to this car that hit you. It never stopped?"

"Not that I ever saw."

Inspector Chang's eyes wandered upward and then darted side-to-side, like he was looking for answers hanging in the corners. Then he focused on Lionel. "Anyone threatening you at work or at home?"

"Employees? They seem really happy. We just got funding and the company is expanding, not laying off."

Chang was still staring. Lionel wondered if he meant something else. *Maybe he meant personally.* "And no, I don't have any jealous rivals competing for a girl, if that's what you mean. No girlfriend right now."

Chang smiled. "I like to ask. You never know what sets people off."

The inspector handed Lionel his card. "Call me if you remember anything more. And be careful in those dark intersections late at night, okay? And I'd skip the music." Chang eased toward the doorway.

"Wait a minute. Is that it?"

"Until you can remember more, there isn't much we can go on. However, we will look for video camera footage from businesses in the area."

"How about checking the paint type? Some must have scraped off somewhere."

"We did find paint on your bike from the car. So far the lab has identified it as common aftermarket black. The car was repainted, so we can't identify the original car manufacturer."

"The car has some damage, then. What about checking body shops?"

"We'll try, but there is no effective way to check every body shop for an unknown make and model with minor side damage." He held his hands out and shrugged his shoulders.

Lionel rolled his eyes in frustration. "Tell me this much—do you think he hit me intentionally?"

"No way to know." The inspector's eyes wandered upward again, searching the ceiling. "Could have been a drunk, driving with his lights off. He may not have even noticed hitting you." He focused back on Lionel and smiled as if the world was a mysterious place. Lionel felt like he was being blown off.

"Seriously, you believe that? You can't hit something as hard as I was hit and not stop your car."

Chang shifted his feet and brought his hands together. "Don't get me wrong, Mr. Lane. Hit and run is illegal and a serious crime. But we don't know the other person's perspective."

"You're right. To learn that, you need to find him."

Inspector Chang looked at his watch and grimaced, then nodded at Lionel. "I agree. Call me if you remember any more details."

Pocketing the recorder, he disappeared out the door. *What is with that guy?* Lionel wondered. *He didn't seem to believe me.*

***

"This website looks like an ad for a strip club. Are they really selling energy drinks? Huge boobs hanging out, tacky tiny outfits—this one looks like she's pole dancing under a tent." Kate was all over the BodyHamr website, pointing at her open laptop perched on Maxine's desk.

"They have been growing over fifty percent per year for six years now. They must be doing something right," Maxine responded, glancing over from her screen.

"Mud wrestling events with girls in bikinis. Wow, what creative marketing, where do I apply?"

"Different strokes . . ."

"Oh wait, here is an event where they actually go topless. Someone has painted the BodyHamr name and logo on their breasts and they parade around. I guess the paint is thick enough to qualify as clothing—that's crazy." Kate spun her laptop to show Maxine.

"She looks cold. But is it effective?"

"Maxine, you have got to be kidding me."

"I'm not asking you to do this. I want you to research and see how BodyHamr is succeeding."

"You call this success?"

"Kate, there are over one hundred forty-six thousand convenience stores in America. I realize those were not primary outlets for your nutritional juice drinks, but they are critical for energy drinks. We need to get into those outlets with the help of distributors. And distributors want to be wooed and convinced we're building demand somehow."

"We've sold effectively through health food stores and grocery stores for years. We're working on drug stores, plus mass merchandisers like CVS, Walgreens, and Rite-Aid. And superstores too, like Walmart and Costco."

"But where is ninety percent of our actual revenue coming from today?"

"Okay, I'll admit, we're pretty much limited to health food stores and a select number of grocery stores. So far."

"So, for energy we have an enormous distribution challenge. We have to crack the convenience stores—it's where the vast majority of consumers buy energy drinks and get exposed to new ones. Places like 7-Eleven, Circle K, Pantry, Speedway, and Casey's. Not to mention all the stores owned by the gas stations themselves—Hess, Valero, BP, Exxon. It's thousands and thousands. And the distributers are the only way."

"Fine. We'll dig into it. Just don't expect us to be tawdry and cheap like BodyHamr."

"We want the success, that's all. Without the bigger budgets. Now what about colleges and universities?"

"I spoke to some colleagues who know that market. They said some energy drink companies are incredibly well organized on campus."

"Is this something we should do?"

"Absolutely."

"Then give me some scenarios. Assume a healthy budget, for discussion purposes."

Kate started outlining numerous campaigns on the whiteboard. Maxine could tell she relished the creative moment.

"We'd have cute cars—like your Mini Cooper, all painted with our logo and a huge can of Double Vision sticking out the back. And we'd organize teams of Double Vision girls, and guys, who are students. We pay them, but not that much. They'd have outgoing personalities and become brand advocates."

"What do they do?"

"They'd attend a master schedule of sporting events, concerts, and parties. They wear their DV outfits, act excited, distribute the product for free, encourage people to experiment with it."

"Experiment?"

"If a Double Vision and vodka became the go-to drink, we'll know we have arrived. Lots of energy drinks are mixed with booze for young people—they want to keep on going through the night."

"Okay, well we have to be careful with that one until they are twenty-one. How about for studying?"

"Red Bull created contests where students searched for energy drinks hidden in fake books in the library, in gyms, and auditoriums. They made games about searching on campus. Fully integrated with mobile applications, tweets, social media. We'd want to create unique fun experiences like that."

"The universities allow this?"

"Oh, and way more. If you sponsor enough on campus, hire students, with a 'responsible' message, you can do a lot. Compared to all the booze these students are drinking, we're saints with caffeine and sugar."

"So you give away a ton on campus to build the demand, for when they have jobs and money?"

"Right. Plus they buy now. Students have some discretionary cash."

Kate started a list of specific college campaigns. Maxine smiled inwardly. *At least she's positive about the market.*

She quickly finished and faced Maxine.

"The key take-away I'm suggesting is this. The leading energy drink companies, like a Red Bull or Monster, spend nearly zero dollars on classic advertising. Instead that money goes into fun event marketing. It's the best way to reach the younger crowd, who quickly tune out conventional ads. Authenticity is huge to them. From campus games to extreme athletes to racecars. It spans from teenagers to the mid-thirties, or more."

"Fine, let's organize our budget that way."

"Right, but keep in mind, creating events takes a lot of time and energy, and people."

"No doubt you will be crazy busy."

"So this is what you want to do, Maxine? Create our version of Red Bull with a conscience? Since we do the one-for-one match."

"That's a clever way of putting it." Although Maxine was sure Kate thought Lionel, and not she, provided the conscience.

Kate nodded her head, smiling. "Maxine, if you set up your own group for the energy drinks, I assume you'll have another marketing director and team. Perhaps they should report to me."

Maxine's dark eyebrows arched over intense eyes. "Two points. One is we don't want the cost of double teams. And the second is, I'm not running energy. Lionel wants to take that lead."

Kate's jaw went slack. It was several moments before she said, "Oh really?"

"So you and I had better get used to working together. Not only that. I'm going to get personally involved in our distribution deals right away, along with Lionel. It no longer will be only you and our sales team. No disrespect, but it's too urgent for us to put it all on your shoulders."

Kate's complexion flushed deep red under her blond hair as she hurried out of Maxine's office.

***

"Lionel, I am sorry to bother you in the hospital, but why didn't you let me know you're leaving and I'm being demoted?" Kate's voice was thick with emotion.

"Leaving? Demoted? What do you mean?" Lionel was fumbling the phone as he filled out the hospital's discharge paperwork.

"To start the energy drink subsidiary. And you and Maxine are taking over the sales lead."

"Ah, you were meeting with Maxine, right?"

"She is such a . . . a . . . I don't want to say."

"Kate, I was going to talk to you about this the other day. Before I got knocked on my ass."

"I'm sorry, you must feel like hell after that accident. It was another surprise bomb from her, which she seems to relish dropping on me. I'm used to working closely with you—we all are. Now it seems you and Maxine decide everything and we hear about it secondhand."

"The team is growing, Kate. It's not intentional exclusion, believe me."

"Really?" Kate said. "Maybe not by you."

"Sincerely, by either of us. Look, I'm actually walking out now. I've been discharged. We can talk more in person when I come back to the office. But can I ask for one thing?"

"Of course."

"Please give Maxine some slack. It's a style issue. She is intense, but you'll always know where you stand."

"Oh, she isn't shy about that."

"True, but I value that. So much better than corporate politics. She can be painfully direct sometimes, but the underlying strategic reasons are remarkably solid and unbiased. Please don't take it personally, okay?"

Lionel heard her choke. He waited, as she took a long breath.

"Lionel, I trust you. I'll bust my tail to make it work with her."

"Thank you, Kate. Now I need to get out of here."

"Wait, important question before you leave. How do you want to handle the PR about your accident? There already have been some tweets."

"Already?"

"Yeah, of course."

"I talked to the police. Some SFPD inspector named Chang. Anyway, it's not the same as on TV, like some Crime Scene Investigation show. It's going to be slow going, at best, to find the guy who hit me."

"Do they have any theories?"

"Chang gave me the impression that someone may have accidently had their lights off, maybe because they were drunk. They hit me, panicked and split. And because I had tunes on, I think he's partially blaming me."

Kate paused a moment. "Honestly Lionel, I think it's best we downplay it. Very unfortunate, probably a drunk driver, but you are okay. Moving on."

"You think if we used social media to try to find the guy, I'd run the risk of being the CEO brat with the headphones on?"

"There is that potential. Plus, I don't want the public to think of you, our young, strong, nutritional-drink CEO as a victim. I mean unless we had a photo and a solid chance to find the guy."

"Chang's pessimistic. You're probably right. Keep it on the down low. I'll see you in thirty?"

"Thanks, Lionel."

***

Lionel was barely through the door of his office when the receptionist announced a call from Jan Swenson.

"Jan Swenson?"

"She said you met at the Entrepreneur of the Year awards."

"Of course." The firecracker. Like a cute cheerleader with brains. She'd heard already? He took the call right away.

"Why Jan, so great to hear from you. How is Sweet Boomerang? Did I get that right?"

"Yes, you remembered. From the awards banquet. A fellow top-five finisher."

"Nice of you to call. And top-five finisher sounds so much better than 'loser.'"

"Positive spin, part of the job description, right? Now Lionel, what in the world happened out there? Are you all right? I saw something scary on Twitter."

He couldn't believe she found the time to contact him. Was she tracking DV that carefully? "The concussion is clearing. And it's a minor miracle, but no broken bones."

"I am so glad to hear that. Are you still in the hospital?"

"I was discharged an hour ago and literally just walked into my office."

"Lionel, you probably should be resting at home, not working," she admonished.

Like she'd ever rest. "What, is this a trick to beat us at the Big Disrupter award?" Lionel laughed.

"You bum, I'm not like that. Although I must admit, the Big Disrupter's had a weird effect on me. Oh, and everyone's starting to call it the Big."

"The Big?"

"That's it."

"I like that. But what do you mean by weird effect?" He started searching Twitter for The Big.

"Something odd. I can't put my finger on it. I'm all amped up."

She's right. I like her honesty. "Is it being nervous?"

"More like anxious. I have a strange feeling about this award. As though a new force is pushing us."

"Yeah, a billion-dollar force. It's a funny coincidence, but I got a call recently from another finalist at C and Y—Raj Singh, with Step-by-Step."

"The clothing company. How is Raj?"

"So supportive. Like you. He sounded a bit stressed—his wife is pregnant, and it may have been a surprise. I think he has a lot on his plate with the manufacturing in India and both the European and U.S. markets." Lionel shook his head, thinking of how difficult it would be to juggle a new family along with that workload.

"It could be this competition too. Maybe that additional force is actually a fear factor. The fear of losing out on a game-changing billion dollars."

That fear sounds so familiar, he thought. "Ignore that fear part, Jan. You really impressed me at the awards. You should be proud, nothing else."

"Thank you. We are growing rapidly. I received the nicest letter from the parents of a man in his late twenties who works for us boxing candies. He has a learning disorder. But he is incredibly dedicated. Anyway, his parents were so thankful, saying he was happier than at any time in his life."

Lionel realized how much Jan differed from Maxine. It was her sweetness. "There you go. Saving the world, one person at a time."

"We all need the positive stories. And is Maxine working with you now? I heard that somewhere."

"You're right on it. Co-CEOs." *This woman is so connected. She must be online 24/7.*

"How is she?"

"We share a similar vision, plus respect the hell out of each other. But our business styles are different. It's a little rockier than what I had imagined."

"Be patient. Maxine is amazing. The results will be worth it in the end."

Jan must see something in Maxine, because the two couldn't have more different personalities. "I'm sure you're right. And don't be anxious about the competition. How can it be anything but win-win as we all knock ourselves out to have a record-breaking six months?"

"Good point. Well look, we're both crazy busy, but I wanted to make sure you were okay."

"So nice of you." As they hung up Lionel marveled at how in tune Jan seemed with the top contestants of the Big.

***

Fanachi studied the surroundings. The Honeycomb, as they called it, was a windowless room with thick acoustic panels padding the walls and ceiling, the floor a dull gray fleck pattern of antistatic tiles. Tall privacy cubicles, each with a wedge-shaped top and back that closed around the operator inside, radiated in an octagon around a core tower. Bright LCD screens attached to the core, tethered with power and communications lines, and flashed at each of the eight operators.

Each desk was monitored by video, a strategy Fanachi used to reinforce the ban on chatter and emphasis on confidentiality. On each LCD, windows continuously scrolled and multicolor boxes popped up. The operators' quick clicks on their keyboards disappeared at the edges of each cubicle, like a sealed island.

Fanachi leaned toward an Asian woman in her thirties wearing a VOIP earpiece, reviewing computer-transcribed conversations highlighted by her Big Data server. The expert system intelligently scoured masses of documents, databases, and digital communications, using filters and triggers based on monitored keywords and actions.

"Analyst Three, you'll message me with any threshold developments on that target? I don't like failure."

"Immediately, Advisor." Her hair was fastened in a bun held by long wooden hair sticks, which wiggled when she nodded.

"Other than the recent miss, how is Igor doing?" He spoke in a low voice, almost a whisper. He brushed back his black and silver hair with thick manicured fingers, then unconsciously rubbed the deep furrow in his forehead. She saw none of this from her cubicle. He watched her face through the desktop camera, but she only saw a black screen with the circular logo of the International Trading Company. Like all the analysts in the Honeycomb, Fanachi was known only as the Advisor, communicating exclusively over one-way video calls. Other cameras mounted throughout the Honeycomb and the entire building fed his other windows, creating a master-view mosaic on the three wraparound LCDs at his desk.

"He creates excellent exploits. We have access to more information than before. He is very smart."

"So you like him?"

She hesitated before answering. Her expression was guarded, but Fanachi knew she wouldn't cover for him if it meant her failure. "He needs field patience, which is typical for these young guys. But online, he's brilliant. He amazes me. He may be a genius."

"Geniuses can be valuable but unpredictable. Keep an eye on him." Then he complained about the slow response time on the communications circuit. "That's it, I'm concluding." As the video transmission faded he noticed her shoulders rise as she breathed in relief. That pleased him. He wanted his employees worried about satisfying him.

A genius, he wondered. The architect who designed the Honeycomb and the villa was considered a genius, a wunderkind of his day. He built fantasy castles in New Zealand for media wizards, bizarre high-tech mansions in Silicon Valley that the press called habitable iPads, and dachas for Russian mineral tycoons along the Black Sea. Too bad he couldn't be trusted to keep the details confidential, thought Fanachi. Fanachi's project was his last.

The genius of the villa, Fanachi reflected, was its invisibility. In plain sight. The lowest part was a plain rectangular building on a dead-end street in a quiet warehouse district. A nondescript stucco entryway with a No Soliciting sign led to a very bored guard who worked daytime hours. Behind him a locked entryway protected a long hallway, lined with doors. The first door housed the International Trading Company, a purported food broker for spices and sauces. It was the plausible explanation for people of many ethnicities and languages to come and go. Down the hallway, every door was triple locked and secured by fingerprint scanners and cameras. The Honeycomb sat in one of those rooms. As far as the security guards and employees knew, the back part of the building was a garage, housing expensive and rarely used antique cars.

The rear of the building backed up to a cliff. It was one of a small group of warehouses that led a quiet, isolated existence in San Francisco. Immediately above but unconnected by roads was Telegraph Hill, an exclusive neighborhood overlooking the bay.

Fanachi thought about his call with Analyst Three. The communications delay he pretended to complain about was actually programmed, knowing his employees would interpret the jerky transmission as an indication he was somewhere distant with low bandwidth.

In reality, his communication with the analysts traveled over fiber optic lines that never left his property. From the Honeycomb, the fibers traveled the entire length of the building, into the cliff and up an elevator shaft. The elevator ascended two hundred feet in solid rock and opened inside Fanachi's Mediterranean villa atop Telegraph Hill. He called it the Rock Elevator, not only for the obvious reason, but because directly across the water lay Alcatraz Island.

Fanachi looked out the arched window from his office in the villa. The sea breeze flicked the Egyptian cotton drapes, soft hues reflecting off the amber mahogany paneling.

He punched in some numbers in an encrypted phone and waited.

"Alpha."

"It's Fanachi."

"I was expecting your call."

"I'm sure you were. We had a problem. We hit him, just not hard enough."

"What? He's alive?" Alpha asked.

"Correct. He survived somehow. He's recovering in the hospital. But they'll have no clues." He walked to an adjacent wall and adjusted the angle of an antique ink drawing of the Ponte Vecchio.

"That wasn't the result for which I pay you handsomely." Fanachi sensed the annoyance in Alpha's voice and imagined his particularly ugly expression as he ground his teeth. Unlike Alpha, Fanachi knew exactly what the other man looked like.

"My people are on it. We'll find another opportunity to accomplish the mission."

"Look, you don't get a lot a chances at this."

"We'll correct the situation. And get him." He watched a group of wild green parrots soar below, then disappear into a cliffside tree.

"That isn't what I mean. Double Vision has raised thirty million dollars, damn it, from a VC and Havermyer. And Havermyer himself has more money than God and bleeds for this young Maxine. If he ever gets wind of something suspicious, he'll leave no stone unturned to find the source."

"You want us to back off?" Fanachi asked coolly.

"No. With thirty million they are going to start growing like a nest of vipers." He wheezed into the phone. Fanachi heard him slap his desk in frustration.

"Then what?"

"Let's mix up the order of things." Fanachi heard Alpha lean closer to the mouthpiece as he began listing names.

10

THURSDAY, OCTOBER 3ʳᵈ

The phone finished the fifth ring before Lionel picked it up.

"Hey, Hugo." Lionel tried to sound awake, but knew his rasping gave him away.

"Lionel, I have it." Hugo's voice brimmed with excitement.

"Are you okay?" Lionel's phone read four a.m.

"Way better than okay. I have the answer to the secret ingredient." He was practically bubbling.

"Huh?" Lionel rolled over onto his elbows, shaking his head. "What?"

"For the energy drinks. The secret ingredient. I have it."

"Oh, of course." He gulped some air. "Cool."

"When is a commodity not a commodity?"

"Um. Yeah. Oh. When you can differentiate. Identify unique characteristics." He rubbed his eyes.

"Excellent. And the biggest ingredient of all, the heaviest, the most volume, and the one we recognize has distinguishable flavor difference is . . . ." Hugo stopped. Lionel realized he was waiting for him.

"Uh. Wait, the heaviest?" He sat up. "Of course, it has to be the water."

"*That*, my good man, is our new secret ingredient."

"The water?"

"The water! Find me special water. An incredible source. Pure, far away from cities or pollution. It's a key ingredient that people differentiate based on taste."

"Yes, yes, I like it." Lionel rolled over to the edge of the bed and stood up. "It's true for all of our products, we just never had the resources to go after the best water."

"Now we do. And the stakes are ridiculously high."

"But Hugo, it's both the water and where it comes from. The setting. If the source is gorgeous, that creates a special image."

"Bring me heaven on earth. Water from heaven. Pure, cold, and fresh."

Lionel started spinning around in his boxers, one hand pressing the phone against his ear, the other stretched out wide. "But we need the plant there, Hugo. We need to bottle this magic elixir right at the source—so our magic leaves this sanctuary intact, then straight to the consumer."

"So be it. Find us heaven's water on earth. And we'll make our energy drinks right there."

***

Later that morning Lionel waited eagerly at the open doorway. Dasha was draped over Maxine's desk, her black bangs skimming her eyebrows like a thinking cap as she pointed at the screen. "And click here to get the details by product line."

Maxine was leaning in next to her, her eyes absorbed in the screen. Their faces were inches apart. "That works exactly the way I wanted."

Dasha nodded. "Good."

"Maxine, when should I come back?" said Lionel.

Startled, the women pulled apart.

"I didn't mean to disturb you guys."

"It's okay." Maxine looked at her watch. "Dasha has already given me way too much of her time explaining this new report prototype. Keep up the great work, Dasha. Thank you."

"I like this system, too. It is an elegant way to present the data." Then she turned from Maxine and stood up, straightening her sweater and jeans. Her amber eyes shined with interest. She smiled at Lionel, then pivoted like a dancer and clicked her heels out of the office.

"Sorry about the interruption," Lionel said.

"You're apologizing *to me* for interrupting?"

"Too true. Speaking of which, I got a four a.m. wake-up call from Hugo."

"You were asleep?" she teased.

"He certainly wasn't. He had an inspiration about the key ingredient that could make our product different. You know what it is?"

She gave him the eye.

"The water. The one ingredient with a distinctive taste. One batch of sugar or caffeine is virtually indistinguishable from another. But water is different."

"Interesting." Maxine nodded. *She likes it,* he thought.

"Consumers—all of us—like the image of a pure source, far away from cities or pollution. And if there is an interesting story that goes with that, all the better."

"Of course. We need the Austrian Alps in America," she said.

She's thinking Red Bull, he realized. "It's a powerful image—putting something unique and unpolluted in your body. Even if it is enhanced with caffeine and sugar and fruit flavor. It's a paradox but true."

"Emotional associations sell. I'm with you," she nodded. "I like the way this balances the one-for-one appeal."

"How so?" Lionel asked.

"Face it, one-for-one is emotional too, but from a compassion standpoint. This association with purity and quality reaches additional consumers. It extends our reach to those uninterested in the one-for-one. It's a best-of-both worlds." She looked at him confidently, eyes shining in thought.

Lionel smiled. "I love it. We decided together."

She brushed a piece of lint out of his hair, then gripped his shoulders for a moment. "It is more enjoyable when we agree, isn't it?" The warmth of her touch surprised him. Then she dropped her hands with a sigh.

"Oh, ironically this relates to my disagreeable conversation with Kate, yesterday."

Lionel took a deep breath. "What did you two talk about?"

"A lot of marketing. We looked at competitors like BodyHamr and discussed ways to develop broader product distribution."

"Those are her strengths. She should be able to nail that."

"So she says. The big difference is the emphasis on event marketing. Promoting and partnering at sporting, music, and celebrity entertainment events. And eventually creating our own branded wacky fun events. That's all new to her."

"We didn't have the budget to do a lot of that before, on a national scale. She'll learn as we grow."

Maxine's lips held a line. "Hopefully. I told her that you and I think the best way for us to get noticed is if we can find a few really successful extreme sports athletes and events. Otherwise it will take years."

"Did Kate disagree?"

"No. What she doesn't like is working more with me and less with you. Plus she wants energy to be a modest product expansion, exactly as several of the Big Four soda companies have done."

"That's not the path to building the next Red Bull."

She nodded. "From the peaks of the Austrian Alps they created the world of energy drinks."

"So true. It will be the ultimate for us to bottle at a pristine source, with extreme athletes representing us, all done with authenticity. Not just being a marketing company, like most of their competition."

"Precisely. We should begin a site selection search right away. I don't think Kate's the right person—are you up for it?"

Lionel smiled. *Maxine knows how to plan and get her way, one way or another. But this would be cool.* "Love to. I'm imagining places in the west, like the Sierras or Rockies or Cascades."

"Makes sense. Some place incredibly dramatic, with outstanding water, and not too far from San Francisco."

"And with a reputation among extreme athletes."

"Start buying plane tickets, Lionel."

11

TUESDAY, OCTOBER 8ᵀᴴ — WEDNESDAY, OCTOBER 9ᵀᴴ

As Lionel steered the convertible Jeep around the ruts and loose rocks, he stole a peek over his shoulder. Far below, Telluride looked like a little Lego town.

The rocky road was wide enough for one vehicle. He wondered what would happen if he met someone coming downhill. It dropped a thousand feet over the edge, and there weren't any guardrails.

High above were imposing red rock walls of sandstone and bright white granite cliffs. With nothing but a roll bar for a roof, it seemed he could reach out and touch the peaks. The wraparound canyon was dotted with evergreens and white aspen, a crystal blue sky painted behind. His excitement climbed with every turn.

For forty-five minutes the Jeep bounced and pulled up the rock-strewn switchbacks like a happy mountain goat. The four-wheel drive and rugged suspension seemed unstoppable.

Then Lionel spotted a vague trail branching above the main road, across a scree slope. It looked like there was an old mine up there. Why not, he thought. He gunned it off-road.

Initially his momentum carried him nicely. Then the road became steeper than he realized, and looser. It faded into more trail than road. Smaller rocks spit out from under his fat tires. He dropped it into low range, crawling. But the Jeep kept sinking, until all four wheels were dug in deep. Suddenly the hillside around him started to move. The

Jeep slid sideways, caught in the downward wave of rock. He tried brakes. Then a little gas.

"No good. Damn," he yelled, as if someone could hear.

The nose turned downhill. He was funneling with the scree toward the road and the edge of the cliff.

Impossible to survive that fall, he realized. He'd have to jump and lose the rental. All around him, the scree chipped like a shaking rattlesnake as he picked up speed.

Now or never. He reached for the door handle. Then an outcrop appeared, stationary among the loose rock. Maybe he can get traction on that. He tapped the accelerator. The front wheels caught on the exposed bedrock, lurching him sideways, away from the flow. The crown was bigger than he realized. He tapped the gas again and went over the edge, wrestling the steering wheel. The undercarriage was punched skyward, followed by shrill scrapes. The Jeep teetered, leaning into a somersault. Then it rebounded and shuddered, finally coming to a wobbly stop on the road.

Holy shit, that was close.

A few feet away the scree washed over the road. The thundering from the rock, flowing like a waterfall over the cliff and bounding down a thousand feet, echoed for minutes. Clouds of rock dust floated upward, like final ashes scattering. Broken rock fragments were strewn across the road like flattened pumpkins. He sat clenching the steering wheel. Damn.

That's it. He was definitely going to stay on the main road, for now. As he gave the Jeep gas, it rumbled, then backfired, lurching forward. Fifty feet of more of the same, and Lionel turned it off. The cacophony bounced around the canyon and then died to silence. He climbed outside, got on his back, and examined the underside. The exhaust pipe and muffler were missing.

"This baby isn't going any further uphill," he announced. He crawled from underneath the Jeep. The sun was warm and air still. There was no human within miles to hear him, he realized.

Suddenly the canyon's quiet hold was broken by whistling. Lionel's head jerked around as he scanned for the source. Then, uphill, he saw furry round noses poked over edges of tiny rock castles.

"Marmots," he laughed. He got up, sat on the front bumper, and tried to imitate their whistles. He watched them venture out, scurrying around the rocks. Their rich gold and brown coats shimmered in the sunlight. He took off his shirt. Might as well enjoy a few minutes before taking this wreck down the hill. The hot sun beat down and relaxed him.

A few minutes later, glancing toward the peaks ahead, a fast movement caught his eye. Something white was streaking down the basin, from Imogene Pass. He stood on the bumper. Wait, it was tracking the road. He studied it. Whoa—it's a white wolf. He climbed up on top of the hood. What! Someone was chasing the wolf on a mountain bike. That's insane.

As the two figures raced toward him he noticed black markings on the wolf's face. It kept turning back to check on the bike, a long pink tongue hanging out, as if laughing. Eventually, on the bouncing bike, he made out a strong chin, red ponytail, and long smooth legs.

They quickly approached. Lionel heard her disk brakes shudder. The white wolf turned toward the marmots above, their loud whistles signaling panic.

"Wolfie, don't even think about it, girl. No, no, no. No whistle pigs for you today."

The wolf whined, but stayed with her master as they slowed.

She rolled to a stop, eying him on the hood. "Car trouble?"

Lionel felt like a vision had descended upon him. "What an incredible animal—not to be dense, but I assume that is a wolf?"

"Wolfdog. Part Arctic wolf, part Siberian husky."

"Beautiful." The wolfdog *and* the owner, thought Lionel, taking a quick peek at the shining face and athletic figure.

"You can come down off your hood now. She won't bite, unless you're an asshole." Then he saw a big bright smile followed by a wicked laugh.

Her comment made him self-conscious, standing in his canvas shorts and climbing shoes on the hood. With a Jeep broken by his dumb maneuver, he felt like an out-of-place flatlander. "Do I look like one?"

She laughed. "No, you don't." She put out her hand.

"Reddi. Reddi Christiansen."

"Lionel Lane." He jumped down and felt the strength in her grip. And realized she must be six feet tall.

"I took this rental off-road and next thing I know, I'm sliding in that scree field and hit the bottom pretty hard on a huge boulder. It's been sounding like a herd of tractors ever since," Lionel explained.

"Yup, that'll happen. I run the welding shop in town. I might be able to fix that for you."

"You do? That's amazing." He realized he was still holding her hand. Wolfie cocked her head toward him.

"Why, never met a girl welder?" He let go of her hand reluctantly. The longer he looked the more dreamlike she appeared. Something about the flushed cheeks and the smile. And the smooth skin, glistening from exertion. She radiated beauty but her freckles were disarming.

"It's like you two floated down from the clouds, like an apparition. I'm in the middle of nowhere with a broken truck, and you appear, with all the answers."

"You're not off this mountain yet, Lionel. Does it run?"

"I think so, downhill."

She laughed.

He loved the sound, like unbridled mirth.

It was warm standing in the high altitude sun. Wolfie whined and nudged Reddi. She pulled a water bottle off her bike frame and squirted some in Wolfie's mouth, as her pink tongue lapped. She saw Lionel watching, and noticed the sweat on his brow.

"Water?"

He hesitated.

"Don't worry, I have my Camelback, this is a spare I squirt for Wolfie. But she has the creek water, too."

"Thanks," he said, taking the bottle. "Wolfie. And Reddi. Your names tell it all."

"Yeah, with this carrot top and kind of a go-hard personality, it stuck."

"Go hard. You mean like always ready?"

"Yeah, that's what Kodiak said."

"Kodiak?"

"Best bump skier in town. Maybe in all the Rockies. As a kid, I was a pesky redheaded ski brat chasing after him, trying to keep up. Always ready for more. So I became Reddi."

Lionel nodded, then guzzled some water. It seemed like sweet nectar. "Wow, this water's outstanding. I'm actually searching for a place with fantastic water."

"Are you a geologist or something?" She unbuckled her helmet, took off her sunglasses, and shook her head. She ran her fingers though her red hair. Her face seemed so smooth and young. But she was a welder? Her blue eyes turned to examine him. He had to look away for a moment to keep from staring.

"Uh, no. I'm with a beverage company, Double Vision. I'm from San Francisco. We want to expand our operations, to someplace with exceptional water."

"I'm no water expert. This tastes really good to me, but I have nothing to compare it to. It comes from over that ridge." As she pointed, he noticed the tight fit of her tank top and lycra shorts on her lithe figure.

"It's phenomenal. Everything here seems amazing."

"You're enthusiastic for a guy who trashed his rental car and nearly punched a one-way ticket down Savage Basin."

"It was worth it. I was supposed to be meeting the mayor to talk about rebuilding a defunct bottled water operation. But he canceled, so I rented a Jeep to explore. And now look where we are." He took a deep breath while Reddi put her shades and helmet back on.

"I know what you mean. This is like a getaway sanctuary for me." Reddi's shoulders arched back with a deep breath. "Anyway, I need to keep moving. My shop is behind Baked in Telluride, in the alley. Near Pacific and Fir."

"I'll find it. Thank you." He held out the water bottle.

"Keep it. You might need it. We'll be down a lot sooner than you."

"On one condition."

"Oh, yeah, what's that?" The devilish grin came back. "Remember, Wolfie has a fierce bite."

"Does she bite innocent strangers who ask you out to dinner? Trying to get to know the locals."

"Hahaha. You're cute, Lionel. First, let's see if you make it down alive and give me back my water bottle."

"And if I do?"

She stood on her pedals and started rolling. He began running next to her. Wolfie bounded ahead.

"Innocent stranger, huh?" Reddi said, watching him run.

"Bring Wolfie to dinner. Bring anyone, I don't care."

She pedaled a few strokes, and he kept running alongside. "Check us out, Double Vision beverages."

With the shove of a powerful hip she jolted ahead. "It's a possibility, Lionel. See you."

He stopped and watched her figure move like uncoiling silk, and then they were a quarter mile ahead, disappearing around the folds of the mountain road. Unbelievable. He took another sip from the water bottle and turned back toward his Jeep. This could be a fantastic place to locate.

***

Reddi agreed to dinner with Lionel that night. They walked the quiet streets together under the soft glow of the streetlamps, to Telluride's Thai restaurant. Meeting Reddi, experiencing the mountain environment and tasting the ideal water had inspired Lionel. He was in a romantic trance, captivated by everything in town.

As he opened the door for Reddi, the heavenly aromas of curries, basil, and cilantro greeted them. The small dining room was noisy, and all of the tables were packed close together and full. Several families were waiting, overflowing the front entrance area. Lionel's serendipity continued when the hostess hugged Reddi and arranged two stools at the bar, where they could dine.

They wedged themselves in. Lionel swiveled toward Reddi, and his legs bumped hers. "Honestly, I'm not trying to hit on you."

"Haha. You have a line for everything, Lionel. Here, how about this?"

She turned her stool sideways, facing him. He did the same. They sat with their long legs spread, sandwiched between each other, close but not touching.

After ordering, Lionel locked into Reddi's blue eyes. "I should warn you. When someone interests me I can't help but ask lots of questions."

"That's okay. If you get rude, I'll push you off the bar stool," she quipped with a smile.

"Can you give me a little warning at least?" he teased back.

"We'll see what the questions are." She cocked her head. Lionel loved the mystery of getting to know someone new, especially someone so attractive and different.

"So have you been in Telluride all your life?"

"No, my family moved here when I was eight. We were living in Austin, Texas, before then."

"I've been to Austin, it's cool. So why did you all move here?"

"It's so different, right? A small remote town, high in the Rockies. I think my parents found this to be magical, especially my mom."

"And what do you think about living here?"

"As a kid, I went nuts over the skiing. I couldn't believe I had a ski area literally in my backyard. I'd ski down the road and jump on a lift and play on the mountain all day."

As she talked, Lionel noticed Reddi's habit of brushing her long hair back behind her ears. It went to the middle of her back, but as she leaned over on the bar stool it fell forward over her shoulders, surrounding her.

I could swim in that red pool, Lionel thought. She was wholesome and radiant. And she didn't realize it. Cute freckles, sky blue eyes with reddish blond eyebrows. Not a bit of make-up on. He tried to concentrate. "What is your favorite style of skiing?"

"Racing gates was a competitive thrill. But now it's slopestyle. For the big air, the bumps, the tricks on rails. I like skiing with style."

"Do you still ski seriously?"

"You mean, why am I working in a welding shop and not skiing in New Zealand and Chile this time of year?" Reddi said it with a laugh, and slapped his leg.

"Sorry, it wasn't meant as judgmental, just curious." There was something unique about her candor. Maybe it was part of being so young.

"My ski career pretty much got put on hold when my mom got breast cancer, my last two years of high school."

"I'm sorry." He felt like an idiot. "I wasn't trying to pry."

"How would you know? It's okay."

"We don't have to talk about this."

She shrugged. "Well, the bright side is how strong Mom was. Even though I had to drop off the Junior National Ski Team, and out of what they call the development pipeline, I got to spend more time with her. Then, she forced me to go to college, rather than stay to help her. So I went to Boulder. I joined their freestyle team the first year." She paused and looked away.

"So you weren't too far away."

She bit her lip. "No, I wasn't. Anyway, the summer after my first year I returned to work for my dad, and the cancer got really bad. I never went back to college that fall. She died late that October, and two years later, here I am."

Lionel was at a loss. "I am really sorry. You're an awesome daughter. She'd be proud." He put his hands on her shoulders.

Her head hung down, shrouded in a curtain of red. He could tell she was trying to control her breathing. Her shoulders were shaking.

Lionel waited, giving her time.

"Reddi, you okay?" The voice vibrated with familiarity, and came from right behind Lionel's head.

Lionel pulled back from Reddi with a start.

"Trig! I didn't know you were back." Reddi quickly wiped off a cheek. She jumped up to hug him.

Lionel stood and turned around. She was holding someone by the arm.

"Trig, this is Lionel Lane. He is a business guy, new to town. Trig is a family friend. We've known each other since forever."

"Pleased to meet you," said Lionel. *Family friend.* He wondered, *what does that mean?*

"Trig Garcia." As they shook hands Lionel noticed the ready stance and solid build, even with the loose pea coat. Thick stubble darkened his square jaw. A black watch cap covered his head, above dark eyes and a brown complexion.

"Sorry to interrupt, Reddi. I saw you through the window when I was walking by, and . . . thought I'd check on you."

"I was getting emotional. With Hannah and Dad gone to California and Mom . . . you know . . . . Hey, why don't you join us?"

"No, thanks, I'm not here to eat. I literally was walking by. Apologies for interrupting. I'll call you tomorrow, okay?"

"Okay, but make sure. I'll come by your place if you don't call. I'll stalk you."

"Okay, okay, I'll call. Bye." He nodded to Lionel as he left.

Reddi perched back on the stool.

Lionel leaned over, but not too close.

"So, basically, since you grew up here, and it's a small town, should I assume that every guy is ready to beat the shit out of me if I get too close?"

"Oh, not really. Trig is kind of like a big brother. A former Navy SEAL. I'll tell you more some time."

Lionel was glad to hear he wasn't her boyfriend. Maybe she was unattached. That would keep things simpler. Why? He wasn't sure. "Okay, back to you. So in your perfect world, what would you like to do?"

"Good question. I'm kind of struggling with that right now. My dad suddenly decided to move to California two weeks ago and took my little sister with him. He left me with the welding shop. But that isn't exactly all I want to do with my life."

"So what are your dreams?"

"My dreams?"

"Yes, your absolute most exciting, adrenaline-pumping, gotta-have-it, totally go-for-it and be-amazingly-happy dream. Not what you *should* do, what you *want* to do."

Reddi answered without hesitation. "Ski in the Winter X Games, kicking ass. Compete around the world in slopestyle, skiing the endless winter. New Zealand, Europe, and the U.S. And then, ski in the Olympics and win some gold."

Lionel jumped off the stool and pumped his fist in his hand. He nearly shouted. "I love it, that's what I wanted to hear! That is so great, having clear and big dreams." He sat and grew quieter. Then he hunched forward.

"Now let me ask a question. You have to be totally honest, and I mean totally. No modesty, no bullshit, just the truth."

"Fine. But you may be in jeopardy of being pushed off your bar stool and beat up by the local guys," she said with a menacing smile.

What a teasing but tough-chick attitude. But here's the key question.

"Are you the best female skier in town?"

Reddi looked slowly around the restaurant, and then leaned close to Lionel. "The people who know, tell me I ski more like a guy than a girl. And that there is no other girl who does what I do on the mountain."

Lionel surged with excitement. In part, she was a goddess he wanted to impress. After all, he did find her very captivating. But mostly, he saw someone who could be a phenomenal face for Double Vision's new energy drinks.

***

"There is a former bottled water plant there, for sale? Insane."

"I knew that would blow your mind, Hugo. Located right in Telluride. It's only three years old. The brand was big in L.A. for a year. They served it at the Academy Awards or something. It even made it into the White House for some events, and then—poof."

"What, pray tell, happened? I hope it wasn't production or water quality issues."

"No, some sort of ownership dispute. And now they are desperate to sell, with all the dough they sunk into the bottling operation. It's relatively cheap, for Telluride. But the historical character and growth restrictions do make construction expensive here."

"Wait Lionel, is this a dump? It'll kill our schedule if we have to remodel extensively."

"No, not at all. It's an old brick warehouse, but totally remodeled by the former owners. Over 25,000 square feet, all tied into the local water supply. Adjacent is a 15,000 square foot building for storing finished product."

"That'll work, for starters. So the zoning is done?"

"Zoning, use permits, environmental studies—it's all grandfathered in the package. I'm meeting with the mayor and planning commission people, but I think we'll win them over quickly."

"Then you'll love this. We found totally functional bottling equipment from a defunct soda company out of Florida. Our deal even includes the former owner helping us to install it. We're using that as negotiation leverage in comparison to buying a brand new system."

"Excellent. We should take an inventory of what comes with this property, and what else we need, and move fast. I'll email over photos and small scale blueprints."

"I'll review it posthaste. If that looks promising, when should I schedule a trip out?"

This is the part he's going to hate, Lionel thought. "Honestly? Hugo, we need you in Telluride tomorrow."

12

THURSDAY, OCTOBER 24ᵀᴴ

It was still dark when Jan Swenson hugged her husband and rolled out of bed. She tiptoed in on her two sleeping children, gave each of their hot foreheads a kiss, and quietly eased downstairs. She went to the back mudroom and pulled on her wetsuit. October, her final month for kayaking. It wouldn't be long before she needed to admit winter was coming and store all the boats.

She carried a bowl of food outside and clipped their golden retriever to the chain. He started slurping happily.

Wind gusts rustled the branches of the naked birch trees. She felt an eerie autumn nostalgia. She strained to see through the darkness to Loon Lake and assess the size of the waves. Unsure, she briefly reconsidered. But she loved the workout and time alone. Plus, there weren't that many days left in the season.

She took one of the life jackets off the line and snapped it on as she walked toward the lake. In a few minutes she had her bright orange kayak off the dock and in the water, the waves slapping. Even this early she felt energetic.

She embarked on her usual route. She liked to follow the shoreline to avoid the rougher water in the middle. If today were typical, she'd complete the five-mile loop in just under an hour.

Many of the cottages on Loon Lake were used only occasionally. Jan's immediate neighbor was a doctor with a large piece of land who lived in downstate Minnesota and visited only on holidays and summer weekends. During the week the cottage was always empty. It was set back from the lake's edge up among some trees on a slight rise. Two small points jutting into the lake afforded privacy and the perfect place for their dock. Jan paddled in that direction, peering through the dark.

Every day was shorter, she noted. And colder. Oh well, at least it wasn't snowing yet. Jan pulled hard on the two-ended paddle, smoothly transitioning from one side to the other, keeping her splashes to a minimum. With each stroke she warmed up, getting into a groove. She started thinking about work and the day ahead. It was 5:45 a.m., over an hour and a half before sunrise in the North Country.

***

In the darkness ahead, wearing full wetsuits with snorkels, fins, and masks, two large men waited. Divers' knives were strapped to their legs. One had a mesh bag clipped to his waist with a hand towel wedged in it. Black neoprene gloves covered their hands.

They bobbed up and down behind the doctor's raft. Peering around opposite corners, they looked for her outline through the darkness. The first swimmer saw Jan approaching his side of the raft. He turned to his companion. He pointed at her and then himself. His companion nodded and drew closer, moving quietly.

The sounds of the kayaking rhythm approached. The splash as the paddle broke the water's surface. Then the gurgling of the pull. The slight sucking sound as the paddle escaped the water's tension. Then the rhythm repeated. The hull knifed through waves, slapping periodically. Adjacent to the swimmers, an occasional slurp came from the raft as it gently tugged against its anchor.

No other boats were out yet. No moon lit the darkness. Only the kayak's sounds could be heard, splashing closer and closer. The lead swimmer waited until he could make out the paddler's shape. Then he exhaled a final breath, sank underwater, and kicked rapidly.

He came to the surface right in front of her. Jan startled. "My God. What?" She twisted her paddle to avoid him.

He grabbed the front of her kayak and shoved the bow toward the raft. She lurched sideways, dropping her paddle. "Stop! What are you doing?" When the second man appeared, she opened her mouth to scream. The first swimmer pulled her off the kayak and plunged her headfirst into the cold water. He shoved the small towel into her mouth and clamped a huge hand on the back of her head, pinning her. The black gloves pushed her downward, and then the swimmer straddled her, his knees pressing her arms against her body. The other swimmer pushed her calves between his legs in a scissors lock. Front and back they sat, trapping her underwater, breathing through snorkels.

After two minutes the struggling stopped. By five minutes the bubbles and twitches were gone. The wind had started to pick up. They let her up, and the waves rocked her body. Her waxen face was unmarked.

The first swimmer removed the life vest and packed it away with the towel into the mesh bag. The second man turned the kayak over and pushed it toward the middle of the lake. The paddle floated near the lifeless body.

A flat-bottomed fishing boat with an electric motor was lashed against the back of the dock. They took turns climbing in. They stuffed the fins, masks, and snorkels in a bag. They unzipped rain suits and booney hats, and within minutes looked like two big fishermen. The waves become larger. They started the electric motor and hummed toward the secluded public boat launch, where their SUV awaited them.

***

Dasha's keystrokes tapped out digital instructions through the cloud to a virtual server sitting in a secure data center. Tasked with building the parallel IT infrastructure for the new energy drink operations, she felt the pressure of the tightest deadline of her young career.

Dasha's Skype ringtone warbled. Seeing it was Hugo, she answered.

"How is the mistress of the computing universe today, and I mean that in the most complimentary interpretation, of course."

Her video window showed Hugo's mischievous grin. She could tell from the background he was in the bottling building in Telluride.

"Aha, I see your breath. No heat yet? Now you know what Ukraine was like, maybe even Siberia," Dasha laughed.

"Indeed, we have an ideal temperature here for storing cold beverages, but not people. I'm working on that." A sudden loud burst from a nail gun interrupted him.

"One second," he yelled.

The sound cut out, and the video jerked as Hugo carried his wireless laptop through the construction activity, over to a storeroom. The background changed, showing baffles of pink insulation and new 2 x 4 framing. Hugo unmuted. "Sorry about that."

"Better," announced Dasha.

"Excellent. As you can see and hear, we are rapidly advancing to a state of readiness."

"So we have all the approvals?" asked Dasha.

"Local people have been great, no problems. Our changes have actually been quite minor. So, no worries." A nearby compressor kicked on. They talked louder.

"I sent comments on your project plan. Anything else?"

"Thanks. I saw them and have a few questions, which I'll email. It will be good to have you out here soon to finalize the IT stuff."

"Thank you. Yes, I'll be there as soon as the equipment and bandwidth connections arrive."

"And the part you didn't want to put in email? What's the mystery?" She could see his eyes widen with drama on her screen.

"Lionel's bike accident. I think we need increased security."

"More than the intrusion security system? What did you have in mind?"

"Security cameras. For each location, no exceptions."

"Aha!" She could see puffs of vapor as he blew on his hands. "Sounds understandable, but there are privacy issues. We'd limit this to the server rooms, entrances, and office space, right?"

"Correct, not in the bathrooms or private offices."

"Very good. And you'd manage this?"

"Yes. Contractors will install, but I'll centralize the feeds for analysis and archiving."

"Sounds good to me."

"Thanks, Hugo."

"Get Lionel's okay and bring on Big Brother. Meanwhile, I've got to get more heat in here."

***

"It's funny. I was riding my bike to work, right behind an Audi at a stop light, and it came to me." Lionel shook his head. "It was as though the fog lifted and there it was."

"It was a silver Audi logo? Black sedan, possibly a wagon?" Inspector Chang asked, typing as he spoke. Lionel could hear the bustle of the Mission Street precinct in the background. A lady complaining, a couple bickering, and a booming voice giving orders. He pictured Chang at his computer in the midst of it, sitting at a gunmetal gray desk.

"Yes, and a red, white, and blue badge of some sort in the upper left corner."

"Not a bumper sticker, but up higher?" He heard Chang suck in his breath as he typed.

"Yes, above the logo on the painted surface itself." He was hoping the driver's face would suddenly appear, just as had the image of the car. As Chang typed, Lionel stared out the window at the traffic below on Townsend Street. He saw a bike messenger narrowly avoid a minivan making a quick lane change, and winced at the memory of his head smacking the car. The sequence of the accident started to replay in his head.

"We'll try to identify the model based upon this." The line was silent. "Hello? Lionel?"

"Yes, sorry, that's good." Lionel came back to the present. "Inspector, how about the videos?"

"Yes. The videos. We searched the neighborhood and were surprised that nothing came up. We thought we had a good lead with two cameras outside a corner grocery, but unfortunately both malfunctioned that night."

"Malfunctioned?" Lionel questioned, his voice rising. "Do you think they were disabled intentionally?"

"It's possible, but that would have taken considerable planning and someone really good with electronics. The units weren't damaged or interfered with from what we could see—they simply had a blank recording for that night."

"Either a strange coincidence or a sophisticated operator," Lionel commented.

He waited for a response from Chang, but heard only something scratching. Back and forth. Then he realized it must be Chang rubbing his mustache, thinking. How annoying.

"These cameras are often flakey. It's hard to say without having an operations history."

"Anything new on identifying the paint or body shop?" Lionel pressed.

"No, as I said before, it was a common aftermarket black enamel. And no shops surfaced with records for this type of repair."

"But now that you know it's an Audi, you can revisit the body shops, right?"

"Mr. Lane, we have limited resources. Please understand that we consider this a serious accident and will do our best."

Was he a lifer burned out on the system? Or was a bike accident a low priority? Lionel shook his head. *This investigation was going nowhere fast.*

13

MONDAY, OCTOBER 28ᵀᴴ — TUESDAY OCTOBER 29ᵀᴴ

"Lionel, it's Leah Barko".
Lionel plugged in his Bluetooth and paced his office. "Jesus, Leah, I can't believe it. You must be calling about Jan. It makes me sick."

"Can I record this?"

"Yes, sure, why not?" he said, slightly annoyed. *It's a tragedy,* he thought, *not a story.*

"You two seemed to hit it off at the awards banquet." He could hear Leah was typing as she talked. It was so impersonal, the recorder and the keyboard clicking. *Well, this was Leah's job,* he reminded himself. *It's not like she didn't care.*

"She is . . . was, great. I talked to her not that long ago. She called me after I was hit on my bike."

"Do you think the two are related? The bike and now the kayak accident?"

"What? I . . . I hope not. She's in Minnesota, I'm out here. Why, is there something suspicious about her drowning?"

"Nothing official. I'm naturally suspicious, of course. Did she say anything to you when you talked?"

"She did say she was anxious. But that's the life of an entrepreneur, I figured."

"What exactly did she say?"

"She felt strange. Something about a force. As though a new force was now pushing us."

"A new force?"

"Those were her words. I thought it was just the extra pressure of the award. We all feel it. Unbelievably great possibilities, but the high probability of not winning. Imagine your disappointment when you fail kids or struggling people counting on you. It's worse than losing your own money. The shame."

"I can see that. But what of her personal safety? For example, did she say she saw people following her?"

"No, nothing like that."

"What about you? Have they found who hit you?"

"No. SFPD has assigned an investigator named Winston Chang, but he's drawing blanks. Frankly he hasn't impressed me."

"Tell me about DV. I'm doing an ongoing series now on the Big with Jules Longsworth, in addition to my other reporting. So here is your chance, what's new?" The abrupt turn in the conversation made Lionel realize Leah must be on a tight deadline. All business today.

"Our big news is establishing the energy drink business in Telluride. A lot of work but it's totally unique. And we are being repped by an unbelievable new talent, Reddi Christiansen. A spectacular free skier. She's bound for the X Games and the Olympics, in my opinion."

"Let me guess. She's a cute blond, right Lionel?"

"Redhead, actually." He thought about telling Leah about the first time they met, high up Tomboy Road above Telluride. He sitting in the sun in his shorts on the hood of his damaged Jeep, she racing down on her mountain bike with her wolfdog. Those cute freckles and winning smile, flushed with exertion. He realized how much he missed Reddi.

"Figures. So now you have the next female Shaun White promoting you?"

"Nice, I like that. She's the real deal. You'd like her, Leah. And Telluride and our new plant are out of this world."

"Hmm. How is the juice business?"

"Fine, great. Maxine is focused on that while I get energy going."

"Kind of challenging reinventing yourself while trying to win the Big, isn't it?"

"But so worth it. Maxine is amazing. She'll have our operations and marketing improved by quantum leaps, no doubt. And energy is a huge growth area."

"Don't forget about the starving kids, Lionel."

"Energy is also one-for-one, so we're still matching sales with nutritional meals. And we'll have a non-caffeinated version, targeted for the younger crowd."

"Let's see how much non-caffeinated you sell."

"Hey, why can't people choose for themselves?" *What's with Leah today? She is so critical,* he thought.

"They can, but let's see what you push."

"I thought you were the one coming down on the Big Four, with their legacy of pushing expensive sugar water and caffeine," Lionel responded, caustically.

"I am, but are you going to become like them?" she shot back.

Lionel started pacing, raising his voice. "Leah, tell me honestly, are we doing more for the world than the Big Four right now?"

"That I'll grant."

"Damn, thank you. So cut us some slack. We need to sell product in order to survive, and to change the model, okay?"

"Touchy, touchy, Mister Adventure Sport."

Lionel finally laughed. "Funny. Thanks for the reminder not to lose my sense of humor."

"Look, I have a deadline."

"I noticed. Let me let you go, then. Bye."

***

Leah immediately called Jules Longsworth.

"Leah, allow me to step away from this luncheon. One moment, please."

That's impressive, she thought. He certainly had many other demands yet was making time for her.

Upon his return Leah steered the conversation directly to Jan's death. His voice sounded as though he took her death very hard.

"A real tragedy. Leaving two children and a loving husband behind. And such an energetic person and entrepreneur, so well loved."

"How were they doing in the standings?"

"Sweet Boomerang was about to take over the top spot. Well, let me correct myself," he suddenly added. "Certainly in the top five. Now, going forward—well, she'll be very difficult to replace."

"Does this strike you as suspicious?" Leah wondered.

Jules hesitated before answering. "I'll leave that up to the police. I assume it was an active person pushing the envelope. An unfortunate perfect storm situation."

"But, what about that other top contender, Lionel Lane of Double Vision, and his bike accident? Accidents to two top contenders?"

"He's another go-hard type. And fortunately Lionel is okay. They appear unrelated, but I defer to the authorities."

"Do you think it's a matter of pushing themselves too hard?"

"Too hard?"

"Working all hours. Focused on the big prize and sacrificing themselves. Is it too much stress?"

"There is that element. But we need to remain positive and focus on the eventual purpose of the Big. I think that's more respectful of Jan and her family, at this point. And the better story." Leah noticed Jules's reverential tone and careful guidance.

Something nagged at her. But she had to hit the deadline. Leah thanked Jules and they hung up. Her editor approved the story for the immediate online edition and for print the following morning.

***

Inspector Winston Chang ducked out of the wet and into his favorite Peet's. After chatting up the barista with pleasantries, he took his drink and sat at a window table. Wind whipped rain across the street and gusts rattled the windows. He shivered under his damp trench coat. He pulled his hot tall cup of chai closer and disabled the public WiFi on his phone, switching to private mobile data. Chang browsed to a server a talented computer geek hacked together using Linux,

C#, and Big Data software. It performed deep search and analysis of conventional and social media. This was his personal unofficial tool, a cyber listening post that helped him with his investigations.

An article by Leah Barko popped up in his alerts. By the time he finished reading, Chang decided to give his counterparts in Minneapolis a call.

***

Race for a Billion—Social Entrepreneur Race Heats Up
National Times Journal exclusive coverage

Tuesday, October 29 By Leah Barko
The announcement of the Big Disrupter Award stirred a lot of controversy in a town already know for big egos and even bigger fortunes. In moves to trump the globally famous Nobel Prizes, numerous other prizes have been created recently, such as the Breakthrough Prize funded by Mark Zuckerberg and Sergey Brin, founders of Facebook and Google, respectively. The eponymous Skoll Awards for Social Entrepreneurship, created by the first employee of EBay, spreads millions among numerous do-gooder organizations annually.

Enter The BIG
The recently announced billion-dollar Big Disrupter Award has kicked the other awards into the kiddie sandbox and now rules the playground. President Jules Longsworth of Schwab and Young, explains. "This amount of money for a single organization is a leadership catapult. A competitive game changer beyond all others."

Standings
Who is in front? Show me the money, says Larry Furtig, CEO of SocialLending, the peer-to-peer lending platform. Unapologetically known for being brash and driven, he credits their first place position to focus and execution.

Wearing the second-place mantle is the charming Raj Singh's Step-by-Step Clothing brand. His company has won over well-to-do consumers with a passion for the environment, featuring products made from recycled tires and plastics.

Jumping into third place is the globetrotting Bill Krause, a pioneer in social entrepreneurship with his fast rising nutritional bar company, Global Bite.

Seen in fourth place is WorldLensFactory. Known as the go-to glasses for urban hipsters, they donate a pair of glasses for each one purchased.

A tragic development befell the fifth place contender, Sweet Boomerang. Their effervescent founder, Jan Swenson, drowned recently in a solo kayaking accident near her home in Minnesota.

Surprisingly, Double Vision has slipped out of the top five. Recent distractions include their controversial move into energy drinks and a bicycle hit-and-run accident that sent Co-CEO Lionel Lane to the hospital. Meanwhile, his new Co-CEO, Maxine Gold, has largely taken a behind-the-scenes role.

The hottest race in the country is full of surprises—stay tuned with updates on my blog and Twitter.

***

14

FRIDAY, NOVEMBER 8TH

I'll be in early tomorrow, the email had said. *Ugh, why she liked such early hours he did not know.* One thing he did know, the most interesting aspect of his new assignment was getting to spy on Dasha Romanyuk. *Ukrainian. Twenty-four-year-old female. Good looking, of course. IT hotshot. Rides a scooter.* He knew she wasn't the primary person of interest for his boss, but she certainly was for him. Igor Vasilchenko dragged himself out of bed at six a.m.

He fired up the Ducati. As it warmed up, the rough rumble between his legs smoothed to a steady vibration. He dropped it into gear and pulled back, rearing toward the Mission District.

He wound through the gears and leaned into the turns, and minutes later he neared Dasha's apartment. It was still dark. There had been no traffic. *That is the only good thing about six a.m.,* he thought.

He positioned his bike next to a van, so he could watch her unobserved. He killed the engine, looking toward her door.

Within moments, Dasha tapped down her front steps on the toes of her low heels. She rounded the side of the apartment, inserted the key and started her blue and gold Vespa scooter. It buzzed like a bee. She zoomed through the alley and dodged a pothole with a quick snap of the handlebars. Igor watched her tight figure lean around the curve and turn onto Mission, a major thoroughfare. The light traffic gave her the opportunity to gun it.

Ah, she was way ahead of me, he realized. He quickly started the Ducati. He had to race to stay within a few blocks range. He could tell she enjoyed quick bursts, the 250cc engine rasping as she squeezed the throttle. She was playful with the machine and with the thrill of speed, and it was hard for Igor to resist pulsing his throttle and racing up to her. The air was invigorating on his cheeks, and by the time they approached the office, he felt wide-awake. He dropped back so she could park before he pulled into the lot.

Igor selected a space close to hers and rumbled to a stop. He watched as she spread her legs and pushed back emphatically, rocking her scooter into its stand. She spun on her seat. Pulling off her helmet her black hair scattered over her face and brushed her snug leather jacket. He was fascinated by her pronounced eyebrows and almond eyes.

"Love that scooter." He pulled off his helmet and looked over.

She ran her fingers through her bangs. "Thanks," she said with a quick glance. She started to walk away.

"Hey, I am wondering, why is the top half blue and the bottom half gold?"

She seemed slightly annoyed with the distraction. Still walking, she answered over her shoulder, "I'm Ukrainian, that's the color of our flag."

He answered in Russian. "That's what I thought. My name is Igor Vasilchenko. From Russia."

She stopped. In Russian she responded, "I thought I heard an accent. Dasha. Dasha Romanyuk."

"I like your helmet. Chernobyl."

She held it out, a half helmet with earflaps, with yellow and black radioactive warning symbols on each side.

He added, "Dramatic graphics, you stand out with that."

"It says, be careful, I am dangerous." And then she laughed. It was a high arcing laugh, and she covered her mouth with one hand as she did.

"I love danger. If you ever want to ride together, just let me know."

She looked over, smiling. "Thanks for asking. But I am so busy these days. See you around, okay?"

He smiled, and saw her look at him a little closer. Then she sauntered away, tight jeans swinging above her heels. Igor felt the thrill of making contact. He glanced at himself in his side mirror. Maybe she liked his short blond hair and blue eyes.

He looked over at her Ukrainian-flag-colored scooter. He knew from experience she was a long way from home. And the U.S. had no extradition treaties and little police cooperation with Ukraine.

***

Later that morning in San Francisco, Lionel saw the Juice Genius hurrying down the hallways. Hugo dashed around, in and out of the conference room, animatedly directing his team. His white lab coat was untied and flew around like a swirling cape.

Lionel followed Hugo into the conference room. He was immediately struck by the organization. Tasting samples sat in front of each chair. Briefing kits for the five new products were tucked in folders, and a color presentation projected on the wall. Just weeks before, these were only concepts. He and Maxine had given Hugo dictatorial powers, and other than a few animated discussions for validation, Hugo ran with the product development. Lionel gently brushed his fingertips over a sample aluminum bottle, struck by its smooth and solid feel. *It's happening.*

"Lionel, can you help me get everyone in here? They'll listen to you." Hugo was kneeling on the floor, frantically unpacking more colorful aluminum bottles.

"I'm on it," Lionel responded, leaving to round up the team. Five minutes later, the twenty people who would help produce, promote and manage the product launch were all crammed into the room.

Kate joined Hugo at the front as he kicked off the meeting. "On September 30th, Lionel and Maxine very generously gave me two months to do what normally takes two years. But, with the excellent team we have, I agreed. And today, about five weeks later, with lots of input, trials and tribulations, and little sleep, we have our five new products to present. The plant won't be online for three more weeks, but we will hit the two-month window." As the assembled group clapped and cheered, Hugo bowed.

"Now as we know," said Hugo, rubbing his hands together, "the only way to stay ahead of the dark side is to out-conspire them." His eyes shined. "And our brew should make the competition quake in their boots." He cast furtive glances sideways, generating chuckles from the crowd. "Kate, are we ready?"

"Oh, yes."

"Then it's time to look at these beauties."

Kate began the product introduction. "We're very close to having the final bottles to show. But today, here are the photo-shopped designs and a few shaped aluminum samples. They are gorgeous, sculpted, and frankly sensuous . . . it's as though we're on a runway with models at New York's Fashion Week. I am *so* excited!" Kate gushed. It wasn't a coincidence she was wearing a new silk top and expensive designer slacks, Lionel thought.

Kate dimmed the lights and the video projected five lustrous aluminum bottles with sparkling beads of liquid dripping down the sides. They were a beautiful burnished gold. A smooth animation spun the tops up and off, then twisted them back on. Images for each of the five labels flashed and zoomed onscreen. Oos and aahs filled the room.

"Sexy, sexy, sexy, right?" Hugo crowed.

Lionel, Maxine, and the rest of the crowded room whistled and cheered. Kate and Hugo held hands and bowed.

"Printed out here and posted on our intranet are all the details and specs. Please check them out. But at a high level, let's review."

Kate began. "First, our core product is DV 24. A fresh fruit flavor with ten milligrams caffeine per ounce, produced in a ten-ounce aluminum bottle. This, like all five products, is delicious."

"Second, DV CLEAR, which has no caffeine, juice infused, and is targeted for the youth audience. It also has electrolytes." Hugo added, "This one is actually healthy."

Kate waved an aluminum bottle with leafy graphics. "This is our Green Tea variant—product number three."

Hugo jumped in. "Approximately seven milligrams of caffeine per ounce. Sodas are between three to five milligrams per ounce. So this has more kick than sodas, but less than a typical energy drink."

"Product four. My personal favorite. DV Java, our coffee-flavored, milk-infused energy drink with just seventy calories per eight-ounce serving. Hugo made me an addict when he brewed this one."

Kate then held up two small aluminum bottles, one in each palm. "And for our fifth and final product, DV Energy Shots. Aren't they cute? Two ounces each. Much more sophisticated than the competition's, which look like little shampoo bottles from a cheap hotel." Snickers and laughter made her smile. "You know it's true."

"Yes, and those sweet minis are laced with 100 milligrams of caffeine. About the same as a standard cup of coffee, but you get it in a quick jolt. Also available as a 'Double' with 200 milligrams caffeine, in the same two ounces, matching some competitors." Hugo rubbed his hands together. "Brewing those made me feel more like a Double Dragon than a Juice Genius, I must admit."

Several members of the team raised objections about the high caffeine levels.

Lionel countered with a question. "Hugo, remind us what a high powered cup of specialty coffee has, caffeine-wise?"

He threw the arms of his white coat out wide. "Specialty coffee averages twenty milligrams per ounce. Way more than this. So your Starbucks sixteen-ounce coffee weighs in at about 320 milligrams of caffeine. But in all fairness, that is hot, and meant to be sipped, not chugged."

"But once you are done sipping . . ." began Lionel.

"Oh, you are lit up." Hugo jumped in the air and pedaled his feet, and the audience cracked up. "But the savior for coffee purveyors is that their products aren't targeted to youth. That is why our youth product needs to be juice, with zero caffeine."

"So, four of our new products are meant to be chilled, and one is room temperature? And one is specifically youth targeted with no caffeine?" Lionel asked.

"You got it. The youth product, DV CLEAR, will look as sophisticated as the others, to further its appeal. The shot is non-carbonated and fine at room temperature. So four will compete with the retailers' refrigerated products while the shot will sit on the counter by the cash register. And hopefully they'll all make it cha-ching."

The Big Disrupter

"What about costs and production complexity among these?" asked Maxine.

"Lionel asked for a report on this, and we're running the production analytics now. Short term, we'll need to limit ourselves to what we can produce in our new bottling plant in Telluride with the excellent local water. Longer term, we can expand our product mix."

"We've discussed the sustainability issues before," said Kate. "I know we have been considering everything—from the carbon footprint of the container materials to our water supply and the other ingredients. Can you update the team on that, Hugo?"

"That, good madam, has been a significant piece of this production design. One key factor is the water, and in Telluride we have what appears to be among the highest-altitude natural spring sources in the country. It is extremely clean water, with literally no upstream effluent, agricultural, or livestock operations impacting it, no residential fertilizer run off, no urban industrial component. It is truly amazing water for us in abundant supply."

"Kate, clearly this can be a key point of product differentiation," pointed out Maxine.

"I love it, all over it," Kate responded. "But we want to be careful about that raging debate on local tap versus high carbon footprint bottled water."

"Totally agree," said Lionel. "But the purity and Wild West origins of the source are powerful images."

"And that will be a huge marketing emphasis," Kate responded.

"What about the container choice? Why'd we choose aluminum?"

"Kate can weigh in here at any time, as our marketing maven," Hugo responded. "But here is my take. The market perception is metal cans are for energy drinks and glass bottles are for juices or healthy drinks. Of course this is ridiculous and not based on any scientific or real business reason, for that matter. It is just perception. It's how Red Bull started, how Monster followed, and how most every one else has entered the refrigerated category. With 5 Hour Energy you have a non-refrigerated shot in a small plastic bottle."

"Did we make the decision based on carbon footprint?"

"Yes, with an asterisk. Aluminum is lighter, transports more readily, and is the more economical and practical recycling material. Glass takes much more energy to recycle. The counter argument is it takes something like twice the energy to make aluminum cans compared to bottles. So, the number of times that aluminum can is recycled determines the eco advantage."

"And plastic?"

"Somewhere in the middle. The Carbon Trust is a good source for this info. And what we know from their studies, aluminum has the lowest footprint, plastic is not far behind, and glass is the worst. So going with aluminum is probably the best choice for us in the energy category, for environmental as well as market reasons."

Lionel rose from his seat. "Thank you, excellent discussion. And a very exciting product introduction. But we're running out of time. To conclude, let's all taste our five new products."

"I humbly await your every command, and shall respond forthwith." Hugo extended a low bow. "Meanwhile, it's back to our bubbling brew."

"Four months left, people," reminded Maxine. "Let's get some winning products and promotion out soon."

***

The meeting had broken up. Lionel caught up on phone calls. Then, something Hugo said triggered a question. Lionel hurried across the office in search of Hugo. He went down the internal staircase to the production floor. Passing through the glass doors and beyond the loud bottling operations, where conveyer belts were moving juice bottles to be filled and boxed, he walked down the hallway to Hugo's lab.

Lionel was immersed in thought as he burst through the closed door. "Hugo, what do you think about this . . . ?" He stopped with a jolt.

Hugo was standing in deep embrace, kissing passionately. His back was to the door. Then he turned, surprised. His partner pulled apart with a gasp. It was Harding Liu, their CPA.

Lionel was frozen.

"Why Lionel, I've never seen you speechless," said Hugo.

"I, I don't know what to say. Other than . . . sorry for barging in." Harding adjusted his glasses, looking very embarrassed.

Hugo turned and tightened his lab coat. "Lionel, allow me to take this opportunity to formally come forward to you and say, Harding and I are a couple. Since we're both senior here, we think it best to share this personal information. We've both been gay forever, but only more recently together."

Hugo looked at Harding. "There, Harding, I told you it wouldn't be difficult to come out to Lionel."

"Congratulations. I'm not surprised about the gay part, but didn't know about you two."

"Normally we aren't this passionate at work, of course. But there is something else. Right?" He looked at Harding for confirmation.

Harding nodded. He straightened his silk tie. The irony of his fastidious business dress and Hugo's mad-scientist informality suddenly occurred to Lionel. Opposites attract, he thought.

"Lionel, we'd like to move in together," said Harding. "For now, that means in Telluride."

"Telluride. You'd move there too, Harding?"

"Yes. But still working, one hundred percent. With your permission, of course."

"That will mean more travel. You know, when necessary."

Harding responded quickly. "You bet. No problem."

"And since we each report to you, and not each other, there is no work conflict of interest," Hugo pointed out. "We certainly wouldn't want a romance to affect the workplace," he added a bit dramatically.

"Right. Of course."

Lionel looked at Hugo's curved eyebrows above his dancing green eyes. *They seem to change color, depending on the light,* thought Lionel. *Especially when he's scheming.*

"So," said Hugo expansively. "When exactly are you and yours coming out of the closet?"

"Me and who?" Lionel asked.

Hugo laughed. "I, of course, am teasing you. It concerns me not in the least. It is indeed ironic that the gay couple is the one that is faster to make a public commitment. You breeders can continue to take your time figuring out who loves whom."

Then he darted over to his desk. He put on a wizard's hat and picked up a long-handled spoon.

"Look Lionel, these are part of an ensemble given to me at the grand opening party for the Telluride plant." He waved the spoon. "The hat conjures magic powers, the spoon stirs our unique elixirs. And I received a kit with a new hydrometer, refractomer, and numerous tech gadgets. I immediately donned the hat and danced around the party."

"Better you than me, brother."

"Evidently, as Juice Genius, I am perceived as somewhere between a Harry Potter wizard and Bill Nye, the Science Guy."

"Hugo, you are incorrigible and insane. But please don't ever change. Meanwhile, I'll shoot you my question via email."

Lionel left the lab. As he headed down the hallway, he wondered what had just happened. As awkward as it was to walk in on Hugo and Harding, he was glad it was now in the open. But then Hugo made that "out of the closet" comment. Then obviously redirected the topic with his wizard hat and toys. How did he know he was hot for Reddi? Had he even met her?

15

TUESDAY, NOVEMBER 12TH

It was one-thirty p.m. and Maxine's stomach had been growling for hours. She had skipped breakfast in her rush to the office at six a.m. But she wanted this meeting to be short, and that meant waiting until after the lunch crowd. She hurried down the block to Burma Superstar, a hole-in-the-wall restaurant with a rabid following. A broad-shouldered man in a long coat waited in the entrance.

"Maxine, good to see you." Blaine Latrell, from Axlewright Capital, leaned into her with a hug.

"Blaine." She hugged briefly, then put her arms on his shoulders, holding him at length. "Good to see you," she smiled.

They took a table and he settled in across from her. "So, it's been a couple of months since the funding. How goes it?"

"I'm continuously overcommitted and living off three hours of sleep. So, it sucks for me. As our investor, that means it's good for you."

He laughed. "Not necessarily. I'd rather have you effective than burned out."

"Oh, I'm effective. Just effective nonstop."

The waitress arrived, a short thin Burmese woman with a charming smile, who greeted Maxine by name. Blaine ordered tea and the same dish as Maxine, and the waitress hurried back to the kitchen.

Blaine rearranged the chopsticks in front of him. "Maxine, I miss our McKinsey days. I was hoping we'd be able to have more time together now that Axlewright has invested in you. And with both of us living here in San Francisco."

He rested his hands near Maxine's. She moved, making a motion of brushing something off her shoulder.

Maxine considered ways to step around his request. "Blaine, consulting at McKinsey was crazy busy. But now that I'm on the operational side at DV, it is insane. With so many employees and operational details, it's a 24/7 situation. Especially in start-up mode."

"Come on, Maxine. I've never known you to be overwhelmed by work."

"Oh, I'm not. I'm explaining why I haven't had time to stay in better touch. With you, or a lot of other people. Don't take it personally. We've got four months until the Big Disrupter is awarded—and that is consuming me."

"That is exactly what I want to talk about." Blaine leaned a heavy elbow on the table.

And exactly what she was dreading. "Really, how so?"

"Maxine, I've participated on several boards for successful beverage and food companies. In each case, I was asked to play a more involved role to help guide the entrepreneurs. To provide vision beyond the daily press of business."

"Blaine, that is why you are on our board as an advisor. We value your experience."

"Perfect, then we are of like mind. I'd like to take that further, to go from an advisory seat to an actual voting seat."

"So soon?" *Why is he focusing on us right now? Shouldn't he be thinking about new deals?*

"Do I have your support on this?"

This was awkward. He knows my response on this has to be no. "Frankly, it's too early, Blaine. Lionel is just getting to know you. Give it some time."

Blaine frowned, withdrawing his hands. "I'm disappointed, I must admit. But let's leave that for a moment. What about setting up time with Jacob for us to meet?"

What was she, his secretary? "Blaine, call him yourself. I assume you want to pursue other opportunities, right?"

"Yes."

"Those are your deals, not my business. I'm swamped with DV. You should reach out to him."

Blaine frowned and leaned forward. He lowered his voice. "The real issue is getting him to take my calls."

Oh. He was striking out. But she couldn't be his Havermyer go-between. "If he is avoiding you, then the timing isn't right. Be patient, I can't change that either."

Blaine took off his glasses and rubbed his temples.

The cheerful waitress arrived with their salads. She took a minute to point out the colorful fresh ingredients artistically arranged on the platter. Then she cut them up, mixed it all together and served.

"Bon appétit." Maxine launched into her salad, famished. With every bite she felt stronger. She wondered about Blaine. Something was bothering him. Were things getting rocky at Axlewright?

Blaine took a few bites, played with his chopsticks, and then smiled at Maxine.

"Here is an easy one. I was wondering if I could get a small office, nothing elaborate at all, in your operations. I'd stay completely out of the way and stop by a few days a week."

"In our offices here in the city?" She stirred a shrimp in her dressing.

"Yes. A small place, a cubbyhole really, with a door." He returned to his salad, twirling the long noodles.

He must have a lot of concerns about our business. Or he's trying to get out of his own office. To go off on his own, maybe? *Either way, it doesn't feel right.* "Blaine, we're bursting at the seams, growing like crazy. Space is at a premium."

"Yes, of course. I understand. But I really am not asking for much, something modest."

"Let me be perfectly frank. I think this would send the wrong message to the team."

He looked at her with surprise. "Meaning?"

She paused, a tangle of noodles and papaya hanging from her chopsticks. "That the investors don't trust us. That they, well really you and Axlewright Capital, are moving in to watch over our shoulders and tell us how to operate the company." She took a bite.

"Oh no, it's nothing like that. I live in the city, and it would be convenient for occasional strategic discussion. It's a matter of support and interest, not a lack of trust."

"It would not be perceived that way." Maxine glanced at her phone and quickly scanned some texts.

"Maxine, I am so disappointed the team would feel that way. Perhaps this is the perfect opportunity for people to get to know me, to help change that perception."

She took the last few bites on her plate. "Blaine, I don't see the value in taking that on, especially right now. We have so many ways to stay in touch, let's use those."

He put his chopsticks down.

Maxine looked up from her iPhone. "I'm sorry Blaine, it's an emergency. A new distributor deal. One of the sales guys sent an urgent text."

Blaine folded his big arms and looked down at the table. Maxine studied him. He was a handsome guy. But when he got that pouty mouth thing going, he seemed so grumpy.

As if reading her mind, Blaine relaxed and smiled. He waved a hand as though dismissing any problem.

"I understand. But, while the waitress brings the bill, one more thought."

"Okay, but I really do need to go." She gathered her bag and sat on the edge of her chair.

Blaine placed his beefy elbows on the table, rocking it with his weight. "I think you are missing the point. I can help DV grow, especially if Lionel is off elsewhere focused on the energy drinks. We've worked well together in the past, and should find a way to do so again."

He wants to fill in for Lionel? "Ah, so that is your concern. Lionel and I are in good alignment and constant communication. So thank you for your offer, but it just isn't necessary at this time. Now if you'll excuse me, I have to run. Okay?"

She hoped he took this as up-tempo, but final.

"Maxine, I really wish . . ."

"I must go. I don't want to lose this potential deal by insulting them and being later that I already am." She reached for her wallet.

"I've got this. But can you call me back afterward? I think we're missing an opportunity here."

She stood up quickly. "Let me give it some thought. We'll be in touch. Good bye."

Maxine patted him on the shoulder, hurrying out of the restaurant and across the street, lost in thought. Did he really think he could add value to their operations? Or was this somehow personal? Deciphering interpersonal stuff wasn't her strong suit. But it sure hadn't take him long to notice Lionel's travels. And why was he so interested in moving in?

She thought back to when they met, after college. She had broken up with Lionel. McKinsey moved her to London as a consultant, and Blaine had already worked in McKinsey's European offices for a few years. He knew a lot of gossip and political inroads for a junior person, far more than she kept up with. Okay, so their relationship did become sexual briefly, very briefly, really more for sport than anything else. But that was years ago. She hoped he wasn't trying to rekindle that now.

***

Blaine watched Maxine's shapely figure in her tight slacks and bouncing jacket hurrying away, her long hair waving. He replayed the image of her dramatic eyes and full lips. He wished she accommodated him more, instead of parrying him with her wicked intellect.

Suddenly he jumped up, dropped some cash on the table, and rushed out to hail a cab. *Damn!* It would take at least fifteen minutes to get to the Axlewright office, but his meeting with Anderson started in five. He crossed against a red light and dodged traffic to jump into a cab.

"Transamerica Pyramid, and I'm late." The cabbie floored it.

Once across town he paid before the cab stopped, then hopped out. He agonized during the elevator ascent, and then hustled down the hallway to the office of John Anderson, Blaine's boss and managing director.

A few years shy of sixty, Anderson had a head full of white hair gelled back with precision. He constantly reminded Blaine he worked out on a treadmill every morning like clockwork. Anderson glanced at his watch.

"Blaine. Take a chair."

He rushed to get seated, smoothing his hair with his thick fingers, feeling Anderson's watchful eyes. *He's like the fashion police, the way he examines me.* Anderson's tailoring was always expensive and crisp. St. Croix. Brioni.

Blaine knew he should be upbeat and super energized, but he had a headache, lunch was topsy-turvy in his stomach, and he was out of breath. He could feel the loose pounds he had added recently. His glasses pressed tight, and he pulled them off to rub the indentations in his temples.

"What's new on the radar?"

Blaine returned his glasses and opened his tablet, looking for answers. "I'm taking a deep dive into coconut water. The market is exploding."

"Humph. Awfully competitive space. Isn't everyone doing that? What else?"

"An emerging company that is flash-freezing fresh fish and scallops and selling it directly to consumers via their website. Arrives in dry ice containers."

"Sounds like Omaha Steaks of the Sea, is that right?" He snorted at his joke.

"The healthy lifestyle version. They are working on celebrity endorsements that could have a geometric effect."

"Competition?"

"Lots, unfortunately. We'll be part of a beauty contest over the next few months. But I'm confident."

Anderson scowled. He swiveled and looked over the bay. He seemed miles away.

"How many years have you been here?"

"Seven."

"And you've had six deals. Three have been losers. Two broke even at best. The only one that remains is Double Vision."

"John, it's been a difficult investment environment. We're just now getting over the effects of the financial crisis."

Anderson spun around and stared across his desk at Blaine. "All due respect, I know your numbers. You are way behind your peers. Several have made partner. They've bought private planes and rented entire islands in the Caribbean for birthday party bashes. You haven't left Disneyland, for Christ's sake."

It actually hurt to breathe. Blaine concentrated on short, shallow breaths as he stared out the window. *Nothing he did was good enough for this guy.*

John rapped his knuckles sharply on his desk. Blaine noticed the clear reflection of his hand on the black wood. *Everything about Anderson is polished,* he thought. *His whole perfect life.*

"Let me tell you something that happened this weekend. I was at a party in Woodside. You know Woodside, the horse country for Valley mega-millionaires with their chateaus and rolling estates. I'm standing on a patio made from hand-cut marble flown in from Italy, drinking champagne grown from the vineyards stretching out below us, and Hank Welcher comes up to me. He's bragging about his firm, Falconvest, and then says, right in front of this crowd of people, that Lionel Lane made a fool of me."

"What?"

"He played me, he says. He said the evening the Big Disrupter was announced he discussed getting ninety percent of Double Vision from Lionel for a measly ten-million-dollar bridge loan. Lionel was that cash strapped. To quote him, he was a cunt hair away from doing the deal. Then his own investment, SocialLending, won that Entrepreneur award, and he figured DV wouldn't make it."

Blaine rubbed his temples. "Sounds like he's jealous."

"Yeah, but he turned down the same deal we took. He called our deal the twenty-four hour immaculate conception. With no foreplay you spent fifteen million and suddenly had an energy drink company with no revenue. A fifteen-million-dollar newborn. That got a laugh." Anderson shook his head. "Welcher sure knows how to piss in your champagne glass."

"I heard he was already committed in the category with SocialLending, that's the only reason he declined."

"He was very graphic in giving other reasons."

"What do you mean?" Blaine realized this was what Anderson wanted to discuss.

"Welcher thinks Havermyer and the sexy black chick, which is how he refers to Maxine, are involved."

"What!? Jacob Havermyer having an affair with Maxine?"

"Well, he didn't put it that politely. He said Maxine was probably giving the old man afternoon blowjobs and a long finger thrill. And then leaning over."

"That's revolting."

"That's Welcher. He loves to paint pictures to prove his point."

"I meant the idea that she'd trade her body for an investment. She isn't like that." Blaine felt like he had just chewed a piece of rotten meat.

"I'm sure Havermyer has his share of eager offers. But that isn't the point." Anderson lifted a thick file on his desk and dropped it with a loud thwack. "I've looked at the financials carefully now, and it's clear they were close to bankruptcy."

Blaine sat up straight. "Look, I admit, they had a severe cash-flow crisis. That was on Lionel. But then Havermyer and Maxine stepped up. And now we're in the running to win the Big for a billion. Not in our pockets, granted, but it's a portfolio company showing a billion-dollar profit. That could kick in significant fees for our limited partnership, on the value side. And we could raise new funds and management fees with that success."

"I'm quite aware of that. And I realize Welcher wants the very same thing."

"You're right," encouraged Blaine.

"My concern is your judgment in acting so quickly, when you should have known they were on the ropes."

So that's where this is going. Shit. "Havermyer made his decision in ten minutes, with probably far less financial rigor than us. The problem isn't me, it's Lionel. He's a classic entrepreneur founder. Not a professional CEO."

"The stakes have changed now with the Big. I may need to get involved."

That could only mean one thing. He would be forced out. "Wait, please. Give me some time."

"There is no time. We're four months away from the Big. And I want to watch Welcher twist in envy at my victory party, surrounded by the very same people who saw me embarrassed by him."

"I can do that for you. I can get Double Vision to perform and remove this troublemaker Lionel."

Anderson leaned forward on his elbows, with a look somewhere between disbelief and greed. "Tell me more."

Blaine stalled for time. "It won't be easy. But, I can split up Maxine and Lionel. She wins as CEO, he loses. Once he's out . . ." Blaine paused. An idea flashed. "In fact, if he is ousted under the right circumstances, potentially we can get his shares at a very favorable price." He stared at Anderson with his mind churning.

The look on Anderson's face improved. *He's still skeptical,* thought Blaine, *but at least the hunt was on.*

"Don't fuck this up, Blaine. This is your long overdue home run. I shouldn't have to tell you, but if you don't get rid of Lionel and win this, you're out."

At this point the acid flushing Blaine's stomach was like an open faucet.

"I have this under control. Trust me."

"Impress me, Blaine. I want to be stomping on Lionel Lane's neck in front of Welcher while I'm celebrating the Big with champagne." He glanced at his iPhone. "We're done here."

16

THURSDAY, NOVEMBER 14TH

Lionel heard the storm pelting the office windows. *Is that hail?* He rushed down the hallway with his suitcase and looked out across Brannan Street. Water was flooding the sidewalks. Sheets of raindrops splashed buttercups right where they'd be walking. They were going to get soaked. And then sit cramped together for five hours, all before this critical meeting. *Perfect.*

"The oceans are rising out there, Maxine, time to leave."

She pulled her roller-bag out her doorway, phone glued to her ear, nearly colliding with him.

"The elevator is backed up. Let's take the stairs." They rolled, carried, and banged their roller-bags down the concrete and steel stairwell. The stale smell of smoke hung in the air.

Lionel pushed open the ground-floor exit and the rain blew in, splashing their faces. Maxine looked at the tempest. "Really? The things we have to do. And where's your umbrella?"

"I'm traveling light." He pulled a Giants baseball cap out of his coat pocket.

She raised her umbrella and plunged into the rainstorm, dragging her roller-bag through the puddles.

He should have planned better, he thought, as he tugged on the cap. Moments later a vicious gust inverted Maxine's umbrella. He started to laugh, then saw her pinched face. He caught up with her and offered his hat. They were both drenched by the time they finally sank into the back of the waiting cab.

"Where to?" the driver asked.

"San Francisco International."

"Okay, but to let you know, traffic is a nightmare."

"Sounds like my day so far," responded Lionel.

While Maxine squeezed in a phone call, Lionel unzipped his bag and pulled out two clean T-shirts. He handed one to Maxine, and they dried themselves as best they could.

The cab pulled up to the curb thirty-five minutes before the scheduled departure. They scrambled through the airport and suffered through the security line. Just past the X-ray machine, Lionel checked his watch and panicked. He whispered to Maxine, "Collect my bag, I've got to make sure we don't lose our seats." He pulled on his shoes and sprinted ahead to the gate just as the agents began giving up their seats to stand-by passengers.

Lionel and Maxine ran down the jet way and the flight attendant slammed the heavy plane door right behind them. The smell of damp leather and perspiration closed in. His shirt stuck to his back. They couldn't move. The aisle was backed up. People bickered, wedged tight. Lionel felt claustrophobic. In fits and starts, they shuffled toward their seats.

For what seemed the millionth time, Lionel waited pressed in the aisle as someone rearranged the overhead space and jammed in their bag.

Maxine examined her ticket. "Why do I have a middle seat?"

"So we can talk, side by side."

"Why don't I get the aisle and you get the middle?"

"I'm taller. Bigger."

"I hate the middle as much as you do."

Lionel pushed his ticket toward her. "Fine, let's switch."

"No. I can take it. Mind over emotion."

Lionel rolled his eyes.

"I saw that."

Lionel snorted, shaking his head.

Maxine looked back at him.

"It has been such a miserable day." He groaned, rubbing his temples. Then he laughed. "Ah, what are you gonna do?"

"You're strange, Lionel."

"And you went into business with me, Maxine."

"I sometimes wonder about that." And then she cracked up.

Lionel's shoulders rocked as he chortled. They were the only people on the plane laughing. They didn't stop until they plopped down into their seats, shaking their heads.

After taxiing for what seemed forever, the plane finally took off for New York. Lionel settled back, ready for uninterrupted talk and computer time. Finally!

Lionel glanced over at Maxine. She was so smart, he was glad she was coming on this trip. He hoped she would be open to his suggestion for their upcoming meeting, rather than argue. Because arguing with Maxine was like arguing with a subatomic particle accelerator. She kept bombarding your logic until it broke up and decayed in front of your eyes. This wasn't going to be easy.

"I never heard the backstory on our meeting tomorrow," she said.

"What do you mean?" Lionel replied.

Maxine leaned closer and said quietly, "How exactly did you get a meeting with Garr Gartick, Merry Cola's CEO?"

"Ah." He lowered his voice. "Look, we know Coke distributes Monster, and Pepsi distributes Rockstar, and so on. Merry Cola is the only Big Four company that doesn't sell or distribute energy drinks."

"Right. So why are they waiting?"

"It's a mystery. But I do know that Merry Cola's global distribution is very impressive."

"So what was the hook to get the appointment?"

"I spoke about people. Not the product per se."

"What people?"

"Jacob Havermyer in particular. And you and me. And the one-for-one offer."

"What did Gartick say?"

"He wanted to talk in person. I told him Havermyer was out of the country but you and I were available any time."

She slapped her hand on his knee. "So he called your bluff and said tomorrow morning, knowing we're across the country. We can thank him for the red-eye."

He tried to ignore the effect of her touch. "Maybe he thought we had a Gulfstream like Havermyer." He glanced down the aisle. "Far from it."

Maxine pressed. "But the real question is, why now? Why would he change his mind and decide to distribute energy drinks? Our energy drinks?"

"Sometimes it's good timing."

"Hmm. I have a theory."

"I do want to hear that theory. But first, a request."

"Which is?"

Lionel glanced around and leaned closer. "Look, Gartick is single and very active, not a suburban family executive. He dates beautiful models. They fly together in his private plane to ski in Alaska and scuba dive in the Cayman Islands. He is big on looks, on image and brand."

"What does that possibly have to do with me?"

"What I am suggesting, asking really, is . . . is . . . difficult."

"Say it, Lionel."

"Maxine, you can be aloof sometimes. So intellectually driven you overlook the emotional or human side."

"This isn't a newsflash, Lionel."

"Tomorrow, not only do I want your theory and brains to be part of the package, but I want your . . . ."

"My what?"

"Your emotions. Let's dummy down the pitch, make it about brand, and make it alluring."

"Alluring? It's a good thing we have five hours to talk about this. Because you are going to need every minute to convince me."

"I understand. But this distribution contract is our only realistic means for winning the Big. We have a billion dollars riding on this meeting."

✱✱✱

After the all-nighter and showers at the hotel, Lionel and Maxine arrived early the next morning at the midtown Manhattan skyscraper.

They were escorted to the private elevator bank, where two uniformed and armed guards in dark blue, one male and one female, reviewed their credentials. The guards performed a tight security search, their gloved hands waving high tech wands. Then they were led to the express elevator and whisked directly to the fiftieth floor.

Passing through the elevator doors into the reception area, Lionel thought he had entered a completely different world. It looked like a five-star hotel lobby, complete with chandeliers, elegant Louis XIV furniture, and collectible art. Classical music played. Two impeccably dressed assistants greeted them. One ushered them toward Garr Gartick's office suite, and as they walked she explained his domain included the entire end of the building.

The assistant paused by the all-glass conference room. "I'm not sure if you'll be meeting here or in his office." This was a calculated stop, Lionel thought. The full-glass-surround views were so dramatic they dared you to keep your concentration.

Parks and rivers framed the far edges of the panorama. It was spectacular in the morning light. From the fiftieth story, the boats and their little white wakes looked like toys. Manhattan itself resembled a chessboard of eager buildings, pushed up like castles, knights, and pawns.

Lionel went right to the edge, tapping on the inch of glass. He wondered what it would be like to climb this skyscraper. He smiled. He was probably one of the few visitors who actually had hung off of granite walls far higher than the polished slabs decorating this tower. How many of these skyscrapers would fit in Yosemite Valley? Then he shuddered at the prospect.

He looked back at Maxine. Her tailored cream silk suit jumped off her dark silhouette. She had her game face on. Nothing was going to distract that woman.

The assistant led them through the lounge area. The décor was lavish with buttery-soft, leather-wrapped chairs and sofas, and original art right off the walls of museums. A full bar and acres of crystal stood ready to serve cocktails to legions of executives. Persian rugs, hand knotted and richly dyed over one hundred years ago, floated on a Brazilian hardwood floor. *It's all about a quality impression*, Lionel thought.

They finally reached his office. Garr Gartick, the CEO of the one-hundred-billion-dollar Merry Cola conglomerate, had his feet up on his massive dark desk. He twirled a glass in his hand. Five large wall screens were lit up with a variety of figures and data, but the one on the left, tuned into Fox News, had his full attention.

He looked over at his assistant. "Thank you, honey. Could you get our guests a Merry Cola, please?"

Garr stood up. "Know what the news is reporting right now?" He proceeded without an answer. "Congressional hearings on energy drinks. You'd think it was napalm in a can. Somebody died, so it must be big business that killed them." He shook his head then squeezed the remote. The screen went dark.

"Welcome to my world, Lionel and Maxine." Garr produced a smile and his thick brown mustache rose. Wavy brown hair, dark eyes, and a square jaw dominated his face. He strode over with easy movements and they shook hands firmly. Lionel knew he was fifty-nine years old, but Garr appeared younger.

Garr led Lionel and Maxine across more hardwood and Persian rugs to his sitting area. He motioned to a leather sofa. He sat opposite, in a wingback chair that rose a foot higher. It gave Garr a good view of all the leg Maxine had showing beneath her suit's pencil skirt. They engaged in small talk until their sodas arrived, then Garr's assistant left them.

"Lionel, why do you suppose I agreed to your meeting request, and had you two fly all this way across the country?"

"Hopefully because you want to add to your considerable success," Lionel responded. "Energy drinks represent the hottest sector in beverages."

"My analysts tell me that at least once a week."

"Plus, energy drinks are stealing some of your soda market share. Especially with the youth market, which is your future," added Maxine.

"Ditto. Look, let's skip the market analysis. I've heard it all."

This wasn't the start he'd expected, Lionel thought.

"If you are aware of the potential upside of energy drinks, then there must be a cost or liability holding you back," said Maxine.

He pointed a finger at Maxine, shaking his hand. "The fact is—energy drinks scare me."

He motioned out the window. "I already have the damn local governments trying to regulate my sodas for size and sugar content." Then he waved to the TV screen. "And now the federal government is going after energy drinks too. How do you fix that problem?"

Maxine turned toward Lionel. "May I take this?"

"Of course, Maxine." Perfect, she didn't sound pushy. Nice job. *He hoped this worked.*

Maxine sat forward. Garr's eyes followed her rising hemline.

"What you want, Garr . . ." She paused for effect.

"What you want is your stock price to go up. That is where you, Garr Gartick, make your money." Her hand unfolded and pointed toward him and their eyes locked.

"And how will *you* do that for *me*, Maxine?" He pointed a finger back at her.

Maxine stood up, legs and all. Her heels clicked as she walked in front of Garr over to a leather club chair and stood behind it. She leaned toward him, her hands resting on the back.

Lionel saw Garr following her every move.

"In its essence, Double Vision is this—the energy drink with a conscience. If Merry Cola is associated with that concept, your stock price will rise."

"The energy drink with a conscience." His eyes squinted. "Explain that."

She glanced back to the sofa. Lionel took the cue. "First, our company contributes to social good with the one-for-one meal donation. We lead in that category. Secondly, we offer caffeine-free energy drink options, suggested for those under eighteen. So we proactively address the over-caffeinated youth issue."

"That's good." Garr nodded toward the TV screen. "I'm not sure that is enough to stand up to a Senate inquiry, however."

Maxine responded. "A lot of politicians use the media to create a positive perception with their constituents, as you well know. Lionel, as a young entrepreneur in his twenties, has already demonstrated leadership in juice products. I'm part of that now too. We're building the entire brand around our young team, our social commitment, and us. That can be leveraged for positive perception."

Maxine walked around the chair and stood in front of Garr. "You need an energy brand that can keep the government off your back and your stock headed up. We are that brand."

Garr gave her his full attention. "Tell me more."

Maxine took several steps toward the window as though taking in the view, then pivoted sharply, pencil skirt flashing. "Above and beyond all the youthful enthusiasm, event marketing, and social media buzz that Double Vision will create, you'll have two Co-CEOs who can take the front-line heat, the media interviews, and frankly the Senate inquiries."

Lionel watched Garr appraising Maxine. The snug tailoring, the long legs, the face that was so easy to watch as she made powerful arguments.

"Not because we have your experience. Because we *don't* have your experience. We bring Lionel's passion for adventure sports and our go-hard entrepreneurship. And let's be candid—I'd walk into that Senate hearing and the cameras would be showing a youthful African-American social entrepreneur. Do you really think any Senator wants to be seen back home by his voters berating me? Especially compared to the giant beverage company executives? I don't think so."

Lionel tingled. Maxine was hitting their talking points with vivid visuals. Garr looked like he was getting it.

Maxine turned toward Lionel and he jumped in. "Garr, I think you invited us here because you already figured this out. You want the energy drink market, but also need a heat shield."

Garr nodded. "You two are on track."

"You strike me as the same type of decision-maker as Jacob Havermyer," Maxine continued. "Jacob made up his mind to support us in one meeting. And candidly, you know this market cold. Plus, Lionel already gave you our financials. Your decision is really about the two people standing in front of you now."

"How long was that meeting with Jacob, before he invested?" Garr asked.

Lionel glanced at Maxine. "About an hour, right?"

"One hour. Twenty-four hours later, we had thirty million dollars."

Garr looked at his watch. Then he stood up.

Lionel's heart stopped. *Was he dismissing us already?*

"I guess I beat Jacob. I only needed ten minutes. I'll have my legal staff contact your lawyers about a distribution agreement."

Maxine broke into a smile.

He committed! But wait, thought Lionel. "An exclusive contract, correct? You wouldn't distribute any other energy drinks?" Lionel said it with a smile, but watched Garr carefully.

Garr cocked his head, chuckling. "If this all pans out with the lawyers, yes."

Lionel rose. "Excellent. I'm sure we can work it out." He strode forward and gave Garr's hand a solid shake.

"I'm impressed," said Garr, "with the two of you."

Then Garr turned to Maxine. As she approached, Lionel moved to the side of the coffee table, bumping a pile of folders. Garr wrapped both his hands around Maxine's outstretched hand. "There are no guarantees, but I hope we can put this together." He seemed to relish looking closely into her eyes and face, as his nostrils flared above his mustache. He slowly pumped her hand. "I like what I see."

Lionel glanced down at the coffee table. Under the dislodged folder a document's title appeared. It read, "Merry Cola and BodyHamr Distribution Contract."

17

FRIDAY, NOVEMBER 29ᵀᴴ

Lionel awoke to a fresh blanket of white outside. *Powder day!* Too good to miss, especially now that he was finally back in Telluride with Reddi. He decided to play hooky and work late that night. Within minutes he was skiing down the snow-covered back streets. He weaved among colorfully bundled kids on sleds and cross country skiers in bright snug fabrics. It was the day after Thanksgiving but everyone was smiling like it was Christmas morning. The parade of skiers thickened on Oak Street, near the chair lift that led up the mountain. He spotted Reddi standing a head taller than the group surrounding her, and he surged toward them.

Three teenaged girls were commenting on her pearl white helmet with red and gold Double Vision decals. Lionel recognized their local ski team jackets. Then the teens began giggling, "All those celebrities!" One girl, with big black curls and a pink headband, shrieked, "Reddi, we saw you on YouTube, competing at Copper Mountain and Aspen!"

Another teenager gushed, "And you're sponsored by an energy drink—do they like buy everything for you now? Are you going to the X Games? It's so great!"

"Ah, yeah, thanks. No, I'm still me, and I'll take it one event at a time. I have so much to learn about the tour."

"Aren't you working out with the slopestyle coach, Bronco, on all kinds of new air? Right? That's what I heard. I'm not trying to be nosey," said the third.

Lionel started to get impatient. "Hey Reddi, we going up?"

She smiled as she saw him. "Lionel, hey hey, come on over, meet everyone."

Reddi introduced Lionel to the group around her, described Double Vision, and the girls checked out Lionel. Someone took a picture. Then Lionel and Reddi slid over to the chair lift. As they rode up the mountain, the girl in the pink headband called after them, "I'm putting your picture on Instagram!"

***

"I'm so glad winter is here. We finally get to ski together."

"No kidding. It's great to have you around. After you signed me up I thought I'd see you all the time, but you travel so much now." Lionel sensed her disappointment. But he also felt conflicted. She was so attractive and he was sorely tempted to get much closer. But they were sponsoring her. And she was barely twenty-one.

"There is this little company we are trying to grow, and we have to get the word out, convince distributors, retailers, get press, create marketing campaigns . . . ."

"I get it," she interrupted. "But at least some time together?"

"All day, all day, I am completely yours." Just then Lionel's cell phone rang.

"If you answer that, I will throw it into a snow bank deep in the friggin' trees."

"Of course, I was just turning it off." He took off his glove and silenced his phone, after sneaking a peek at the caller ID.

"Thanks for making the time for me, but I have to train with Bronco in an hour, actually. I'm working on a whole bunch of inverted moves with an air bag he has set up."

"Oh, look who is the busy one now."

"Okay, okay. We're about to get off the lift, so what would you like to ski?"

"How about down Mammoth to warm up? Then cut through the trees to the Spiral Stairs and then rock the lower Plunge?"

They flew out of the chair and headed down Mammoth Run. Lionel felt a sudden competitive drive take over. He'd never been out-skied by a girl. He went his fastest on the top part of the run, and then pulled up. Reddi was right behind him.

"Nice turns, Boss," she said with a bright smile.

His heart was pounding and his breathing harder than he thought it would be. "Fun! Great to be out here with you."

"Over to the Stairs?" she asked. They immediately pushed off, went around the bend and cut through the woods. Reddi looked like an Indian gliding through her private forest. Branches sprung up in Lionel's face and he pushed through them aggressively. They popped out of the woods and headed down to the Spiral Stairs. This was one of the steepest bump runs on the mountain, he remembered.

They hit the top of the run in parallel, and Lionel took the line by the trees on the left. He did three nice turns and glanced to his right toward Reddi. She flew over four bumps, landed on the backside of one, then moved her feet so fast he could only see her steady upper body leaving him behind. Suddenly she was up in the air again, doing a twister spread eagle before landing in the bumps full speed, straight down the fall line, feet a blur as they touched edges from tip to tail. He had never seen anything like it. Then she waited at the bottom of the run.

After what seemed an eternity to him as he turned through all the bumps, he finally arrived next to her. He felt like a stiff wooden puppet in comparison. But he was crazy excited. For her.

"*That*, that was so rad! I have never, ever, seen anything like that before. You don't ski. You fly, dance, and fly again. Where did you learn that?" He was leaning over on his poles, breathing hard, bubbling with enthusiasm.

"Around here."

"Is that a local style? The ski instructors I've seen here don't ski like you."

"Remember that guy Kodiak I used to chase growing up? He was the coolest on the mountain. He makes his own clothes, sewn with a treadle sewing machine, all custom. An off-the-grid type. Anyway, he skis bumps like that."

"Man, I used to think Lionel was a pretty different name. But your coach is Bronco and your childhood mentor is Kodiak? I am totally outclassed on this mountain."

She laughed. They started skiing again, but toned it down. They'd take short bursts, then stop and talk. Lionel had nothing to prove anymore. That was already established. He knew he was not in her league.

They skied for an hour, until Reddi had to head down to the lower mountain where her coach Bronco had set up the air bag next to a half pipe.

Lionel hung back, watching from a distance through some aspen trees. She went through jump after jump, continuously trying new things. Many times she came down wrong. She took some hard tumbles that looked painful and dangerous. Bronco tried to get her to slow down, take more breaks, but her determination was fierce.

Lionel went off to ski with some members of the town council, working them for special concessions for the bottling plant. He returned several hours later. He was whipped, between the altitude and the steep terrain. Reddi was still working it, pushing to land new inverted tricks perfectly. Some of her landings on the bag were complete blow-ups, and he could hear the impact with the bag from afar. That must hurt, he thought. He suddenly realized she lived in a different world. The risks and the challenges of the aerials demanded much more than he realized. And he felt something he had never felt before. He was very afraid for her.

***

"There's a band at Pandora's Box Saloon on Main Street, tonight. The snow is epic, winter is in full swing, and there'll be a lively crowd. Are you coming?" Reddi asked.

Lionel had promised he would, but only after he finished a few hours of work.

Reddi looked at her watch. It was ten p.m., hours after he had promised to show up. Wherever he was, he could probably hear the music blasting away. The band was vibrating the back room, and all around her was deafening chaos. Everyone was loose, waitresses with full trays of shots balancing between the hats and elbows, someone doing upside-down margaritas on the bar, and two girls dancing on a table in their bras. Couples were grinding and dancing with passion, zipless sex in full swing. Reddi returned to the dance floor.

Connie and Tina were Reddi's childhood friends, recent graduates from the dance program at Boulder. As the three girls danced together, they laughed as Reddi lifted up Connie and dipped her upside down. They pirouetted and swung each other around with abandon. Eventually the DJ wrapped the set. "Beautiful movement out there people, especially the ladies. Let's chill for five."

Reddi pulled off her black cowboy hat and wiped her brow, eying the long line to the bathroom. *Ah, screw it.* She walked to a dark corner and turned her back, unbuttoning her handmade leather vest. Then she peeled off her turtleneck and sports bra and tossed them in a heap by the big speakers. Connie and Tina huddled around her laughing as she buttoned her vest back up. It rode above her low-ride jeans, her taut midriff showing. She shook her bare shoulders and arms, feeling refreshed from the heat. "Thanks for the cover, girls, I was sweltering from the dancing. It's steaming in here."

"We always have your back, girl. Naked or not," Connie said, grabbing her hand.

"Don't worry, I'm done stripping for the night." As they all giggled, Reddi offered to get another round.

"This round has to be on us, you got the last one," insisted Connie. She and Tina wiggled through the crowd after a waitress.

Then Reddi saw him. Gonzo, the sponsored skier from BodyHamr energy drinks. He swaggered toward her. Midheight, muscular, with a platinum dyed Mohawk, he eyed her with his best sultry look. Two close-cropped blond guys trailed, reminding Reddi of the Hitler Youth. All three sported BodyHamr armbands in platinum and neon orange.

"You look hot Reddi, in more ways than one."

His groupies laughed.

"I was. But now that you've arrived, I'm feeling a chill."

He leered at her, openly drinking in her bare skin. His pale green eyes followed the line of her shoulders, and then slowly crawled down the front of her vest. He lingered over her belly button, tracing the smooth skin to her jeans, as though undressing her.

He stared at her crotch. "You're the total package, girl." He looked back to her eyes. "You're rocking the ski scene. You should hang with us on the BodyHamr team—we're kicking ass. Screw Double Vision. We're the next Monster, baby."

This guy is such a prick. Hassling her for weeks, trying to get into her head and pants. Wearing his BodyHamr custom clothes everywhere, bragging about his skiing and swanky lifestyle. She turned away and picked her hat off a nearby table. She pushed it on and stepped closer, standing over him.

"I have no interest in you or the way you all brag about yourselves." She squinted at his posse. "I think you are all overrated and obnoxious. So back off."

Gonzo stared at her. "Just making an offer to help you flash some cash. And afford some decent clothes. Looks like you need them."

His little Nazis laughed on cue.

"Fuck you, Gonzo. I'm giving you three seconds before . . . ."

Connie and Tina suddenly arrived with three overflowing cocktails and weaved in between Reddi and Gonzo. Connie lifted a dripping stemmed glass to Reddi.

"Cocktail time, Reddi."

Gonzo's eyes narrowed. "You and your big mouth are gonna get tamed one day. Big time, bitch." Gonzo turned and his posse followed him through the crowd.

"Whew! What was that all about?" asked Connie.

"Just those BodyHamr vultures," she said, taking the drink. "Cheers, girls," and she chugged it.

The music began again.

***

Lionel walked down Main Street and pushed through the doors of the saloon. He scanned the crowd, then headed over to the bar at the opposite end from a group doing shots. As his beer arrived, he felt a hand on his shoulder.

He turned to find Reddi with a devilish smile. Her lake blue eyes were lively and her black cowboy hat was tipped back cockily.

Man she looks sexy tonight. "Hey hey, Reddi."

She gave him a big kiss on the lips as she wrapped her arms around him. He tried not to spill his beer.

"Welcome, partner," she said, after finally pulling back.

"Nice to see you too." He looked at the tight vest. Her bare shoulders and sculpted arms glistened from dancing. In the hat and cowboy boots she was taller than him.

She saw him checking her out. "It's hot in here," she said by way of explanation. "I was wearing a shirt, but that got all sweaty. So I stripped."

Lionel laughed. *She is definitely feeling no pain.*

"But look," she explained, with her thumb hooked under the vest by her breast, "high armholes and front buttons, so my tits aren't hanging out."

"Maybe whoever made the vest can fix that?"

She laughed and punched him in the arm. "Kodiak made it. Probably guessed I'd do something stupid like wear it naked." And she laughed again, and started dancing in place.

"Glad you are here. That asshole from BodyHamr—who thinks he is a hotshot freestyler—keeps hitting on me. I'm going to rearrange his front end one day."

"He's desperate, like their company. Total losers."

The DJ started a new song. "Come on, let's dance," urged Reddi, more an order than a question. He left his beer on the bar. Four fast dances later as they transitioned to a slower and quieter number, his ears were ringing, back sweating.

"If I had a vest I'd take my shirt off, too" he told her. The crowded dance floor was radiating heat and sexual energy, and as the inhibitions dropped, so did the clothes.

Reddi held onto him heavily, and they moved together in a tight slow grind. He got hard under his jeans, which only made her push her pelvis tighter against him. The long slow song ended.

"Take me home," she said, "I'm ready."

He managed to find her coat but not her shirt. They buttoned up and walked holding hands across the snow banks and slick streets.

They went inside her crib and she checked on Wolfie in the kitchen. Wolfie sniffed Lionel and curled up. Reddi dropped her butt on her bed heavily. She managed to pull off her boots and wiggle out of her jeans, but her underwear and vest were still on. She looked at Lionel, with her eyes nearly closed. "Take off your boots at least," she said. He kicked them off.

She stood up and they hugged, and started slow dancing, the music still echoing in their heads. He felt a chill. He grabbed the top blanket and pulled it over them as they circled, on the verge. Her head rested on his shoulder and her hat fell off. She was fading fast.

They fell into bed in each other's arms. Reddi passed out.

***

Lionel awoke feeling a warm tongue on his neck.

"Mmm."

Her face moved closer, made it wet behind his ear, and eagerly moved across his cheek.

He opened his mouth in anticipation. Her tongue was rough, and really, really long. He reached for her face and felt a handful of short soft hair. Everywhere.

What!? Lionel sat up and opened his eyes. He was looking directly into Wolfie's blue eyes.

"Jesus, Wolfie!" He sputtered, spitting toward the floor. He rolled out of bed and wiped out his mouth on the blanket.

Wolfie sniffed him, pushing her wet nose against his underwear, turning her head with a quizzical look. She pushed again.

"Wolfie, you're practically sexing me."

Lionel looked for refuge. He heard the shower running and saw the empty bed.

He rubbed her behind the ears. "Good girl, stay." He eased toward the bathroom. Paws clicked on the wood floor. He quickly closed the door behind him.

Inside, clouds of steam warmed the bathroom, and through the swirling mist the high walls and ceiling dripped with condensation. His feet sank into a soft rug. Directly in front of him a white shower curtain was being pounding by water, encircled by a long porcelain tub.

He turned on the sink faucet and scooped fresh water into his mouth, gargling and spitting.

His sounds caused Reddi to open the shower curtain and peer out.

"You get tongued by Wolfie?"

"Practically raped."

"Sorry, forgot to warn you. She can be very insistent."

Lionel turned toward Reddi. His underwear was pointing straight out.

"I see she got you pretty hot and bothered," Reddi giggled.

"Oh, sorry, reflex." He considered grabbing a towel.

"I like that you didn't take advantage of me last night. I woke up with my underclothes on."

"When it's time it should be your choice, right?" he said, meeting her eyes. "And besides, I'd want your full heat." He arched his eyebrows and smiled.

"The water feels good. Want to come in?" He could see through the narrow opening of the curtain. She nonchalantly tipped her head back, long wet hair falling to the small of her back. She reached back and squeezed her red rope. Water dripped onto the rounded crescent of her pink butt. Drip, pink. Drip, pink.

"As long as I don't have to bring Wolfie."

"No, just you." She pushed open the curtain with a flourish, the shower splashing off her body. Her muscular figure glistened, the shoulders and arms dotted with freckles. Her upturned breasts were pert, the nipples red and firm. Water streamed down the taut torso to her small waist, then flowed into a red triangle of pubic hair.

Lionel's groin literally jumped. He started bobbing like a hunting dog in point. Reddi grinned as she watched him thread off his underwear and step to the shower. She pulled the curtain closed behind them.

18

TUESDAY DECEMBER 10TH — WEDNESDAY, DECEMBER 11TH

Lionel pulled the sliding door and walked into the darkness of the deck overlooking the City. Christmas music drifted over from the nearby department store. He leaned on the railing, looking at the bright holiday lights framing the Embarcadero Center, the thin and wide skyscrapers like fanciful chocolate bars on edge. Trees and stars sparkled from building rooftops.

December had disappeared in work. He hadn't even begun to think about shopping or vacation. It would be cool to buy something exciting for Reddi. Something she didn't expect. She missed her dad and sister Hannah now that they had moved to California. Christmas would be complicated. He sighed. He wondered if that Trig character was hanging around her. Or was he still off doing that Navy SEAL stuff? He stared at the spectacle of holiday lights, thinking. The fresh air reminded him he hadn't been outside today since six a.m. Reflections twinkled off puddles on the street. Maybe it's snowing in the mountains. Then a gust of wind blew. He shivered, retreating through the door and into the DV kitchen. Maxine was foraging for dinner under the bright florescent lights. She looked weary.

"I can't believe Christmas is coming so soon," he said, sliding the door behind him.

"I thought it already came. The signed contract from Merry Cola." She pulled two DV Javas from the fridge, and handed one to Lionel. "Merry Christmas from Merry Cola."

"Cheers." They clinked bottles. "It is great news, but what an incredible time sink. God, I'm glad we got it done before meeting the board tomorrow." Lionel's chest tightened, thinking of all he wanted to get done tonight. And it was already eight p.m.

"That contract was worth the late nights. I worry more about all the valuable time invested with our board," Maxine replied, shaking her head. "We really don't need this group's approval, Lionel." She took a sip of her drink, and then pulled a yogurt out of the refrigerator.

"True, their ownership percentage is so small their votes aren't a requirement. But, they work for big name brands and that brings credibility."

"For our audience?"

"At the very least, we need their influence with the media and industry leaders. Plus their industry knowledge and feedback."

"But what if this new contract backfires somehow? What if that *was* a signed agreement with BodyHamr on Garr's coffee table, and not a failed proposal?" She took a couple bites of yogurt. Lionel dropped a banana and strawberries into a blender.

"I told you, when I spoke to Garr directly, he absolutely confirmed our exclusivity clause. It's in our contract. He can't have a deal going with BodyHamr. Whatever I saw must have been a draft that never happened. I couldn't ask him about it, and admit I was spying on his papers during our visit in his office."

"Fine, fine, fine. But something has me nervous. Let's try to keep this board meeting tomorrow short and sweet, okay?"

"I agree. It should be a walk in the park. I don't see any problems." He thought about the part of his presentation where he'd show the promotional campaigns featuring Reddi. Kate's marketing had gone over the top with her. It should be huge.

"It's the holidays. Get with the mood, Maxine." Lionel suddenly thought of Christmas trees, snow in the mountains, seeing Reddi and skiing with her. And then her warm down-covered bed afterward. Exploring, sex, out of breath . . . the memories were so real.

Maxine walked out without a word. Lionel shoved the blend button.

***

The following morning Lionel was at the conference table updating their board of directors. They were a collection of successful business executives and insightful nonprofit leaders, with long resumes and lots of gray hair.

"The team pulled off a miracle in getting the new bottling plant operational in Telluride. They were able to lease a former plant, get permitting, and build out the factory in two months."

"Bravo, well done," chimed in a director. "At one of my former employers, they fought for two years about who would get the credit before starting."

"Thank you," Lionel acknowledged with a laugh. "Hugo, our Juice Genius, really deserves the bulk of the credit. And speaking of deserving credit, allow me to present Kate Zell, our marketing director, to show you our new product masterpieces."

Kate pressed a button and a metallic curtain shimmered open. An energetic beat vibrated out of black speakers on slender chrome stands. Colored lights powered up to a high glow. A slide show started on a fifty-five-inch screen mounted directly behind the pedestal displaying the bottles.

Kate began with a flourish, showing the newest versions of the five products. The music, videos, graphics, and burnished aluminum bottles all shined. Lionel watched the reactions carefully, but he knew behind the scenes Kate had prepped nearly all of them privately, so there were no surprises. She spent twenty minutes reviewing the details.

She finished by reinforcing the overall messaging and passing around samples. Numerous questions were posed. In the end they gave Kate a round of applause. The advance buy-in had worked.

Lionel transitioned to promotion. "First, some of you know from our social media exposure and website, our first Double Vision athlete, Reddi Christiansen, won the women's slopestyle bronze medal in Colorado. She blew away the judges with her acrobatic spins, flips and big air."

"Sounds like something I'd like to watch, but not try," commented a director, to laughter.

"You're right, it's a great spectator sport. And we have exclusive sponsorship rights with Reddi. Credit Kate's team with pushing the exposure for DV, and you can see it on YouTube, Facebook, our website, and more. Here is a picture of Reddi on the victory stand and some stills from the competition we have on Instagram and Flickr. Additionally, taken in a studio in Telluride, here are other shots of Reddi with the new DV products and branding. Just a sample."

Reddi's radiance, emerging in young-adult life, was beautifully captured in the slide show. There were action ski shots in DV logo wear. Casual scenes by a hot tub. Playing around with Wolfie in the snow on a sunny day in a halter top and Uggs. And the DV logo everywhere. Kate had pulled together Hollywood star-level promotion that clearly pushed Reddi's healthy sex appeal.

"Lionel, you have chosen wisely. It is clear she has that star quality of wholesomeness together with an edge of sexiness," observed Jackie Snow, the director with the deepest marketing experience. There was quite a bit of murmuring and excitement about the photos. "Stunning, a great image, she should be the permanent face of Double Vision."

Maxine then stepped to the front. "Thank you, directors. We're pleased with her, but remember, everyone, these athletes are very unpredictable. We hope they represent us well, we hope they win, but they are extreme, by definition. We continue to recruit many others as well, so we can have a balanced portfolio of them, for broad appeal. I'd like to move on . . . ."

"Excuse me, Maxine, please." It was another director, Dirk Manafee, formerly with The Gap. He stood to be heard. "I appreciate what you are saying, but there is quite a bit of appeal right there." There were several chuckles from the fellow directors.

"No, I'm serious, and I'm not being a dirty old man. I have a daughter about her age, who skis quite well. Yet she tells me this young woman Reddi is unbelievable, in a class of her own. And Lionel said we have exclusive sponsorship. I'm just saying this is a special opportunity for DV. If she goes to the X Games or the Olympics, so does DV without all the expense of traditional advertising."

Maxine nodded briefly. "Dirk, we'd all welcome that but I'm trying to manage expectations. This is a person in a very competitive and frankly dangerous sport, and only twenty-one years old. She's one of many in our active portfolio of athletes we are sponsoring and branding."

"I defer to your judgment, of course. I want to reinforce that she represents a potentially huge opportunity, and that all athletes and celebrities should not be considered the same in drawing power. Typically a few are exponentially better, drawing considerably more exposure than hundreds of others. And that striking redhead with those cute freckles may be one of the exceptional ones." Dirk took his seat.

"Maxine, if I may?" Lionel saw Maxine's annoyed look. "Dirk, we'd love it if Reddi goes viral. Kate and the team are all over that from the TV and social media front. In fact it'd be great if a number of our athletes blew up." Dirk and the other directors nodded in agreement.

"Let's move to our final topics please. You all have our report on our nutritional side, the present source of most of our revenue. We're a little below plan in juice sales, due to the distractions of the energy launch. Meanwhile energy has only been shipping for a few weeks so no revenue to speak of yet. But we are very optimistic."

Lionel closed his laptop and looked around the room. He smiled, hoping his excitement showed. "We've saved the best for last. It is very special news. We are pleased to announce we have signed an exclusive distribution agreement with the Merry Cola Company. This will provide access into an enormous number of convenience stores, and much more. The exhausting negotiations, which took seven weeks, were completed just hours ago."

"Merry Cola!"

"Why would we choose them?"

"I wasn't consulted. Was anyone?"

The directors became agitated, talking among themselves heatedly.

Then Blaine Latrell, from Axlewright Capital, stood up.

"Lionel, while on the face of it this is good news, it's so sudden. I anticipated this, but evidently none of the other directors were in the loop. They were shut out."

Another director jumped to her feet, holding her iPad like a club in the air. "My problem, and I know others share my concern, is we are immediately sucked into the Big Four, large corporate entities that frankly don't hold the same social values that I believe we have at DV. We're the good guys."

"I beg to differ. We aren't losing our social entrepreneurial spirit," Maxine said defensively. "This distribution allows us far more leverage."

Another director yelled out. "But at what cost to brand value? Now we are going to be thought of as a subsidiary or pawn of Merry Cola."

A former Coke executive pounded the table with thinly disguised frustration. "I, for one, think much more highly of the Coke brand than Merry Cola, and many others in the industry agree with me."

It went from bad to worse. Blaine spoke up with another idea. "I would have preferred that DV raised more money and built its own distribution network, trucks and all, and not given Merry Cola a piece of the pie."

Lionel tried to bring order. "Can we have one meeting here? People, let's talk this through together." He was completely ignored.

Maxine stood up. "Directors, please, how can you not see the inescapable logic here? Several competitors gain a significant sales advantage over us by using large distributors."

The room erupted, people yelling at Maxine, Lionel, and each other.

A flash mob of controversy had ignited.

Suddenly, above the din a piercing high-pitched whistle sounded, circling the room. It warbled and rang in waves. Heads swiveled, eyes and ears strained to identify the source.

"What is that?"

"Oh no, do we have to evacuate?" The fighting quieted.

Lionel pointed at the high-tech triangular speakerphone in the middle of the conference table. "There."

"People, people, this is Jacob Havermyer. May I have the floor for a moment please?"

The group stared at the black triangle.

Lionel shouted, "Please go ahead, Jacob."

"Thank you, Lionel. Excellent points one and all. I personally apologize for demanding complete secrecy while these delicate negotiations were carried out. Please think of this new announcement in the context of advice from the wise Chinese philosopher Sun Tzu. 'If you know both yourself and your enemies, you can win numerous battles without jeopardy.' We will learn a lot in this new relationship, and then choose our ultimate path."

A muffled background voice was heard. Then Jacob returned with his fast-paced delivery, and Lionel noticed how his tone resonated with both empathy and urgency. The faces of the directors around the table beheld the triangle as though an oracle.

"Right now I am standing on a tarmac next to a jet destined for the Sudan on a time-critical humanitarian mission. The pilot tells me I must board immediately or we will lose our departure window. So with that, and my sincere apologies for being in such haste, I personally move to support this announcement by Lionel with a vote of confidence. Can I ask my fellow directors to support this initially, subject to review down the road?"

Lionel held his breath.

Blaine immediately spoke up. "Aye, Jacob. Blaine Latrell of Axlewright here, voting with you." One by one the majority of the other directors then fell into line.

Lionel exhaled, and it felt like the pressure blew out of the room. He dug down deep to close the meeting with a final burst of enthusiasm. Kate provided the directors with clever bags filled with drink samples and promotions, and ushered them from the offices.

***

Maxine closed the door to Lionel's office and watched him sink into a beanbag chair, spent.

"Four more months? I'm not sure I'll make it."

"Those idiots. I warned you last night."

Lionel stared at the ceiling. "I think we all want the same thing. A diverse group has a hard time agreeing."

"You'd think we were fighting over the Middle East."

He grabbed some squeeze balls and started juggling them. "Admittedly, you warned me, and I underestimated our board's reaction. But, you didn't have that personal charm today, Maxine, like you turned on for Garr of Merry Cola. Just an observation, not trying to piss you off."

"Any more than I already am, you mean?"

"Yeah."

"Look, Lionel. Signing with Merry was brilliant. I really wanted that. But I'm not comfortable schmoozing, playing up the sex appeal like you're pimping out of Reddi."

He caught the balls and stared at her. "Hey, come on."

"It's not who I am. I'm not into branding my cute black ass for everyone. Or wasting my time placating over-the-hill directors. That shouldn't be necessary. What I think and plan and execute—that is who I am. And it should be enough."

"I'm not trying to sell you out," Lionel replied. "I want all that brilliance to be appreciated. It's hard to get people to change their thinking. It's hard to get them to agree with you. It takes emotion, not just logic."

"There are leaders and there are followers. This board needs to realize that."

"It's a team effort. I believe we can convince this diverse group, and the market, that you can be generous and do good while enjoying consumption." Lionel stared out the window running his fingers through his hair. "But I definitely don't want to become a corporate clone selling caffeine and sugar water."

Maxine put her hands on her hips and stared at him. He felt her laser eyes. "You are such an idealist, Lionel. We need awareness, product execution, and broad distribution. Our revenue growth is the best way for our social cause to benefit."

Lionel sighed. "I wish the board understood that. And, I wish I believed in our energy products more."

"With the board's help or not, and whether our product is a magic elixir or not, we need huge revenue in the next four months. To win and do good. Period."

19

THURSDAY, DECEMBER 12TH

Blaine took a deep breath, threw his shoulders back and walked through John Anderson's door.

"Boss, a moment?"

"Sure. I have a call in five, but talk to me. How is Double Vision?" Anderson's feet were on his desk, hands behind his head.

"May I?" Blaine motioned to close the door.

"Okay. But I do only have five minutes. We can schedule something, you know."

"Five is perfect. Thank you." He'd do anything to avoid a long meeting with Anderson, with his biting criticism and crude humiliation. Hell, he couldn't even be bothered to sit up properly.

"John, I've got things moving in the right direction at Double Vision."

"How so?" Anderson asked, still reclined.

"Now this is between us, not to be shared with anyone. Okay?"

Anderson nodded.

"I coached Double Vision on how to approach Merry Cola as a distributor. Then I got them an appointment with Garr Gartick, Merry's CEO. And voilà—now we've got a deal put together."

"*You* know Garr?" Anderson looked surprised. He brought his feet down.

That got his attention, thought Blaine. "We've been at some events together. But I primarily work through his people."

Anderson looked less impressed.

"But it worked. Perfectly."

Anderson shook his head. "What do you mean?"

"At the board meeting yesterday, they announced the distribution agreement and Lionel took all sorts of heat. The DV independent directors, opposed to the Big Four powers, were all ruffled. And the other directors, who have competed with Merry, thought Lionel handled the situation poorly by failing to get buy-in."

"Net it out, would you?" He looked at his watch.

"Unquestionably, Double Vision is going to increase revenue with Merry. But, the meeting today showed Lionel is weak as a true CEO. He doesn't even know how to work a board of directors."

"He is still firmly in control, even if he is unpopular with some board members."

"So far. And he's useful in moving us toward winning the Big. But meanwhile, I'm laying groundwork to get him out of the way to settle your score with Hank Welcher."

Anderson stood up. "Blaine, don't disappoint me. You know the consequences."

***

Alpha read the press release that morning about the Double Vision and Merry Cola distribution deal. Goddamn Double Vision. With that kind of leverage, they could become formidable. Their sales could grow exponentially. He felt his blood pressure rising. Slamming his fists, he spun himself into a frenzy. Damn it, they could win the Big!

He reached for his encrypted phone.

"Fanachi."

"I want you to reprioritize. I want Double Vision to become a nonfactor."

"Hello Alpha. Let me remind you that you said to be discrete. We have a plan to eliminate them, but the time and place has not lined up yet."

"Change it up. Move faster."

"You want accidental. That takes time."

"Aren't you capable of working faster?"

"There are many risks. That costs a lot more."

"Jesus. How much?"

"You work with a lot of Silicon Valley companies, right?"

"How do you know that?"

"It's true, correct?"

"Whether it is or not, it isn't relevant."

"If you want future work done by me, it is."

"Why? I don't understand. You're being cryptic."

"You're the one not answering the question. The reason I asked, is because I am interested in high tech intellectual property. IP. The type gained via high level executive access in Silicon Valley."

"Look, I want to focus on Double Vision and the fee. To speed this up, how about an additional 100K?"

"Thank you, but no. I'm not interested in just a fee."

"Why not?!"

"I told you. IP. Product plans, growth strategies, M & A activity, patent applications, and customer details."

"That's against my best interests. I have relationships with these companies. And besides, I'm not a spy."

"You make money betting on more than one company all the time. That's all I'm asking."

"I didn't realize IP was an interest of yours."

"There is a lot about me you don't know."

Alpha was feeling uneasy. This was not at all what he expected, and he didn't like surprises. And he certainly was not used to his money failing to solve a problem.

"This is not a negotiation I would consider. Not at all."

"Perhaps it's just a matter of time."

"I want to keep it simple. Cash for accidents."

"That is how we started. But going forward, my muscle will cost you IP."

"Why this sudden change? What's wrong with cash?"

"You make your money on the really big opportunities, right? It's maybe one in ten deals that becomes something big like a Facebook or Google or a smaller version of them. The same is true for me selling IP. The right client, especially a government, will pay vastly more for the right company's IP than I can get in years of providing muscle."

"This isn't where I want our relationship to go. I am not comfortable at all in this direction. I said, I'm not a spy—and I don't want to be."

"My people will do the online work—your involvement would be much simpler than you realize. A few emails, a few conversations we monitor, not much really."

The back of Alpha's neck tightened. He clenched his teeth to keep from yelling at Fanachi. The son-of-a-bitch was a doublecrosser. "I'm signing off now. But you'll do what we agreed to originally, right?"

"Of course. I'll honor my commitments. But any changes, any new priority for Double Vision, that's a new deal."

Alpha jammed the End button. He dropped the phone before the urge to smash it against the wall overwhelmed him. Fanachi reminded him of a boa constrictor, smooth and calm, but slowly wrapping around him. Fanachi's words echoed in his head, *perhaps it's just a matter of time.*

20

WEDNESDAY, DECEMBER 18TH

Toast, a start-up with a smartphone app for ordering bar drinks without the bartender lines, was very publicly seeking a new round of venture capital. Their lobby in a remodeled warehouse in San Francisco was jammed. VCs and private equity investors, dressed down casually, had shown up in hoards to help provide money. Attractive salespeople were vying to help spend the imminent cash, representing everything from new office furniture to marketing services. They crowded the reception desk in expensive natural fabric outfits. Others typed or talked animatedly on smartphones as they waited for their appointments. Blaine watched as employees in T-shirts rode by on skateboards and juggled soft toys. They really did think anything was possible, and all new ideas awesome, he thought. The smell of money and success was in the air. This was a scene.

Blaine perched on the edge of a short mushroom-shaped stool, his knees in the air and suit hitched up awkwardly. He felt like a dad at a kindergarten open house.

"Blaine, congratulations, you're here too."

Hank Welcher's shiny bald head appeared through the crowd, his grinning front teeth working up and down. "How the hell are you?"

Blaine forced his enthusiasm. "Hello, Hank." Of all the bad luck, to have to meet with Toast after Welcher, who was having such a stellar year.

"Who are you guys meeting with? And where's your boss, Anderson?"

"John is in the restroom." Blaine paused. "And, we'll be meeting with someone major."

"I just came out of Costello's last meeting of the day. If you're not meeting with him, you're wasting your time. No CEO meeting, no funding."

"It's a top VP. I'm assured he's someone key in the process."

Hank Welcher raised his hands and said, "Okay," with a smug smile of victory.

Then he surprised Blaine.

"A word privately?" He waved a hand toward a less crowded corner. Blaine hesitated, then followed.

Welcher lowered his voice. "Look, I'm not trying to piss in your pocket about anything. We compete, and we accept that, right?"

"Sure." Where was he going with this?

"But the word on the street is Double Vision is make or break for you at Axlewright. This could be your last rodeo if you don't win the Big Disrupter."

Blaine went on the offensive. "Hank, I have plenty of success . . . ."

Hank quickly put a hand up. "No, allow me. Listen for a moment. Please."

Something about the gesture stopped Blaine.

"Thank you." Hank glanced around, and then continued. "You see, personally, I think you should be supported. The word is you were the one behind Merry Cola backing DV. You must have a hell of a relationship with Garr Gartick."

The compliment, especially from Welcher, warmed Blaine. He certainly wasn't getting them from his boss. "Thank you. I can't comment on that, but I do take personal pride in my involvement there. But, that's between you and me—let's allow the Co-CEOs to continue to take the credit."

"Smart strategy. I like that—I'm impressed. I suggest you continue to impress me. It may open a door you'll need one day."

Blaine didn't want to reveal how risky his situation was at Axlewright. *But he'd love a Plan B.* "Hank, all due respect, but this is a bit awkward given we're competing for the Big."

"Today we're competing, tomorrow you never know. Blaine, if things start to go in a direction you aren't comfortable with, be sure to give me a call. That's all."

Right. Spill his guts and play his hand? "Hank, what exactly are you offering?"

"That depends on what you're bringing with you. *Or what you do for me.*" He took Blaine's elbow and squeezed it. "Stay in touch."

Then he saw John Anderson across the lobby returning from the restroom.

"Anderson," Welcher boomed, "how am I supposed to make a living with you guys talking to my prospective clients? How the hell are you?"

I can't believe Welcher bumped into us here, and recruited me under Anderson's nose. Was this a coincidence or not? *And what did he mean by what I do for him?*

***

The listening device was a quarter the size of an iPhone, and stuck underneath the IKEA desk in her bedroom. Voice-activated to conserve its small battery, it transmitted to a larger recording device Igor had hidden in the laundry room in the basement of Dasha's building. Tonight, the recording device was on the floor of his car, between his legs, the speaker turned up. He had parked his Audi at the end of her block, and sat listening alone. Igor was picturing the conversation as he leaned back in his front seat. Dasha was at her desk using Skype.

"Hello Dasha. What's happening in San Francisco, California, U.S.A.?" Igor noticed the family resemblance in the girl's tone.

"Hello Lilia. Your American accent is getting better every day."

"Oh, now you have five pierced diamond earrings, Dasha. Present from a boyfriend?"

"I don't have time for men. I'm busy with work."

"Me too. I haven't met a real man yet, just silly boys."

"Lilia, you are seventeen. Don't rush things. Be a little patient, okay?"

"Don't worry, I am very careful. Oh, and I have big news."

"Yes?" *Dasha sounds worried,* thought Igor.

"I have been accepted at the University of Kiev. I am going to study computer science, like you!" Igor heard the younger sister clap her hands excitedly.

"Wow, congratulations," Dasha said, sounding relieved. Then her voice rose higher with enthusiasm, "I'm sure you'll do even better than me."

"Better than you? Well, only if I get to go to America like you. Silicon Valley, Hollywood, Las Vegas, you know, all that stuff."

"More like programming all the time, late nights and early mornings, a lot of strange customs, and having to understand everything in English. Plus, I miss you all."

"I miss you too. But if I came to U.S., I'd be near you."

"Yes. But first your education. So, how is the rest of the family?"

"Everything is same. Mom and Dad worry too much and our little sister is driving me crazy."

"Nothing strange going on? No one bothering you?"

"No, of course not. Why?"

"Just checking. Remember to walk in groups and don't go out at night in bad neighborhoods."

"Come on, don't sound like Mom."

"Okay, sorry. I am really happy for your school success. But, I have work soon, let me talk with Mom, okay?"

"I love you."

"I love you, too."

Igor heard the mother come on the call, as they switched to Russian.

"So you have a boyfriend?"

"No, I'm too busy."

"Not anyone?"

There was a pause. "There is this one handsome guy."

"Really?"

Igor sat up. He turned up the volume.

"What is he like?"

"Blond hair. Blue eyes. He's very smart."

Igor's hand went to his chest. She was attracted to him. He had been making a point to time his arrivals on his Ducati so they could talk briefly as she got off her scooter. She has been playing it cool. He thought of her tight jeans straddling his engine, arms wrapped around him. He needed to ask her out.

"What does he do?"

"He is a programmer."

She remembered. She was interested in him. His leg jiggled.

"Does he work at your company?"

"No."

"Then where?"

"Google. He lives here in the city. His name is Andriy Bubka."

Igor felt his face flush hot. He glanced out the window, as if checking to see if anyone witnessed his humiliation.

"Mom, I've got to go. I'm sorry. I'm so busy with work."

"We love you."

"Yes, I love you too. Goodbye."

She didn't even mention him. It was all about someone else. She hadn't given him any thought.

Moments later, Igor saw a new BMW screech around the corner. It expertly wedged itself into a parking place. The door swung open and a young man emerged carrying flowers and strode up the stairs with a sense of purpose. He had blond hair.

It was self-inflicted torture as Igor listened to Dasha greet him in her apartment.

"It's so good to see you," she said, and then they engaged in small talk. As their Russian chatter slowed, he turned up the volume. Then he heard soft moans. Shades were rolled down. He heard zippers sliding. He imagined her wiggling and pulling down her jeans. It meant only one thing—she wanted to open up her legs for him. Despite his jealously Igor became hard. Their passion became louder. He heard furniture scraping; something fell over, maybe a lamp. The guy was grunting and exhaling like a wild pig, in between slurping sounds. "Deeper, deeper," he yelled. Then he bellowed like a fat beast, like he was being gored.

It was quiet. Then she started moaning. For minutes he listened as she continued, her voice rising and falling. "Yes, yes, there. More. Don't stop." On and on. Her breathing was thick, and she exhaled in low vibrating moans. Then he heard her voice jump an octave. He imagined her naked and overwhelmed with sensitivity. Her voice cascaded like a harp, as though little tickles that built up deep inside now rushed out of her mouth.

It went silent. A noisy truck drove by and he leaned his head closer to the speaker. Then she commanded, "Let me on top." The bed started squeaking in rhythm. Something thumped, like the headboard hitting the wall. Then he heard her say, "Now you are my little boy." She moaned, her breaths longer apart, her voice lower. For minutes. Then her breathing quickened. Her voice rose as she called, "Now, now, now!" and then shrieked.

The room quieted. After five minutes Igor turned off the recording device with a hard click. He desperately wanted her. He was better than that Ukrainian Google wimp.

21

THURSDAY, DECEMBER 19ᵀᴴ

The morning TV talk shows across all the major networks were promoting the tragedy, reporters were providing continuous live updates, every news website had anguished images and video clips, Facebook was jammed with camera phone updates, and it was Twitter's leading trend. National television showed ambulances with flashing lights, young women breaking down on camera with raw emotion, close-ups of youthful faces twisted in pain, discolored by sobbing and tears.

Lionel was at the office, and every computer on every desk was showing the TV shows, then automatically switching to the internet activity and Instagram pictures. Running from desk to desk, each monitor flashed in synchronization, speakers echoing the sirens and emotions. The entire office reverberated. No one else was there but Lionel, all alone.

He rushed into the conference room and the whiteboard was a giant TV screen. It grew larger, taking over all the whiteboards, wrapping the room and swallowing him. Suddenly he was standing in a sorority house, next to a sobbing brunette in a Theta sweatshirt.

"It was a stupid initiation. I don't know why we did it, but all the girls had to chug four energy drinks in a row, and Sandy and Elaine were trying so hard to be in the sorority. They wanted to be popular, so they chugged six of them, drank them one after another. And now they are dead . . . dead . . . it's so unfair." The young woman put both hands over her face and sobbed uncontrollably.

He was spun around into a TV studio with intense lights, watching a seated newswoman with a mass of black curls. It was Leah Barko from the *National Times Journal*. She looked into a massive rolling TV camera with a sad face and tragic tone.

"Two young woman died today at Western Montana State after rapidly downing six Double Vision energy drinks in a sorority initiation. Officials are testing the manufacturer's products now to determine what ingredients might have contributed to the deaths of these bright and popular coeds. Angry parents are calling for the drinks to be pulled from the market immediately, while others are pressing for criminal charges to be filed against Co-CEOs Lionel Lane and Maxine Gold."

The scene disappeared. In its place a bright backdrop of the Washington Capital dome emerged. Sitting in front was a newscaster with polished hair, square jaw, and brown mustache. It was Garr Gartick. He stared into a camera with the words *Merry News Broadcasting* in large type behind him.

"Co-CEO Maxine Gold made a statement to the press today supporting their right to promote and sell energy drinks wherever legal. She was unapologetic about their products connected to the deaths of the young girls, citing 'individual bad judgment' as the source of the problem. She challenged the media to publish the names of the alcohol brands contributing to DUI accidents or alcohol-related violence."

Then the newscaster morphed into a board member, waving a pen in front of a digital map of the country, drawing lines like a weatherman.

"Co-CEO Lionel Lane has literally vanished into thin air. He was seen in Colorado piloting a helicopter with twenty-one year old Reddi Christiansen, an attractive redhead extreme skier. They landed the helicopter on top of Aspen Mountain and witnesses report seeing them dive off a cliff and fly away together in red and black wing suits, holding hands. The search continues...."

The news was drowned out by the sudden ringing of telephones. Lionel spun around, back at the office, surrounded by vibrating phones. The sound became an angry mix of ring tones competing like warring birds, screeching and fighting. No one answered as the cacophony built to a crescendo.

"Someone needs to answer!" he shouted. "It might be a customer. Where is the receptionist, why won't anyone in the office pick up the phone?" He grabbed a phone, shouting, "Hello, hello, hello?!"

There was no one on the line. The ringing stopped and the doors of the office opened to reveal tall stacks of Double Vision drinks lined up, shrink-wrapped, and loaded on pallets. He walked toward the stacks of inventory and the room flipped open like a transformer and grew longer and bigger, expanding into a huge warehouse in both directions, with forklifts sitting in the aisles. It was deserted. A computer screen hung from a wall in the long corridor, flashing: NO SALES—INVENTORY OVERFLOW—NO SALES—INVENTORY OVERFLOW. The stacks of shrink-wrapped aluminum bottles started growing higher and higher, tall walls closing in on him. Then the inventory covered the lights. The ceiling went black. The phone started ringing again. Ringing. Ringing. The pallets crashed down on him.

Lionel bolted up in his bed. The sheets were twisted around his bare legs. His face was hot and sweating. He was gasping.

The Colorado winter blew against the window of his apartment in Telluride. Reaching over, he tapped the pane to make sure it was real. He pressed his palm against the cold glass to be extra sure. Moonlight brushed the swayed wood structures outside. They looked abandoned, blue and gray in the snow, weathered like a ghost town. He shivered.

Light from his iPhone alarm flashed off the pane. He turned. Four a.m. He shut the alarm off before it rang again.

***

The moonlight streamed through the window of the condo. *It's an invitation to play,* he thought. Hugo sat up. Five a.m. He couldn't sleep. Across the bed, Harding breathed quietly, embracing a huge down pillow. Hugo pushed the curtain and admired the pale blue of the valley floor, imagining the silent and invisible nocturnal animals. Perhaps the absence of police sirens and garbage trucks kept him awake, he mused. Just then an owl hooted. *Aha, it's his fault. Maybe it is a Boreal owl, looking for company.* He had been studying the local flora and fauna for amusement. *Oh well, must be time for another blog.* He pulled out his computer.

He hadn't blogged for the teenagers recently. Maybe he'd reference some of those Mayo Clinic articles and NIH studies on the effects of caffeine. What title would catch their attention? Hmm. *Your Mama's Crack? No, no.* Aha. *Breaking Bad Lite—Confessions of an Energy Drink Mix Master. Better. I don't know why Maxine calls my blogs self-destruction manifestos. People like them.* Thousands of people, actually. He started typing and didn't stop until the moon was low in the valley and the blog was posted to the Double Vision website.

He looked over. Harding wiggled, then slumped deeper into the pillow with a little snort. Hugo sighed. He loved Harding and their life together. But what if something happened? He worried about the company unraveling. *Would the world buy this? He didn't know. Will they win? Didn't look likely.* He reminded himself not to worry about the things out of his control. But he didn't want be the one to screw it up. What if Lionel did create a skyrocketing demand? Improbable as it was, what if? They wouldn't have the product to respond quickly. Not for months. Not until after the Big. *Unless he started now.* How much could they possibly manufacture and warehouse in the next three months?

He started speculating on how much space he'd need to stockpile a volume of product double their highest predictions. He had been talking to a local carpenter, who had worked on their new bottling plant. A gearhead, he drove a beautifully rebuilt Porsche. During the winter snows he stored his Porsche in a large abandoned mine tunnel, with hundreds of other vehicles. It was right off the road to town. There were lots of tunnels. Cool, dark, and so big you could drive a truck right in. And inexpensive. *Perfect for beverages.* He began working out the calculations.

***

Maxine pulled her red and white Mini Cooper into the garage at five-thirty a.m. She swiped her card through the scanner in the dark, and walked down the quiet hallways flicking on lights. She was alone in the San Francisco office. By the time the sun peered through her open blinds at seven-thirty, she was into her second java drink, hammering away on her laptop and talking to the East Coast. When eight o'clock came the office was mostly full. She smiled in satisfaction recalling the nickname given her by an admin, from a conversation she had overheard. "She's like La Machine. I swear, she never sleeps, just showers and changes clothes, then drives back in to work."

Kate entered Maxine's office at eight-thirty, with one of the board directors, Jackie Snow, in tow. Maxine greeted Jackie and observed her elegant Armani silk jacket, colorful scarf, and Prada shoes. Retirement and silver hair didn't slow her down, she noted. And Kate kept up, with her subtle Burberry ensemble. Well, they were marketers. They were supposed to look stylish. Her J.Crew would have to do.

"Thank you, Jackie, for coming today. Your advice continues to be invaluable."

"As long as I can be helpful and not in the way, offering advice is part of my role as a director. And it has been terrific to work with Kate."

Jackie was a welcome foil, thought Maxine. With Jackie's support she could get her way in marketing without the sparks from Kate.

"What's on today's agenda?"

"Maxine, there are two key items in the marketing plan that frankly only you can address," Kate answered.

"What did you have in mind?"

Kate glanced at Jackie who smiled encouragingly. She plunged ahead. "First, more exposure with celebrities. We'll do the grunt work if you can commit to the meetings and a little follow up."

This wasn't my idea, thought Maxine. *Where did this come from?* "What return do we expect?"

"Results will vary. Unfortunately, a lot of PR is unpredictable."

"If we can't measure the results, how will we know the value of the investment of time?" Maxine raised her palms and looked at Kate and Jackie.

Jackie responded with a pleasant smile. "This will be very worthwhile, Maxine. As you know, many celebrities are branching out into beverage endorsements, whether it's Jennifer Aniston's Smart Water or the rapper, 50 Cent, and Vitaminwater. Some involve equity. With our social cause, we may get endorsements from some celebrities without a steep price tag. But *you* will need to impress and convince them."

Maxine sat back, eyebrow raised and head tilted. She crossed her arms.

Kate pressed on, unfazed. "And this celebrity PR feeds into the second request."

"Which is?"

"We want you, as well as Lionel, to be more of the story. More of the brand."

"Sorry, Kate, no extreme skiing or wing-suit stunts for me."

Jackie laughed and smoothly stepped in. "No, not that sort of thing. But making your voice heard, as young, notable, hip CEOs. Like Blake Mycoskie of TOMS shoes. You become intertwined with the brand, and you get lift out of it. Steve Jobs did it for Apple starting from an early age."

"What do I need to do? Do you have a plan?"

Kate responded. "I do." She motioned to her tablet. "Lots of them."

"But the most important aspect is letting your personality show through more," Jackie added.

"Are you sure about that, Jackie?"

Jackie looked at Maxine, puzzled.

"Seriously, are you aware that I can be scary? I have friends, friends mind you, who say I make Condoleezza Rice seem like Mary Poppins. And by the way, Condoleezza is one of my heroes."

"We'll work with you on this, Maxine. Maybe we'll do it over a glass of wine or two."

"You better bring a case."

Jackie laughed as Maxine remained straight-faced.

"See, it's working already. If we trade out your 'all business' stare with a smile accompanying your dry humor, you'll go from scary to witty, from threatening to charming. We aren't saying change your beliefs; we're polishing the edges. We want more of you, your personality and emotion, to come out in ways that resonate."

Maxine's intercom buzzed. "I'm sorry for the intrusion, Maxine."

"I'm in a meeting," she barked.

"I'm so sorry, but I have Garr Gartick, CEO of Merry Cola on line three."

"Oh." Maxine looked up. "Can you give me a moment?" They began to rise. "No, don't bother. Stay."

Maxine picked up the phone.

"Hello, Garr. This is a pleasant surprise."

"It's my pleasure. Since we have a contract now, I'm following up to make it work."

"Garr, do you know we've doubled our efforts in promotion ever since signing the contract with Merry Cola? I thought you'd be pleased to know."

"That helps. But you have read my mind."

"How so?"

"You remember that article last month by Leah Barko, about the standings in the Big Disrupter Award?"

Maxine's stomach soured. "Yes, but of course we dropped in the standings because we hadn't started shipping energy drinks. You can help with that."

"Help me help you, Maxine. Did you see the part where Leah says, and I quote, *'Co-CEO Maxine Gold has largely taken a behind-the-scenes role.'*"

"I think that was a backhanded compliment to Lionel."

"That's one view. But I personally think you have to move up front. Join Lionel in the publicity. You are part of the package, right? We want a high-profile brand that boosts our stock and keeps the government off our backs. Isn't that how you put it?"

"Yes, indeed." She couldn't believe the timing. With Kate sitting right in her office, pushing for the same. Were they conspiring?

"Very good. Well, how about you all start a Double Vision music studio? Like Red Bull's? Maybe one out here in New York and one on the West Coast. You can recruit popular, hip performers to get behind the product."

"Garr, perfect timing. The marketing team and I have been working on several concepts. We have waves of promotions rolling out."

"Excellent. Can't wait to see you stir things up."

"And how are your orders lining up for our drinks?"

"I've greenlighted the national convenience store roll-out. But my distribution managers are the ones looking for more brand demand for your product. The ball is in your court. And it won't stay there long."

"With doubling our promo I'm surprised they haven't seen more demand. Maybe they need to prime the pipe with more product on the shelf?"

"Maxine, I have a small army waiting for me in my office. I need to get back to them. Just thought I'd let you know what I'm hearing internally. Bye."

"Thanks, Garr." Maxine hung up. Not good. Merry Cola distribution was rolling slowly until DV generated more publicity and demand. And Garr and the marketers wanted her to suck up to celebrities and pimp herself. Talk about a personal nightmare.

22

MONDAY, DECEMBER 23ʳᴅ

Raj Singh, the young CEO of Step-by-Step Clothing, focused on his arm movement and stride. Like an Olympian, he told himself, smooth and efficient.

Running on the Golden Gate Bridge was epic he thought, even in the dark. The smell of the fresh air blowing from the Pacific. The rust red towers, washed by spotlights against the black and purple sky. He looked toward the top of the approaching South Tower. As his head bent backward he saw a red light twinkling at the top, warning aircraft. Then he glanced down, over the railing. He saw the flicker of a light in the dark waters below. *It must drop hundreds of feet*. He tried to make out the light source. Maybe a barge? He veered toward the railing, almost tripping. *Whoa, he needed to focus.* He centered back on the sidewalk, looking and running straight ahead.

As he neared the North Tower he saw a large dark figure in the shadows. The tower was where he liked to turn around. But the person made Raj nervous. *Maybe I should turn around sooner.* Stubbornly he continued forward, wanting to reach his goal. He was annoyed at this interruption of his routine. There was no one else out. And this person was right where he wanted to stop. As he got closer he made out a large African-American man on a bicycle. The man reached behind his waist to get something. Raj panicked. He began to stop. The dark man pulled the object forward and held it in front of him. Then Raj recognized the walkie-talkie and the shiny badge on his chest. A cop. Golden Gate bridge patrol. He panted in relief.

"Good morning, sir."

"Yes, good morning officer." He sucked in several breaths. "Nice to see you." He touched the smooth art deco tower, then put his hands on his knees for a moment.

"Beautiful, isn't it?"

He turned for a quick look at the view. "It sure is."

Raj noticed the security camera mounted above on the tower. He suddenly felt foolish for feeling afraid. He gulped more air, waved at the police officer, then began his return loop.

***

Below, nearly three miles away in the Marina Green, a wiry man in a tracksuit approached Raj Singh's parked car. He removed the remote from his pocket and aimed it at the passenger door. The lock clicked and the interior lights came on. He quickly entered and turned off the overhead light.

Sitting in the console in the cup holder was a fresh bottle of water, unopened. Keeping his thin gloves on, he pulled out a flat case from a zippered pouch sewn into his track top. He carefully opened it. Suddenly flashing red lights broke the darkness. He froze. In the rearview mirror he saw white headlights and pulsing red flashers. Then two bicyclists rode by. *Damn.*

As the darkness returned he breathed again, calming his pounding heart. Through the windshield a low barge with winking bow and stern lights motored slowly toward the bridge. He returned to his work.

He wrapped a thin towel around the top of the bottle and inverted it, wedging it firmly in the cup holder. He removed a long syringe from the case, plunging the needle into the bottom of the water bottle. Pulling the plunger back he filled the barrel with water, then emptied it on the floor under the seat. Taking a clear glass vial from his pouch, he placed it firmly in the case, flipped open the top, and punctured the foil seal. He filled the syringe, withdrew it, and injected the clear liquid into the hole of the water bottle. With a small drop of transparent silicon glue he plugged the entry point. He waited five minutes for it to cure, then inverted the bottle.

He exited, used his remote to lock the car, and did a few stretches nearby. Then he began jogging, disappearing into the neighborhood.

***

Raj had been running through the yellow glow of the lampposts on the Bridge. He looked up to take in one last view of the sparkling lights from the skyscrapers downtown, then wound his way through the Presidio. Minutes later he was running along the water's edge, the waves of the bay breaking gently along the shore. The air was tangy with salt. Seagulls were calling their high plaintive tones and skimming along the beach. In another ten minutes he approached his car. It sat in an empty row of parking spaces, along the rocky breakwater that held back the bay. He stopped, sweating and breathing hard. A few early morning joggers passed.

He should hurry back home, he thought. His wife was pregnant and she might need his help. To the east the predawn glow was pink and gold. *So beautiful.* Moments later he retrieved his bottle from the cup holder. He paused, thinking of her and the joy of the new baby. The baby would be like a new sunrise for them, he thought. He drank eagerly, finishing the water as the sun emerged.

He began his drive across town. Normally he felt invigorated. But today, with every minute his energy disappeared. He started to feel lethargic. Strange. Maybe he'd pushed himself too hard. Raj worried his wife would be upset with him. With her first pregnancy and morning sickness he had felt guilty leaving to exercise, but she insisted. Now he regretted the run. He needed a nap. Maybe he could lie down briefly when he got home. A minute later he didn't know if he'd be strong enough to make it to work. But he had so much to do, he couldn't possibly stay home. Then he wondered if he could even make it home. His body wasn't responding properly. He pushed himself, concentrating, as he slowly lost muscle control and his breathing labored.

Raj's car ran off the road, crossed a lawn, and plowed into a tree. By the time the police and paramedics arrived, his running clothes were covered in blood, and he was slumped over the steering wheel near death. The paramedics attached a defibrillator immediately, treating him for cardiac arrest.

He died on the way to the hospital.

In his apartment, the wiry man in the tracksuit monitored the local news and traffic media, until he heard the reports of the accident. He pumped his fist in victory. He took pride in his work. He knew the key was to make the accidents explain themselves, so authorities and family had logical causes, and fewer questions. Most people wanted a simple answer and didn't want to dwell on unpleasant thoughts.

Today he had used succinylcholine bromide. In fatal doses it gave the appearance of a heart attack, and with the proper scenario, that conclusion would rarely be tested. It was a powerful fast-acting muscle relaxant and paralytic agent, commonly used in hospitals in small doses. In larger doses it was used to euthanize horses.

When the newscaster returned from a commercial with confirmation that the accident was fatal, he called Fanachi.

23

TUESDAY, DECEMBER 24TH

On Christmas Eve, Inspector Winston Chang visited Maxine in her office. Lionel joined from Telluride on a Skype video call. He had to give Chang credit, Lionel thought, he was working right up to the holiday.

"I'd complain about working, while most people are off shopping and celebrating. But then I think of Raj," said Lionel. "I can't imagine a more likeable person."

"I'd like to hear more about him," Chang replied. "As much as you two know." He looked away from the screen, and rubbed his mustache. "And also the other competitors in this Big Disrupter contest. Maybe start with the people supposedly in first place, SocialLending, and work your way down please."

After fifteen minutes, Lionel and Maxine had told Inspector Chang everything they knew regarding their competitors. It made Lionel realize how little they really knew about Raj, and Jan Swenson and the other entrepreneurs. They could talk about their business models more knowledgably than the people themselves.

Chang scratched his head. He seemed lost in thought. It annoyed Lionel, reminding him of an absent-minded professor he had in college. "Inspector Chang, is any of this helpful? I'm looking for some feedback here."

Chang nodded slowly, then smiled. "It's helpful. But we are missing a lot of pieces."

"Okay, well what about the bike accident?"

"Based on that new info you remembered, we narrowed the vehicles to a short list of Audis."

Maxine broke in, "And where has that taken you in the investigation, Inspector? Do you have any suspects identified?" Lionel could hear the frustration in her voice.

"Unfortunately we need more facts. I was hoping to get more from you, and the other business people in the contest. But so far, they too have limited information." Lionel saw Maxine's lips form a firm line.

"Was Raj Singh's death accidental?" Lionel questioned.

"The preliminary conclusion is cardiac arrest, which then led to a fatal car accident."

"So you *don't* suspect foul play?" Maxine asked. Lionel sensed the storm clouds coming.

"I have recommended an autopsy to the medical examiner, but they are very, very busy. Budget cuts, you know. And his wife is opposed for religious reasons."

"So you *are* suspicious. So that means Lionel and I may be in serious danger?"

"The events surrounding Mr. Singh, Ms. Swenson, and you may be totally unrelated. In which case, you have nothing to worry about. However, a billion-dollar prize is significant motivation for criminal behavior. I wish we had the manpower to watch the hundreds of people involved in this contest, but that isn't feasible. You'll need to exercise caution. Don't go out alone, especially early or late in the day."

"Inspector Chang, it's Christmas Eve," Maxine barked out. "You know what I'm doing tomorrow? I'm on a plane. And the next day, and the next. We have three months to build outstanding company results. That means working twenty hours per day, and constant travel. Caution is the very last thing we can afford. We'll do anything to help, but if we're in jeopardy here, you have a job to do, and fast."

***

Chang didn't recognize the caller, but that happened frequently as a cop. He picked up.

"Inspector Chang."

"Inspector Winston Chang, of the San Francisco Police Department?"
"Yes."
"Leah Barko, reporter for the *National Times Journal*. I got your number from Lionel Lane."
"Oh, I see. I'm not sure I can be of much help, but go ahead."
"I'm writing an ongoing series about the Big Disrupter. I work directly with President Jules Longsworth reporting on the progress of the contest. You are aware of it, of course?"
"Yes, I am." He liked Leah's writing but dreaded media interference during investigations. It stirred up so many distractions. Or worse, gave the perpetrators warning.
"Can I get your take on the latest tragedy, the death of Raj Singh?"
"Ms. Barko, we don't comment on ongoing or potential investigations."
"Off the record, can you at least say if you think this is related to the Big Disrupter?"
"It's too early to speculate."
"We have a young runner die by heart attack, a kayaking death and a late-night bicycle hit-and-run—all in a matter of months. And all three victims were leading contenders for a billion-dollar award. Don't you consider that suspicious?"
"It's not that simple. Raj Singh died from cardiac arrest, after suffering trauma in a car accident. Jan Swenson drowned in windy cold October waters kayaking alone, something she typically did in better weather. And Lionel Lane was hit in the dark of night by a vehicle, but we don't have the full context. All in different cities. Given the number of contestants for the Big, and all their employees, there is a very reasonable possibility these are random. Very unfortunate, but random."
"Inspector, does that mean you have no suspects?" Chang could hear her exasperation.
"I wish I could be more helpful, but I can't comment."

***

Leah's next call was to Jules Longsworth. He was in a meeting. She took a chance and hopped in a cab. She was on her fourth cup of coffee, but still threw down an energy shot as she drummed her fingers on the back seat. She was juggling multiple story deadlines, but Raj's death obsessed her. Fifteen minutes later she was walking into Jules Longsworth's office. His desk was neatly organized, as she remembered from before. A small silver laptop sat atop gleaming dark wood. Several shopping bags from Gump's and Nordstrom filled a corner, brimming with colorfully wrapped Christmas presents.

"Jules, thank you for squeezing me in, especially today. So I'll come right to the point. Do we have a crisis here? Do you think the magnitude of the award has bent the values of even those who purport to be socially conscious?" She suddenly realized she was still standing and practically breathless.

Jules seemed a bit taken aback.

"Leah, please, have a seat." He motioned to the wingback chairs. She placed her laptop bag on one, the recorder on his desk, and sat down.

"Thank you. And the recorder is running, per our protocol. Still fine?"

"Of course," he replied, arching his fingertips together. He squared the shoulders of his blazer. "Now, starting at the beginning, are you assuming that there is some sort of plot here? A plot which interconnects these tragedies?"

"It is very much looking that way."

"If we take that assumption, hypothetically, then are you further assuming the actors in such a drama are potential recipients of the award?"

"Who else would possibly have more motivation? As they say, follow the money. Although I suppose it could be other industry players, concerned about a powerful competitor emerging."

"External competitors?" he asked, his eyes searching.

"One example. Hypothetically, perhaps one of the Big Four beverage companies, maybe even Merry Cola itself, could be trying to sabotage Double Vision. But obscuring their intent with unrelated victims, like Jan Swenson and Raj Singh."

"Does Lionel think this?"

"This is my own speculation, a possibility, thinking outside the box."

"Murder for profit? I don't see it, Leah."

"It wouldn't be the first time. If not, then what is your explanation?"

"I think we have coincidence combined with . . . with a high degree of scrutiny."

"So, it's the media's fault? Or are you blaming the Twitter and YouTube speculation that is popping up now?"

"The Big is the world's largest award. People are learning what social entrepreneurs do. These entrepreneurs are suddenly in the limelight, their companies are receiving terrific exposure, in no small part due to your coverage. That's the better story. Not the tragic deaths of some hard charging, active entrepreneurs with some unfortunate lifestyle risks."

"A kayaker drowning in her backyard lake? An unexplained heart attack? Getting run over on a bike in an empty alley? You call these 'lifestyle risks'?"

"They represent an anomaly. Statistical flukes. No one could have predicted this. It's the same thing I told Inspector Chang of the SFPD, and he happens to agree with me."

"He interviewed you?"

"Of course, wouldn't you expect that?"

"Yes. Yes, actually I'm glad. But I wish he'd be more aggressive. Why am I the only one with suspicions here?"

"It is what it is, Leah. Nothing more. Very tragic but isolated accidents, in my opinion."

"Jules, you are an esteemed professor, as well as a businessperson. Can you please put on your questioning academic hat, for a moment? Does it strike you that perhaps the business people want to allay any suspicion of a conspiracy here? At the same time, the police want to keep the press out of an ongoing investigation to make their lives easier?"

"That has occurred to me."

"Aha." She leaned toward him in satisfaction.

"Similarly, in the same objective mindset, is it possible that an aggressive reporter would link together isolated circumstances in order to create a sensational and career-vaulting story?"

What?! What sort of opinion did Jules Longsworth have of her? Or was he trying to squash the story?

24

SATURDAY, JANUARY 4TH

Lionel stepped off Reddi's front porch and immediately dialed into the conference call. Maxine and Kate were already online. He walked up the street, slipping on the packed snow, trying to concentrate. It was midday Saturday, but weekends had been sacrificed long ago.

"Where are you?" asked Maxine.

"Telluride. Walking to the office. Thought I'd take the call there. And you?"

"New York, JFK, waiting to board. On my way to L.A. for meetings tomorrow." Lionel could picture the crowded airport waiting area, families trying to make cranky kids happy, exhausted revelers going home, unhappy road warriors traveling on the weekend. And Maxine, in some stiff worn seat, trying to carve out a cone of silence.

"How'd the presentation go yesterday?"

"Fine, but an insane day. I've got a ton of follow up. Anyway, should we get started?" She sounded irritated and tired.

Kate interrupted. "She was awesome. Her session at the American Marketing Association conference was packed, and there must have been fifty people who came up afterward to talk. She nailed it. The crowd loved the one-for-one approach and products."

"Thanks. However, the endorsement deals were another story."

"What do you mean?" asked Lionel.

"We had several appointments with celebrities that afternoon. They were all gushy and excited, and then their business managers took over and demanded either millions in cash, a big percentage of the upside, or a huge chunk of company stock. As though their hoisting a DV energy drink during a show constituted an enormous effort and would compel millions to buy." Maxine sounded disgusted.

"Bummer. It's a numbers game. We'll find the right match with more socially conscious celebrities. They've gotta be out there," said Lionel.

"You know I don't suffer fools gladly."

Maxine sounded burned out. A sudden inspiration hit Lionel. "Look, before we start our sales and marketing update, Maxine, why don't you think about coming to Telluride? You've never even seen the new bottling plant. Plus you can have a short break and recharge your batteries."

Maxine sighed. "Let me think about it. Blaine is bugging me about visiting Telluride and our operation, as well. Look, I have to board soon. Let's do our update and I'll let you know."

Twenty minutes later they wrapped up the conference call as Maxine walked down the jet way to her plane.

Half an hour later Lionel got a text.

***

Still on ground. Okay, maybe I will meet you in T-ride?
Sure, when?
Next Thursday?
Great! We'll take a day and ski- then work like crazy.
I need it.
I'm traveling until Wed, back on evening flight.
Okay, good.
FYI-Plane only two seats across. Highest airport in country. Can be bumpy. (lol)
NP. Can't wait to leave craziness behind.
Perfect. I'll book it in the calendar.

***

"Hey Geek," greeted Nicco, the darker of the two hunks guarding the front table. Igor acknowledged them as he entered, then hooked the braided rope behind him. The body guard swung his blocky head with a nod toward Fanachi's table, against the back wall of the private dining room. Walking past the empty tables, Igor realized he had never seen any of them occupied. The faded paintings and gilded mirror looked like they had been there as long as the building.

Igor saw Fanachi stare as the waitress in the red skirt and low-cut blouse leaned toward him. He said something in Italian. She laughed while she poured his coffee and he gave her backside a rub.

Igor approached slowly. The waitress turned to him, and with no concern about Fanachi's hand still lingering on her soft parts, said, "Café?"

"Grazie," he nodded. She poured him a cup and wiggled around Fanachi and back into the kitchen.

Igor sat and waited for Fanachi to bring the cup down from his thin lips. His eyes stared through the steam rising from the brim, and Igor noticed he was only smelling it, not drinking. It clattered on the saucer and then he spoke.

"You had an idea that is so good you had to rush over right now?"

"Analyst Three pinged me. We have new real-time algorithm using the Apache Hadoop server searching everyone's calendars . . ."

Fanachi waved his hand and Igor stopped.

"What's the point?"

"Lionel and Maxine will be together in isolated environment. The ski town where they make the drinks. Telluride, Colorado."

"So?" Fanachi took a sip of coffee. Igor waited until he finished.

"Accidents in the mountains in winter are common." *Don't bother him with details*, he reminded himself.

Fanachi sat back and put his hands together. The planes of his big face hardened as he thought.

Igor spun his coffee cup in the saucer and waited for Fanachi.

"You? Why not Calabrese? He is our expert for these things. Like the job he did on that jogger."

"He agreed that I am well suited for this one. I have experience in winter mountain conditions. But I will follow his directions, of course. Just like the big guys followed his plan for the kayaker." Igor's leg started to jiggle under the table.

"There is no need to rush this." Fanachi took a sip of his coffee. Then he leaned forward on his elbows and his black eyes stared at Igor. The huge forehead and cheeks were motionless. Igor slowed his breathing. And stopped wiggling his leg.

"Tell me what you are thinking," Fanachi said quietly.

25

THURSDAY, JANUARY 9TH — FRIDAY, JANUARY 10TH

The bells on the handle jingled as Reddi opened the door.

"It's my favorite smell, Helga's cinnamon rolls," exclaimed Hannah, running over to the glass bakery case.

Reddi closed her eyes and breathed. She loved the sweet smells mixed with the pungent herbal teas and strong roasted coffee. The Roast was like her second home. The light that filtered through the large-pane windows onto the worn oak floor seemed soft and comforting. She surveyed the collection of colorful but mismatched sofas, worn plump chairs, and pillows. The cafe was starting to fill up with other patrons.

"Look, look at my beauties," Helga called out. Helga's knit snowflake hat was a blur as she came rushing from behind the counter.

She hugged Hannah, then stepped back and exclaimed, "Taller than me now. And only twelve years old."

"I'll be thirteen in two months. Practically a teenager." Hannah beamed.

"Oh, no, please don't change." Helga hugged her again with a laugh, pressing her round face against Hannah's cheek. "And how is California? And your dad?"

"We like Santa Cruz. Dad's busy. The people are nice. But I am so glad to be on vacation so I can ski with Reddi. And see Wolfie."

Reddi, Hannah, and Helga looked toward Wolfie, sitting contentedly on the front patio as snowflakes dropped on her fur. Beyond the high storefront windows heavy snowfall descended on Main Street. Ajax Peak, the giant snow cone defining the end of the valley, was barely visible. The red canyon walls were turning white. As if sensing their attention, Wolfie cocked her furry head to check inside.

"I have treats for her, but first let's get you two seated."

"Someone is joining us. My other boss at my sponsor, Double Vision. Her name is Maxine. We've never met."

"Wonderful. She is going to love meeting you." She gave Reddi a kiss on the cheek. "Find a comfortable sofa, and a chair for her, and should I bring you . . ."

"Wait, don't say it. Let me say it, okay?" Hannah's eyes were round with anticipation.

"Of course," said Helga.

"Bring us *the usual* please, Helga," Hannah requested, with a dramatic swing of her arm.

"You get such a kick out of being a regular," Reddi chuckled.

"I don't get to do it in Santa Cruz."

"Maybe one day, bookworm."

Helga clapped her hands and disappeared behind the counter. Reddi and Hannah made themselves comfortable on a sofa. They sat with legs crossed facing each other on the bouncy cushions, like old times. Reddi relished the shining excitement in Hannah's face as they talked.

"Can we take Wolfie skiing with us, maybe somehow?" asked Hannah.

"No dogs on the mountain, you know that."

"No fair. Ski patrol has their dogs, and Wolfie is even better."

"No argument from me on that, but those dogs are for mountain rescue, they're working dogs. But," she said, drawing out her thought, "maybe we can do some Nordic skiing up Bear Creek in the morning. Wolfie is allowed there. Then in the afternoon we can go up on the ski area."

"Yes, can we, can we?" Hannah bubbled with excitement, bouncing on the sofa. Reddi was reminded of how much she missed her little sister.

"As soon as Maxine arrives we can ask her, okay? I did promise to spend some time together with her."

"Okay, but I'm sure she'll want to come with us. After all, you are the best skier on the mountain and we have wonderful Wolfie."

Reddi wondered. *What will Maxine be like?* She was interrupted by the arrival of their drinks and cinnamon treats, and then she and Hannah continued their talk.

Minutes later, Reddi looked out and saw a striking African-American woman walk down the street. The woman stopped and looked at the sign, then noticed Wolfie and jumped back. She hurried inside.

A red beret topped the thick black hair that flowed to her shoulders. A fitted tan ski jacket tapered to her waist, and her wool pants were tucked into tall Uggs. Her bright eyes searched the room.

That has to be her. Reddi jumped up and worked her way around the tables and chairs. "Excuse me, are you Maxine Gold?"

"Yes. You must be Reddi," she said, extending her hand. "A pleasure to meet you in person, finally."

She looks so sophisticated, Reddi thought. *Those dramatic eyes and dreamy smooth chocolate skin.* Well, her smile seemed friendly. But she'd been warned.

They exchanged pleasantries as Maxine unbundled and Reddi introduced Hannah. They fixed Maxine up with a homemade scone and chai, and she sat next to them in an overstuffed chair.

"I have to ask—is that your wolf I've heard about, on the front patio? He is absolutely gorgeous, but terrifying."

"She, actually. And technically a wolfdog," explained Hannah knowingly. "Wolfie looks a little scary but really is very nice, once you become friends."

"I look forward to getting to know her better," Maxine answered.

Reddi smiled. "In fact, Hannah and I were hoping to do a little cross country adventure with you. You know—Nordic skiing, and bring Wolfie along. We'd walk up a beautiful canyon, using skins underneath our skis for traction, and then we take off the skins and ski back down to town. It's up an old mining road in the bottom of the valley, so it isn't that steep."

"Really, something in these mountains that isn't that steep?" asked Maxine, tilting her head to the side. She looked out the window at the canyon walls disappearing into the storm, and raised an eyebrow.

"Okay, I confess, the sides of the canyon are steep, where it goes up to the tops of the mountains," explained Hannah. "Like a V," and she made a V shape with her hands for Maxine. "But we stay in the middle along the river and that is not steep at all."

"A ski adventure is such a nice thought, but I'd really hate to slow you experts down. Especially since you are here on your holiday, Hannah." Maxine smiled at her.

"Actually the uphill is more of a walking and gliding experience," replied Reddi. "And I can break trail. Then, when we turn around, it's a pretty gradual downhill. So it's a great way for us to be together. We can talk as we go."

"What did Lionel think?"

"I texted him. He thought it would be a fun way to spend half the day together. And then see what people feel like in the afternoon."

Hannah gave Maxine a hopeful look.

Maxine chuckled. "Do you know when Lionel is arriving?"

"He's on the seven forty-five flight tonight from Denver."

Maxine nodded.

Reddi glanced out the window at the falling snow. "If this breaks he might make it, otherwise he'll be stuck because they won't fly through the storm."

"Stuck?"

"Yeah. He's on the last flight. If they cancel he'll have to wait a day. But either way we should go. If it's a powder morning, it'll be an amazing experience."

Maxine looked outside, skeptically. Hannah started bouncing up and down on the sofa, rubbing her hands together excitedly. Maxine turned to her and broke into a laugh.

"Okay, I'll take your word for it. You're the expert, er, experts," she said with a nod at Hannah. "I'm willing to try almost anything once."

"You'll love it," Hannah promised, clapping her hands and then squeezing Maxine's knee.

"How about we meet you at your hotel at seven a.m.? Then we'll pick up additional rental equipment for you and Hannah, and start from the base of Bear Creek Canyon at eight-thirty a.m."

"What about Lionel?" Maxine asked.

"I'll let him know. He's got all his gear already, he can meet us at the base of Bear Creek."

"We have a plan, then. Meanwhile, can you point me in the direction of the Double Vision office? I've got some things to finish before the end of the day."

Hannah jumped up and down. "I am so excited you are coming tomorrow. Powder is heavenly soft, Maxine."

"Thank you, Hannah. I really am looking forward to a relaxing adventure away from work."

As they made their way through the packed restaurant, other customers smiled at Hannah's cute antics as she tugged on Reddi's long scarf. Even the unfamiliar out-of town faces seemed interested, Reddi noticed. Helga blew a kiss and waved good-bye from behind the crowded counter.

Outside, Wolfie leaped to her feet. She shook off the snow blanket on her bushy fur and nosed Reddi, taking one of Helga's treats. They parted with words of encouragement about their coming morning adventure.

***

The alarm rang at three-thirty a.m. He hadn't slept. As he dressed, Igor limited himself to a few thin layers. He shivered, bracing for the cold plunge outside the glass door. Lunging forward he stretched in place, then switched sides, repeating the exercise, warming and calming himself. He envisioned the vigorous uphill climbing on his Nordic skis that lay ahead. In his mind he broke trail in the deep powder, and eventually the reinforcing motion began to heat him up. Then he knew he was ready.

In his pack he gently placed a dozen custom explosives of varying sizes and a 22-caliber pistol with a silencer. He placed his Swarovski binoculars and a pair of military-grade-night-vision goggles on top. He double checked the remaining contents and ran down the list he had made with Calabrese, Fanachi's top lieutenant. He had to be careful. Finally he zipped the individual pouches and closed the pack.

He slid open the glass door and stepped into the deep snow on the deck of his rental chalet. It was quiet as he adjusted his headlamp and skis. A few light flakes swirled down, melting on his face. The storm must be over, he thought.

Within moments Igor was striding on his route. He thought of his past two days in town, and the roads and trails he explored. At night he memorized the map Calabrese had given him, and read about the slide history on mountaineering blogs. It was very fortunate that he overheard Reddi's plan at The Roast, the cafe where he had followed Maxine. Now, he knew exactly where he wanted to go.

Telluride was still dark and silent. He glided through town on a side road, dimly lit with streetlights. He branched off and made first tracks along the river toward the trailhead. A wooden bridge and locked vehicle gate lay ahead. He crossed and left civilization behind as he moved into the black of the canyon.

It was soft and slower going on the Bear Creek trail. He stopped by a group of pine trees. Opening his pack he swapped the headlamp for his night-vision goggles. He snugged on the head harness, rearranged his watch cap, and pulled up his hood. The goggles extended beyond the hood like a heavy beak. Night suddenly became day. The features of the canyon appeared much closer and clearer. His world changed to a green tint, with shades of white and black. He felt powerful, like a glass-eyed superhuman.

The hunt had begun.

***

Reddi made coffee and hot chocolate. In the dim light out the kitchen window she saw the soft white of a fresh foot of snow blanketing every roof, car, and tree. The town was still, slowly awakening.

The hush was broken by explosions. Ski patrol, she thought. The patrollers were already exploring the steepest slopes of the ski area, skiing cuts and throwing bombs into the slide-prone chutes. Then she heard the Howitzers and avalaunchers shooting charges far into the inaccessible slide zones. They won't open the ski area until it is completely safe, she realized. It sounds like they are busy this morning.

She woke up Hannah for breakfast, fed Wolfie, and by seven a.m. they were at Maxine's hotel. They trudged through the heavy snow to Crazy Jack's shop and got outfitted. They emerged from the shop on their cross country skis. By eight-thirty, Reddi, Maxine, and Hannah were at the bottom of Bear Creek, as the red alpenglow brightened the snow-covered peaks. Wolfie was prancing like the powder was a field of fresh daisies.

"Look," said Hannah, "tracks."

"Yes, it looks like several people headed up before us. So that'll make the going easier."

"Is this part of the ski area?" asked Maxine.

Hannah answered as Reddi checked her pack. "Nope. Past that side of the mountain is the ski area." Hannah pointed to the right of the canyon. "Bear Creek is our own special valley. No vehicles or chair lifts. Not many people. But don't worry, it's fun," she added, restlessly stamping her feet.

"Everybody has their beacons turned on?" asked Reddi. She double-checked the equipment, which included lightweight collapsible snow shovels and emergency kits.

"It seems like we're gearing up for a real expedition. Is it really only a two-hour trip?" asked Maxine.

"It may take longer with the deep snow," admitted Reddi.

"I can't wait," beamed Hannah, pumping her poles eagerly. Her brown pigtails wiggled below her pink wool hat.

"Remember, with all this new snow, we need to stay together. Safety first."

Maxine shook her shoulders to warm up. "Well, I can't believe I'm doing this and Lionel is stuck in the Denver airport."

"That's the mountains. Unpredictable," said Reddi.

"I'll finally have an outdoor adventure where I can tell him—you should have been there."

She and Reddi laughed. "You don't get outdoors as much as he does, right?"

"Not a fraction. But I'm ready to have this one adventure over him."

"Let's do it," said Reddi, as she took the lead, sliding into the tracks ahead. Hannah followed closely behind, while Wolfie bound through the snow to the side of the trail. Without skis, her paws sank into the snow, and her chest and belly made a deep trough.

Maxine made up the rear, gamely swinging her arms, poles sinking deep into the snow.

"Use your hips more than your arms," advised Reddi, demonstrating the ideal motion.

"Fine by me. I'll get this butt in shape. Too many restaurants and plane seats."

Town quickly faded behind them and a wonderland emerged of tall green pines, Douglas firs, and white aspens laden with snow. Every turn up the canyon revealed new crystal formations on logs, rocks, and the frozen creek bed.

As they ventured deeper in the canyon the snow piled higher. The canyon walls loomed larger. High above, red cliff-bands jutted out, plastered with white. Occasional powder wisps blew off the rock and disappeared.

Reddi and Maxine talked as they strode. Hannah raced in front, singing to Wolfie. Reddi looked up the trail and saw Hannah distancing herself uphill. "Hannah, don't go too far ahead."

Her little voice called back. "Okay, I won't," as she continued smoothly, following the group of tracks.

"Wow, what a natural. Hannah just floats up the hill," exclaimed Maxine. She stopped, her breath coming in quick gasps.

"Aw, you'll get acclimatized in a few days, then it will be easy for you too."

"I seriously doubt that," she gasped. "But thanks for the encouragement." Maxine took a few breaths and then they resumed.

"Reddi, I want to get to know you better. Tell me, what are your goals?"

"Goals? I love to ski and compete. Slopestyle competition skiing is letting me see lots of amazing places. Not only Colorado, but mountains across the U.S. and Canada. Maybe one day I'll go ski in Europe too."

"You have a flair for the promotional side too."

"Thanks. But that really is Kate. The videos and social media. The articles she gets in the magazines, the help writing my blogs and tweets, the TV interviews. It's the whole marketing team."

"Glad you appreciate the team. That's good. So where would you like your career to go?"

Reddi hesitated. "Not sure I follow you."

"Do you want to maintain the life of a ski bum, working at your shop in the summer and getting enough sponsorships to compete on the slopestyle circuit in the winter? Or more?" Maxine stopped for a moment, sucking air.

"Oh, bumming has been fun so far, no question. But I have another plan. Well, dream, I guess."

"What's that?"

"To be a slopestyle champion, in the X Games. And the Olympics."

"I've heard. You know that takes tremendous personal sacrifice. Are you willing to do that?"

"I already am. I train a lot with my slopestyle coach, Bronco. You may think I just show up at meets, but there is a lot of air bag, foam pit and water training behind the scenes."

Maxine started ahead. "What about your education? Finishing college?"

"Right now, skiing comes first."

"So it's either win the X Games and go to the Olympics, or bust?"

"Sure, why not? Have you ever gone for something like that?"

"No. I never had the talent. I always preferred to use my mind to get ahead, or at least that was the only realistic alternative."

"You went to college, right?"

"Uh-huh." Maxine was starting to pant heavily.

"With Lionel, at Harvard?"

"Right."

"Did you know each other?"

"Yes," she said, between puffs, the vapor like little clouds as they spoke. "Were you friends? Or more?"

Maxine stopped. "You're not shy." She gasped several times. Then she raised her head back and exhaled slowly. "It's not fair grilling me when I can't even breathe. I should ask the questions and let you talk." She took several breaths. "Evidently you don't need oxygen."

Reddi laughed. "Friends or more?"

Maxine growled. Reddi chuckled.

"We were friends for a while, then lovers." She took a deep gulp. "After graduation, we went apart because we were working on opposite sides of the world."

Reddi thought about that. They continued uphill.

"How do you feel about Lionel now?"

"We're colleagues. It's all business."

"That's funny. Because in some ways you two seem so compatible."

"Compatible for business, perhaps. Although even there, we have our differences."

Suddenly Reddi realized she had lost track of Hannah. She looked up the trail. "Hannah, wait up!" There was no response.

Reddi frowned. She turned back toward Maxine. "I don't know exactly what Lionel has told you, but he and I recently started having sex. And it was long after you all decided to sponsor me, so it wasn't like that."

"Whoa, hang on. That's not why I'm here." Maxine stopped and leaned heavily on her poles.

"Maybe not. I do feel a little awkward though. I don't want it to get in the way." Reddi waited.

"It could be a real issue if you were an employee. Nepotism and all. But as a sponsored athlete, it's not quite as complicated." Maxine started up again.

"Good. We enjoy each other's company, and I'm not involved with any other guy romantically right now. I'm not sure where it is going, but so far it's working."

Reddi exhaled, feeling pressured by the topic. She was getting a funny feeling, a sense, and it seemed more than the awkward conversation. "Maxine, hang on for a second."

Reddi cupped her hand and called out, "Hannah, Hannah, wait up! Stay closer." She turned to Maxine. "I need to pull her in. There is a lot of new snow above us. We should be closer together. Conversation to be continued, okay?"

Reddi pushed off and started gliding gracefully. She turned her head back momentarily, "Keep on coming, okay Maxine?"

"How do you do that?" Maxine muttered as Reddi kicked uphill, quickly leaving her behind.

It took several minutes before Reddi had Hannah back in earshot. Wolfie was at her side still romping around. Reddi drew closer, while Maxine was approaching slowly from below.

Two distinct bursts, muffled by the blanket of snow, echoed. Reddi spun her head. There was open slope, without trees, above to their right. She saw a line at the top, a deep crack that extended across the field of snow.

"Slide!" yelled Reddi. "Shit!"

Below the crack the snow began moving downhill, picking up speed.

Close above Reddi and Hannah were dense groves of aspen and spruce. The trees should protect them, if the slide to the right didn't widen out, Reddi thought.

Reddi looked downhill and immediately knew what they had to do.

She turned to Hannah. "Hannah, keep going uphill, and take Wolfie. You'll be safe that way. Wolfie, stay with Hannah. Now! Fast!"

Reddi spun and started downhill toward Maxine. And directly into the path of the oncoming avalanche. Maxine was still climbing slowly. Above her, hundreds of tons of snow gained momentum.

Reddi dug her poles and kicked her legs in powerful skating motions. Thank God she didn't wear skins like everyone else. Her waxless backcountry skis were faster. But the deep snow slowed her. She frantically pushed to build speed.

"Stop!" she yelled at Maxine. "Turn around."

She saw Maxine look at her and stop. Then she looked uphill.

Reddi yelled again. "Turn around!" This time Maxine understood.

Maxine began turning around, but in her rush, one ski went on top of the other and she nearly fell over. She uncrossed them, pointed them downhill and immediately started sliding.

Then she fell backward. She looked as though she had fallen in a deep hole, butt first. She flailed with her poles and feet.

"Hurry Maxine!" Reddi yelled. She saw her struggling to get back on her feet in the soft powder. Maxine threw her shoulders forward and pushed her hands down on her skis, wobbling into a crouch.

Reddi looked up toward the avalanche. The early morning sunlight lit the advancing wall of white. With speed, the slab had disintegrated into a boiling wave of powder. A plume churned up in the center, and the front edge foamed. *It's only a matter of seconds.*

Faintly she heard "Stop, Wolfie, come back," behind her. The wind blast in front of the slide whistled by. She pumped her tiring shoulders and arms.

Maxine stood awkwardly, adjusting her goggles, her poles pointed upward.

"Crouch down, bend your knees," yelled Reddi, closing fast. Just before impact, Maxine bent over, wobbling. Reddi slid her right ski between Maxine's two legs and slammed into her, her right thigh and hip mating with Maxine's butt, as she wrapped her right arm around Maxine's waist. The impact shot them downhill together. Reddi felt Maxine press heavily against her. Swirling powder choked their noses.

Why was Hannah calling? A sudden panic made Reddi look back.

It was her worst nightmare. Hannah was coming down the trail, skiing frantically, chasing the bounding Wolfie.

"No!" Reddi screamed. *Wolfie, why are you following me?*

"Hannah, no, back," and then she realized it was too late.

The avalanche washed over Hannah and Wolfie.

26

FRIDAY, MIDMORNING, JANUARY 10TH

Inspector Chang drove by Peet's, picked up a tall hot chai, and brought it back to the Mission Street precinct in San Francisco. He was eager to see his research results. But he maintained his routine, greeting colleagues and chatting as he arrived. Once at his desk, he grabbed his keyboard.

He logged in via a back door to his private listening post, the Big Data server that helped him sort through enormous amounts of social media. He had started a social media sentiment analysis, examining tweets, blog posts, and comments made about Jan Swenson's and Raj Singh's death. He also included Lionel's bike accident. Using keywords and context analysis, the software categorized each of the tens of thousands of comments, tweets, blogs, and articles. The server was finally done, after crunching through the night.

He made sure no one was watching. Then he looked at the graphical reports, rubbing his mustache. The sentiment was overwhelmingly skeptical that the running and kayaking deaths were accidental. Perhaps the predictable personalities of those two also figured in, he thought. However, the bike accident was less conclusive—a much higher percentage thought it could be accidental. Was it because riding bikes was considered more dangerous in cities? Chang wondered. Or that Lionel was considered a daredevil? What he didn't find, however, were any clues about the perpetrators. Not yet.

Chang kicked off another query. This one would take minutes, not hours. He settled in his creaking chair and wondered how to link the clues to the Big Disrupter. He thought back to his interview with Jan Swenson's husband.

It had been a phone interview. He hadn't the departmental resources to fly to Minnesota to interview Steve Swenson in person, which he would have much preferred. It was an emotional discussion, although Chang had been through many similar painful interviews in his career. Jan Swenson's husband was left with two young children and the memory of a wife he believed died doing what she loved. And running a company that everyone admired. They were a family with a private tragedy, and Chang's inquiry opened the wound.

He could still hear the edge in the husband's voice.

"What do you mean you have more questions? I have two young kids without a mother. We're trying to heal, remember the good times, get on with our lives."

"There have been new developments, sir."

"You mean you don't think it was an accident?"

"According to the reports her life jacket was never found."

"Like I told the local investigator. You don't have to wear it. It only needs to be in the boat. Sometimes we'd sit on the life jackets. They cushion the hard plastic seat . . . ." He stopped talking. Chang could tell he was struggling with his composure.

He finished the thought for him. "So you think something happened with the wind or a wave, she capsized, and the cushion floated off."

"Yes," he said quietly, his voice shaking.

Chang waited. Finally Steve asked, "Why are you involved? San Francisco is a long way from Minnesota."

"We've had other incidents involving people in the same contest as your wife."

"Contest?"

"The Big Disrupter."

"Oh yeah. I'd lost track of that. That really excited her. She'd dream about what Sweet Boomerang could do with the money."

"Like what?"

"Oh, more locations, better training for the workforce, and less cash flow stress. You know, no one cared about employing people with disabilities like Jan did—she said it gave meaning to their lives."

"What else did she say?"

"Look, with her job, my job, and two kids we don't . . . *didn't*, have a lot of free time to share all our work details. Our time together was mostly about the kids."

"I see. Of course. But did she mention anything in particular about the contest?"

"She did mention some guy who has an energy drink company, like Red Bull. They give one away for each they sell."

"Double Vision?" prompted Chang.

"That's the name. And their CEO got hit by a car. And that was before Jan . . . ."

"Yes. Lionel Lane."

"That's the guy. They talked. She said he was really positive, a win-win guy. Not an obnoxious competitor."

"What about other competitors?"

"After she came back from the awards ceremony she said the irony was the guy who won that night, you know, the one who got Entrepreneur of the Year, had the worst personality. Really obnoxious and competitive."

Chang thought a moment. "SocialLending? Larry Furtig?"

"Yeah, the financial company guy. But I'm not accusing him of anything. You need to understand, Jan is really positive." He sighed. "Was really positive. And she sometimes wondered if she should be more pushy and assertive. After meeting that guy, she told me, no matter what edge it gave him, she didn't want to be that person."

Chang's computer chirped, signaling the end of the search. His reverie interrupted, he studied the results for several minutes. Nothing appeared that he hadn't already seen in Jan Swenson's case. And no suspicious links to SocialLending or Larry Furtig.

Chang rocked back. He stared upward, annoyed by the ceiling's stained acoustical tiles for the millionth time. He hated ceiling stains. Why didn't they fix them? Then he slowly leaned forward. He began another search for clues on Raj Singh, the CEO who died of cardiac arrest. Something his wife Anala said triggered his curiosity.

It too had been a difficult interview but for unexpected reasons. She was a composed and articulate woman. They had sat in her small living room in modern curved-back chairs, a woman friend of hers hovering in the background.

"It is painful, but part of a cycle. See, I have a beautiful reminder of him on the way." She patted the bulging belly under her embroidered maternity blouse.

"One life is coming into the world and one left. It is so sad they won't get to meet each other, but think of how wonderful it is that Raj will have a son or daughter to carry on. And hopefully with a stronger heart."

She shook her head, the long, fine hair wafting like a black veil. "His father died young as well. I always knew something like this would happen. Yet I hoped we'd have more time." She took a sharp breath.

"I'm very sorry, ma'am." He nodded his head and paused a moment. "May I inquire, what are your plans for the future?"

"I am not going to let the business stress me out. My job right now is to have a healthy child. After that, I look forward to helping the poor via the business. The thing about helping the poor, Inspector, is you have a lot of customers. They aren't going away with a fashion change or new technology. They will be there when I come back to work in a year or so, karma depending."

"Of course." He saw her friend looking impatient. "May I ask you about that day? I've read the report, but was there any small thing that may have been different?"

"No, Raj's routine was very consistent and efficient. He woke up early—no coffee or tea, no breakfast. He always laid everything out the night before. Shoes, socks, shorts, two long-sleeved microfiber shirts, and a water bottle. He drove to the ocean or a park to run, for the fresh air. The Golden Gate Bridge was his favorite. Then he ran his loop. Back at the car he drank his water—that was his treat for the run, he'd tell me. And then he would come home, shower, and we would leave for work."

"He had a water bottle?"

"Inexpensive bottled water. We buy cases of them at Costco."

"Do you have any more?"

"Probably. We keep them in the garage. I don't drink them. I use tap. He would drink the whole thing down at once. He always did."

His laptop chirped again, interrupting his thoughts. The query report had come back. Another strikeout. No reported problems from the bottler of the water, nor from Costco customers. And the tests on of the remainder of the case from her house came back negative. *He had nothing to convince Anala to go contrary to her Hindu beliefs and do an autopsy. Another dead end.*

27

FRIDAY, LATE MORNING, JANUARY 10TH

The whipping snow blinded Maxine. She crouched in limbo. Suddenly she was slammed forward, pushed between her legs, clamped around her lower back and waist. It was Reddi, tight against her rear. Maxine leaned into her. She felt like a baby carried by the big skier's strength. The wait was endless.

Then the turbulence faded. The furious sideways wave of pressure disappeared. It became smooth, like they had passed through a doorway. Maxine heard Reddi's snowplow as they glided to a stop.

Her face was a frozen mask of snow blast. She shook, sucked cold air, and a dry pain burned her throat. Then she felt Reddi's hands on hers hips gently pushing her way. As they separated, Maxine felt the warm strength leave, and she collapsed in the snow.

"Gotta go find Hannah right away. She's buried and that means she only has a few minutes."

Maxine scraped her goggles, trying to see Reddi standing above her. She had dodged certain death. Her only wish was to return to civilization. "You're going back up there? It can't be safe."

"It isn't. Something's making the snow unstable. Maybe warming temps or winds, something. There could be more slides."

Maxine jerked off her goggles. Reddi was scanning the cliffs, squinting in the diffuse gray light. Maxine saw the stress lines, like little cracks, in her face. Reddi's eyes had lost their lake blue—they looked steely gray.

Maxine lay shaking.

"Go over to those trees." Reddi pointed to a tall clump of aspen. "You'll be safe. Move around enough to stay warm."

Reddi started uphill. Maxine's teeth chattered. "What are you doing?"

"Getting my baby sister out of this motherfucking avalanche."

She pushed away, pumping ferociously.

"What can I do?" called out Maxine.

Reddi yelled. "Stay safe. You're the frigging CEO. We can't have you die. Too much money at stake." And with that, she kicked violently toward the slide rubble.

The words didn't sound bitter, just factual. Reddi was right. The company and their mission depended on her. The conditions were unsafe. Plus she was exhausted and out of her element. She felt sick.

Maxine looked at the gash on the side of the mountain where the snow had slid off. Then an image of Hannah appeared. *She is buried somewhere at the bottom, pressed into a knot in the dark. Freezing and choking to death.*

She threw up. The bile rose so suddenly it left her mouth before she could think. Vomit landed on her skis and dribbled on her jacket. She just stared at it.

The nausea swept over her and she twisted sideways. She shivered as she lay in the snow.

"I don't know what to do," she moaned. She looked up where Reddi was headed. Above her wings of white were blowing off dizzyingly high cliffs. Nearby sloughs still inched and shook precariously. It was treacherous. *Completely stupid for humans to come here in the winter.* Her shoulders shook uncontrollably. She heard tapping and realized her hands were vibrating and banging her poles together.

"Damn, damn, damn it! Insane snow," she yelled out to the canyon.

Maybe Hannah was okay. Just lost somewhere. That wolf and Reddi would find her.

Another wave of nausea flipped her stomach and vomit filled her throat, without warning. She spat it out weakly and wiped her chin. She sputtered and her jacket stained.

Dizzy, she rolled over. She felt her face sink down, pushing into the snow. Her forehead felt soft and cool at first. Then the snow compressed, and her head became encased in the dark. Suddenly she couldn't breath.

Jesus, she was suffocating!

She struggled to move her arms and free herself. The deep snow was like quicksand. Every time she pushed, she sank in more. She started panicking, wedged downhill and sinking. She pulled off her mittens and rolled over in her puke. Her feet were pinned into her skis, and she couldn't stand.

Then the image came again. Hannah, and now Wolfie too, drowning in the snow. Their light being sucked into the ice. She convulsed but nothing was left.

She swore and shook and finally fought her way to her feet. *Stupid, stupid, stupid.* Against her perfect logic, and in spite of her trembling fear, she started stomping uphill after Reddi.

***

Without slowing, Reddi unzipped a small pouch she had strapped on her side. She grabbed her yellow beacon and flipped it into search mode. *Come on little Pieps, find my sister.* It blinked at her, searching.

She shoved it back in the pouch and surged forward, angry at the burning in her thighs. She stole glimpses of the cliffs above, scanning for more avalanche signs. The snow underfoot was the hard base layer, compacted chunks left after the top layer slid. She fought over the uneven surface until she reached the spot she last saw Hannah and Wolfie. This looked right. She jammed one of her poles in between chunks of snow.

A faint voice called out behind her. "What can I do to help?" She saw Maxine, gamely trying to catch up. She didn't look too good, but she was trying. Reddi felt her breath catch. Her emotions surged. Maxine cared for Hannah.

But they had to hurry. Without slowing, she called back. "Follow me. Starting from here, I'm going to walk a grid with lines about fifty yards apart. I'll work my way down through all the deposition. I've got to find her beacon and . . ." Suddenly Reddi's beacon started beeping.

"Got her!" Reddi stopped and pulled her beacon from the pouch. "She's fifty yards away. Back toward you . . . . Wait, that doesn't make sense."

Reddi's face fell. "Damn, it's you," she said quietly. She turned and yelled. "Maxine, find the side switch on your beacon and slide it off of transmit and into search mode."

She pocketed her beacon and looked back. Maxine had pushed her goggles up on her head and was struggling with the beacon harness. Then she began yanking off her mittens.

"Two minutes," Reddi called. "That's how long she has been buried. We've got to find her fast. Maxine, you find transmit mode?"

"Transmit mode. Got it." She saw Maxine gathering her gear and pushing uphill.

She was about seventy-five yards ahead of Maxine. "Hurry up here, and I'll tell you what to do."

Reddi studied the scene. About fifty yards below, the scraped layer of snow transitioned to a pile. Twisted and chunky, compressed and hard, it was the upper edge of the slide deposition zone. It continued another one hundred fifty yards to the creek. That was where the avalanche slowed down, piled up, and stopped. Several huge boulders, the size of small houses, marked the edges of the frozen creek. Big and dark, they had white caps from the fallen snow and piles of chunky deposition at their bases. The very center of the run-out crossed the creek and came to a rest near the bottom of the opposite upslope.

Reddi realized the deposition was quickly setting up and hardening like frozen cement. It would become a dense morgue. She skied down fifty yards, stopped, and planted her skis in an X at the point she would begin her search grid.

"Three minutes," she called, fighting to keep her voice calm, focusing on her training, pushing away images of Hannah suffering.

"Maxine, when you get up here take off your skis and walk." She scanned the surface for any little sign of a glove, wool hat, ski tip—anything. Nothing from Hannah nor Wolfie was visible.

As Reddi scrambled over the chunky deposition, beacon in her front harness, she thought about the situation. Hannah had a tracking beacon with fresh batteries. And, she had an Avalung. She was so glad the rep comped her that new model. But was Hannah able to pull its snorkel mouthpiece into her mouth? So she would have oxygen and the carbon dioxide wouldn't build up? *She hoped so.*

She made a turn, following her mental grid. She saw Maxine arrive at the edge of the deposition zone, the left flank going downhill, and take off her skis. She crossed them like Reddi. She extended her shovel handle, carrying it in one hand, poles in the other. *She's copying me. Smart girl.* Reddi was walking downhill along the opposite side of the deposition zone. Maxine tried running across the deposition toward Reddi, angling downhill. She slid and fell on the hard, lumpy surface. She picked herself up, and resorted to a fast walk. Reddi saw the rapid puffs of her breaths.

As Maxine approached, Reddi updated her. "Four minutes. Hannah has an Avalung, so hopefully she put the mouthpiece in and is breathing. At this point, after four minutes . . . ." She stopped, not wanting to finish the part about brain damage. "At this point, we're counting on an air pocket."

"Tell me what to do."

"Your beacon's in the search position?"

"Yes, I slid that switch on top."

"Okay, Wolfie doesn't have a beacon. So if we get a signal, we'll know it's Hannah. I want you to walk below me, back and forth on this rough crap, starting at the creek and working your way up. Across the full width, come up twenty-five yards, then across again, all the way up to my crossed skis. Go as fast as you can. Got it?"

Maxine moved her hand back and forth in the air. "Like a big square S shape, back and forth, right?"

"You got it. Scan the surface looking for clothing, a glove, a ski or pole, anything. Okay?"

"I'm on it."

"We're hoping you spot something closer to the surface. Hannah knows to swim to the top while the avalanche is still moving, so maybe she'll be up near the surface somewhere. And make sure your volume is up high on your search beacon. I'm moving more slowly to scan deeper, while you cover the wider surface with your eyes."

Maxine started scrambling downhill.

"Five minutes," called out Reddi.

Maxine fell and hit hard on the chunks. Reddi glanced over and saw her get up and run again, like a wild woman. She didn't say anything. Her face was cold, tight in concentration, and her mouth was pinched in a hard straight line. She kept reviewing mental checklists.

Reddi strained to hear the beacon. The scattered snow on top made loud crunchy sounds as she walked over the deposition. She felt waves of panic alternating with hope.

"Six minutes." Reddi struggled to push away the guilt that overwhelmed her. *If Hannah doesn't have a pocket of air, if she was knocked unconscious and couldn't get the Avalung in her mouth, she has probably asphyxiated by now.* She gritted her teeth and hummed loudly, trying to block the thought.

"You okay?" yelled Maxine.

"Yes. Nothing yet." She followed with a weak, "Seven minutes."

She made another turn, following her grid, and saw Maxine fall face-first, dropping her beacon, poles, and shovel. "Total yard sale," muttered Reddi cheerlessly. Nothing was funny right now. Maxine forced herself up.

Suddenly Reddi heard beeping. Her heart pounded. She oriented her beacon and followed the arrow. She tried to remain calm and note her location. It had been eight minutes. The display read fifty yards and the arrows pointed to the center of the deposition, downhill toward the creek. She scurried and the beeping got louder. The beacon kept showing she was getting closer. Forty-six, forty-four, forty-two.

"I may have her over here!" Reddi yelled.

Maxine was sixty yards downslope and bent over, near one of the giant boulders. Reddi saw her jam one of her ski poles and then begin scrambling uphill. She had a pole in one hand, shovel in the other. "I'm twenty-five yards away," Reddi called.

Reddi was moving much faster than Maxine. "Six, five, four, three, two. Ah, three, four." Reddi backtracked two yards, and hollered, "Right here, burial depth two yards." She dropped her pack and grabbed her shovel.

Reddi dug frantically. The snow was dense, making the shoveling difficult.

Maxine ran up, panting. "Move about nine feet that way and dig down. We've got to find her soon." She glanced at her watch. "Ten minutes."

They both hacked furiously at the snow. Chips and chunks were flying as the mélange came apart unevenly. Suddenly Reddi struck something. She probed again next to it, not as deep, then scooped out a wedge of snow. Pink. Pink wool.

"Thank God! Hannah's hat!" She surged with relief.

She attacked the dense snow, reinvigorated. Maxine pounded away. Reddi by the head, Maxine near the feet. Some chunks were impossibly large and hard, so they had to work around them. Then Reddi spotted the upturned collar of her sister's ski suit.

"Hannah, hang on, we're coming."

It's been eleven minutes now. Is she dead? Oh please, God.

As she scraped around the pink wool she found more black fabric. What? Gloves. Two of them. "She put her hands in front of her face," Reddi yelled, even though Maxine was right next to her.

"Oh my God. Please be alive. Please. It isn't fair God, not twice. Be alive Hannah."

They saw the hat wiggle.

"Good girl," shouted Reddi. "I think she made an air pocket. Hang on Hannah, we're coming."

They dug ferociously. In another sixty seconds the snow and icy chunks were cleared around the head. Reddi grabbed the remaining large chunk and strained backward with her hips. It released with a crack, sending her flying backward.

Hannah's face appeared, pale and bluish. Her goggles were on and her mouth clenched the Avalung mouthpiece. Her cheeks shivered.

"Hannah!"

Reddi pulled off her gloves, crawled over, and rubbed Hannah's cheeks with her hands. Then she removed the mouthpiece.

"Hannah!"

"Hi. Hi Reddi. I'm, I'm sorry."

"Honey, you are alive! We'll get you out. Breathe slowly."

"Yea, Hannah!" Maxine yelled. "You are a strong girl." Maxine continued to dig, trying to shield Hannah's face from the chips and debris.

"Thank you," she said in a small voice.

"We're going to dig you out. Keep talking to me, okay?"

"Thank you," she repeated. Then she bowed her head, slowly shaking it. "It was so scary under there." She looked up suddenly. "Wait, where's Wolfie? Is she okay?"

"Wolfie will have to wait until we get you out. You are far more important." She paused, realizing how difficult it would be to find Wolfie without a beacon. She had considered it, but a beacon on an animal could lead to it being rescued before a human. "Wolfie will be okay, we'll find her."

Hannah hung her head again.

"Hannah, I want you to stay alert. Tell me what happened, while we dig you out. Look at us and tell us everything. And remember, you're okay now." She felt herself smile for the first time in what seemed a really long while.

Hannah started slowly. Reddi could see she had to concentrate to keep her teeth from chattering. "I, I started up the hill. But then Wolfie decided to follow you." Hannah's eyes moved slowly over toward Maxine. "Sorry, Maxine, it isn't your fault. Wolfie follows Reddi everywhere."

Maxine nodded. She sat down and rested her chin on the end of her shovel, and made a smile. Reddi looked at her and thought, *she is running on fumes.* Rescue adrenaline crash.

"Keep talking. What next?" Reddi returned to chipping away.

"It wasn't the smartest, but I followed Wolfie. I thought I could get her to stop and come with me. Like you said."

"You were trying to help. I understand. What next?" She kept digging.

"The avalanche came. Even before the snow, there was this really strong wind. You know, the snow blast?"

"Yep." *The bookworm probably read one of my mountaineering books,* she thought.

"At the last second I turned downhill, hoping to outrun it. Suddenly I was flying forward, so I tucked and started somersaulting. Then I remembered what you told me."

Reddi was gulping air in between surges of shoveling. She looked at Maxine, who literally was moving in slow motion.

"Keep talking honey. A few more minutes, okay?"

"You told me to swim, remember? To let go of my poles. To, to try to keep my arms in front of me." She took a big gulp of air. "And to get to the surface."

"Good girl. You're right."

"Once the somersaulting slowed I put my hands in front of my face. Then everything stopped. It was really dark. Then I remembered the mouthpiece. I wiggled my hands and got it off my coat. Once I got that in my mouth I was able to think about you guys and Wolfie. And hope."

The pain in Reddi's back was excruciating. "Five more scoops and we got you, sweetie. Help us count them." She and Maxine swung in rhythm. "Five, four, three, two, one . . . ." She dropped her shovel and pulled on a remaining piece of ice. It wouldn't give. Then Maxine put her hands on Reddi's shoulders. Reddi felt the force of her grip yanking her backward. The last chunk snapped, and they tumbled in a pile.

Hannah slowly climbed out of her frozen position. Reddi and Maxine rolled over and crawled on all fours to Hannah. They collapsed together in a dog pile, panting and shaking.

"I feel like a spent rag doll," said Reddi.

"Me too," said Hannah. Reddi pulled her pack over and covered Hannah with a reflective blanket. Her back ached from bending over the short shovel, and her hands were cramping like bird claws from gripping and pounding.

"Reddi, is Hannah okay with you now? If so, I want to check something by that big rock." Maxine rolled over and slowly crawled to her feet.

"Like what?"

"Maybe some fur in the snow. I was starting to dig there when you found Hannah. I stuck a pole there."

"Wolfie. Wolfie," whimpered Hannah, in a small voice. "Oh, please Maxine, can you find Wolfie?"

"We're good here, Maxine. I'll call search and rescue. And then I'll move Hannah into those trees. But if you think you saw Wolfie, please try."

Hannah's teeth chattered as she begged, "P-P-Please rescue Wolfie."

"I'll try, honey. Reddi, you're sure it's okay if I leave?" Reddi saw exhaustion on Maxine's face, her skin dry and chalky. But her dark eyes shone with a freakish intensity.

"We're fine here, now."

"Okay." Maxine grabbed her shovel and pack, then started running down the uneven slope.

It took ten minutes to check out Hannah and walk her up to a grove of aspen. Reddi was thrilled that she seemed only bruised and shaken, and without any broken limbs.

Reddi scraped the snow off some logs and fashioned a makeshift shelter with branches. She draped a second emergency blanket over it.

Reddi sat next to Hannah and hugged her, rubbed her skin, and gave her water and snacks.

Then they heard Maxine, far below. "I see her!"

Hannah raised her head off Reddi's shoulder. "Wolfie! Please go help Maxine rescue Wolfie."

Reddi kept holding Hannah. "Let's make sure you're okay, first."

Maxine called out again. "She looks good. Air pocket."

Hannah wiggled herself away from Reddi and stood up. "Yea, Maxine! Get Wolfie. Please." Hannah waved both arms over her head at Maxine.

"Okay, okay. If you are sure you are all right."

"I'm positive. I feel good. I won't move. Promise."

"That didn't work last time."

Hannah hung her head.

"It's okay, I didn't mean it like that. Just stay, okay? No matter what?" She put her fist under Hannah's chin.

"Cross my heart." She looked up at Reddi, her face hopeful.

Reddi put on her skis and raced downhill. When she arrived, she saw Maxine pounding at the snow with her shovel. In a chopped-out pocket beside the house-size boulder, a black nose stuck out. Then a pink tongue. She heard whimpering.

"Wolfie!" Reddi pulled her shovel out and dropped down next to Maxine, swinging away. The boulders had slowed the deposition and the snow was softer. Within minutes Wolfie was freed from her snow grave. She stood up, shook herself and flung snow on both of them. Then she leaped over to Reddi, and started dancing around her feet, zigzagging back and forth.

"Being alive is good, isn't it Wolfie?!" Then Wolfie went over to Maxine and nuzzled her.

"Yes, you do owe her, big time," said Reddi.

Reddi packed the shovels and skis and started walking uphill. Wolfie led the way, still prancing. It made Reddi realize how tired she felt. Then she thought of Maxine. She waited for her to catch up, then put her hand on her shoulder.

"I'm so glad you came back to help. I didn't expect that."

"I had no choice. I got sick thinking of Hannah being buried." Maxine leaned over, sucking air.

"How do you feel now?"

"Okay. I can make it."

"No, I mean . . . like your heart. You should feel really good. You helped save my sister's life."

Maxine looked up and said quietly, "It's strange, almost euphoric. Unlike anything before."

Reddi took Maxine by both of her shoulders. "Thank you for bringing back Wolfie. I know it's terrible to think of a dog when there are people at stake, but I couldn't help it. It would have been horrible to lose her like that."

"You saved my life. Not only that, you risked your life for me."

"I shouldn't have brought everyone up here. It was on me."

"You are such a good person," Maxine said, tears streaking her cheeks.

"Helping you was the right thing, until Wolfie . . . ." She didn't finish the thought.

Maxine kissed Reddi, pressing her face to hers, as tears mixed in. They clung to each other, exhausted.

Then Reddi squeezed Maxine so hard her back popped.

"I'm so sorry," Reddi said, and they both laughed. Maxine gently wiped her tears off Reddi's cheek.

The rumble of a snow cat coming up the valley interrupted them.

"I'll bet that's Will Masterson, the sheriff. He runs search and rescue. When I called he said they'd be rushing out."

"Wait," said Maxine, still holding Reddi's coat. "Before they get here." Their faces were close.

"You are the most selfless and brave person I have ever met," whispered Maxine. "I owe you my life. I will do anything for you."

✳✳✳

The inside cab of the giant red snowcat felt warm and safe. Reddi was relieved to get Hannah, Maxine, and Wolfie inside, away from the extremes. As they ate, Maxine kept Hannah talking and covered in blankets. Reddi watched the Sheriff and several recue team members looking over the site, from the crown to the deposition.

Once the rescue team returned to the Cat, Reddi rode with the sheriff on his snowmobile. Will Masterson had been the sheriff for many years, and was respected by the townspeople. Famous for his refusal to prosecute marijuana offenders, he was even better respected for his search and rescue operations. It was a challenge with constrained resources for him to keep up with a town full of extreme athletes constantly pushing the boundaries.

As they rode on the snowmobile, they talked in bursts, whenever he cut back on the throttle and the loud revving dropped.

"Will, I didn't want to say it in front of Hannah, but I swear I heard a couple of explosions before the slide. At first I thought it was a tree limb or echo from the ski area blasting. But then the fracture opened up, and everything started sliding. Something had to make that slope move."

He nodded. "Normally I'd be lecturing you on the dangers of Bear Creek. But we found something weird up at the top of the slide."

"Like what?"

"Off the record, Reddi, I found ski tracks and two small craters at the fracture line. You're right, it looked like small explosives created the slide."

"Explosives? Could the ski patrol be working here?"

"We are way beyond the boundaries for them. This is Forest Service land. No one blasts here, not even my group."

"You know, after the slide, when we were in search mode, I thought I saw something moving through the trees up high."

"We saw tracks up there. They had to be from this morning. I could see why someone might go off the main road to go up there to ski first tracks. But to blast it? Doesn't make sense, especially that low on the mountain. That's a run out zone, not some high traverse. And why would someone blast when you were clearly down below?"

"I don't know, it's crazy."

The snowmobile edged around a curve, then approached an ice bridge over a frozen side creek. Masterson crossed and then stopped, waiting for the snowcat. He turned his head to Reddi.

"It makes me think, is it possible that someone is out to get you all?"

28

SATURDAY, JANUARY 11ᵀᴴ

Alpha hissed in frustration. "Your avalanche missed them both?" Fanachi calmly spoke into the encrypted phone. "No. Only one showed up, the girl, Maxine."

"But you proceeded anyway?"

Fanachi let him vent. He waited a measure before his reply.

"These projects are difficult to line up. We thought getting one of the two would be worth it." Fanachi carefully clipped another fingernail with his Swiss manicure scissors.

"Now Maxine is wondering who is trying to kill her. What about the police?"

Fanachi could hear him rapping something nervously on his desk, probably his pen or mouse.

"It's a small town way up in the mountains. These avalanches happen all the time up there. The local cops are not a factor." He snipped another nail.

"What if they talk to San Francisco and put it together with the bike accident? Or link it to the other ones? This reporter Barko of the *National Times Journal* is sniffing around like a bitch in heat."

"They have no evidence. They've got nothing on my people. Relax." He pushed back on a cuticle.

"I will not relax. I want professional results, not some idiotic comedy of errors. How dare you try to extort me to do cyber crime when you can't even perform like a man."

Fanachi could feel the back of his neck start to heat up. "We'll get them. All things in time. I did not commit to a specific calendar." He put the scissors down as his jaw tightened.

"I am not paying for your botched efforts. If you can't do this, maybe I need to find someone qualified, not the clowns working for you."

"I don't like your tone."

"I don't give a damn! I'm not letting you play me any more." Alpha's screams vibrated the phone. "Fix the goddamn problem, you incompetent greaseball!"

Fanachi flared. "Now you're being insulting. Okay, we'll drop the two targets with a silencer and bullets through their brains. Execution style."

"No, you fool, it has to look like an accident. We've talked about this."

Fanachi was pacing now. "You want an instant accident? Then I'll have them disappear. People will ask a lot of questions. They'll look for motives. Some detective will make a life career out of finding the do-gooders. But they'll never connect it to me. Just you."

"No, don't do that. The cops will swarm everywhere. The prize won't . . . ."

"Watch me."

"Don't do it. Damn you, Fanachi!"

Fanachi heard the sound of Alpha's phone whistling through the air before the line went dead.

***

Reddi had taken a long hot shower and her crib was steamed up. She rocked by the glowing gas stove wrapped in a thick robe, soft slippers, and a shearling blanket.

"Wolfie, I think we need some help. Someone who deals with bad guys." She picked up her phone and saw Wolfie following her every move.

"Maybe Trig. I know he handles the worst types of situations. Navy SEAL stuff. He can probably do anything, really. I'd feel safer if he was involved. Okay?"

Wolfie cocked her head and Reddi rubbed her fingers into the thick fur behind her ears. Then she dialed Lionel.

"Hi Lionel. It's me. Still stuck in Denver?"

"Reddi. Hey, hey sweetie. I heard from Maxine. You're a hero. Avalanche Queen."

"Yeah, right. When are you coming?"

"Hope to fly out in a few hours. But the airport is jammed with stranded travelers all fighting to get the same seats."

"Do what you can, please. It's . . . it's been intense. I am thrashed."

"Seriously, Maxine thinks you are a star. I can't tell you how much you frigging impressed her."

"Me? I shouldn't have taken them up there in the first place."

"Maxine doesn't praise people often, believe me. You are in very elite company."

"At least there is one good outcome from that total disaster of an adventure." Reddi's voice lowered and cracked. "I was so afraid of losing Hannah. Oh God." She breathed in short, shaky pulls.

"But Hannah is okay, right? And she came on vacation to ski with you. You can't beat yourself up, babe."

Reddi choked. "Yes, she's fine." She added quietly, "Sorry, now that I get to talk to you I'm a mess."

"It's okay. You deserve to let your feelings out."

"It was scary. And I almost lost Wolfie too. Maxine found her."

"She did? I didn't hear that. I want you to tell me everything, in person. I feel really bad about missing it."

Reddi shook her head, suddenly angered. "Why, so you could have been buried too? Missed your chance?"

"No—I feel responsible. I told you I thought the trip was a good idea. And then I wasn't there to help. Instead I was stuck here in the airport and worthless . . . . But you carried the day, and everyone is very impressed and thankful."

"That's nice of you to say." Reddi brightened.

"I'm serious. And I want to help you, in any way."

"Lionel, there is something about the avalanche. I'm not trying to make excuses. But I think there might be a problem."

"Tell me."

"Sheriff Masterson believes two explosives set this off, and not the kind used by ski patrol. Basically he thinks someone purposefully started that avalanche."

"What?! That's insane. The avalanche nearly killed you guys."

"Yeah, it's a creepy thought."

"Has that happened before?"

"Slides? Yes. But intentionally setting slides to hurt people? No. In fact the sheriff was asking me if there was someone out to get us."

"Oh shit. Not good."

"I know."

"Can he do anything to find these guys?"

"He can help locally, but it is a small department. If this is someone from outside of Telluride, he won't be able to do much."

"Outside of Telluride? Why does he assume that?"

"Well, Telluride has barely two thousand full-time residents, but more than one hundred thousand visitors each year. And with Maxine being from out of town, it's just the odds."

"Got it. That sucks."

"I have an idea. But it may cost some money."

"Sure. What is it, honey?"

"Do you remember just after we met, when we had dinner the first time, at the Thai place?"

"Of course."

"You met a guy that night who might be able to help. Trig Garcia."

"Huh? Oh, that tough-looking dark guy who almost beat the crap out of me for hugging you?"

"Trig would not do that."

"It looked like he could have. You told me he was a family friend and former SEAL."

"That's right."

"How could he help?"

"Well, after SEAL duty he worked for the cyber security team at Fort Meade in Maryland. Now he works for Ancill, some private security contractor. I think he could help track people down. I'm sure he'll offer to do it for free, but . . . ."

"The cost is not what I'm worried about, Reddi. I just want the right people to help us stop these attacks."

"Although most of Trig's work is overseas, I bet he could help here."

"I'm not sure this is soldier-of-fortune stuff. Let me think about it. And keep this extremely confidential, okay sweetie?"

"You got it boss." She suddenly felt odd about bringing Lionel and Trig together. But they were both such important guys in her life.

"Thanks, hon. I can't wait to see you. I'll call once I'm confirmed on the flight."

***

As Lionel looked out the airplane window the cobalt blue sky was so clear it was hard to imagine a storm had recently dominated the area. Mount Wilson sparkled in cinematic grandeur, a symmetrical diamond-shaped peak. Below, the snow-covered mesa glared like a second sun, and the cut of the runway shimmered.

Minutes later the loud twin-engine plane landed with a bump, and taxied within fifty feet of the terminal building.

As he walked toward the terminal Lionel saw his reflection in the doorway. He ran his fingers though his hair in anticipation. Inside the building he saw Reddi and lit up. She ran to him, her white jeans gliding with grace. Her sweater and long French braid bounced as she hurried. Without a word they began kissing.

Eventually they pulled apart. "I can't wait to spend some time together," he said.

"Finally!" she answered.

Just then Maxine came through the door, all in black, looking over her tortoiseshell sunglasses, phone to her ear. She hung up and greeted Lionel.

"Evidently Blaine has Axlewright's private jet and will be landing in a few minutes. He'd like to see our bottling plant, so if you don't mind, let's wait and take him through."

Lionel groaned inwardly. "Sure, I understand. He's been talking about this trip for a while."

"He has," responded Maxine, in a resigned tone. She turned to Reddi. "Sorry about the interruption, superstar."

Lionel saw the disappointment on Reddi's face.

"This gives me a chance to tell Lionel firsthand what a hero you are. Let's grab a seat so I can tell this story right." Lionel could see Maxine's excitement as she took Reddi's arm.

Lionel interrupted. "Not to be a killjoy. But Reddi called and told me Sheriff Masterson now thinks this was intentional. Set off by someone with explosives."

Maxine's eyes widened. "This was criminal? Not a random mountain avalanche?"

Reddi shook her head. "I made a recommendation to Lionel to hire a private investigator I know, a former Navy SEAL named Trig Garcia."

Maxine looked at Lionel. "Well?"

"I'm thinking about it. He sounds a little more like a special ops contractor than a private investigator. No offense, but I don't know if he is the right guy."

Maxine turned. "Lionel, we are in this woman's hometown, in her environment. If she knows the right guy to hire, then that is the right guy to hire. Now. Before whoever it is does something else, damn it."

Lionel had seen that look on Maxine's face before. The arched eyebrows, the set jaw. "You're right. Uh, Reddi, can you give me Trig's number?"

"It's probably best he calls you."

"Anytime. ASAP, please."

Twenty minutes later the Gulfstream 150 arrived. Blaine deplaned and walked into the building with his big frame swaggering in a rawhide jacket, cheerfully calling out their names in a loud voice. A white cowboy hat sat atop his head. Orange aviator glasses, red gingham shirt, and shiny new cowboy boots completed his new look. He laughed and greeted everyone with hugs.

"Business first, then pleasure. Can we visit the bottling plant pronto?"

"Sure," answered Lionel. "It's on the way into town in the valley."

"I rented that mondo red pickup over there," he said pointing to a shiny 4WD Escalade truck. "Maxine, why don't we ride together?"

Minutes later, Blaine raced off full throttle, the oversized truck tires spitting snow. Behind them Reddi and Lionel carefully navigated the switchbacks down the mesa to the valley floor below.

Lionel called Hugo, the Juice Genius.

"I realize this is a Saturday and I apologize for the interruption, but any chance you could give an unscheduled tour to Blaine Latrell, our VC from Axlewright?"

"Sadly I must report, Lionel, that a of couple guys on the production team and I are spending our Saturday . . . at the plant. We'd be happy to take a break and switch to tour guide impresario mode."

"You are amazing, good sir." He paused. "A bit of warning. Blaine flew in on the corporate jet. He's all hyped up, and dressed like he's headed to a dude ranch."

Hugo laughed. "I'll restrain myself from any commentary on his insufferable ways."

Fifteen minutes later the vehicles pulled up at the bottling plant, housed in two faded brick warehouses. At the top of each building the Double Vision logo in red and gold was prominently displayed, surrounded by industrial iron and heavy-duty timbers. The facility looked like it had been there for years.

Hugo and several plant people greeted Blaine outside.

"Welcome to our rapidly expanding energy drink epicenter," Hugo beamed.

"It certainly has that ghost town rustic look," observed Blaine.

"From ghost town to boom town," countered Hugo. "Let's go inside and you'll see the centuries leap forward with our modern technology and shining stainless steel." As they walked toward the entrance, Blaine pulled Lionel aside.

"Lionel, I heard from Maxine about the avalanche. I can't believe you weren't there when they went backcountry."

What a rude thing to say, thought Lionel. "Yeah, I was snowed in," he replied, nonchalantly.

"But you were so close in Denver. You probably feel rotten about the whole mishap."

"I do, you're right." Lionel turned and walked though the door, trying to shrug off the jabs. He focused on Hugo.

"Normally it is much louder, but the line isn't running on this particular Saturday," explained Hugo, as they walked the production floor. Blaine followed along for a few minutes. Then, as Hugo described the storage tanks, Blaine turned to Maxine and Lionel.

"This is a gorgeous setting, but getting all this equipment up here and servicing it must be expensive."

"Not as bad as you'd think," replied Lionel.

"But don't you have to truck everything out of here, all that product? Aren't the roads closed by avalanches and snowstorms sometimes?"

"Imagine all that Red Bull, five billion cans per year, coming out of Austria and the Swiss Alps," replied Lionel.

"They have economies of scale. Speaking of which, how is Merry Cola?" asked Blaine.

"Contract is all signed, a major accomplishment."

Lionel looked at Hugo, who had stopped talking.

Blaine ignored him. "Are you shipping to their distribution centers yet?"

"Some. The first order was one hundred thousand dollars, and we expect a lot of follow on orders."

"That's peanuts. Do you think those guys are playing you?"

Hugo interrupted. "Excuse me. Are there any questions in the back from our esteemed guest?"

Blaine turned around. "Yes, Hugo. What is the maximum revenue you can pump out of this facility?"

"The maximum revenue? Well sir, that depends upon our pricing, discounts, and the product mix of course. It's not a facilities issue *per se*."

"I'm curious how long this facility will last until you need to build another one, maybe closer to your customers."

"I understand your question, sir. Allow me to answer it in this way. We are very focused on the Big Disrupter Award, of which I'm sure you are aware?"

"Absolutely."

"Excellent. We have two months left to win said award." He smiled at Maxine and Lionel. "And we are producing an abundance of product which is inventoried in ancillary warehouses. This facility will manufacture enough product to win that award. That, sir, is the production objective with which I am most concerned."

"Great answer," Lionel enthused, clapping his hands. "With that, we'll let you all get back on task."

As they walked out to their trucks, Lionel wondered what Blaine really had in mind for this trip to Telluride.

***

Reddi drove her old Jeep along the San Miguel River toward town. Lionel peppered her with questions about the freestyle tour, the avalanche, and her family. His curiosity fed her enthusiasm. His single-minded focus kept Reddi talking the entire drive. Suddenly they were stopped in front of Lionel's apartment, the engine running.

"You're coming in, aren't you?" Lionel asked.

"Should I?"

"Absolutely. Maxine can entertain Blaine. Right now is our time." Lionel put his hand on her knee. "We've barely gotten started."

"Good, I wasn't sure." Reddi smiled and shut off the Jeep. Lionel grabbed his bags out of the back.

She looked up at the historic brick building, with tall windows and stone ledges. Reddi loved the views he had from his apartment on the top floor. She climbed the stairs in anticipation as Lionel raced ahead, banging his bags against the stairwells.

Once inside, Lionel dropped his bags. Reddi was drawn to the glow coming through the windows. The pink and purple sunset reflected off the snow-capped peaks in a spectacular show. Lionel followed her to admire the view, then pulled her into an embrace.

He was tantalizingly slow as he undid every button and snap, gently slipping clothes off her, following the bare skin with nibbling kisses. His warm breath tingled her skin. As his fingertips stroked and lingered she shuddered in anticipation. By the time the last piece of clothing dropped she wanted to burst. She twirled around the room, with nothing on other than her long braid trailing down her back. He never took his eyes off her. Then he was naked and his fingers explored her contours. She let him take the lead. She thought about closing the blinds, but didn't want to break the spell. Besides, Lionel seemed to like being naked and daring three stories above town. As they cavorted in athletic positions around the room, she moaned and shrieked, and made him groan. Finally, she felt a chill through the windows, and led him under the covers on the bed.

Afterwards they lay spent. Reddi leaned back against the pillows trying to get comfortable under the fluffy down comforter. She wanted to snuggle and talk more, like they had in the Jeep ride into town. But Lionel was sound asleep.

She stared out toward the impossibly close mountains, as if they held an answer for her. She felt happy, but not at home. *It was so comfortable having Lionel's smell surround her. She loved being with him. But he felt like a passing visitor in her life. A wonderful guest who breezed in and disappeared. Not someone who would stay forever.* She looked over at him. The day replayed in her mind. *Being with Maxine felt a little strange after he arrived. Something changed. But she is so supportive of me.* She drifted and worried about the avalanche. *Would Trig be able to help solve this mystery?*

***

Blaine suggested they skip dinner and instead check out the bar scene. Maxine texted Lionel, but he never responded. She hesitantly climbed in the high cab. Blaine drove around Telluride's icy streets like a cowboy just arrived to town.

He parked the red truck next to a high snowbank. As they walked over packed snow toward the Roma Saloon, Blaine's new cowboy boots slid and he wiped out, scattering his hat and sunglasses. Maxine managed not to laugh.

Inside, the bar was abuzz with young faces three deep, and crowded tables erupted in loud laughter and wild antics. Girls danced in the aisles and guys jumped from chairs showing off moves from their day. Layers of fluffy down, colorful fleece, and long flowing hats bulged from the wall hooks. Loud music boomed from the back room. People leaned within inches of one another, straining to be heard.

Blaine and Maxine lucked into a small table in the far corner. Blaine had the waitress bring three double scotches and a glass of wine for Maxine. Maxine was still sipping her wine when Blaine turned to his third scotch.

They nearly yelled in order to hear each other.

"Maxine, do you know why Telluride is like Las Vegas?"

"Like? I can't imagine two more different places."

"Because what happens here stays here. We're way up in the mountains, away from the world."

"Tell me about it. I'm the one who nearly left this world permanently in an avalanche." She took another sip of her wine.

"Exactly. It's a place of extremes. Danger and fun. You had the danger. Now you deserve the fun." He looked across the table into her eyes.

"Blaine, think you should ease back on that whiskey?" She looked at the glasses on the table.

"It's smooth stuff." He picked up his glass and examined it, swirling the amber liquid over the ice cubes.

"Promise me you won't drive."

"Oh, that's no problem."

She saw him stare at a couple grinding on the dance floor. He finished the scotch with a wince, slammed the heavy glass down, and looked at Maxine from under the brim of his cowboy hat.

"Maxine, it's not like we haven't fucked before, you know."

She stared at him silently before glancing calmly at the surrounding tables. If anyone heard over the loud music, which was very unlikely, they weren't reacting.

"You are drunk. And you're getting rude and obnoxious. I'm going to leave if you continue."

He leaned forward. "I'm sorry." He put his finger to his lips. "Shhh. Our little secret." He glanced sideways. "Is Lionel here?"

"Look, the fact that we had a one-night stand back at McKinsey is no big deal. We were consenting adults. It's over and done with. But gentlemen don't go bragging about their private affairs publicly. Understand?" She glared as he looked away.

Eventually he broke their silence. "I'm sorry. Look, I haven't bragged about that. But I want things to change. With us. I believed in you and invested in DV and . . . I don't know." He fluttered a hand vaguely.

"That was smart. So is Jacob Havermyer, your fellow investor."

"Yeah? Well, a lot of people in the valley think I was fooled. They call the deal the twenty-four-hour pregnancy."

"What? I don't get it."

"It doesn't matter. An expression that jerk Hank Welcher was using. Trying to humiliate my boss by saying he got pregnant in a deal with no foreplay, no taste test, just a twenty-four-hour ultimatum from Havermyer. An immaculate conception."

"That's competitive bravado. He's jealous." She was staying out of that. It wasn't smart to get caught in a pissing match between the VCs, she thought.

Blaine yelled over the music. "Lionel ran Double Vision into the ground until you and me and Jacob saved him. He was out of cash."

"Wait a minute. He started Double Vision, poured all of his money—several million—into it. And built a recognized brand with forty million in sales. That's impressive."

"But he is an entrepreneur. He gets things started, but isn't the right one to continue. You are."

So that's where this is going. "We complement each other. It's a team effort."

The music blared and Blaine waited. Then he leaned forward. "Look Maxine, people are talking."

His vagueness was starting to annoy her. "What exactly about? And who? And why should I care?"

"I don't want to say, nor honor their catty remarks by repeating them. But I think you need to prove yourself as CEO. Alone. Lionel nearly went bankrupt and you need to distance yourself from that."

"Damn it Blaine, we're killing ourselves, literally, to win the Big. Hell, isn't that enough?"

"Between you and me? No." He slurped an ice cube out of the drained scotch, then lined up the three glasses between them.

"The word in the VC community, and I have never repeated this, is that you and Havermyer are having an affair."

"What!?" She flushed with anger. Then a creepy chill came over her. It was unnerving.

"And," he continued, "That Lionel misled you all about the state of his finances. Hank Welcher says he could have had ninety percent of the company for ten million dollars the night the Big Disrupter was announced, but turned it down."

"That's bullshit. He's trying to undermine us so he can win the Big."

"Maxine, I'm trying to help you."

"By buying into slanderous rumors and splitting up the team that is building the company?"

"By separating the professional CEO, you, from the entrepreneur who is holding you back."

"Why would getting rid of Lionel help us?"

"You'd demonstrate your strength alone. Otherwise there always will be questions."

"Blaine, look at me. Do you seriously believe I'm having an affair with Havermyer? And that I'd sleep with him to become the CEO and get his investment money?"

His cowboy hat swung side to side. "No."

"Did I offer you sex to invest?" She grabbed his jacket, twisting it with her hands.

"Come on, Maxine."

"Answer!" She pulled him, leaning into his big face.

"Of course not."

"On that McKinsey trip in London, by the Tower Bridge. Years ago. That night at the hotel. Did I hand you a fucking bill afterward? Or is that what you're telling all your VC friends?"

She released him, sitting back in disgust.

Blaine looked down, the hat shading his eyes. "That was one night. And I have not told anyone. Not a soul."

"So why am I suddenly being accused of sleeping my way to the top?"

He looked away.

"Is someone putting you up to this? Tell me!" She pushed aside the empty glasses that sat between, leaning forward.

Their faces were locked. "This deal has to hit for me, Maxine, or I'm fired from Axlewright. And probably washed right out of the valley. Back to Des Moines."

"I can help you with that. But back off of Lionel. I need him. *We* need him, to win the Big. I'm serious." She gave his jacket one last shake.

Maxine was so furious she trembled. She rose and shoved out the swinging doors of the saloon without looking back.

Blaine sat stunned. He hunched over and rubbed his temples in a slow massage, his big hands covering his eyes. He brushed the corners softly.

With a sigh he pulled out his phone. Above the din of the bar he yelled, "Hello, Jake? Jake the Rake? This is Blaine. Yeah, I'm in town now, at the Roma Saloon. I want to talk about that job I have for you. Yeah. No, not here. We need to meet somewhere private."

29

SUNDAY, JANUARY 12TH

Lionel woke up to his phone vibrating on the bedside table. He didn't recognize the number. "Lionel Lane."

"Mr. Lane, sorry to bother you early, sir. This is Trig Garcia."

Lionel rubbed his head. "Wow, that was quick."

"My apologies, sir. I have a limited window. Is this a good time to talk, or should I call another time?"

"No, thanks. Appreciate your being so responsive." He sat up and pulled the comforter around him. Reddi must have called him last night. He took a deep breath.

"Yeah, this is a fine time." He glanced over at Reddi, still sleeping. He rolled out of bed to pull on some pants.

"You know about the avalanche?"

"Affirmative. Reddi said Sheriff Masterson suspects someone threw some charges to set it off intentionally."

"Right." Direct to the point, Lionel thought. He started walking downstairs to the kitchen.

"Telluride seems an ideal place to hire someone with knowledge of backcountry skiing and avalanches."

"True, could have been a local operator. But here is the bigger picture. In San Francisco, about two months ago, I was hit on my bike late at night by a hit-and-run driver. The cops have no suspects. A month later, near the end of October, Jan Swenson, a fellow CEO of another company in the Big Disrupter competition, drowned mysteriously while kayaking."

"Still unsolved?"

"Yeah. Like us, her company was also a top contender for the Big, so it made me wonder. Wait, you know about the Big, right?"

"I do. I also read about the other CEO, Raj Singh, dying of a heart attack."

"Right. Raj started Step-by-Step Clothing. I can't be sure the deaths are related, but after this avalanche, I'm obviously worried about Maxine and Reddi."

"Sir, unfortunately you appear to be at the top of the list of targets."

Lionel took a breath. "Probably. And if this is related to the Big, then we're looking at a hairy two months."

"Understood."

"Trig, candidly, can you handle this? All the necessary travel and time? I'm not looking for a part-time commitment."

"That is not a problem, sir."

"So you have extensive electronics and computer expertise?"

"Yes sir, those are my specialties. Software, Internet, security, counter intelligence. And deployment of force as needed."

"Nothing illegal, of course," said Lionel. "You'll have to coordinate with Sheriff Masterson and Inspector Chang of the SFPD. But I can't wait on their resource availability. The stakes are huge."

"Certainly. No problem."

"How do we proceed?"

"A standard engagement letter. I'll email it now."

"Then what?"

"I'll do everything I can remotely. I'll need access to your current computer systems. And what can't be done remotely, I'll do in person."

"Why our computers?"

"In Maxine's first visit to Telluride someone managed to prepare and lay an elaborate trap deep in a canyon. Hacking online schedules or scanning emails is a great way to acquire the necessary advance intelligence."

"Holy shit. So they may be spying on us internally?"

"It's a good place to start looking, sir."

"I'll get you full access right away. And Trig, thank you. I realize this is a favor because of your relationship with Reddi."

"I've known her family since we were kids. Great people. A privilege to serve them, and you too, sir."

"Thanks, Trig. And please, it's Lionel."

As he hung up, Lionel felt a surge of relief. *We're finally doing something.*

He walked over to the kitchen counter and quietly started a pot of coffee. His phone buzzed and he groaned. He had hoped to go back and snuggle with Reddi, but it was Leah Barko calling. *How did she find out so fast?* He answered and she launched in immediately.

"Let me get this straight. You were supposed to be there, along with Maxine, but you were stuck in the Denver airport?" Leah asked.

"It was a major blizzard. Shut the airports down all over the state."

"And this extreme skier of yours rescued Maxine, and then they dug out her little sister?"

"They both would be buried without Reddi. Dead."

"Incredible. So level with me. Accidental or intentional?"

"Are we off the record? I don't want this conversation showing up in the *National Times Journal* or your blog tomorrow."

"For now, yes."

Lionel took a deep breath. "The local sheriff and Reddi are both very suspicious."

"I knew it. If you had been there, maybe Reddi couldn't have rescued you both. Seriously, you and Maxine could have died."

"I hear you."

"What's it going to take before you advise Jules Longsworth to stop this contest until they can make sure someone isn't trying to kill off all the leading contestants?"

"What? I don't think that could happen. The front-runners would claim gamesmanship."

"You better do something, Lionel. This is insane."

"We hired a private investigator. To help out the local sheriff, and supplement whatever Inspector Chang is doing in the City."

"Or not doing, you mean."

"The investigator's name is Trig Garcia. He'll also provide our people with additional personal security. Look, I'll let you know whatever Trig learns. But until then, how about a little love about Reddi's heroic rescue?"

"The redheaded snow bunny?"

"Leah, her mother died of cancer when she was nineteen. She dropped out of Boulder to help take care of her little sister and work in her dad's welding shop. Frigging blow torches and sparks and big heavy metal pieces. And she is on her way to the X Games. Give her a little credit."

"Okay, okay. I'll stick with the avalanche rescue angle for now, if you let me know what your new investigator finds out. Deal?"

"Deal."

30

MONDAY, JANUARY 13TH — TUESDAY, JANUARY 14TH

Sheriff Will Masterson answered his phone on the fifth ring.

"Good afternoon, sir, Trig Garcia calling. Is this a good time?"

"Apologies, but do I know you, Mr. Garcia?"

"Not officially, sir. I am a private investigator hired by Reddi Christiansen. I'm in town occasionally, but all my prior work has been in other locations."

"I see. Well, I know Reddi and her family well. Great people."

"Yes, sir."

"Yeah, I have time. I'm sitting here in my office trying to catch up with mounds of paperwork," he said. "This high snow count has resulted in a record number of backcountry accidents and emergency responses." He sighed. "Anyway, go ahead."

"Yes, sir. Reddi is being sponsored by Double Vision, the beverage company, as an extreme athlete. They have hired me to help out with an investigation involving Reddi and their CEO, Maxine Gold."

"The avalanche in Bear Creek."

"Yes, sir."

"What can I do for you?"

"We're concerned that this accident may be related to other incidents outside of your jurisdiction. We realize you are stretched for resources, sir, so I'd like to help."

"How so?"

"Sir, Double Vision is competing for a huge award called the Big Disrupter. The prize is one billion dollars. Two other CEOs in that contest have died in recent accidents. I'm looking for connections, sir."

"Hmm. You have a service background, young man? All the *'sirs,'* you know."

"Navy, sir."

"And you know Reddi?"

"Reddi's dad and mine go way back to Austin, sir, before they came to Telluride. She and I met as kids."

"Oh, now I know you. You're a Navy SEAL, right?"

"Guilty as charged, sir. Former Navy SEAL."

"Now I understand." Trig heard him typing for a moment. "Here we go. There are three rental shops in town that provide alpine touring gear for the backcountry. I checked the records of the people who had rented for that day and the week prior, without finding anyone suspicious."

"Any witnesses in Bear Creek that day, or near the trailhead, who saw anything?"

"We interviewed a few people, but no luck."

"If they didn't rent, and they are from out of town, it could show up as checked baggage."

"Correct. So I checked with the airlines here in Telluride, in Montrose, and in Grand Junction. I reviewed all the passengers who checked skis, which isn't that hard, since they are oversized baggage."

"Anything, sir?"

"I can't say for sure, but there were no obvious matches. I do plan to check Aspen and Durango, also."

"Sir, can I send you a list of people from a Double Vision competitor called BodyHamr? There have been concerns about them."

"I can't get into private vendettas. Tell you what, I'll check on all of the Double Vision people as well as Body Slammers."

"Sir, sorry to interrupt, BodyHamr sir."

Sheriff Masterson paused for a moment. "Okay. Send me that info. And I'll check the Double Vision people too, so I'm not playing favorites."

"One other thing, sir. We have a potential connection with a bike hit-and-run in San Francisco. Someone ran into Lionel Lane, the

Co-CEO of Double Vision. He survived the accident, and believes they were driving an Audi."

"You are thinking it could be the same person?"

"A possibility, sir. Giving you all I have presently."

"Give me your number and I'll call in a couple of days, Trig."

***

Twenty-four hours later Sheriff Masterson called Trig.

"We looked into two guys from BodyHamr who rented Alpine gear. They partied hard until closing at the Loose Moose according to several people. It seems unlikely they could have skied up the canyon at six a.m. and carefully launched explosives."

"Yes sir."

"We ran a check on the other local airports I mentioned. The search came up empty."

"Appreciate that, sir."

"And one more thing. I got a call from an Inspector Chang from the SFPD. He was interested in info on the avalanche, because it involved Double Vision, and maybe that Big Disrupter contest. Evidently that contest has everyone all worked up."

"Yes sir, a billion dollars means a lot to these social entrepreneurs."

"I'll tell you the same thing I told Chang. A guy was flagged in our state highway patrol database. Seems he was going at least one hundred twenty miles per hour outside of Grand Junction two nights before the avalanche. Patrolman was getting coffee in a truck stop and saw some guy fly by. By the time he caught up with him the perp had slowed down to seventy. His car didn't look street legal, so the officer flagged it. Gave him a ticket for eighty-three. Name is Igor Vasilchenko, California license. But otherwise a total mystery man. No record."

"What kind of car, sir?"

"Some unusual euro screamer wagon, called an RS2. An Audi."

***

Alpha stared out the window of his Silicon Valley office as the wind whipped across the rolling hills. The long brown grass was beaten down by the heavy rains. He hadn't spoken with Fanachi since their blow-up, but the topics had swirled in his mind, like the storm outside. He couldn't let Fanachi piss him off. They were already in bed together, and now he realized Fanachi was a beast with his own rules. His money and social hierarchy didn't intimidate Fanachi, as it did with others in his universe. That was a disturbing revelation. He had to adjust.

He lifted his new phone and dialed.

"Fanachi," came the answer.

"It's Alpha."

There was a pause. "Are we going to discuss this like intelligent business people today?" Fanachi asked.

"Yes." Alpha clenched his teeth. "I apologize for our disagreement the other day." There. He said it. He watched the rain pelt his window.

"Apology accepted. I appreciate the call," Fanachi answered.

"First things first. It is true I have relationships with people and companies having considerable intellectual property. However, my access to my clients is not on the table." Alpha braced for Fanachi's response.

"Fair enough. I'm a patient man," came the reply.

Alpha sighed inwardly in relief.

Fanachi continued. "As for the present project, we have a revised plan. However, I think it is time for us to meet and discuss this in person." Then Alpha heard a loud crack, followed by the unmistakable click of balls dropping in pockets. Was he in a pool hall?

"What's that sound? Are you alone?" Alpha questioned. "It sounds like you are playing pool somewhere."

"Excellent deduction. I do have a billiards table. Right here in my den on Telegraph Hill. It's a pleasant villa, perfect for a private conversation. One that we should be having in person."

Alpha shifted in his leather chair. "I appreciate the gracious offer. But I absolutely cannot honor the request. It is too . . . compromising for me to be seen with you, given your background. Especially with all your recent activity on my behalf. I have no interest in allowing the police or FBI an opportunity to put together clues."

"I understand," Fanachi replied. "However, there comes a time in a relationship, especially one like ours, where our mutual abilities need to become clearer." Alpha heard another click, and after a pause, the clunk of a ball drop.

Alpha worried about Fanachi's villa. Was it watched by the FBI? "The phone will work fine."

"As you wish. But I am not interested in a conclusion similar to the last one." More clicks peppered the background.

"Nor I. You mentioned a new plan. Stop playing billiards and tell me what you are thinking," said Alpha, annoyed.

"Very well," Fanachi replied. "We'll enjoy the game together another time." Alpha heard a rapid succession of clicks and clunks of balls shot into pockets.

"We have agreed on a four-hundred-thousand dollar fee if Lionel Lane and Maxine Gold are eliminated. Correct?" Fanachi asked.

"Yes," replied Alpha.

Fanachi continued. "I plan on collecting that sum, by doing a well-executed lover's quarrel."

"What? A lover's quarrel?" Alpha sat up straighter.

"Heat of the moment. Passion. The result of jealousy and anger. In this case, fatal for both of them."

Alpha took several breaths, calming himself. "I don't want the FBI to start a major investigation."

"I understand. They have no reason to do so. And the victims are young social entrepreneurs, not major corporate executives or D.C. politicians who would demand the FBI's attention. We'll continue to make these events perfectly believable." Alpha heard the confidence in Fanachi's voice, and imagined him standing like a Roman general with a cue stick as a sword, overlooking the storm. Except Fanachi was ignoring the fact that he had missed Lionel twice already.

"No intellectual property required from me, right? Just the four hundred K?"

"Correct." Alpha heard the sound of Fanachi sinking heavily into a leather chair.

"And this will look accidental?"

"Yes. So plausible it explains itself. However, I will have to invest more resources to make it happen sooner, as you requested. Consider that a gesture on my part, toward future business."

"That's a good investment. But to be clear, our original cash deal stands. No IP."

"Yes." A match struck, crackling. He heard Fanachi sucking in smoke deliberately.

"And you are confident this will be clean? The headlines will quickly disappear?"

There was a pause as Fanachi exhaled. "The kayak accident and the runner's heart attack were perfect, right?"

"Yes. Those were very good. You earned your money."

"Trust me. A jealous lover's quarrel will be very convincing. And with them gone, you'll get what you want."

The fire of Fanachi's cigarette burned like a long whisper. Alpha grimaced in distaste. He hated working with Fanachi. He didn't trust him. But he was getting the original cash deal he had negotiated, not the IP angle Fanachi had tried. And Double Vision had to be stopped quickly.

***

The Ducati revved as it surged toward the oncoming traffic. At the last minute the motorcycle turned hard right into the parking lot, stopping with a squeal.

Igor cut his engine and looked over the row of bikes. "Hi Dasha. How's the scooter running?"

"Ah, Igor. Hi. Fine, like usual." Dasha was clipping her helmet onto her backpack. Igor could see people bustling to work in the nearby plaza.

"My Ducati is temperamental. I drive my Audi most of the time. That's why you only see my bike here occasionally." He took off his helmet and ran his fingers through his hair.

She nodded.

"You know, my girlfriend has a scooter like yours, in Russia. Moscow."

"Really?" she replied, without much enthusiasm. She started to walk toward her building.

"Yes. Her name is Lilia."

Dasha stopped. "I love that name. That is the name of my little sister. Back home in Dnipropetrovsk."

"What a coincidence. Once I save up more money, I hope my Lilia can come here and join me in the States."

"Oh? What do you do?"

"Programmer. Back-end databases. SQL server. So, how old is your sister?"

"Seventeen. Just entering university."

"An exciting time. So many possibilities."

"Yes. But I miss her. And Lilia is always in trouble with our parents. Sort of rebellious."

He began his carefully prepared invitation, which he had rehearsed repeatedly to sound spontaneous. "Yes, I worry about my Lilia too. So far away. You know, I don't usually have much time at work, but it might be nice to try to laugh a little about families back in Russia and Ukraine. One of my favorite restaurants is nearby, Burma Superstar. Maybe sometime we can grab a quick bite there, for lunch. Talk about our Lilias. Life back home. Something different from work."

He held his breath, waiting for her reply.

"Sure. We could do that sometime."

"Should I text you?"

"Uh, okay."

"If you don't mind, tell me your number. I can remember."

He saw her pause for a moment, considering. Then she told him.

"I won't forget. Anyway, sometime when we aren't too busy."

She headed toward her building. His eyes followed her tight black jacket and jeans as fantasies ran through his head.

31

TUESDAY, JANUARY 21ST

Trig stepped off the elevator at the San Francisco offices of Double Vision. He checked out the card scanner operating the door, and noticed the absence of video cameras. Then he realized the door was unlocked. He walked inside and the busy admin barely paused.

"Trig Garcia, ma'am," he said, as he handed over his business card. "I have an appointment with Dasha Romanyuk."

The admin at the front desk logged him in, called Dasha, then escorted him down the hallway and opened a door.

Way too easy, he thought. He could be anyone and now they'd be in the main computer room. He stepped through the doorway.

The room was a cave—smooth hard floor, no windows, and dim. Rack-mounted servers lined the walls, their green and blue LEDs flickering like a wraparound city nightscape. Three large screens sat atop a tall desk in the center, their glow highlighting Dasha's face. She peered at Trig under her dark bangs. Music played in the background and Trig felt the coolness from the air conditioning.

"Welcome, Trig Garcia." Dasha came around her standing desk and shook Trig's hand. High cheekbones framed her Slavic eyes, an unusual clear amber color that absorbed light, without reflection. Trig felt their intensity pulling him inwards.

He handed her his card. She took it without taking her eyes off him. "So you are Navy SEAL and security expert trained at the Cyber Command in Fort Meade, Maryland."

"Just a consultant now," he responded. "And with your impressive background in engineering at the University of Kiev, I am not surprised you have thoroughly researched me."

"Here I am and this is our computer room." With a dancer's carriage she waved her hand around the room. He noticed the meticulously labeled servers, firewalls, and high-speed fiber optics. Not only an impressive technical education from Ukraine, but she was also well organized. Trig had done his research and Dasha's credentials were impeccable, especially for someone who was only twenty-four.

She pursed her lips. "Can we be direct with each other?"

She stood in front of him in a tight gold sweater and black jeans. Her low black heels added European style, he thought. Unafraid to be feminine even though she was a techie. And with techie bluntness.

"Of course."

"Is there a concern that I am not doing my job correctly?" Her eyes never wavered as she leaned toward him.

Trig stood steady, feet from her. He quietly replied, "Not at all. I am evaluating the systems for vulnerabilities. Every system has them, so don't feel personally challenged."

She crossed her arms over her chest.

Then Trig transitioned to Russian. "The real concern is protecting Lionel and Maxine and others in the company. I am here to work with you. I come to help."

She smiled for the first time, her large eyes leaping at him. "You speak well. How is it you know Russian?" she replied, also in Russian.

"A personal interest that became part of my work. Security projects."

"What a nice surprise. Now we can really talk."

For the next hour they discussed plans for an assessment of cyber and physical vulnerabilities. Dasha surfaced a proposal she had for video cameras in and around all the DV locations. Trig found they both shared a healthy paranoia about security. They never stopped speaking in Russian.

"I'd also like to do a bug sweep of Lionel's and Maxine's apartments and change their locks. And have security systems installed with motion and window alarms."

"In Russia and Ukraine, they put dashboard cameras in their cars. Maybe this would be good for Lionel and Maxine. In case someone attacks them with a car again."

"Good idea," he agreed. That reminded him of Igor Vasilchenko, the Russian caught speeding in an Audi in Colorado. He started to bring his name up, but caught himself. Something about the Russian and Ukrainian connection worried him.

***

His instructions today were to go to Fanachi's villa. Igor wondered why they wanted to meet there, on Telegraph Hill. From the cab window he watched the tile rooftops below as they wound up the prominent peak. Steadily they climbed above the City. The view swept to the distant waterfront and then suddenly, in a tight circle, they jerked to a stop in front of Coit Tower, the popular tourist destination.

Igor stepped out, paid, and walked to the adjacent overlook. He heard three different languages being spoken by the tourists jostling for the perfect camera spot. He took some photos with his smart phone as he scanned the surrounding gardens. Then his eye caught the path mentioned in his instructions. He wandered over and disappeared in the dense oaks.

Igor passed through overgrown vines and ducked under twisting branches. The path was intersected by several small roads, but he pressed on, following the directions through the disjointed segments. Eventually he emerged on a narrow street with beautifully painted villas and modern mansions. The imposing houses were shouldered together, and between them were little slices of dramatic water views. He realized the entire block was built on the edge of a cliff. Ships and bridges lay far below on the bay.

Igor walked down the street, admiring the expensive cars that lined the driveways. He located Fanachi's address on a gate. He sucked in his breath. Wow. Now he knew why Nicco called the villa a Venetian castle. The terra-cotta tile roof floated above stone terraces and columns, surrounded by colorful gardens, statues and wrought-iron accents. He noticed the matching garage. Nicco had let it slip there was a red Ferrari 458 inside, worth two hundred fifty thousand dollars. He wanted one of those some day.

Igor buzzed, announced himself, and the gate opened. At the door Nicco motioned Igor inside, then pointed down the tile hallway, past the marble statues. There was a stone staircase at the end. Igor spotted the well-placed security cameras behind the elaborate ceiling molding. At the top of the stairs, Fanachi's other huge bodyguard, Tomas, stood like a giant redwood tree.

"Put your phone in the box." Tomas' block-like head motioned toward a table, which made his shoulders swing. Tomas and Nicco had been born with no necks, Igor concluded.

As he pulled his phone from his pocket, Igor noticed there were zero bars. Must have a cell phone jammer working in here, too. He dropped it into a lead-lined box on the table.

Tomas opened the double arched doors. Fanachi sat behind a large desk, inlaid with dark wood. Pictures of Mediterranean cliffs, old Italian bridges and churches covered the walls. He hadn't seen any family pictures or personal effects anywhere.

As he walked closer, Fanachi motioned to a chair in front of his desk. His large flat face both fascinated and worried Igor. The furrows that created the different angles seemed deeper today, especially the one in the middle of his forehead. His black hair was combed back and held in place like a helmet.

He sat, feeling on edge. Fanachi wouldn't have invited him here if he was in trouble, would he?

"You didn't accomplish everything I expected of you."

Igor immediately felt his chest hammering. His mouth went dry. True, the bike accident and avalanche hadn't worked. He wanted to respond, but didn't know what to say.

"However, the feedback on your hacking skills is very good. That's our future. I want you to be part of that."

He sucked in a breath of sweet air. He heard himself say, "Thank you."

"I plan to expand our operations. To target the intellectual property of the most valuable companies, here in Silicon Valley. Google,

Facebook, Genentech, Intel, and Apple. Much more sophisticated than Double Vision and those other companies we've attacked. Do you think you can hack them?"

Fanachi had done this to him before, several times. First he crushed you with fear, then he rescued you with a job to do for him. Something challenging. This man was clever. But Igor felt confident. Hacking was his passion. *Analyst Three must have told him about me.* "Everyone is vulnerable," he responded.

"Good. Those companies are where I want to put your talents to work in the future. Your talents combined with the talents of other hackers you recruit for us in Russia and Ukraine. Maybe other eastern European countries too. Understand?"

"Yes. This is possible."

Fanachi stared at him.

Igor wondered what to say. Then he realized he should be more positive. "Yes. I can do this. We will talk about a plan whenever you are ready." He immediately thought of Dasha.

"Good. First we have to finish a job, in order to gain access on the inside with these companies. So I'm going to show you something very few people get to see."

Fanachi nodded at Tomas and Nicco. "Let's go downstairs."

"Into the tomb?"

"Yes."

Fanachi pushed a button and a wood panel slid to the side. Behind it was a brushed metal elevator door.

"I hate this part," said Tomas.

"Jesus," said Fanachi. "As tough as you are? Igor, come down with me. The big boys go one at a time."

He stepped inside the narrow elevator, feeling uncomfortably close to Fanachi. He saw there were two levels below this one, labeled 0 and 1. He heard a hum and felt the drop in his legs. Fanachi was silent. Igor glanced at him sideways, and his expression was stone-like. The elevator hum turned into a cyclical grind as they dropped deeper and deeper. He started to sweat. By the time they passed level 1 his armpits were soaked. *This could be the end.*

Finally they shuddered to a stop. Level 0. The door opened and Fanachi stepped into a windowless hallway. Igor followed. Dim lights washed the uneven ceiling and walls and Igor realized they were cut rock. Three short hallways branched out, leading to sealed doors. To the right of each door were glowing keypads with blinking red and green lights. Their footsteps echoed in the stone chamber and Igor shook with a chill. *This is a tomb.*

Igor began imagining the worst. They were completely isolated. No one could hear or witness anything. *Are they going to kill me?* His eyes searched for an exit.

"Straight ahead," said Fanachi.

Igor's mind was racing. *Should I run?* Was there a code for the elevator to get back up? He glanced back at the elevator. Retina scanner. Hard to hack.

"Relax. We're having a private meeting." The hallway ended at a metal door. Igor waited as Fanachi swiped his finger on the keypad and the doors whisked open with a low swoosh.

Igor slowly stepped through the metal doorway, rimmed in an eerie blue light. *What is happening?* Scenarios flashed through his mind. Beyond the threshold, inside the room, he saw a cart with medical instruments. A stainless tray was stacked with plastic gloves, syringes, and vials. A tanned man with a shaved head bent over the cart. He looked very athletic. Igor's heart was hammering inside his chest. The shaved head turned upward and Igor immediately recognized him. Calabrese. Fanachi's first in command.

"Igor. Welcome." Igor nodded. He gulped the dry air.

Four chairs were situated around a whiteboard. Displayed on a metal table were an array of knives, gag pieces, and restraints. Black cases lay open, with 22-caliber pistols and silencers resting in foam inserts.

"Calabrese is planning the next operation," said Fanachi.

"Complete privacy here," said Calabrese. "Each of these rooms is a Faraday cage. Between the rock and the metal shielding, no electromagnetic radiation can penetrate."

"So no cell phones or remote surveillance frequencies?"

"Exactly. Even if someone suspected there was an operation here, they'd never be able to detect or monitor it."

Then it clicked. The International Trading Company offices were in a warehouse that continued not just to the edge of the cliffs, but deep below. And the rear area wasn't only for storing old luxury cars. It led to these stealth offices—and the secret elevator connected to Fanachi's villa. Fanachi would never be seen entering or exiting the lower building.

"This all connects?" Igor asked Fanachi. "Your villa and the Honeycomb?"

"For some people. That little ride you took needs to remain completely confidential. Understand?"

This was some sort of test. No one in the Honeycomb had any clue Fanachi was in the same country, let alone an elevator ride away. He nodded as his mind raced.

"Understand?" Fanachi repeated.

"Yes. I understand."

"Good." Then Fanachi sank into a big leather chair.

Nicco and Tomaz came in, greeted Calabrese, and sat down.

Nicco turned to Igor. "Me and Tomas and the director are going to show you how it is done, little geek."

"Director?"

"Yeah, like a movie." He held his hands like a camera and looked through the circle his fingers made. "Calabrese is beautiful planning all the details. And me and Tomas finish the job. You'll learn, geek."

Igor took the teasing with a shrug. *We'll see who brags once I hack Facebook,* he thought.

"Listen up," interrupted Fanachi. "Calabrese is in charge of this particular operation because it is complicated. You guys need to follow his plan very specifically. You'll be practicing over the next few days. Take it seriously. Am I clear?"

Igor nodded like Nicco and Tomas.

"He'll review the entrance to the apartment. How you disable the targets and make sure you don't leave any marks on them when you initially subdue them. Or leave any of your hair, or DNA, or any other crap. Got it?"

"Yes, boss."

"And Igor, Calabrese will review cutting the apartment power and the alarm system with you. Then re-engaging those systems when the boys are done, so no one is the wiser. Understood?"

"Yes."

"We also need their iPhones to be hacked so we can play a loud fight enactment. The victims will already be dead, the big boys will be gone, but we want witnesses to hear a fight. The audio files need to then disappear off their iPhones. Igor, can you do it?"

"Interesting. I will try."

Fanachi swiveled his head.

"If it is possible I will do it," Igor said quickly, his voice rising. "There are details about access to their devices to work out. But yes, I am on it."

"Okay. Nicco, tell me the status so far," said Fanachi.

"Boss, we had keys made for both apartments. Then some dude comes to town and changes their locks. No problem, we got new keys made. Then he installed the stupid alarm. Such a pain-in-the-ass. What's his name again, Igor?"

"Garcia. Trig Garcia."

"Go figure, some spick is helping them. I thought, okay, must be cheap. Then the geek tells me he saw some email that says the guy is a damn Navy SEAL."

"So what?" said Fanachi.

"So they is gearing up, that's all I'm saying. Getting more careful."

"Did you wire their places?"

"Yes, boss. We put in wireless microphones, so we can listen to whatever is going on inside."

"How's it look?"

"These two, Lionel and Maxine, are always traveling. If they're in town, they work like dogs. Sleep for four hours. Then back to work. They don't teach them how to sleep in college, I guess."

"Separately?"

"Yeah, he's in the Marina, she's across town in the Mission. So far they aren't screwing around in the same apartment. I think Lionel has a thing for that skier Reddi. Not Maxine."

"The avalanche one, right?" asked Fanachi.

"Yeah."

"No brown sugar for him," piped up Tomas.

"Shut up, Tomas," growled Fanachi.

Tomas dropped his head like a wounded dog.

Fanachi continued. "We know based on archived social media that at one point Lionel and Maxine had a sexual thing in college. And frankly, a lot of people assume they still are involved. But there also is this relationship Lionel has with the skier and that is gossiped about in social media. So that's the love triangle. It's the cover for our operation. Tell them, Calabrese."

"We're planning a lover's quarrel between Lionel and Maxine that ends badly for both of them. He'll choke her to death and she'll stab him fatally as she nears passing out. We'll stage it at one of their apartments." Calabrese moved as he talked, like an acting coach.

"Why will people think it's a lover's quarrel?" asked Igor

"You've got his email passwords, right?"

"Yes."

"We're planning on Lionel sending an email to Reddi that night. It will be open on his laptop in the apartment. So it's like Maxine discovered the email after he sent it, and they started fighting over it."

"What could make them get this angry?" asked Igor.

"Don't worry. I'll have it prepared for you, Igor. You'll need to hack in and paste in the words and send it. By the time Reddi sees the email, the other two will already be dead."

Igor looked at Calabrese blankly. There was a prolonged silence in the room.

"Calabrese, tell them some of your ideas," Fanachi said.

"Okay. In this email Lionel tells Reddi they have to stop dating for now. He starts off saying, 'I'm emailing because I am so emotional I can't talk. I had a wicked fight with Maxine. THE BITCH.' He goes on to say he really loves Reddi, not Maxine, but Maxine has insisted he break off his relationship with her."

"Okay, so far," said Nicco.

"It gets better. Then he says, 'Reddi, you are my true love. Maxine is a machine, but I want to keep her happy until we win the Big

Disrupter. After that I will break up with her and fire her. I want her out of my life. I can't believe what a total bitch she has become—no one in the company supports her.'"

"Ooh, that's cold," howled Nicco.

"Nice," said Tomas, nodding his big crew cut.

"Remember, he has to upset Maxine when she discovers this email. Here is where he gets personal. Like this. 'She is nothing like you. You are the passion of my life. Working with her is enormously painful. Even worse is the robot sex with her—I hate every minute of it. Sometimes I want to choke her and finish it. I can't wait until after we win and I can return to only you, my one true love. Forever yours—Lionel'"

Igor clapped while Nicco and Tomas whistled. Calabrese did a mock bow for them.

"What do you think, boss?"

"It's good. That would start a hell of a fight for any couple. And some of those fights would end the way ours will."

"Absolutely," agreed Nicco.

Igor felt a chill, but this time it was in excitement.

"Here is the point," said Fanachi. "Track them online and monitor those apartments like hawks. When they go to one of them together, then you move. Be ready."

"What if they don't?"

"I have a Plan B," answered Calabrese. "But let's make Plan A work."

Fanachi rose, his shoulders square, head erect. His black eyes bore into all three and ended up lingering on Igor. "Be ready to execute this perfectly by the end of the week. No mistakes this time. Or there will be consequences."

As he walked past them a shudder went through Igor. The metal doors sealed behind him with a thud. Then Igor realized they couldn't escape this chamber until Fanachi decided to return. He felt beads of sweat form on his temples.

32

WEDNESDAY, FEBRUARY 12TH

Reddi received a text on her cell at eight a.m.

***

Hi Reddi—Last minute scratch due to injury in the Slopestyle event. Congratulations—you are ranked next highest. Ready to compete in Slopestyle at X Games? Pls let me know ASAP. Nigel Thickett, Winter X Games Manager

***

Reddi called her coach immediately. She was jumping up and down screaming, while Wolfie spun around her. "Bronco—Unbelievable! The X Games!"

"Reddi, it's an honor. But you have the option of waiting, you know."

She landed with a thud. "Why would I want to do that?"

"So you can prepare more."

"What do you mean? You don't think I'm good enough?" She loved that Bronco was cautious about injuries. But the X Games? This was her chance.

"No, of course I know you are good enough. You scare me sometimes, you're so talented."

"What's the deal? Why are you hesitating?" Her temper started rising as her joy deflated.

"You are still working on perfecting your new big-air routines."

"Oh, you think I'm going to get too excited and try to go too big?"

"Any inverted air is dangerous. You should have the tricks down cold in practice before even thinking of pulling them off in the excitement and pressure of a competition."

"Maybe I'm different. I ski better when I'm pushed and I have someone to beat. You know that."

"Promise me we'll work out your routine and you'll stick to it."

"Okay, I'll meet you on the hill at ten-thirty. But I'm going to master a trick to blow them away, like the double rodeo 900."

***

Reddi couldn't wait to tell Lionel. As she rode the lift chair up the face of the mountain, she called him. He finally answered after she redialed the third time.

He was talking quietly. "I'm with a customer in a conference room. In Boston. Are you okay?"

"Guess who is skiing slopestyle in the frigging X Games next week?"

She heard him gasp. "Wait, let me get to the hallway." A moment later he came back on. "Is it that really cute girl from Canada? No, maybe that beast from Eastern Europe? Or the Scandinavian . . . ."

"Very funny, dude, you are talking to the one. It's so cool."

"It's official?"

"Got the text from the X Games manager himself. Bronco is getting the low-down now."

"How do you feel? It's major, right?"

"I know I have a whole headache of stuff to think about, but right now, I'm psyched. I'm riding Lift 9 up the mountain, heading over to the Terrain Park to work out with Bronco. We've got epic plans."

"I am so excited for you. We've got to blow this up big, publicity-wise. Okay?"

"Heck yeah, let's roll some video and socialize it."

"Awesome. Kate will be all over this X Games exposure with marketing programs."

"I'm pumped. And you'll be there, right?"

Lionel paused. "I will do *everything* possible to be there."

"You better."

"Talk soon."

***

Lionel got on a conference call with Maxine and Kate, filling them in.

"Fantastic, we can use the publicity," said Maxine.

"Tweeting it right now," said Kate as her fingers flew over her phone. "Let's blow it up."

"Are you two good with pulling the trigger on the new creative agency for videos? The timing could be perfect to bring a videographer for X Games footage near Aspen, and Telluride the following week."

"Are we still within budget?" Maxine asked.

"Yes, it's all in there. And we have budget for the other campaigns like the music performances, college campus events, and some other extreme sports."

"Okay, then let's add the videos. But we'll need to work on scripts and storyboards with them, right?" asked Kate. "That sucks a lot of hours."

Lionel exhaled. "How are you two holding up?"

"Other than no social life and the bags under my eyes?"

"I would love, love to sleep in my own bed. And get some exercise other than a Stairmaster in a gym full of staring strangers."

"How are the events treating you, Lionel?"

"I'm doing two per day, and it's okay. I'll probably travel thirty thousand miles this month. I've met the Merry Cola distributors in the largest twenty cities, and we have advertisements, events, and in-store promotions coordinated in every single one. How about you, Kate?"

"We're bringing on ten to twenty new promotional people per week on the college campuses. I'm visiting two schools a day, attending rallies, interviewing and hiring the top people, then circling back as they put their teams in place. It's cranking. Nonstop action."

"Maxine?"

"I've signed up five additional distributors for the holes in Merry Cola's distribution coverage. They are second-tier cities at best, but the distributors are motivated to keep up now that Merry is on board and we are committing serious local promotional dollars. This will be my twenty-first consecutive day on the road."

"Twenty-one straight?" Lionel groaned. "Maxine, you win this week's blues fest with that travel schedule."

"No complaints. We're in it to win it," Maxine replied quickly. "Look guys, we've got six weeks. And frankly I am nervous with our sales trend. Merry Cola isn't placing stocking orders as fast as we need."

Lionel's cell chirped. "Guys, sorry, but it's Leah Barko texting me."

"What is it?" asked Maxine, frowning.

"She needs an immediate response on a new Big Disrupter article."

"Deal with it," Maxine suggested. "I'm worried about what she will say."

***

"Lionel, how is Maxine doing?" Leah's mass of black curls and designer cat-eye glasses filled his screen, as the Skype connection came live.

"What? Oh, the avalanche? She's way beyond that. She's been traveling for twenty-one days straight, pumping up our distribution. We're on fire over here." He flashed an enthusiastic smile. *No time to be shy,* he thought.

"Glad to hear."

"So Leah, what about the standings in the Big? Calling to get some more background as we move up toward first place?" Lionel looked confidently at Leah.

"Can we talk confidentially?" She glanced away.

Oh no. She doesn't look like she had good news. "Always."

"Schwab and Young still doesn't have you guys in the top five."

"What? Come on, seriously?"

"I'm sorry, Lionel. I don't get to vote. I'm letting you know before the announcement."

"After signing the deal with Merry Cola? We're on plan to sell thirty million beverages. Thirty million meals. Who else is doing that?"

"I think there are two issues. One, the whole energy drink controversy."

"Our products are so much healthier than the competition—and we have an entire juice line too."

"It's a controversial category. And the other issue is Merry Cola. Big beverage companies are synonymous with big corporate America. They aren't typically associated with social entrepreneurship."

"Merry is simply a distributor. A channel. A way for us to do good."

Leah's face softened. "I get it. And the rules are not totally clear. I think some judges favor contestants who are philanthropic and address solving the actual problem."

"How is feeding someone not solving a social problem?" Lionel looked at Leah in disbelief.

"It is, but some think that ideally, you should feed them and in the process eliminate the social causes behind their hunger. Don't give them fish, but teach them how to fish."

"Nice theory. Totally legitimate concept. But I think I'll take thirty million meals today instead of a tiny fraction of that and a truckload of fishing poles in a desert." Lionel threw up his hands, groaning in frustration.

"Look, it isn't over. You still have time."

"Time? It's six weeks until the end. Leah, we are feeding starving people and using local farmers and processing to do so. Sure, we're riding the consumer energy drink trend in the wealthier nations. But we are providing healthier options."

"Lionel, I understand that." Leah sounded annoyed.

"If you write a story focused on our being knocked out of the top five, our brand will take a huge hit. People will assume we're a passing fad. It could become a self-fulfilling prophecy."

"Give me an alternative then."

"Maybe right now the bigger story is all the tragedy happening to the contestants. We're like gladiators dying in the Coliseum in ancient Rome."

"What has your investigator surfaced? Talk to me, Lionel."

"Off the record, our investigator Trig Garcia is working with the Telluride sheriff and Inspector Chang, of SFPD. They have determined the same Audi that hit me on my bike in the alley later was driven to Telluride by the avalanche bomber."

"Seriously?" Leah looked over her glasses in surprise.

"Leah, you can't write about this."

"Lionel, you can't dictate the story."

"We can't blow the criminal investigation."

"It's a balance. I can't write without background details. And you're the one who is nearing the final stretch and far behind." Leah tilted her head with a take-it or leave-it look.

Lionel shook his head wearily. "Okay, I'll tell you everything we know, but you promise not to compromise the investigation. Deal?"

"You have a deal. Start talking."

***

The next morning the cover-page article came out in print and online. Lionel, Maxine, and Kate spent hours on the phone spinning their falling fortunes in a positive direction. Leah received a call from a disappointed Jules Longsworth, threatening to cut off further interviews unless her coverage became less sensationalistic.

Gladiator Tragedies Raise Suspicions in BIG Battle for a Billion
National Times Journal exclusive coverage
Thursday, February 13 By Leah Barko

There was another life-threatening attack on a leading contestant for the Big Disrupter Award. Maxine Gold, Co-CEO of Double Vision, was caught in a deliberate and near fatal avalanche in Telluride, Colorado.

Earlier last month, Ray Singh, the charismatic CEO of Step-by-Step Clothing, suffered a heart attack while driving home after a long run. He was 28 years old. Four months ago, Jan Swenson, CEO of

Sweet Boomerang, drowned while kayaking. And prior to that, CEO Lionel Lane of Double Vision was hit on his bicycle in a late-night hit-and-run mystery.

President Longsworth of Schwab and Young commented for this article. "We have some of the highest energy people running phenomenally socially minded organizations. They are active and engaged people, and unfortunately risks accompany such outgoing activities."

Our take
Must our best social entrepreneurs be sacrificed like ancient gladiators? This latest attack appears to be part of a tragic specter haunting the competition. Is the lure of one billion dollars disrupting the competition even more than expected? And in the wrong ways? Should this contest be suspended until these tragedies have been fully investigated and explained? Or is our blood lust too ingrained?

Standings
The race is in the final stretch, with just over six weeks to go.

SocialLending continues to be the first-place leader. They have expanded operations to three additional countries in this past quarter, and issued millions of dollars of loans to needy emerging businesses and individuals.

In second place is Global Bite, the nutritional bar company. They have expanded their outreach to 20,000 new consumers and 4,000 beneficiary recipients.

In third place is WorldLensFactory. They have added 10,000 new customers and donated the same number of glasses to needy recipients.

Fourth place has been awarded to Global Lightz, a small footprint solar collector manufacturer using recycled parts to create solar collectors for rural homes without power infrastructure.

Fifth place is currently held by Step-by-Step Clothing, shaken but not down from the recent death of their founder. Their clothing, made largely from recycled plastics in India continues to sell well in fashionable boutiques with numerous celebrity endorsements.

The complete list of the top fifty social entrepreneurs vying for the Big Disrupter is below. Check back on my blog for updates.

***

33

FRIDAY, FEBRUARY 21ST

Garr Gartick looked across his huge desk and pounded his hand. "Lionel, this is not a passive process."

"We have been anything but passive. We're promoting nonstop." Lionel jumped to his feet and swept his arms wide. He had flown to Manhattan and talked his way into a meeting with Merry Cola's CEO without notice. *He was not going to roll over.* They had to increase sales.

"You've got to build the brand, generate awareness, make people want to reach for one on the shelf. I can put Double Vision on the shelf but I can't make your products fly off of it."

"My concern is there isn't enough product on the shelves. In over half of the stores we sampled, customers can't find DV in stock." He jabbed a finger at a color chart he had on his tablet.

Garr waved his hand dismissively. "My people assure me we're giving you full coverage. Complete distribution and service in-store. Look, rather than squabble, tell me what you are doing to promote the new products."

"We're doing everything but driving your trucks for you. In-store promotions, local events and advertising, and we're blanketing college campuses. In fact, one of our promotional athletes will probably be the star of the X Games."

"Your star is in the X Games, you say? The lady welder with the red hair?"

"Absolutely. They're going on right now. With national TV coverage. So Garr, we are doing our part. Now, can we please review our product inventory in your distribution chain?"

Garr ignored Lionel's question. He spun his chair toward the wall and clicked a remote. Lionel watched as the five screens flickered.

Then he punched another remote. As the window blinds descended, the towering view of Manhattan disappeared. The inventory reports would have to wait, Lionel realized. His eyes adjusted to the darkness.

The center screen popped to life in high definition. "There it is," said Garr. "X Games. Aspen, Colorado." The surround sound boomed.

They saw a crowd scene, people bundled in bright coats, hats, and mittens. Snow drifted downward. Then the camera zoomed in, showing hand-painted signs, banners and animated faces, steaming breath and frosted mustaches. The spectators cheered, packed behind a fabric fence alongside the finish line.

"Wow, great turnout," said Lionel.

Garr nodded. "I wonder what the ratings will be?"

"Shoot, it's snowing hard there. Look."

The camera's view transported them to the starting gate of the slopestyle course. The horizon was whited out. Close by, through the flurry of flakes, were colorful rails, flat elongated boxes, and jump ramps. Further below they saw sets of huge snow mounds.

"They go over those mounds?" asked Garr.

"They ski off one, perform their aerial tricks while flying through the air, and then land on the downslope of the next hill."

"Jesus—how far is that?"

"Eighty feet or more in the air," Lionel replied. He felt a nervous chill.

The announcer started in. "Welcome back to the Slopestyle Finals of the X Games. It's been an exciting day at Buttermilk Mountain in Aspen, despite the difficult conditions."

The standings for the women's event flashed on the screen.

"Oh man, Reddi ended up in fifth place." Lionel took a deep breath, bummed. Still, fifth was okay, he told himself.

The announcer continued. "We have two competitors remaining. Marla Vanden, a veteran and favorite, and Reddi Christiansen, a newcomer on the scene."

"Wait! Reddi has one run left." He couldn't believe their luck at tuning in for this moment.

"Well then, let's see your star perform," replied Garr.

His words sounded like a challenge. Truthfully, he had talked Reddi up a lot. Her beauty, the drive to overcome her mom's death, and her working-class grit all made for a great story. But still, she needed to win. And she was far back. Lionel's stomach churned.

The camera focused on a stocky brunette with a platinum and neon orange ski suit. The announcer began. "At the top of the run, about to start, is Marla Vanden, sponsored by BodyHamr. She presently is in third place, looking to move up."

"Looks like the BodyHamr competitor is ahead of your girl, Lionel."

"We'll see. That's Reddi on deck, on the sidelines. With the red and gold helmet and the flames."

"That's a long red ponytail. Is it natural?"

"Of course it is," Lionel replied. "You've got to meet her one day."

"We'll see."

The BodyHamr woman jumped on the course. Lionel tensed, feeling he had to do something. As the announcer described her moves, Lionel gave Garr some background.

"You see the cameraman skiing parallel to her? He does that at the start, to film close-up. He gets the early moves on the rails—the jibs—when they are going slower. See how tight the coverage is, like you are skiing along with them?"

The announcer commented. "Marla Vanden is playing it conservatively here at the top. She and the final competitor have it tougher than the rest of the field, as the visibility has significantly worsened. The snow is really starting to come down."

Then the coverage switched to an aerial view as she flew down the course. "See that? The big jumps are coming up, mound to mound, and the cameras are mounted high up on scaffoldings."

"Now for the first of three jumps for Marla," intoned the announcer. "She looks good heading on the cannon box, that big blue rail that extends twenty feet into the air. She's launched . . . oh, she's cut back on her routine. She did a 360 rather than the 540 she planned, probably because of the bad visibility."

Lionel shook his fists. "Yes!"

"Let's see if Marla stays with the switch 540 and grab she has planned on the second jump," said the announcer. "She may drop out of third if she doesn't maintain her degree of difficulty."

Lionel and Garr stared intently.

"She is up, nice spin, oh, no . . . over-rotated . . . she's down. Marla Vanden has lost a ski, and is rolling down the back side of the jump. She appears to be okay. Yes, she's up. The crowd is giving her nice applause. She is actually skiing down along the edge of the course, on one ski. What a competitor. But her day is over. Now, we'll see our last skier of the day, who has come out of nowhere to create quite a sensation. Reddi Christiansen, from Telluride, Colorado."

The TV programming returned to a close up camera shot, at the top of the mountain. Reddi's image filled Garr's TVs. All five were showing the same picture in a wall of color.

The announcer continued. "You can see the snow sticking to the red and gold colors on her helmet. It's got to be tough for a rookie competitor, first time in the X Games, facing the worse conditions of the day. Evidently she is a welder who loves to ski, and barely made it into the games, after another competitor was scratched. Let's go to our announcer, Sonja, standing slopeside. Sonja?"

"Thank you, Jim. I love Reddi Christiansen's style. Something about the curve of the jacket, bright colors, and sleeker fit of her pants gives her a very feminine figure. Trust me, that is difficult to do with insulated ski clothing! We'll see how she skis, but with that long red hair and pretty face, we have the female version of Shaun White on skis here at Aspen."

"Thank you, Sonja. Now it is up to her skiing. Her chances are pretty slim to move up to third place, given the conditions. There she goes. Reddi has pushed off from the top and headed straight for the first box. She is on with a 90, off with a sweet 270, and heading downhill. She's on the next rail with a blind 270 spin and off with another 270. Very risky. She's heading backward over the next rise, and look at her—she has a big smile on her face! And going quite fast. She is on the rainbow rail with a 450 spin, picking up speed across the full length, and now off with a big 450. Wow! Listen to the crowd screaming. We haven't seen any woman do that in this competition. This young woman is taking some big risks on the rails. I don't think she is trying for third—she is going for first place!"

"You go girl!" Lionel yelled.

"Her competitor Marla cut back on this next jump. Let's see what Reddi does. The crowd is getting louder with her approach. She's heading backward, looking over her shoulder, going awfully fast. Oh, my goodness, look at that air. A huge arc over the gap, one, two, two and a half helicopters. She's done a 900, sweet backward landing, and roaring on to the next one. This young lady is very impressive."

"Yes!" Lionel shouted, jumping out of his chair.

"Here is her second jump," said the announcer. "Huge air again. This girl loves to fly! It's a switch 540 with a grab, landed effortlessly. How does she even see in these conditions? Her air was huge, much higher than any of the other women. You can hear the crowd roaring. And she just pumped her hands overhead. She's having fun!"

Watching from New York, Lionel suddenly saw the problem. She was going into the last jump too fast. Worst of all, a gust from the snow storm made visibility terrible.

"Back off, Reddi. Do a simple jump. Shit, she won't be able to see the landing," Lionel whispered. Images of broken bones and a concussion swept over him. Then the worst fear came—what if she was paralyzed? He went cold. *What have I encouraged?*

"Reddi is up," began the announcer. "Oh, my God. She has exploded, like she was launched right out of a cannon. Two and a half spins plus a double flip. It's a double rodeo 900. But she has completely disappeared in a cloud of snow."

Lionel's chest caved inwards. Why wasn't he there to help?

"Wait, there she is, she landed, backward, out of control," he announced.

Lionel gripped his chair frantically.

"Her skis are wobbling, head bent nearly to the snow . . . she's . . . she's holding on. Unbelievable. She has spun around and is pumping her fists to the sky. Reddi Christiansen. Oh, my goodness!" The announcer was bubbling over.

"She did it!" Lionel yelled, as he watched Reddi come to a spraying stop at the bottom. The spectators were roiling in excitement. Someone knocked over the snow fence and the crowd poured out into the skier's waiting area, past the finish line.

Lionel threw his arms high and turned to Garr. "Unbelievable!" He pumped a two-handed high five with Garr, then danced around the room whooping. Garr actually cheered. His assistants ran in to check on them and he waved them off.

The video image went to a close-up, across all five screens. Reddi pulled off her helmet and goggles and gave her hair a big shake. It fell down over her shoulders. The camera zoomed on her face.

"Look at this young woman, only twenty-one years old," said Sonja, the announcer. "She is glowing after that run. And deservedly so. I can't wait to interview her after the results come in."

Then Reddi stood with her coach, Bronco, waiting. The camera followed their every expression. Bronco looked like a nervous elf next to Reddi. She hugged and shook him, and waved to people in the crowd.

The announcer returned. "Her score is about to be revealed," he intoned dramatically. "How much did that performance impress the judges, today? We'll see. It is flashing on the screen now. It's 98.5. That is enough to move her into first place! Ladies and gentlemen, we have a new Slopestyle X Games Champion!"

Reddi practically threw her skis sky-high, showing off Double Vision to the cameras. Then she jumped up and down with Bronco, and got gracious hugs from her fellow competitors.

Garr was transfixed as she was interviewed. She brushed off the fallen snow from her eyelashes. She shook her hair occasionally as she spoke. Her enthusiasm and smile were irrepressible. Her cheering fans waved behind a snow fence in the background. She dedicated the victory to her deceased mother. And she explained the welding torch flames on her suit. The entire time she made sure the Double Vision graphics on her skis and helmet were prominent.

"My God, look at her. She really is a young beauty," said Garr. "How do you keep your hands off her?"

"She's the face of the company. Look at that crowd go wild," said Lionel, ignoring the question.

"Faces sell products. And that one could sell a lot."

When the first interview finished, Lionel saw Reddi scanning the crowd and waving. She seemed to be looking for someone else. *She's looking for me*, thought Lionel. His joy immediately became tinged with guilt.

Lionel suddenly noticed a burly guy with a black watch cap in the crowd behind Reddi. Was that . . . Trig? He whipped out his cell phone.

His text was short.

Trig—Please tell Reddi I saw her victory live on TV from NYC. She launched herself and DV. So happy. Lionel

He watched for her reaction on the screen.

Trig leaned close to a security guard and flashed something. They let him pass through the gate toward Reddi. He showed her his cell phone. Lionel could see Reddi reading it. Then she took off her gloves and grabbed the phone. It looked like she was texting.

A new text appeared on his iPhone.

Thanks. But you missed it.

Lionel looked back at the TV. Reddi had her arms around Trig, hugging him.

Garr paused the coverage. The blinds and drapes came rolling up. Lionel squinted, trying to return to the present in New York. But his heart was in Colorado, hurting.

"Are you prepared to capitalize on her?" Garr asked.

He needed to make Garr commit, Lionel told himself. But the guilt of missing her victory, after his promise to be there, was agonizing.

"Lionel?"

He pulled himself back to focus on Garr. He had to get some results from him. "Absolutely. As we speak we have mobile campaigns running on Twitter, Instagram, and Facebook. An entire website has been launched."

"I'd go huge with her. From TV ads to in-store promotions. Print and online. Get her face everywhere. And get her prepped for doing appearances on TV shows. National first and then global." Garr was waving his big hands.

"Fantastic. And what will Merry Cola do?"

Garr paused. He squinted over his bushy mustache while pointing a big finger. "You do that, then we'll double the size of our orders with you."

"Double? Right away?"

"As soon as we see the promo. You have my word." Garr leaned back and stared at the close-up of Reddi's face, paused on his screen.

34

SATURDAY, FEBRUARY 22ND — SUNDAY, FEBRUARY 23RD

Trig took the late flight back from Denver to San Francisco. He validated the address for Igor Vasilchenko provided by Sheriff Masterson and examined it with Google Maps. But when he finally visited the apartment building in San Francisco on Saturday morning, there was no sign of Igor, and no listing for Vasilchenko. He knocked on the door of a neighboring apartment. An elderly woman answered, her head full of curlers covered by a bright pink scarf. She peered through the small opening of her double chains.

"Never heard of such a name," she replied in a wavering voice. A strong smell wafted into the hallway. Then, through the crack of the door, he saw cats. And more cats. Short-haired, spotted brown and black cats, fleecy Asian cats, a sleek Abyssinian, and fluffy Persian cats. A thin white cat eyed the door hopefully. "Sounds Polish. No Polish people in this building."

"Yes ma'am. It's Ukrainian." The smell from the litter boxes became overpowering, and Trig's eyes began to itch.

"None of them here either. Chinese, Greeks, and gays. And me and my cats."

The cat lady slammed the door. Her latches snugged into place behind him as he walked to the peeling wooden staircase. He had struck out. He considered contacting Inspector Chang from SFPD. This was his backyard, after all. Then he decided to save that for later. First he wanted to find this guy's physical location, and hack into it.

Once he knew more, he'd contact the police. But if he used the police's info first in an illegal op, it could get messy.

He'd have to use his ace in the hole. Trig found a local cafe and used its WiFi to access TOR, a secure remailer. He emailed a former NSA employee he had met while working at Fort Meade named Slurp. Slurp now worked as a security contractor for the San Francisco city government. Trig knew Slurp had access to an impressive bank of data, even though he was technically only a contractor. Brilliant and eccentric, he was completely uninterested in interacting with most people. Trig got along just fine with him.

Trig's email got a quick response, also encrypted via TOR.

- - - - - - -

Subject dude, one Igor Vasilchenko, address is 1171 Tennessee Ave, apartment 5, San Francisco. Surprisingly little info on this guy, he must be low profile for a reason. I'd have to tap into Russian intelligence to get more. Slurp1024

- - - - - - -

Trig rented a van later that day. He drove to Igor's apartment building and parked nearby. With a blue baseball cap, windbreaker, and forged cable company badge hanging around his neck, he walked into the apartment building. He carried a canvas tool bag and test equipment hung from his hip belt. He identified the ISP, routers and cable delivering Internet to apartment 5. Then he tapped into the service.

He retreated back to his van. Now for the complicated work, he thought. He fired up his laptop and server. Using WiFi, he executed a software compromise of those specific versions of firewall, router, and OS. This exploit gave Trig access to all internet traffic to and from Igor's apartment. He fabricated an email from a trusted source, and inserted a bug, undetectable by standard commercial products, that launched mirroring software. It was a sophisticated variant of the Trojan Citadel bug, called AZ99, which installed when the user clicked on a link. Trig headed back to his hotel, for his first sleep in thirty-six hours.

The next day, Sunday, Igor made the fatal click. It was embedded in a bogus version of a status email from VK, the Russian social media platform, a widely popular clone of Facebook. Within minutes, Trig's mirror software had access to Igor's personal laptop. What he found surprised him.

35

WEDNESDAY, FEBRUARY 26ᵀᴴ

Blaine typed with gusto, filling out the questionnaire. With practiced exaggeration, crafted to impress in an offhand way, he described his successes as a venture capitalist at Axlewright Capital in California. He concluded his personal status as single and seeking adventure, jetting between helicopter skiing and surfing on private islands. He read it a final time, smiling as he smoothed a wrinkle here and there, as though primping in the mirror. Satisfied, he attached it to an email to his former girlfriend and high school classmate, the organizer of their fifteenth high school reunion. The reunion would be at the Holiday Inn in Des Moines, Iowa. *She's been married a while,* he thought. *Maybe she's bored and would leave her husband at home.* He was renting the presidential suite. He started dreaming of her long hair, flirty smile, and all the fantasies they could play out in his suite.

He wrote some notes in his personal diary, savoring the moment. His diary chronicled his ups as well as his downs, an old habit that he maintained as a way of keeping things straight in his personal and work life. His friends and colleagues seemed to shift a lot, and this helped ground him.

The chime of a calendar reminder popped his dream. He groaned. *He had to make Double Vision a huge success.* He couldn't possibly face his old friends, or his family, as a washout. Not after all this hype about his career and the way he boasted about his personal connections with famous business people. No way he'd let Anderson end his career in San Francisco and Silicon Valley . . . and force him to slink back home as a local bank branch manager. His stomach soured as he thought of his boss.

Blaine reached across his desk and placed the call. It rang in a second-tier suburban mall in New Jersey, headquarters of BodyHamr energy drinks. From the pictures of their office celebrations he dug up on Flickr and Facebook, it looked like a drab collection of worn-down cubicles. Young people posed with holiday hats, red cups and glassy smiles. In the background, posters of scantily clad promo girls covered the walls. The bulletin board featured the BodyHamr ski star Gonzo, performing a daredevil stunt.

"Mr. Latrell, will Mr. Shamitz know what your call is pertaining to?" The admin had a bored tone.

"No, he won't. But once he does, he'll be very glad we spoke. I am a vice president in the leading food and beverage venture capital firm on the West Coast. It's Blaine, Blaine Latrell of Axlewright Capital."

"One moment, sir."

Nearly two minutes later a speakerphone crackled with a fast talking New Jersey accent. "The leading venture capital firm in food and beverage. Interested in my little company? Well, funny how things change."

"Mr. Shamitz? Blaine Latrell here, Axlewright Capital."

"It's Sid. So Blaine, what's going on? You guys printing so much money you want to give some away to regular guys like me?" Sid laughed loudly at his own joke.

Blaine glanced at his computer window with the holiday party posting of Sid Shamitz. He sat with his feet up on his desk, industrial smokestacks appearing in the background. An open Hawaiian shirt displayed a thick mat of prominent chest hair and a gold chain. He held a cigar in one hand and a bottle of champagne in the other, grinning at the camera.

"Sid, I understand BodyHamr is doing quite well in the energy drink space. Even with this economy you are doubling every year."

"I don't know where you get your numbers since we don't release them, but we are managing. Why do you care, if I may be so bold as to ask?"

"In the spirit of full disclosure, my firm Axlewright Capital has a sizeable stake in Double Vision."

"Jesus H. Christ, the competition. What are you calling me for? Giving up?" Sid laughed extra hard at that one.

"Are we able to have this conversation in confidence?"

"Confidence you say?" It sounded as though Sid had leaned closer to the speakerphone. "Certainly, you, me, and the wall."

"We both know the competitive landscape has the energy Big Four, with Red Bull, Monster, Rockstar, and 5 Hour Energy. And then there is a big gap. Would it make sense to have discussions about ways to combine efforts to muscle into the top tier, make it a Big Five of energy?"

"Combine? You mean like merge? I can tell you right now, there is no possible way I want to work for anybody else. Period. You know what I mean?"

"Anything is open to discussion."

"Look, this business is a gold mine. Hardly no industry has margins like we do, except for maybe software and drug companies. If we can keep these freaking kids excited, buying enough of this caffeinated sugar crap, with enough tits and ass and crazy extreme people doing nutty shit to keep them coming back, it's a money machine. So Blaine, I don't see any reasons for me to sell out. Every year is more bucks than the last. The owners of Red Bull, and Monster and Rockstar—and that Indian guy at 5 Hour Energy, are making billions. It's fabulous."

"Allow me to suggest a hypothetical, a scenario for discussion. What if, hypothetically, we merged Double Vision and your organization and you ran them both?"

"Huh? Why would the present owners do that? You know, the lion guy and that black chick . . . ."

"Lionel Lane and Maxine Gold?"

"Yeah, right. Why would them two throw in the towel?"

"With the pressures of competition and the need to scale more quickly, this might become a board of directors mandate."

There was a brief pause. "Oh, kick them out. But they gotta own the majority of stock, don't they?"

"I'm not at liberty to say. Given that we are having this conversation, there clearly are several considerations."

"I dunno. Seems complicated."

Time for the big gun, thought Blaine. "You have heard of my good friend Jacob Havermyer, no doubt?"

"Jacob Havermyer. Your head would have to be under a rock not to know about him. A fellow member of the tribe of Israel, and holy shit, is he rolling in the dough? As they say, a real alrightnik."

"He too is an investor in Double Vision, like myself. And we investors have a responsibility to make the right changes to grow the company. Jacob certainly knows how to make an investment profitable."

"Jacob Havermyer, yes, I can see he would want this to be world class. You know, to make it worth his time. He's a big money kind of guy, for sure." Blaine could hear the wheels turning in Sid's mind, maybe picturing himself smoking cigars with Jacob on a porch somewhere, planning to overtake the Big Four.

"So whaddya want from me?"

"How would you respond to running the whole show, knowing that Jacob Havermyer was a supporting investor?"

Sid didn't hesitate. "I tell you one thing. You can tell Jacob Havermyer I could run the whole thing with my eyes closed. Get you better margins, simplify that poverty program one-for-one giveaway crap. We could still do some, whaddya call them, charity events, you know, get some deductions, and get a bunch of press about it. Beat the drum about saving some kids somewhere. It's all PR bullshit anyway. Yeah, so it can be done, but at a much lower cost, ya know?"

"That is good to know."

"And say, coincidentally, between you, me, and the wall, what are Double Vision's revenues?"

"I am bound as a fiduciary to hold that confidential, of course."

"Ballpark." He heard Sid pick up his handset. "Between us, since we are, you know, collaboratin'."

"Really, I'd like to but . . . ."

"Annually, between us, so I have some idea if this merger would even make sense for me. Is the annual revenue in seven or eight figures? If I don't know something about them, well there is nothing for us to talk about."

Blaine hesitated. Then caved. "Eight figures." Then he waited a beat and said, "And the first digit is a four."

"Not bad, I suppose. Is that includin' the nutritional stuff, too?"

"Oh, those are the total numbers, for all products. In fact, ah, the bulk is nutritional sales, although energy is growing rapidly."

"Oh, I thought that would be all energy," said Sid, sounding disappointed, as though he would ever be saddened by a competitor's sales numbers being lower than expected. "That's the whole kit and caboodle, eh?"

"Yes."

"Let me say this. I got suppliers who bottle all this stuff right here in New Jersey. They can squirt out anything on contract, cheap. But stop trying to be your own bottler, for God's sake. It's a money-losing waste of time. This game is all sales and marketing. It's promotion, baby. You tell that to Jacob. And that is what I am about, in a nutshell. Fire up the kids to run around all day and party all night. And once they experience it, and had a good time, they always come back. And you take care of your distributors real good, like Merry . . . ah, whatever." He stopped.

"Jacob would be very interested in your advice, no doubt."

"Anyways, hypotheticals, like we was saying, something to tell Mr. Havermyer about."

"Sid, thanks. Sounds like you have some great marketing plans. But, confidentially, how would you compare your numbers with those of Double Vision?"

"Blaine, I dunno."

"Sid, please. To help me convince Jacob Havermyer."

"As you know this is very, very confidential. And I share this with you only because we are having a simpatico kind of conversation with possibilities for future . . . ah, how do you say, alignment . . . yes, alignment between our organizations."

His voice lowered as he delivered his precious information. "Our numbers are similar to the entire line they have, the whole enchilada. But ours is pure energy. BodyHamr is the next Monster, trust me."

"So your energy revenue is in the forty millions?"

"For the purposes of this conversation that is a safe number to use, yes." Blaine had anticipated BodyHamr's numbers would be half that. Once they started due diligence, they'd sort out the actuals.

"You tell Mr. Havermyer he gets that advice from me free of charge, and I got a lot more where that came from. And I look forward to meeting him one day. I think we have quite a lot in common, ya know?"

"Great talking to you Sid, thank you. Are you going to be out on the West Coast for the BevGlobe conference next week? I know a number of the energy drink companies will be there."

"You betcha. We always have a real classy booth, kick ass sexy booth babes, some, shall we say, foxy entertainment for our favorite distributors, the whole nine yards."

"Excellent. Let's make a point of getting together then."

They hung up. The hook was baited. Now for his next call.

***

Jacob looked down at the ringing phone. He frowned, then answered. "Havermyer."

"Jacob Havermyer, it's Blaine Latrell, of Axlewright Capital."

"Blaine, yes, your calls have been very persistent, so it must be something important."

"Yes indeed, I think it is important for us to be in touch. We share an important investment in Double Vision, something we both care about personally." Blaine paused for effect. Getting no response from Jacob he continued.

"It strikes me that the beverage space has infinite upside, a significant trajectory opportunity, but I am not sure we have attained the angle that is truly possible."

"What exactly do you mean?"

"I think Double Vision's pace of growth could be accelerated and the focus sharpened. Without that, the top four energy drink companies, let alone the Big Four beverage companies, will never be overtaken."

"Coca-Cola was started in 1886. That is over one hundred twenty years ago. Even Red Bull is thirty years old. Double Vision is in its fourth year, and literally months into introducing its energy drinks. And growing above the projected numbers."

"The energy drink tide is rising quickly and that is making DV look good. I want to make sure we expand even faster than average in the space. Like BodyHamr, for example."

"Hmm. You feel that BodyHamr is a competitor comparable in size and growing more quickly? What are their numbers?"

"They are very difficult to pin down. Due to a special relationship I have with their CEO, I was able to learn they are doing at least our total revenue, but strictly in energy. And they have some efficiencies by outsourcing their product manufacturing, and limiting their charitable contributions."

"Where are they located?"

"New Jersey."

"So they outsource their production and they don't do the one-for-one offer, and they don't offer a nutritional side. I'm looking on their website right now. A lot of very scantily clad women. And eight years in business. Blaine, I am failing to understand what about them is so compelling."

"Double Vision needs growth. If we invest more, acquire BodyHamr, blend the best of industry practices, the most aggressive management and sales people, we end up with a company poised for higher growth."

"Blake, what you . . ."

"It's Blaine."

"Yes, of course. Blaine, I understand what you are suggesting. Let's get right to it. You want more ownership, more control, and a blowtorch at the back of management to grow revenues as fast as possible. The typical VC deal. There are times for that. I don't think change is justified right now, and certainly not the kind of change BodyHamr would bring through an acquisition."

"It's our job to guide the growth of the company."

"I understand. But let me make a suggestion. Learn everything you can from BodyHamr and their CEO, your buddy. And share this at the next board meeting. If there are ideas we can use to grow Double Vision, then let's talk about them."

Not what he wanted, but at least it was some progress with Havermyer, Blaine thought. "Very well, I'll work the competition, and will personally update you."

"Be sure to keep the management team in the loop."

"Absolutely," Blaine promised.

***

"Come on in, Blaine." John Anderson pointed him to a chair. His shock of white hair was cleanly parted on one side, his face drawn tight around noncommittal eyes, part of his Teflon look. This wasn't a scheduled meeting. It was Friday afternoon, and John was known for delivering bad news on Fridays.

The rain outside was pounding against the windows. Long rivulets clung to the glass of the Transamerica Pyramid before plunging down forty stories. Blaine tried to show upbeat confidence, but his stomach felt like he was making the same forty-story fall. He hadn't exercised in months. His collar pinched his neck, and as he sat he felt the belly roll hanging over his belt. He smelled his own body odor, and clamped down on his armpits.

"Blaine, let me get to the point. Frankly, none of your investments have eager customers showing up to the party. The deals you have put together are duds. And it's time to face these facts."

Typical Anderson, a black hole sucking out his energy. "John, if I may, I have a fresh update."

Anderson's face registered no response. "Go ahead," he said warily.

Blaine adjusted his heavy glasses. "I spoke with Jacob Havermyer, personally, ten minutes ago. We are pursuing an active strategy together that I have crafted. This is designed specifically to grow Double Vision through acquisition, and coincidentally, replace Lionel. We have interest from the CEO of BodyHamr, Sid Shamitz. We've talked, and he might be the guy to run the whole show. Under our direction, of course.

"What does Havermyer think of this?"

"He is onboard." Blaine left it at that.

"What about the Big Disrupter prize?"

"You nailed it," Blaine enthused. "DV has fallen far behind. This could help them rebound. We could win the prize and be in fantastic shape."

"And if they lose?"

"It's Lionel's fault. And there will be several good reasons to replace him."

Anderson was silent. He looked out the window. The water streamed down the glass.

Suddenly he turned and waved a finger at Blaine. "I'll give you *one month* to make this happen."

Blaine nodded confidently.

"One month. Either you get rid of that embarrassment of a CEO, Lionel, and use DV to demonstrate you are a money-making deal-maker, or you are terminated at Axlewright."

Blaine's face fell as fast as the acid hitting his stomach.

"One month. No more discussions. I've defended you long enough. I suggest you get to work."

Blaine stood and walked out in a daze, the words "one month" rebounding in his head.

***

That afternoon Trig sat with Lionel in his office in San Francisco. The door was closed. Trig swept the room for bugs prior to beginning the conversation.

"Sir, we have the AZ99 mirror software running on Igor Vasilchenko's laptop."

"Trig, please, can you call me Lionel? Between the 'sirs' and the counterintelligence measures, I feel I'm on a military mission."

"Of course. Ingrained habit . . . Lionel."

"Great. So what have you learned?"

"Cyber crime. Igor has ongoing attempts right now to get into thirty different companies in the U.S., collecting proprietary commercial intelligence. He uses a database template that he populates as he proceeds." Trig moved next to Lionel and showed some examples on his laptop. "See? He is trying to steal business plans, forecasts, product strategy documents, patent applications, and info on M&A activity."

"What's the connection to us? Why Double Vision, and why now?" This seemed so unrelated, like they were caught up in someone else's deceitful plots.

"I don't know that yet. The person he seems to be working most closely with is named Zebra. Does that name mean anything to you?"

"Zebra? Not at all."

"Probably a random code name then. They email in English. Zebra must be here in San Francisco, because they've talked about local meetings. He appears to be the boss with the money."

"Trig, why would these guys cause the avalanche and the bike hit-and-run?"

Trig shifted in his chair. "I don't know yet. But I discovered one other thing."

"Yes?"

"He is running a stealth monitoring application. And he is targeting our servers, here at DV headquarters."

"Wait a minute. The guy we're spying on is actually spying on us?"

"Yes." Trig nodded slowly.

"How!?"

"It is very clever malware that hides in sectors of the server, cloaking itself. The scanning software never treats it as a possible threat."

"Wait—if we root it out does that mean he might realize we are onto him?"

"Exactly."

"So what do you suggest?"

"He has already downloaded what he wants. Now it appears he is monitoring the scheduling software and email, probably to track your and Maxine's whereabouts. I think you and Maxine should use your phones to text or call people about your locations. We'll block you out on the schedule for the next month as 'traveling,' no details. The same for Reddi."

"That's a hassle." Lionel drummed his fingers on the table. "But it seems like a smart precaution. And he won't know we are on to his monitoring of our corporate network."

"One more thing. Igor has a lot of information on his drive about Dasha. Pictures and details on her family back in Ukraine, and some background on programmers at Google and Facebook. Young Ukrainians, her age. I don't understand the connection, but I'm concerned.

Lionel sat up in surprise. Dasha? *No way.* "You don't think she is working with this guy Igor, do you? She seems so dedicated."

"My gut says no, but he has a lot of private information on her. I'd like to keep her out of the loop on this investigation until we can remove any suspicion."

"Damn." Lionel rubbed his temples. "Okay. But I can't imagine Dasha working against us." He thought of her incredibly long hours, early and late, often working alone in the computer room. They trusted her with all their data.

Lionel stood up, pacing. "We've got to track down the guy giving Igor his orders. This Zebra guy."

Trig's dark brow creased. "That's my top priority."

36

MONDAY, MARCH 3ᴿᴰ

Reddi was curled up in her bed with her phone, waiting on hold for Lionel. Luggage was strewn on the floor. Her tablet lay opened to a story with the headline: "X Games star loses, fails to place in Canadian ski challenge." Used tissues were scattered on her down comforter like powder puffs.

Lionel eventually returned. "Sorry, Reddi, I couldn't avoid that call." He sounded rushed. "Now where were we?"

"Lionel, sometimes I wonder if I'm doing the right thing. It's not just losing. Traveling alone sucks. I hate leaving Wolfie behind. Plus customers are complaining about the welding shop being closed."

"You'll bounce right back," he said. She heard muffled whispering in the background.

"Lionel?"

"What was that honey?"

"I know you have so many things going on as CEO, but I feel like we aren't communicating. We hardly ever talk anymore."

"You're right. But can you hang on for one quick second, please? I've been trying to get hold of this Merry Cola VP for days, and he's finally calling me back. Sorry, this will be quick."

The wait dragged on. She started to come to a decision about the question agonizing her for weeks.

He returned, sounding out of breath. "I'm back. Insane day. I apologize. I definitely want to talk with you."

"Lionel, you know I care for you, that I totally appreciate everything you have done for me."

The phone beeped. "I am *so* sorry. Be *right* back."

When he came back on the line, she continued. "I know you don't like long conversations on the phone. But sometimes it's three or four days and I haven't talked with you. We just have short texts or emails."

"It's been a little crazy recently. We're both traveling all over the place, business is blowing up, and your career is exploding."

This is so hard to do over the phone. I hate this, she thought.

"Lionel, when I am with you, you are so attentive. You look at me, you make me feel like I am the center of the universe, you ask me crazy and embarrassing questions."

"Is it too much?"

"No, I like that. It's outrageous. You try to understand who I am. And my new success is because you believed in me and made all sorts of things come together so I could compete."

She heard him pacing. "I have nothing to do with your talent and your drive. That is one hundred percent you. You deserve all the credit for your success."

"You are the one who convinced everyone at DV to support my efforts. And without that . . . I can't go on."

"Signing you to represent us was one of my smarter business decisions. It has been *great* for DV. Why are we arguing about this anyway? What are we talking about?"

Reddi grabbed another tissue and wiped her eyes. *She couldn't even talk. She was too choked up.*

"Reddi? Are you okay? What's up? I'm twisting in the wind here."

She spoke haltingly, her voice breaking. "Lionel, this isn't . . . enough for me. I want someone steady . . . Someone who puts me at the center of his life . . . and has time to keep me there."

She heard him inhale. He asked quietly, "Are you saying . . . we're breaking up?"

Reddi whispered in a little voice. "Yes."

***

Reddi hugged Wolfie a long time, talking and crying some more. *Had she made a huge mistake?* She hated feeling uncertain. Yet that was one of the reasons she had broken up with Lionel. Wolfie licked her tears.

"You always understand me, Wolfie." She smiled and gave her one last rub. She didn't want to be alone and unhappy. She composed herself, fed Wolfie, and walked up to Telluride's Main Street.

"Reddi!" came a shout. Tom Funkmeister, sporting a Cat in the Hat top hat above his curly beard, pushed opened the door of the Loose Moose and threw his arms up wide.

"You Nordic Wonder Woman. Goddess of the Deep. Like a returning Viking you must come in and regale us with stories of travels and conquests!"

"The Funkmeister. How are the Epoxy Queens?" Reddi opened her arms and they embraced, laughing.

"Crazy as always. Skiing backcountry, breaking gear, and gluing it all together."

"You working?"

"Nah, we're skiing. Snow's too deep to work. Slowly burning down that fine summer stash of cash from construction."

"How's the house? Still at the end of town in the old miner's cabin?"

"All ten of us." He started laughing. "We were doing flips off the roof today, and Big Yan's ski popped off and crashed right through the kitchen window."

"No way! Is he okay?"

"He's inside wearing a grass skirt, queen for a night, entertaining us all."

"And your girlfriend Mona?"

"Better than ever. She's bartending tonight."

Funkmeister leaned back, examining her face, still holding her. His cheeks were red and curved like apples above his beard. "Come inside. Everyone's dying to see you."

"Inside?" She glanced at the saloon. "I'm not in the mood, Tom."

"Reddi, you're not gonna win every single competition. And these are the very times your friends are here for you." He gently tugged her toward the Loose Moose. "Come. We'll make you laugh. The other queens will be heartbroken if you don't have a round and watch at least one grass skirt dance."

She rolled her eyes. "Okay, one round. I'm in training you know."

"Mademoiselle, you delight us with your company, however so brief." He bowed and opened the door. The sounds of merriment and music washed over her, and a rowdy throng of ski bums yelled greetings and pulled her in.

Reddi sat next to Funkmeister at the bar, as his best friends and housemates crowded around. They replayed the video of her X Game victory on the TV screen above the bar, time and time again. Several of the guys wearing grass skirts started jumping off tables trying to imitate her moves. Chairs scattered everywhere, amidst tumbles, rolls, and laughter.

"Who thought up the name Epoxy Queens?" Reddi asked.

"I did," came a chorus.

"It's unanimous," said Tom. "We all invented the handle for a bunch of ragtag skiers from Vermont who love the steep and the deep. And we love you, Reddi. Three cheers for our Freestyle Queen. We anoint you an honorary member of the Epoxy Queens!" Cheering, the friends slammed down yet another round of tequila shots.

Two hours later, without ever spending a dime, Reddi was hammered. Her head began to spin. "I gotta go home." She pulled on her wool hat. "Thanks Mona," she said to the bartender, with a flopping wave of her hand. She pushed the bar and fell off the stool backward. Funkmeister and another Epoxy Queen rushed over.

"Oh dear, our comrade has copped a complete buzz. Let's walk her home. Come on, Reddi."

"You betcha," she slurred. They picked her up and she threw her arm around Funkmeister, still wearing his Cat in the Hat top hat. Leaning on him and another Epoxy Queen, they stumbled out of the Loose Moose and into the snowy street. It was dark, and only a few blocks to her crib. But the falling snow made the road slippery. With all the booze, she could barely hold her head up. But she knew Wolfie was waiting for her.

***

Gonzo, BodyHamr's ski champion, had been watching this spectacle from the back of the bar, pretending to be busy online with his phone. He drank slowly and seethed at her popularity. When they staggered out, he got his coat and slipped into the street.

He followed in the shadows. As the two guys helping Reddi approached the front door of her crib, Gonzo heard Wolfie's whines. Gonzo crossed the street and watched as they opened the door. Light streamed onto the porch. Wolfie nosed Reddi, then began jumping around. The room looked chaotic as they struggled with Reddi. After Funkmeister closed the front door, Gonzo moved closer to spy through the window.

"It's too crowded for all of us, Wolfie." Gonzo saw Funkmeister rub Wolfie, then lock her in the kitchen. "Good Wolfie. Stay girl."

They dropped Reddi into bed and tugged off her coat, wool beanie, gloves and boots.

"That's a beautiful girl."

"Yeah. And hammered. She's out cold."

Funkmeister dragged the down comforter over her.

Seeing that, Gonzo retreated to the shadows.

The two friends left her, pulling the door behind them.

"Is it locked, dude?"

Funkmeister rattled the handle. "Yup, she's tight." And they wobbled up the street.

Gonzo stretched his black ski mask over his face. Then he slipped behind the crib. The new snow was quiet underfoot. He inspected the first window in the back. Seeing the kitchen, he continued. He crept around a small shed and found the second window, the one that opened to the bedroom. He saw a shape on the bed.

The hunting knife clicked as it unfolded into the locked position. Its sharp blade easily punctured the visqueen insulation covering the window. Gonzo sliced the taut plastic with the smoothness of opening a zipper, down one edge, across the bottom, then up the other side. The outer plastic hung like a flap now, and the window was accessible. Standing on the piled-up snow, the window was at his waist level. The moonlight was at his back, illuminating his work, but the shed hid him. The window was old single-pane divided-light construction. Placing his heavy jacket against a single pane, with a pop of his elbow the glass gave way. He waited, holding his breath. No one stirred. The lights remained dark. With his gloved hand he removed the larger pieces and dropped them quietly in the snow. Then he reached in, turned the latch, and pushed up the window.

He boosted himself inside, closed the window, and put the open knife on the bed stand. As he stood over Reddi's comatose form, his eyes grew accustomed to the darkness. Details emerged.

She was on her side, her face turned away from the moonlight on her hair. The veins in his neck pulsed against the tightly stretched mask. His lips whispered through the small opening, "Reddi you nasty bitch, you want me, don't you?" The thrill of hearing the words out loud sent a shiver down his back. She lay submissively. "You want me to dominate you, I know." He trembled with attraction and anger.

He sucked in air as he stroked himself, his rasping breaths deepening. The pressure welled up as he grew harder, pushing against his jeans.

He turned to the bedstand and took the knife. In the moonlight he slid open the window, cut off the hanging plastic flap, and brought it back inside. He closed the window and placed the sheet on the thin rug that insulated the cold wood floor. He sliced it into four long strips.

He tied a strip on each of the four bedposts. A floorboard creaked, and Reddi moaned. He froze. And waited. Her eyelids twitched. But she slept, and he started moving again.

He fingered her coat and boots on the floor. He found her wool beanie and placed it on the bed, next to her head.

He pulled the top part of the comforter down to her waist. Rolling her over on her back, he stretched one arm toward the strap. She tugged her arm, but he held her wrist, tying it in place. Her head rocked and she moaned. She reeked of alcohol. But her eyes remained closed. He crept around the bed to the other side. He fingered her thick hair and studied her face in the moonlight. All those freckles. He took the hunting knife and ran it down the length of her face, grazing the skin. Then he jabbed it into the top of the bedstand. He slowly forced her other arm up. She moaned again, and her breathing became faster. As he finished tying her second arm, she twitched and blinked her eyes. He grabbed the beanie from the bed and stuffed it into her mouth. She gagged, and started shaking her head, snorting.

Moving quickly, he slid the comforter off her legs. He heard her choking on the beanie. She began jerking her feet. He grabbed an ankle and wrapped the plastic strip around it, cinching it tight to the bedpost. Only one foot left to have her completely spread eagle. He reached for it.

***

Warning signals were screaming in Reddi's brain. But the heavy blanket of alcohol smothered them. Something was keeping her arms above her head. Uncomfortable. She couldn't get up. She pulled harder, confused.

She struggled to open her eyes. Everything spun as she blinked. Her mouth was so dry. She gagged. *What's in it?* Stuffed full of something scratchy. She lifted her head. Her wrists were pinned down. She couldn't breathe.

She grunted in panic, thrashing her head back and forth, yanking her arms and twisting her upper body. She kicked. Only one leg could move.

I'm trapped. Can't breathe. She panicked.

Your nose. Use your nose. She inhaled. The air felt like life itself, and she sucked in short, desperate pulls.

Where am I? She twisted her head and recognized her room. Her temples throbbed from the movement. *What is someone doing in my bedroom? Who?* And then in the moonlight she saw the black ski mask.

She tried to scream but nothing came out. Bucking, her arms and wrists strained against the straps, gouging her. Her tendons and muscles felt like they would pop from the effort. Then the hole in the middle of the mask opened in a grin. Terror seized her gut.

The black figure moved toward her. She was paralyzed, staring at it. Then she saw the knife blade gleaming in the moonlight. It sliced toward her eye. She twisted her head to the side, wincing.

He pressed his hand against her breast as he leaned on her. She felt his stale breath as he whispered in her ear. "Quiet, you bitch. If you don't stop, I'm going to take your eye out. And then you'd be ugly and no one will like you."

The cold knife blade pressed flat against her cheekbone, below her eye. She shivered. *She'd heard that voice before.*

Suddenly, from across the room, behind the kitchen door, she heard whining and scratching. *Wolfie.* The ski mask turned. He pushed off her and walked toward the kitchen. "Good dog, Wolfie. Everything is fine, be quiet. Good Wolfie." The whining stopped.

He turned back to the bed. He put a vertical finger over the mouth hole. With the knife in his other hand he made a cutting motion under his throat. The masked head looked like a snake. *He knew Wolfie's name.*

He grabbed her other leg and quickly pulled it to the post. He sat on her leg as he lashed it tight. She was spread wide. *What was he going to do with that knife?* Each breath was a struggle. She felt underwater, sinking deeper.

He sat on the bed by her waist. "Now for the fun part. If you move you get cut. If you stay still, you won't get hurt." Reddi saw the knife move toward her belly and she reflexively sucked in. She felt his knuckles on her skin as he slid his hand up her middle, cutting the buttons off her flannel shirt. She squirmed.

He whispered in her ear. "Don't move. Or I will cut you."

Who was this evil sonofabitch?

He jerked the shirt open with his other hand. She felt his hand grab her bra. Her eyes were focused on the knife. It came toward her chest and nicked her. She noticed the trembling blade. Then it sliced the strap fastening the bra cups in the center. She felt the chill of the air on her breasts. The knife fell on her belly and then each of his hands grabbed a breast, pinching the nipples hard. She grunted and turned away, wiggling. He squeezed harder, pulling her.

She felt a burning liquid erupting, filling her throat. *She'd die choking on her vomit if she puked!* She willed it back down. Her nostrils wheezed as she sucked them tight, straining for air. The room started to spin. Hammers pounded at her temples. She fought to stay conscious, while part of her wanted to close off and shut down.

His hand grabbed her jeans. As he unbuckled them she forced herself to look at the mask. She saw his eyes as he struggled with the zipper, cursing. Then she realized who it was. *It's Gonzo. Fucking asshole. He hates me.*

Her kicks and twists were barely more than wiggles. He jerked hard on her waistband, then got the zipper down. With the knife rising and falling on her heaving stomach, he put both hands on the top of her jeans and jerked down. She felt his fingernails rubbing through her pubic hair.

"Who's in control now, you cunt?" He lifted her up by her bush and she screamed a muffled cry.

He pulled on the pants again, but with her legs spread out and tied, he couldn't get them down any farther. "Well bitch, we'll skin them off you."

Her abdomen was trembling, vibrating the open knife. The thick blade was serrated near the hilt, with saw-like teeth. *What was that knife for?*

He got on the bed, kneeling between her spread legs. She felt him put one arm under her butt and grab the back of her jeans. She felt the pressure under her as he raised her hips in the air. Then his other hand brought the knife under her butt.

Reddi's heart pounded as she snorted for air. She contracted every muscle in her lower body.

He plunged his arm downward, cutting and sawing. He slipped and scraped her and she winced. She tensed as his hand rubbed her backside. She heard the jeans tearing.

He stopped. "Hold still." Then he grinned. She closed her eyes. *Was he totally insane? What was he doing?*

He had hacked the entire backside of her jeans. With one final grunt he split them in two. She felt him grab her panties and slice them in half. He pulled the split jeans down each leg. She felt the cold air.

Is it rape? Mutilation? Then murder? The tension took her to the edge of passing out, and she wavering on a dark cliff, awash in alcohol. Her head pitched and rolled.

He stood above her, knife in hand. Then he placed it on the bed stand. She saw him eying her through the sockets of his mask as he undid his jeans and zipper. He pulled out his erection. Then he returned to the foot of the bed, staring through her spread legs.

"You see who the master is here? Me, you bitch."

She struggled for breath. The room kept moving. She gagged. Every wiggle and tug on the straps seemed to amuse him. He watched as his lips twisted in a grin.

She heard whining and scratching again. Wolfie. Wolfie. Reddi snorted desperately. Her eyes suddenly came into focus. *It's now or never.* She sucked in until she choked. Then coughing and vomiting at the same time, the beanie flew out. She screamed. "Wolfie, help me, Wolfie."

Gonzo lunged at her. She swung her head away and screamed again. Scratching and growling came from the kitchen.

"Its payback time, bitch," Gonzo spat into her ear, grabbing her hair and jerking her head. He shoved the soaking Beanie deep down her throat. She gagged. He straddled her. She felt him squeezing her breasts as he worked his way backward. His disgusting breath blew on her skin, faster now. Groping fingers pushed at her crotch. Her head pounded as she bucked her hips.

Then the room exploded in splintering wood. A white blur flew in behind Gonzo, as Wolfie snarled and clawed the floor.

Gonzo spun backward. "Shit!" He rolled off the bed, searching for the knife on the bedstand. Then he turned to Wolfie.

Wolfie's growl rumbled like she owned the room. Her white face and black mask pointed into him like an arrow, eyes glimmering as though possessed. Her sharp ears were wound back like coil springs. She lashed her fangs at him.

"Bitch! Get away!" he screamed, swinging the knife.

He backed toward the window and flung it open. As he bent to escape, Wolfie lunged. She snapped her teeth on his butt. She twisted her head tearing a bloody chunk out. She snapped again and again.

Gonzo was screaming. He swung an arm backward and Wolfie shredded it to the bone. Crawling and crying, he grabbed the window ledge and pulled himself out headfirst, falling into the snow below.

Wolfie snarled out the open window, her teeth stained red. Then she turned back to Reddi. She came close and put her paws up on the bed. She nosed Reddi and put her teeth on the beanie, pulling it free from her mouth.

Reddi sobbed and shuddered as she drank in the sweet cold air.

"Up here, Wolfie." Wolfie jumped and nestled next to her, her thick coat against Reddi's chilled skin.

"I love you, girl. Thank you, thank you." She trembled as she rubbed her head against Wolfie's fur.

Reddi could hear Gonzo moaning outside, lying in the moonlit snow, trying to contain the life oozing out of him.

***

Minutes later sirens were wailing and a vehicle raced to a stop outside the crib. Reddi heard Sheriff Masterson shout, "Police! Open up!"

Reddi called back, "Help, Sheriff."

Masterson kicked down the front door, gun drawn. Wolfie's hair was on end as she stood on the bed growling.

"It's okay, Wolfie. He's a good guy. You know Sheriff Masterson. Down girl."

Masterson holstered his weapon. He picked up the comforter off the floor and carefully approached the bed.

"Good Wolfie. I'm friendly. Good girl."

He gently put the comforter over Reddi. He cut the straps binding her, then got her some clothes.

As she returned from the bathroom, the sheriff was looking through the window at the crying form in the snow below, now handcuffed. Lights were flashing outside, emergency vehicles arriving. "Sheriff, it's that asshole Gonzo, from BodyHamr."

"Not surprising, actually," he replied, shaking his head. "Most rapes or rape attempts involve people who know each other."

He turned back and looked at Reddi. "You've clearly been through hell. But I need to take you to the medical center right away, as well as get a statement. I have the feeling you won't want to leave Wolfie for a while, so we can bring her along."

"Thanks, Sheriff."

As they rode in the back of the sheriff's SUV, Reddi curled up with Wolfie in her arms, holding her tight, trying to control her trembling. She whispered in her ear. "How would you like to have a new trick named after you? Maybe the Midnight Rescue. Or the Flying Wolfdog? Or, how about the Big Bite Roll?"

37

TUESDAY, MARCH 4TH

Wolfie howled at the knock on the door.
"It's Trig, Reddi. I just got to town."
Wolfie quieted and sat still, ears and head cocked toward the door.
"Oh, you know him, don't you? We love Trig." Reddi threw the door open. Trig stood with his arms out.

"I didn't expect you," she said. His brown eyes were circled with concern. He seemed tired. She hugged him. Big, strong arms. His stubble was rough and he smelled like fresh soap. He was such a great guy for showing up like this, she thought.

"Come in, please. Wolfie, it's okay." Reddi pulled on Trig's arm and led him to the small table in the kitchen. She suddenly wished she had space for a sofa in her crib, instead of just kitchen chairs and her bed.

"It's good to see you. Did you hear . . . ?"

He nodded. "A friend on the sheriff's response team called me. Then I cashed in a favor and got a ride on a private jet." He rubbed a hand on the edge of the table. "So, how are you doing?"

"It's a good thing that door was old and Wolfie is strong as hell." She looked at the broken hinges hanging in the doorway. She had cleaned up the bulk of the shattered door and changed the sheets and covers. Now she found herself staring at the bed.

"Oh, God. I can't believe it was twelve hours ago that Gonzo had me tied up to that very bed."

Trig glanced inside the other room. He moved his hand closer to hers. "Why don't you and Wolfie come stay at my place? I'll sleep on the couch. Just for a few days."

She sat back. "I don't want to put you out. I can sleep in the welding shop."

"Reddi, the point is to have some company. For a little while. Give yourself some time."

"People might talk," she said, shaking her head.

"What do you mean? I'll be on the couch. I'm an old friend. And given these circumstances, everyone will understand why you might want to stay with someone you know."

"Oh, maybe. It's a little more complicated."

He watched her with his patient brown eyes. She decided to tell him everything.

She took a big breath. "Yesterday I broke up with Lionel. That was part of this whole disaster."

"Sorry to hear that."

"And it was hard. He is a great guy, super smart, and he did a lot for me personally. I got very emotional, and let myself get in a funk."

"That's understandable."

"Yeah, but I was also pissed because I skied like shit in the Canadian contest. Didn't even make the top five."

"I hate it when I'm not perfect, myself."

"Oh, cut it out." She shoved his arm. He smiled at her.

"I was pretty depressed. I took a walk to clear my head, and went by the Loose Moose. Funkmeister saw me, we got to talking, his girlfriend was bartending that night, and the next thing you know I'm inside getting free drinks."

"I know a free drink with friends is hard to turn down."

"Gee, thanks. Did you fly all this way just to make me feel dumber?" She wondered if he was going to lecture her.

"I'm joking. Keep going." He patted her hand.

"The Epoxy Queens were trying to cheer me up, but then I drank way too much. Tequila shots." She shuddered. "I'm in training. I can't waste myself like that." She shook her head slowly. "And then goddamn Gonzo."

"Gonzo. I'd like a few minutes with him myself."

She saw his jaw tighten. He had a very scary look in his eyes. It frightened her to think of what he could do to a man given his training.

"Trig, it's okay. He's an asshole, but now he has some chunks bit out of his butt and is locked up."

"Oh, he's going to serve time, we'll see to that. Maybe he'll be dancing for a big nasty dude and get some of what he was trying to give."

"Trig, you're not going to do something to him that will get you in trouble, are you? I mean, I'd like to roast Gonzo's testicles over a fire. But, thanks to Wolfie, he didn't rape me. Or worse. He terrified me, and I'm still very freaked out. But the sheriff has him now. Just because I did something stupid doesn't mean you should too."

"What did you do that was stupid? You were just partying."

"I lost it at the Loose Moose. Got out of hand, and made myself vulnerable."

"I talked to Funkmeister. Yes, you had way too much to drink. But considering you were four blocks from home, and walking, not driving...."

"More like being carried, you mean."

"Fine, helped along. But every one of those guys has been in a situation like that at least once in their lives. And they didn't get attacked."

"Yeah, well they aren't girls. I'm not saying it's right—it isn't. It's screwed up."

"My point is, the problem is Gonzo, not you. Don't feel guilty for being you. Ever."

She looked into his warm brown face, with the lines of concern. She suddenly felt safe. In every way. Instead of a lecture he reaffirmed her. This guy was here for her.

She put both of her hands on his broad jaw and pulled his face close to hers. And kissed him on the cheek.

***

Trig left to talk with the sheriff, and Reddi decided it was time to turn her phone back on. She had dozens of missed calls and voice mails. Word must have quickly spread in town with all the late night commotion. She began scrolling through the messages.

Hugo had left a very sweet voicemail. He offered Reddi his condo. He went on to say workers at the local DV bottling plant had told him the news this morning and he then informed DV headquarters. The next message was Lionel's. He sounded very upset, so she sent him a text. Kate was very supportive, assured her the news was still mostly within DV, but wanted to discuss a PR strategy ASAP. Maxine simply said: "Call me, sister, when you can." Maxine's was the first call she returned.

"Reddi, I am so glad to hear from you. How is my Wonder Woman?"

"Not feeling like I have superpowers today. That peckerwood Gonzo had me in a real bad position."

"You are unbelievable. To fight back from that and win."

"It was Wolfie with the midnight rescue. Thank God for her."

"After I couldn't reach you, I called Trig. He gave me the lowdown about the attack. I'm still shaking. I can't imagine how you feel."

The emotion in Maxine's voice surprised Reddi. Then she remembered. "You know how we felt after the avalanche? Once we had Hannah back from under the ice, and Wolfie too?"

"I'll never forget. Walking up that slide path together, once everyone was safe."

"That mixture of relief and anger and guilt. But mostly thankfulness? I feel that right now."

Maxine was quiet for a moment. "That was so intense. I'm sorry I'm not there with you, to give you a hug . . . but Trig is there, right?"

"Yeah. After the whole ordeal, I was back home and not able to sleep . . . then I heard knocking at the door. There was Trig. He was so supportive, and made sure I didn't blame myself in some stupid twisted way. He is really special."

"He is an amazing guy."

"Did you know I broke up with Lionel?"

"Yes, he told me."

"We just didn't talk or see each other enough."

"You don't have to convince me. He wants a perfect mate, some impossible combination. Yet he is unwilling to compromise his dreams."

"Maybe one day he will."

"Let's talk about you. You're the one who went through hell."

"I'll say this. I'm never, ever, going to let myself get that hammered again. That vulnerable."

"I hear you there, sister."

"And you know what else?"

"What?"

"If you hadn't rescued Wolfie from the avalanche, then she couldn't have saved me. And I'd be . . . ." Reddi shook her head. "Maxine. All I know is, now I owe you."

**

The light from Sheriff Masterson's squat brick building disappeared out the window into the dark sky. The quiet of his office was broken by footsteps.

A figure appeared at the doorway. White snowflakes glistened like stars on the black watch cap and across the broad shoulders of the jacket.

Masterson startled. "Trig Garcia? I thought you were in San Francisco."

"I was, sir. Just arrived. Sir, would it be possible to question the rape suspect?"

"Trig, it's eight o'clock at night."

"Yes, sir."

Masterson leaned back in his chair. "Someone must have called you about the attack?"

"Yes, sir. I'd like to talk to him for a few minutes. He may have information relevant to other investigations. For example, the avalanche. And the hit-and-run. Time is of the essence."

Masterson took a closer look at Trig. Everything about him was tense, from the forward tilt of his broad shoulders, the slight pulsing of his hands, to the tiny muscle in his jaw that twitched.

"Given how fast you got here, you must have figured your way via some private jet. I won't even ask. You beeline at eight p.m. to my office, and you want to march in and question a suspect who attacked a woman that you have known for over fifteen years. And you are a trained SEAL."

"Yes sir. Just some questions."

"Trig, if I wanted to make sure this suspect Gonzo never walked on this earth for another day, then I'd let you see him. But I can't do that. Anyway, he's in intensive care, guarded under lock and key."

"Predators like him are cowards. I could get him to talk pretty quickly."

"Tell you what." Masterson pushed away his paperwork, and leaned back in his chair. "You clearly want action on this case. Do you know this Inspector Chang from SFPD?"

"Not yet. I've been meaning to contact him."

"We've talked a few times. He called today. It's still seven p.m. in SF. Let's get him on the phone and bring each other up-to-date. Who knows, we might solve something together, okay?"

Trig nodded. Sheriff Masterson reached Chang and turned up the speakerphone.

"Inspector, are you still in the office? It's late there."

"No. I pulled my car over to take the call. It's dark and raining here. I'm curious about what you've found, though."

"You bet. Late last night we took an attempted rape suspect into custody. He is a professional skier sponsored by BodyHamr named Gonzo Sonders."

"Isn't BodyHamr a rival to Double Vision?"

"Yes. And the person he attacked, Reddi, is sponsored by Double Vision."

"Ah, yes. I've read about her. Hmm. I wonder, was this Gonzo character in town when the avalanche occurred?"

"He was. Initially we didn't suspect him, as he was reported to be hammered at a local bar at closing time."

"Which made him an unlikely suspect at that point?"

"Correct. Now, with this attack, we've got some questions for Gonzo."

There was a pause.

"Sheriff, let me ask about Igor Vasilchenko. How do you see him fitting into this?"

Masterson leaned toward the speakerphone. "We know his Audi places him speeding across Colorado prior to the avalanche. And his car matches Lionel's description from the bike accident."

"Could Igor be in the employ of BodyHamr? Is that what you're thinking?"

"Maybe so," said Masterson, with a sideways glance toward Trig.

The call went quiet for a moment.

"Trig, do you know any more about this Igor character?" asked Chang.

"Nothing definitive, sir."

"Uh, huh. Trig, a little birdie told me you have formal training in cyber crime. Hacking, that kind of stuff."

"I worked at Fort Meade in Maryland, sir. Three years. Part of the Cyber Command."

"Is any of that useful here? Just wondering." Chang sounded offhand, like it was a casual query.

"Sir, I am safeguarding the Double Vision computers and network. That is part of my responsibilities."

"Oh, I see. Anything interesting coming up?"

"My apologies, sir. I'm not at liberty to discuss the company's internal security measures at this point."

"But you have Igor on your radar, so to speak?" Chang persisted.

"Yes sir, I believe him to be a viable suspect."

Masterson spoke up. "Inspector Chang, do you have anything on Igor?"

"I did check Interpol and other European databases. Vasilchenko was part of a Russian gang smuggling drugs. Evidently the gang was recently wiped out by a rival gang, butchered and dropped into the Black Sea. But they never found Vasilchenko."

"That's gruesome. But Igor could be alive? He might be the guy they ticketed?"

"Right. And one other thing."

"What's that?"

"He is an explosives expert. Army trained."

"What?" Masterson drew closer to the speakerphone. "Now that is interesting."

"Yet BodyHamr isn't in the Big Disrupter contest," replied Chang.

"But they are rivals. And it's a billion-dollar prize. No way you want your competitor to win that," Masterson noted.

"Well then, gentlemen, we may have our motive and our guys."

38

FRIDAY MARCH 14TH

As the Boeing 757 jet lifted off the runway at LAX, Maxine and Lionel looked over at each other.

"Sure you are fine with the middle seat?" he asked.

She gave him a mock glare, and then a weary smile. "You need the aisle, less self-control."

"A little humiliation is worth the extra comfort."

She pushed his leg playfully.

Lionel reclined wearily, his head rolled toward Maxine. He recounted their travels. Before LA it was Austin, before that Boston, Chicago, and Atlanta, Miami, New York.

"Hopefully this burnout is worth it," he said.

"I don't see an alternative. Although you probably miss your skiing in Telluride."

"No time for that now. And Hugo is on top of the Telluride production, big time. Plus with my breakup, even less of a reason to go back."

"Your breakup with Reddi?"

"Yeah."

"How are you handling that?"

He groaned. "I should have seen it coming. We've all been so busy. You and I are crisscrossing the country. She has blown up with her publicity and contests. We weren't talking enough, I guess."

Maxine nodded.

Lionel sighed. "Anyway, she said she needs a guy who puts her more at the center of her life. And I don't, evidently."

"Bad timing. Sorry about that." Maxine didn't sound that surprised.

"Yeah, thanks." He paused. "And now, with that attack on her, I feel even worse."

"Trig's been with her, right?"

"Yeah, ever since the attack he's either been with her or checking in on her. He says she's doing well, all things considered."

"He's making her the center of his life."

"Trig? He's always been protective of her."

"Uh, huh."

"What does *that* mean?"

"We'll see. Don't be surprised if those two become a real couple."

"Oh, thanks. Now I'm exhausted, dumped, *and* replaced."

Damn, she was probably right. He'd wondered about Trig before, but Reddi insisted they were strictly friends. Maxine. What else was Maxine right about? He sank deeper in the seat and fell asleep, thinking of her.

A few minutes later he felt her hand shaking him. He started to wake up.

"Lionel. Lionel."

He remembered her warm touch. Her smell next to him. He was dreaming of their intimate moments during their senior year of college. Rolling on a blanket under blossoming sugar maples in New England. It was a warm spring day. And as their clothes gradually came off...."

Maxine shook him hard. "Lionel. We're going to be in San Francisco soon. Tell me about your speech this afternoon for BevGlobe. What's it like?"

"Huh? Oh, yeah." He opened his eyes. "I've got that covered." He stretched in his seat, and discretely tugged at his pants. The warm memory receded.

"The BevGlobe conference is full of beverage manufacturers, suppliers, and distributors—so we have both our key partners and our competitors in attendance. Of course I can't share our internal information. Instead I entertain, present industry trends, and share some of our own video. With all our recent video promotion we have plenty of funny mistakes, stuff that got edited out. Kind of our 'B roll' footage."

"And that's good for the brand?"

"I pump the brand indirectly. In a humorous and self-deprecating way. This crowd hates speakers giving thinly disguised sales pitches."

"That's your style. If they like it, I guess it makes sense."

He realized they didn't agree. He decided to change the topic. "You know, the LA meetings went well. You rocked it."

"I did?" She sounded pleased.

"You were passionate, clever, and credible. I think all three meetings went incredibly well."

"Come on, it was both of us. Flanti, the musician, was my favorite. And it will be huge if she follows up on her promise to promote us in her concerts and social media, gratis."

"She is gorgeous."

"You noticed?"

"The two of you looked beautiful together."

"Charming." But she smiled anyway. "Is that all you think about?"

"Of course not. I'm thinking about three weeks to go."

"Now you're talking like a man who gets my interest."

"Yes ma'am, I do know your interests." He ran his fingers through his hair. "How about that Bull Delaney, the movie producer?"

"He was a character. With the Cadillac with the horns on the front, driven by that muscular guy?"

"The Vin Diesel look-alike in the tight T-shirt?"

Maxine giggled.

"I was a little more interested in his girlfriend Anka, the super model," Lionel said.

"Figures."

"Come on. She was very funny. I think she was behind placing our product in his upcoming movie."

"I agree. Very sharp. But you and tall Nordics kind of have a thing."

"Hey, it's mostly because the brilliant brunettes ignore me."

"Ignore?" she said with an arched eye. "We've been traveling together for ten days."

"You're right. And it's been good." He stretched in his seat. "Should we talk about Merry Cola? They'll be at BevGlobe. Their orders are rising, but we have a long way to go."

"No way they have doubled them yet, like Garr promised," she complained.

"Is it their ponderous size that takes so much time and effort?"

"Or is Merry playing us? Stringing us along, planning to introduce their own product?"

"I don't know. What if they did something stupid like bought BodyHamr?" Lionel worried.

"That would be bad. BodyHamr was behind the attack on Reddi, right?"

"At least their sponsored skier was—Gonzo."

"Has Trig spoken with Gonzo yet?" Maxine asked.

"No. Trig said the sheriff was afraid to let him question Gonzo. Trig promised not to waterboard him, but it wasn't enough."

"Very funny. Do you think you can have a conversation with the BodyHamr CEO without punching him out?"

"Sid Shamitz? Now Maxine, there is a good example of a cheesy opportunist who is totally focused on money. Is that your type?"

"From his picture he's a little old for me. But let me reserve judgment until I meet him in person at the show."

"Sure, if you can make your way past the pole dancers in their booth."

Maxine shook her head in disgust. "Despite the emotions, we can't focus on revenge. BevGlobe is a great time to boost distribution and get back on track for winning the Big."

"I totally agree. It's all about business."

***

Kate stood in the aisle of the enormous BevGlobe exhibition hall in Moscone Center. She scrutinized the various company signs hanging from the ceiling, marking their display areas and booths below. Seeing the BodyHamr logo, she peered at their display, and scowled at the scantily clad dancers gyrating out front. She had insisted Double Vision's booth be located a considerable distance away from BodyHamr's prominent corner location. "Sleazy creeps," she muttered.

She glanced at her watch. Lionel's presentation should be over now. She had checked on his session, and it was packed. Maxine was in a sales meeting with an international distributor in their private conference room. She worried about getting one of them back to the booth in time to meet the VIPs she expected.

Kate returned her focus to their booth. An intern handed out pre-autographed photos of Reddi, as she shook hands and chatted briefly with the long line of interested attendees. Sales people offered samples and chatted with the visitors. Videos played on several flat-screen TVs nearby. They looped between extreme adventure shots and young people with high-energy lifestyles. But the star of the booth and most popular draw at BevGlobe was definitely Reddi.

It was impossible to miss the red wave of flowing hair. Especially being six feet tall and wearing high-heeled Uggs. Kate complimented herself on the custom show outfit she had created. Reddi rocked it, from the logo scarf, short-waisted vest, to her snug flame-trimmed pants. God, she wished she had a nineteen-inch waist. And everything else that firm. If Reddi weren't such a sweet kid, Kate would hate her.

Kate walked over and pulled Reddi aside for a moment. "You look fabulous. And I am thrilled with that line of fans here at the booth. But how are you holding up?"

"I could do this all day," she smiled. "I'm trying to make sure they know about the good DV is doing with the nutritional donations. Although a lot of people prefer to talk about skiing, the X Games, and going to the Olympics. And they want to meet Wolfie."

"God, if we'd brought her, you two would suck all the life out of the show." Reddi's fresh enthusiasm was endearing, she thought. Suddenly Kate noticed someone approaching. "I'll be right back." She patted Reddi's arm. Then she added, "And if I am accompanied by an executive with a bushy mustache, ask him about skiing." She dashed away.

Minutes later Kate returned, shepherding Lionel and a well-preserved middle-aged man with a strong jaw, thick brown mustache, and impeccable suit.

Lionel pulled Reddi away from the crowd with an apology. "Reddi Christiansen, I'd like to introduce Garr Gartick, CEO of Merry Cola and a big fan of yours."

"This is indeed a pleasure, young woman." He wrapped both of his hands around hers, shaking slowly. "I didn't think it would be possible for you to look even more radiant than the images on television, but indeed you do."

"Thank you," Reddi replied with a smile. Then she stepped closer. "I understand you are quite a skier, Mr. Gartick. Is that right?"

"Please, call me Garr. And yes, I ski. Principally by helicopter. In Alaska."

"Oh man, I'd love to do that some day."

"Perhaps we can arrange that. We can take my Gulfstream from Manhattan to the Chugach range, outside of Valdez. The best guides, our own helicopter, and powder all day. And then we retire to a beautiful private lodge." He smiled and rubbed his mustache.

"Garr, trust me, based on my experience trying to ski with her, you'd only see her for five seconds before she disappeared far ahead of you," said Lionel.

"That sounds impressive," Garr replied, as he looked her up and down, his nostrils flaring.

Lionel turned to Reddi. "Thanks, Reddi, but I'm going to steal Garr away now and see if we can talk a little business."

"What a pity. Reddi, a pleasure meeting you." Garr kissed her hand. "And when we decide to do that helicopter trip, let's not tell Lionel, okay?"

She laughed. "As long as I can bring my wolfdog."

Lionel chuckled, then steered Garr to a small meeting table in the back of their exhibit space. Kate followed behind them within earshot, watching for snooping competitors.

"Very impressive. The face of Double Vision is even more wholesome, more perfect in person than I imagined."

"She is. That's why we need Merry Cola to step up. Garr, I appreciate you are busy. But you have to complete your commitment to double your order."

"I assure you, the boost in orders is rolling through the system. I don't have the details, but the process is ramping up. Once our giant machine is in motion—watch out. If you build the demand, we'll be fulfilling in outlets everywhere."

Kate heard Lionel raise his voice. "We've only got weeks until the Big. You've got to be able to speed this up."

Garr slapped the table. "Dammit Lionel, you could offer me a week of nights with your redhead over there, and there is nothing more I could do."

Kate saw Lionel launch to his feet and storm away.

***

This has dragged on twenty minutes longer than needed. Maxine nodded respectfully at the potential Asian distributor, as DV's international sales director chatted interminably about minutia. They sat in a stifling private conference room with a cheesy chandelier, faux cut-glass wall sconces and overly bright carpet. A phone call from Jacob Havermyer gave her the perfect reason to politely excuse herself.

"Hello Jacob." She walked down the wide hallway toward a sitting area.

"How are sales?" It was classic Havermyer directness, but she noticed a slight edge.

"Right on target. If we could get Merry Cola distribution to move faster, we'd be over the moon. We had a recent surge in interest, but a hard time getting the product to all markets fast enough. Why, what's up, may I ask?"

"I'm trying to understand why Axlewright Capital thinks DV would benefit from merging with BodyHamr."

"What? Merge with those misfits? You must be kidding me. Unless," and she started to reconsider it, "Unless they are available really cheap?"

"I don't think it's that. Blaine's sounding an alert about DV not growing as fast as the competition. And the suggestion is that BodyHamr is killing their numbers."

"You know those guys are going the easy route. Very little new product development, no nutritional products, and 'me too' marketing. Plus, no one-for-one offer. They aren't doing anything innovative."

"On the record, let's agree I called to check on the numbers and encourage you. But off the record, beware. At the end of the day these fishing expeditions usually indicate someone wants to change a CEO. So make sure your performance doesn't afford Blaine an opportunity to bring this to the board from any position of strength."

Maxine's stomach dropped. Why was Blaine still going after Lionel? And maybe her too. "Got it. It does sound like a witch-hunt. Thanks for the heads up."

She hung up and collapsed in a chair, exhaling every air molecule in her body. They were under attack from all corners.

***

At eleven p.m. Dasha received a priority alert. It came from the new video system she and Trig had installed. For each DV location, they monitored entrances, the racks of computer and network equipment, and the bottling operations.

The alert was from the Telluride office. The software Dasha had configured learned typical behavior, such as the janitor's movements, and recognized known faces. This alarm indicated something abnormal.

She sat barefoot in a T-shirt and flannel pajama bottoms in front of her Mac, her apartment dark except for the computer's pale glow. She opened a new window for the streaming video. She saw a tall Caucasian male, with a ski cap pulled over a long ponytail. He wore a suede jacket and nervously rubbed his angular nose. He moved desk to desk, rummaged through drawers, looking at papers. In one desk he inspected a box of business cards. Then he slid a plastic baggie full of white powder in the rear of the drawer.

"Looks like Lionel's desk," Dasha muttered.

The intruder went to the security panel, entered in the code rearming the office, and left.

Dasha gave Trig a call and sent him a link to the video. Trig alerted Sheriff Masterson in Telluride immediately.

Dasha also called Lionel. She was surprised his phone was off. She left an urgent message. Their office had been compromised.

39

SATURDAY, MARCH 15TH— PRESENT TIME

When he regained consciousness he was on his back. A crowd of faces stared down at him. The faces began to spin as he raised his head. He closed his eyes and sank back to keep from throwing up.

The fire escape. *Did he fall down the fire escape?*

Eventually the faces slowed and molded into one stationary old face. It was a man. He seemed very curious, bent over, staring at him. A worn corncob pipe hung out of a toothless mouth, and dry gray cracks creased his dark skin. A faded blue watch cap was pulled over his head. The whites of his eyes were streaked with rust-colored veins.

"Yer butt naked," came his high and amused voice.

"What?" he croaked. His head was pounding and he felt like he was floating outside his body.

"Well, at least yer talking." The ancient man straightened and slowly shuffled away. He made it to an upside-down crate, next to a blanket-covered shopping cart. He eased down, like it was home.

He pushed up from the ground. An enormous orange debris box loomed.

"Truck never saw ya. Dropped his debris box and drove off." The old man waved his pipe down the alley.

He shook his head, trying to remember.

"Yep. That sucker came sliding off da back of da truck and hit you like a fly swatter." He cackled and blew some smoke. "That'd make you the fly." The man started laughing, then launched into a coughing fit.

He heard the sounds in waves, louder then softer. Finally the coughing stopped.

The man tugged on something from the bottom rack of his cart. A filthy green plastic poncho emerged. "Ya might like this."

He took it. He stood uneasily, naked and shivering. He pulled the wrinkled poncho over his head, tugging down on the edges. It gradually occurred to him how important this was. "Thank you sir, I'll bring it back . . . plus some money . . . later . . . soon."

The old man pointed down the alley. "There's a church thataway. They got clothes. And mebbe some food."

"A church. With clothes."

"Doan forgit yer phone." He nodded to a smashed iPhone near his feet.

"This is mine?"

"Yep."

He picked up the cracked device. It didn't turn on. He nodded his thanks then drifted down the alley. The few people he saw looked away and walked by quickly.

The alley did lead to a church, of sorts. It was a converted house, ranch style, with a draped vinyl sign out front that read: *Evangelical Mission, Everyone Welcome.*

All the lower windows were covered with metal grates. A tall wrought-iron fence surrounded the small lot and in the middle were a gate and buzzer.

He couldn't remember the last time he was in a church. Not many options today. *He could use a revelation right now.*

The buzzer led to a welcoming voice, an open gate, and someone with sympathy. He explained what he could. With some hand-holding, lots of prayers and advice not to ever binge on liquor again, he got a warm meal. Then he left the church with a pair of blue high-water sweatpants, a red sweatshirt advertising the mission's "BBQ with Jesus" picnic, and a pair of old wingtip leather shoes.

He knew he had someplace to be. And he knew there was a person he wanted to be with very much. He just didn't know their names or where they were.

He followed his feet. They kept taking him in a direction along the bay, toward downtown. He saw ships and sensed he was going the right way. It got darker and he moved under a freeway onramp, making a pad from discarded cardboard. Other people shuffled in under the ramp's protection, some with carts. Others with bags. Street grime covered them head to foot.

He smiled and said hello to everyone. Most ignored him. Occasionally a new fact would surface from his memory, and he'd add that to the puzzle of his identity. Finally, he fell asleep.

40

SUNDAY, MARCH 16TH

Maxine called Lionel early in the morning. It went directly to voicemail. *The same as yesterday*, she thought. She checked email and texts. No luck. He was still missing.

There had been times when their travels put them out of touch. Especially on weekends. *But this felt different.*

Worried, she called Trig.

"I could notify the police, but maybe that's overreacting."

"Ma'am, when did you see him last?"

"Friday afternoon, at BevGlobe. We flew in from LAX and he gave a presentation. I met with an international distributer. He was at the booth for a while. We planned to get together at the cocktail reception that evening."

"Did anyone see him there?"

"Kate did. Then he disappeared."

"That's thirty-six hours. I'm going to call Inspector Chang right now. I'll also file a report with Missing Persons. Meanwhile, as soon as I get back to San Francisco I'll visit the hotel and reception facilities and start asking around."

"Thanks, Trig."

"Please keep your phone handy. They may call you to follow up."

"Of course."

Maxine tried reading and watching TV online, but nothing held her interest. Panic seized her one moment. Then anger would take over, as she imagined Lionel off on an adventure. He could be helicopter skiing in Alaska right now, she thought. Somewhere with no cell service. Or playing with some new love, rebounding from Reddi. Another redhead, she fantasized, growing angry. He could screw around however he wanted, but he needed to be responsible. They were two weeks away from the Big. So many things needed to happen for DV to win.

Why had she shown up late to that stupid cocktail party? Damn that long meeting!

What if BodyHamr people were behind his disappearance? And that creep Igor. The one with the Audi who started the avalanche. She spun in circles, worried. She had to do something. She had to get out of the apartment and look for herself.

She showered and pulled on jeans and a sweatshirt. Her hair was wet and up in a towel when she got a call. *Unknown number, San Francisco.*

"This is Maxine."

"You don't know me. But I'm calling about Lionel." It was a woman's voice.

"Yes, what about him?"

"Is he back yet?"

"Who's asking?" Maxine demanded.

"You want help or not? If he's there I ain't wasting my time." It sounded take-it-or-leave-it.

"No, he isn't."

"Okay then. Look, a prank got out of control. It wasn't his fault. Anyway, he might be a little goofy. The last I seen him was in some alley near the waterfront. In the industrial district."

"What address?"

"Um... call it Hunters Point. Third Street. Anyway, he was naked."

"What? And what do you mean by goofy?"

The connection went dead.

Maxine stared at her phone. Then she grabbed her purse and ran downstairs to her Mini.

Twenty minutes later she was in one of the poorer neighborhoods of the City, wandering the alleys. She called Trig and left a voicemail, knowing he was probably in flight to San Francisco.

She started going up and down alleys, driving around trash bins and dumpsters. She saw homeless people huddled on corners. Pit bulls and German shepherds chained up in back yards. She came to a block with kids playing football in the rain. She stopped and showed a picture of Lionel, asking if they had seen him. She got all sorts of responses, but nothing helpful.

She drove into one alley and came upon a group of men in hoodies standing around a fire in a barrel. When they saw her in the Mini they took interest, swaggering over on both sides of the car. Several rubbed their crotches as they strutted. She floored it in reverse and spun out of the alley. They laughed and jeered at her. "Come on back, sister. We show you a good time."

She stayed on the streets for a while. She saw black people, whites, Latinos, and Asians. In one block several families had barbeques going, a tarp strung high to ward off the light rain.

She ventured back in the alleys. A pack of barking dogs chased her as she maneuvered around strewn trashcans. Block by block she looked for Lionel.

She called Trig again. This time she got through and described what she knew.

"This lady who called said Lionel was naked and goofy."

"Ma'am, Lionel is in good shape. So even if he's naked and goofy, whatever that means, he can walk."

"What would you do, Trig?"

"First, I'd get some clothes. Anything. Off a clothesline or out of a dumpster. Then, I'd go somewhere familiar. Either home or work. Knowing you all, probably work because he could get inside. Naked means he's got no apartment keys, no wallet, no phone."

"Okay, good thinking. I'll head closer to the office."

"Even with rags on, he's a go-getter, so you'd think he'd borrow a phone. Or seek out a cop."

"Right. That's what I expected."

"But the fact that he hasn't, might mean he's impaired."

"Impaired. What do you mean?"

"Maybe he was hit and has a concussion. He could be drugged, or some sort of trauma has him scrambled."

"Jesus. All the more reason to keep looking."

"I have notified SFPD Missing Persons. And Inspector Chang. They have a photo of him and are aware he is missing in that general neighborhood."

"Thanks Trig."

"See you in a couple of hours, ma'am."

Maxine turned left and headed toward the waterfront, following along the piers. She drove slowly, scanning. Sunday morning was quiet in this part of town. She stopped at a red light.

An old person slowly pushed a cart down an alley. Stringy black hair whipped around his shoulders in the wind. He shuffled in a long grimy coat and heavy boots. And then Maxine saw the torn dress. It was an old lady. Three teenaged boys circled her. Juking and poking, they toyed with her. She moved like an old turtle trying to escape, protecting the cans and bottles piled in the rusted shopping cart. With a kick they sent the cart toppling sideways, and bottles shattered while cans cascaded down the alleyway. The teenagers walked off laughing, kicking cans as they went. Maxine shuddered in disgust.

Across the street she noticed a tall, longhaired guy wearing a hooded red sweatshirt. A pair of blue sweatpants rode several inches above bare ankles. He waved woodenly at a cab as it rushed by.

"Lionel?" she said out loud. She strained to recognize details. How could she be in doubt about Lionel? He didn't dress or act like Lionel. But it could be him. She glared at the red light impatiently. There was little traffic, but she was stuck behind a Grand Marquis with a bent rusted bumper.

The woman struggled with her shopping cart. She pulled and tugged as it spun on its side. Cans and bottles were scattered all around her. Then the guy in the red sweatshirt shuffled into the alley. He moved stiffly like an old man. He righted the cart and stooped to pick up the cans and bottles that hadn't broken.

Maxine shook the steering wheel impatiently. "Damn it." Just as she decided to run the red light, it turned green. She raced to the strewn cans, stopped the car, and jumped out. She wanted it to be Lionel, but also feared this person was damaged.

"Lionel?"

The figure paused and stood up with a vacant stare. The eyes were dull behind heavy lines, the face streaked with grime.

Maxine's heart stopped.

Then his face lit up. "Maxine?"

She ran over and hugged him.

"Lionel, are you okay?"

"I don't know."

"You've been missing for thirty-six hours."

"Missing?"

"You look pale. And dirty. Are you all right?"

"I'm not sure. But this lady. Her cans. Recycling money. She needs help."

"Oh, yes. Let's get those." Maxine bent down, scooping up cans. She took a twenty out of her purse and put it in the old woman's hand.

"Thank ya," she croaked, looking up at Maxine. A dirty scarf was knotted above her forehead. Below it a young face was overlaid by an old woman's mask, weathered into deep folds. A few stained teeth remained. She was probably in her thirties, thought Maxine sadly.

Maxine took Lionel by the arm. "Let's get you home, okay?"

"I am so glad you are here. I don't have anything anymore." He shifted from one foot to the other, holding his empty hands out to the sides.

"How about a shower and some clothes that don't freak me out. Then we'll talk, okay?"

"Okay. But I am very lucky to have these clothes, believe me."

Maxine opened the car door for him.

"I don't know what happened. I don't remember."

"It's okay." She hugged him gently. "Come home with me. Everything will be all right."

***

As Lionel showered, Maxine called Trig.

"I found him. He was wandering in an alley."

"In an alley? How is he?"

"He doesn't remember what happened. He's spaced out. Should I call the police?"

"Does he have any signs of violence? Bruises? Cuts—that sort of thing?"

"He has a bump on his head and a nasty bruise. He said a man told him he ran into a debris box that came rolling off a truck. I'm not sure if it was intentional or not."

"Any blood on his clothing?"

"I don't see any. I think he got the clothes after he was hit. He seems really passive. I've never seen him like this. Dreamlike, but wistful. He said he wants to stay here and sleep."

Trig paused. "I'll call Chang and Missing Persons. Sleep is good but check on him every three hours. I recommend taking him to a clinic tomorrow and having him tested for a concussion. And also for drugs, especially Rohypnol. Roofies."

"Roofies?"

"I think so. That would explain his memory loss. And passivity. Roofies loosen inhibitions. That might fit into this prank the woman on the phone was talking about. I'm sure Chang will want to interview him."

"Makes sense. He's coming out of the shower now. I'll check in later. Thanks, Trig."

Lionel emerged from the bathroom.

"Hungry?"

"Starving."

"All I have is leftover pizza. Want me to get something else at the store?"

"No, please don't leave. Pizza's perfect."

He sat, slowly eating. She pulled down the blinds and closed the curtains. Even though it was only two in the afternoon, he lay down. She covered him with a blanket.

"Promise me you won't leave me," he said.

"I'm not going anywhere."

"Promise? I don't want to wake up alone."

"I promise." She sat next to him on the bed and rubbed his shoulder. He finally let his head sink into the pillow.

"Can you help me put myself together again?" His eyes had a far-away look.

"Yes, of course."

"I feel undone. Erased. Guilty for a night I can't remember."

"We'll figure it out. It isn't your fault." She shook her head slowly.

"Thank you." His voice lowered and slowed. "For taking care of me." His head sank deeper and his eyes fluttered. "You . . . rescued . . . me." A moment later he was asleep.

Maxine ran her fingers through his hair. It was strange. She didn't feel put out. Or angry. She adjusted his blankets. She liked taking care of him. She was so glad he was back.

***

The wireless microphones had been working perfectly. Nicco listened to Lionel and Maxine's conversation in her apartment. He alerted Calabrese.

"He sounds hung over or something. He's spending the night there."

"Finally," Calabrese responded. "Tell Tomas and Igor. Get ready for Romeo and Juliet. And you know how that ends."

***

Maxine put down Sheryl Sandberg's latest book. She stretched as she walked to the bathroom and got ready for a night on the couch. After putting on a camisole and sweatpants, she quietly checked on Lionel. He lay in the bed, slowly breathing under the covers.

She went to the front door and set the apartment alarm that Trig had installed. Then she returned to the couch and spread out a sheet and blankets. The neighborhood lights peeked around the edges of the blinds, but not enough to bother her.

She checked the time. Ten p.m. She set her iPhone alarm clock. She smiled, thinking about scrounging for something for Lionel to wear after his shower. There was nothing that would have worked until she found his old Harvard gym shorts. Somehow she had kept them. He had put them on chuckling, "I've seen these before."

"Senior year. Springtime," she had reminded him.

Now she shifted around on the couch, snuggling under the blankets. Finally she got comfortable and fell asleep. She dreamed of their spring trip to the maple syrup farm.

The Sunday evening traffic quieted down early, as the neighbors settled in, exhausted from active weekends. Several hours passed. The streets were deserted, except for a few shadows.

Something woke Maxine. She sat up and listened, looking around the darkness of the apartment. Chilled, she pulled the blanket over her exposed shoulders. Must have been a passing truck. She started to ease back down. Just then the alarm keypad lit up in a surge. Then it went dark.

She peered across the room. That was strange. It always had a low glow. Maybe a glitch. Her eyes started to close. Then she jerked her head. *Lionel.* Lionel was here.

She rose and walked through the dark, over to the keypad. None of the keys responded. It was dead. Then she tried the light switch. No power. She started to panic.

Wait. Through the edge of the blinds she saw light. Another apartment in the building had lights on. She sighed in relief. That was good.

The floor creaked outside her front door. Her stomach tightened. She listened, straining. Then it creaked again.

Get Lionel. She hurried on her bare tiptoes to the bedroom. She tried the light switch. Nothing. She stood near Lionel. *She should have grabbed her phone by the sofa.*

"Lionel." She shook him.

He didn't stir.

She shook him hard.

He didn't respond.

Then she heard slow footsteps up the back stairs. *Both entrances?* She thought she saw movement outside the window.

That can't be a coincidence. She pulled off the blankets and grabbed Lionel's shoulders, shaking him.

"Lionel," she hissed as loud as she dared. Nothing.

"Lionel!" She shook until his head bobbled.

"Umh?" His eyes opened slightly. Then his head rolled to the side. How could she wake him? He lay unconscious in the old gym shorts. Then she remembered. Pain. Pain is a powerful stimulant.

"Sorry, Lionel. But I have to wake you up somehow."

She spread his legs apart. Her hands trembled as she raised a fist and swung it down as hard as she could, right between his legs into his privates.

His knees jerked up. She clapped her hand over his mouth as he groaned. Then his eyes opened and he started to gasp.

"It's Maxine. Sorry. Don't talk. Someone is outside. I'm worried."

He struggled up, still moaning.

"The power is off in the apartment, but not the whole building. The alarm is dead too. And I heard something outside the front door. Maybe the back door too."

"Attacking? Us?" He moaned quietly.

"Yes. They might be armed. Careful. Let me get my phone in the other room and call 911."

"Wait. Let me see," he whispered. He stood up and hobbled to the hallway.

He took her hand and they tiptoed to the back door. He stood on a chair and looked over the transom. He pointed outside, nodding his head.

Not good, she thought.

Then they heard the latch to the front door turning.

"They have keys," she whispered. Oh God.

"Follow me!" he hissed. He took off running toward the front door. Maxine ran after him in the dim apartment, lit only by the streetlight edging around the blinds.

She saw him grab a lamp and snap it violently from the outlet. Just then, the front door opened and a long barrel appeared.

In full stride Lionel swung the lamp, base first, onto the hand holding the gun. The metal edge of the circular base crushed downward and the gun went crashing to the floor.

Lionel leapt at the door, shoving it. Maxine saw him slamming it, but the door wouldn't close. It flung open suddenly, sending Lionel backward, and a huge man filled the doorway.

Lionel staggered. She saw a mask on the huge man, and he was pulling something from his waist. Lionel ran at him like a wild woodsman winding up an ax. The arc of the lamp's base ended at the top of the huge skull. With a grunt the giant went to one knee.

She heard footsteps behind her.

Lionel raised the lamp again. Maxine sprinted to the door.

"Let's go," she yelled, and she jerked his arm forward.

Lionel dropped the lamp and she pulled his hand past the groaning hulk. They ran down two flights of stairs, bursting through the building's small lobby and into the street. They kept sprinting, Lionel in shorts, she in her pajamas.

"Call 911!" yelled Lionel. "Call the police!"

They ran without stopping, calling out to the darkened windows, hoping someone would respond. She realized they looked like lunatics in their nightclothes. An all-night grocer lit up a nearby street corner. A metal grate covered the entrance.

Lionel pounded on the window as Maxine yelled, "Emergency! Please let us in. I live nearby. It's life and death."

The owner approached the grate, staring at them.

"Please, someone broke into my apartment. You know me. I shop here."

The owner recognized her and slid open the metal grate. Lionel shoved it closed behind them.

"Don't let anyone else in. Call 911."

Maxine's chest didn't stop heaving and she didn't let go of Lionel's hand until the police arrived five minutes later in a swarm of flashing red lights.

41

SUNDAY NIGHT, MARCH 16ᵀᴴ — MONDAY MORNING, NARCH 17ᵀᴴ

It was three a.m. in the Metro Division's Mission Street station. Lionel and Maxine sat in hard plastic chairs facing Inspector Chang at his battered gray steel desk. The fluorescent lights were unflattering, making everyone look even more exhausted, and the office was uncomfortably hot. Stained coffee cups sat half full. Chang touch-typed his notes on a tablet while carefully watching Lionel. His encouraging smile seemed permanent. *He's almost annoyingly friendly*, thought Lionel. *But they had just barely escaped, no thanks to him.*

Trig arrived. Lionel wondered if Chang would object, but he politely directed him to the coffee machine and a chair. As Trig took off his coat and sat down, his broad shoulders rippled through his T-shirt and his arms popped out like a linebacker's.

Chang's phone rang. "Ah, CSI. One minute please."

He nodded into the phone, asked a few questions and took notes. Then hung up.

"The Crime Scene Investigators are going over the apartment thoroughly. The perps were quite careful, leaving nothing other than the blood where Lionel hit the large attacker by the front door. But we did discover something else."

"What's that?"

"Two surveillance devices. Microphones. An expensive auto-sensing model, using both WiFi and 4-G cellular. Alerts listeners to activity so they then can monitor you via cell from anywhere." He studied the ceiling, then asked, "Do you know about these, Trig?"

"Not mine, sir," he responded. "I recently swept the apartment. These must be new."

"What does this mean?" asked Maxine.

Chang rubbed his mustache. "Someone has been listening to every word you've spoken in that apartment."

"My God."

"Probably the same people who attacked last night."

"This means they must have known I was there," said Lionel.

"Right. They want both of you," said Trig grimly.

Lionel stood up. He started pacing.

"Is it unusual for you to be at Maxine's apartment?" asked the Inspector.

"Yes. I've never spent the night there."

"How about at your apartment, Lionel? Do you two stay together there?"

"Never. We're business colleagues. Not a couple."

"I see." Inspector Chang rubbed his head. "I agree with Trig, then. They were waiting for both of you together."

Lionel turned and looked at Maxine. Her eyes were lost in thought.

"There's more," said Lionel, turning to Chang. He took a deep breath. "I think I was drugged on Friday night. That's the reason I was at Maxine's place. She found me wandering near the waterfront."

"We think he might have been slipped some roofies," Trig added.

Chang studied Lionel. "Walk me through this, please."

Lionel dropped back down into his chair. "I woke up Saturday afternoon in a strange apartment with no memory of where I was. People were banging at the door. I climbed down the fire escape, and ran naked through an alley, escaping the building. Then I got hit by a debris box and knocked unconscious. I woke up, got clothes, wandered until dark, spent the night under a freeway ramp, and the next day Maxine found me in an alley."

"You are a lucky man to have her as a, a . . . colleague," said Chang.

"The luckiest."

"So that's why you were at Maxine's apartment?"

"Yes."

"With these bugging devices, the attackers may have known you were weak. And chosen that moment."

"Sure. But who gave me the Roofies? And if I was high on those, why not take me out then? Why did they wait for me to be with Maxine?"

"Good questions. We need more information." Chang glanced upward before focusing on Lionel. "Tell me more about Friday night."

"I was at the BevGlobe trade show. I gave a speech. Double Vision had a booth. The last thing I remember was a cocktail party after the trade show."

"Where was that?"

"The Presidential."

"Then what happened?"

What did happen? Lionel wondered. It was a blank. "I don't have any memory of the party."

"Our marketer, Kate Zell, saw him there around seven p.m.," Maxine offered. "I was hung up in a customer meeting and by the time I arrived, he was gone."

"Your next memory is waking up at this unknown apartment?"

"Right."

"Who else was there?"

"Some guy pounding down the door. And a woman, with brown hair."

"A woman? Was she with the guy pounding down the door?"

"Ah, no. She was in the bed with me." Maxine was going to give him crap about this, he knew.

"I see," said Inspector Chang slowly. "So presumably you met her at the cocktail party and ended up at this apartment. Maybe her apartment?"

"It may have been. Look, I woke up feeling like death. I'm naked. She's naked. But I have no recollection of her or any . . . interaction at all." *Oh, God this sounded bad.*

"This is new," said Maxine, crossing her arms.

"I woke up and the guy pounding down the door said to open up, or he'd shoot."

"He threatened to shoot you with a gun?" Chang asked.

"Definitely. That's why I insisted on trying to take this woman with me. I thought he might shoot her and me." He looked at Maxine for approval and black disks stared back at him, expressionless.

"But she didn't come?"

"No, I got her as far as the fire escape outside. But she was too afraid. And then she admitted she was with them."

"She said she was with them?"

"Yes. That's when I left her." Lionel decided to omit the part about the smashed iPhone. He had left the iPhone in Maxine's Mini after she found him, and she had already given it to Trig.

"So you ran down the fire escape and into an alley. Did the man follow you?"

"I saw him on the fire-escape balcony as I ran away. He had a camera with a long lens."

"A camera?"

"Yeah, like sports photographers use. A really long lens."

"So he stays, the girl stays, and you run down the alley?"

"Right. I'm running as fast as I can, feeling like hell, looking back to see if they are following, and then suddenly—bam. Next thing I know I'm waking up with a homeless guy over me, seriously concussed, and he tells me about the debris box."

"This was still Saturday, right?"

"Yes. He gave me a green poncho. That's all I was wearing until I went into the church, where they gave me some clothes."

"Was there a reason you didn't call the police at that point?"

"I had no idea who I was. Or what had happened. But I had this sense that if I walked along the waterfront, I'd find someone. Someone who would take care of me. I didn't know at the time, but it was Maxine I was thinking about." He looked at Maxine. She was biting her lip.

"But she didn't find you until Sunday."

"I wandered all day and spent the night under the freeway ramp. She found me Sunday morning."

Trig spoke up. "Inspector, I called you on Saturday, as well as filing the missing person's report."

Chang nodded. "After Maxine got that phone tip." He studied the ceiling again. "Lionel, do you think the woman who called was the same one in bed with you? The one you were trying to help escape?"

"It could be. She said she was with the attackers, but she didn't seem happy about it. And she didn't try to keep me there."

"Friday you get drugged and they try to take photos. By Monday, at one in the morning, they're trying to kill you both in Maxine's apartment with a silencer pistol."

"I don't understand it, but that's what happened," replied Lionel.

"Someone is putting a lot of resources into trying to stop you two," said Chang. "Do you have any reasons to suspect anyone, based on recent developments?"

Lionel and Maxine exchanged a look of frustration. Then Trig spoke up. "I spoke with Sheriff Masterson about the attempted rape on Reddi Christiansen," he said. "Gonzo of BodyHamr says he was drunk and under stress. He claims he knows nothing about the avalanche nor Igor Vasilchenko."

Lionel stood and spun around his chair. "Inspector, have *you* come up with *anything*? You've been investigating for several months. I'm fine with answering all these questions, but it would be great to hear your conclusions." He leaned forward on Chang's desk. "At least a theory. Maxine and I almost died last night." He stared at Chang.

Inspector Chang answered calmly. "First, Sheriff Masterson has a suspect in custody who broke into the Telluride offices and planted the drugs. One Jake the Rake. He hasn't talked yet, but your company video camera recorded his break-in, so hopefully he'll crack soon."

"Who was he working for?"

"We don't know yet. We have learned that Igor Vasilchenko, the Audi driver, has sophisticated Russian military training. That could explain his ability with avalanche explosives. Also that could account for the security intrusion and surveillance devices. He was part of a criminal gang operating out of the Black Sea."

"Is he part of a local organization now? Along with the two big guys who attacked last night?" asked Trig.

"That would seem a likely combination. Tech skills and muscle. But why?" asked Chang. "Is it the Big Disrupter prize?"

"All the competitors are social entrepreneurs. They're do-gooders. It seems crazy," said Lionel.

"A billion dollars is an enormous amount of money," said Chang. "All the deaths have been accidents. Perhaps the reason for the apartment break-in, was to get the two of you together, for an accident."

Wait a minute, what about Furtig? "Inspector, do you think it's SocialLending and Larry Furtig? They have been in the lead the entire time and no one is attacking them."

"Have you looked into him?" asked Maxine.

"Yes. I've seen nothing suspicious. Other than being unpopular for his . . . style."

"How about the other companies at the top?"

"The standings keep switching. But I haven't found any connection yet to Igor."

"What about investors in these companies?" asked Lionel.

"Such as?" asked Chang.

"Double Vision has Jacob Havermyer and Axlewright Capital. Everyone has investors. They have huge incentives to help their company win."

"Why? Doesn't the money go to the company, not the investors?"

"Yes. But indirectly, a win provides huge advantages," answered Lionel, pacing faster.

"I'm just a detective. How does that finance angle work?" asked Chang, his head cocked to the side.

"VCs make their money two ways. First, they get two percent each year for managing money once they raise a fund. So if they raise a five-hundred-million-dollar fund, each year they get ten million dollars just for breathing. Literally. They call this their management fees."

"Okay, keep going."

"So if you win the award, the company you invested in shows a one-billion-dollar profit. And that company becomes a dominant player in its industry. Serious star power. As an investor, your ability to attract your next one-billion-dollar fund, generating twenty million in annual fees, improves significantly."

"Nice work if you can get it."

"Okay. Now for part two. Carried interest. VCs typically create a limited liability corporation, or LLC. They raise money from institutions, endowments, pension plans, wealthy investors, and the like and that capital is what is invested in companies, maybe ten of them. Then, once the collective LLC shows a profit, the VC starts collecting their profit, usually at least twenty percent. Getting a billion-dollar profit creates a lot of value for the LLC. The VC will be able to start recognizing twenty-percent profit on the earnings of the whole LLC right away."

"So every investor who owns some part of these companies competing for this one billion dollars, they want to win pretty bad. Right? Whether it's the one in first, SocialLending, or your own investors at Double Vision?" asked Chang.

"Yes," responded Maxine. "But the list doesn't end there. There are other potential suspects."

"Like who?" Chang asked, his hands typing on his tablet.

"Take our primary distributor, the huge Merry Cola. Sometimes they buy smaller companies with innovative products. Other times, they work as a distributer for the smaller company and gradually suck all the product plans and market ideas out of them. Then they cut off the smaller company and suddenly announce their own version of the very product they were distributing."

"I see. So even Merry Cola is in the mix of suspects?"

"Inspector, with the dollars involved, there are a lot of suspects," said Lionel. "And if we don't find the culprit behind this soon, Maxine and I are done for."

***

The meeting with Inspector Chang concluded near sunrise. Maxine and Lionel left in a cab to find temporary accommodations. Trig saw them off, then began walking. The wind picked up and he pulled his Navy peacoat closer. He headed toward a worn down industrial neighborhood, South of Market, crisscrossing and backtracking to make sure he wasn't being followed. He ducked into a derelict courtyard. Several stripped and corroding bicycle frames stood locked to a rusted bench. Broken bottles were piled around them, like the remains of target practice. An intrepid Abyssinian cat eyed Trig from atop an abandoned couch, licking its paws. She was the only elegance he noticed in the neighborhood.

In a basement apartment behind a metal door and multiple blinking alarm systems, Trig met with Slurp, the former NSA programmer. His messy apartment fit right in with the abandoned courtyard. He needed a shower. Long greasy brown hair topped off a splotched black T-shirt and enormous crusty overalls, enveloping what had to be three hundred pounds. His refrigerator had an Anchor Steam Beer tap the size of a small baseball bat mounted in the center. Old pizza boxes stacked up in the corner.

The Abyssinian cat snuck in the door with Trig. He started to reach for her but Slurp waved him off.

"I like her. She's my mouser. Keeps it tidy."

Trig nodded, glancing around the apartment. He wondered where the tidy part was. "Good relationship."

Slurp sat with a grunt in a massive rolling chair. He retrieved something from his desk.

"Success?" Trig asked.

"Yep." Slurp slid a silver bubble pouch across his desk. "Was able to suck everything off that drive. That baby was pretty cracked up, too."

Trig was pleased. When Lionel handed him the smashed iPhone dropped off the fire escape, he had his doubts.

"This new facial recognition software I've been poaching from Homeland Security is crazy good. They call it BOSS, for good reason. I saved a file on that drive with the name and profile info of the chick that owned the phone and twenty-three other people. BOSS ID'd them from her photos and videos." He put both hands behind his greasy head, and rocked back in his chair with a pleased grin.

"Mind if I take a quick look at her now?"

Slurp leaned forward and tipped like a giant keg. He wheezed as he stabilized in the creaking chair. His hands barely extended beyond his girth, but his fingers were surprisingly nimble on his keyboard. In a burst of clicks he summoned up the file.

"There is the babe who owned the phone, one Maria Monrovia. If I got out of the apartment more, I'd go see her act. Whew. She's a pole dancer at the HungryLady Strip Club."

Trig scanned the text and the images. One was a selfie and the other from the strip club where she worked. Both pictures showed the same full face, long brown hair, and alabaster skin. There was a vulnerability buried below the sexy poses.

"You *are* the man, Slurp." Trig slid an envelope over.

He left and the cat followed him out, returning to her post on the abandoned couch. Trig circuitously made his way through the neighborhood, then across town to the landmark Presidential Hotel.

***

Trig walked into the Presidential's foyer, loosening the buttons of his coat. From the lobby he passed into the adjacent Glass Court. Overhead, metal arches curved gracefully, supporting the glass dome. Italian marble columns and elaborate chandeliers surrounded brilliant green palms. Nice place for a reception. Must have cost a bundle.

He approached the security guard positioned at a velvet rope across the entrance.

"Private investigator. I'm working with Winston Chang, SFPD."

He held out his card along with a carefully folded twenty-dollar bill.

With a nod he walked into the closed restaurant.

A bartender was prepping behind the bar. The wait staff was arriving for their shift, a parade of attractive women and guys who looked like aspiring actors. They headed to a back door to change. Trig approached the bar. The bartender moved deliberately, organizing and polishing. Dark brown eyes behind a square jaw gave little away.

A twenty didn't help free up his memory of the night. "Nope, don't recognize him," he said, after looking at a picture of Lionel. "I remember the BevGlobe conference and working that private reception. Another crowd of business people. We have a lot of private parties. They all seem the same." He shrugged.

A couple more twenties appeared on the counter.

"Anyone else who worked that night who might be able to help?"

He stopped his polishing, squinting as he brushed his mustache. "No. Sorry about that. We used a lot of floaters that night."

Trig continued with some small talk until the flow of arriving wait staff ebbed. As he left, walking toward the exit, he saw a woman hurrying in. He briefly caught her eye before she disappeared beyond the service door. *That's the one.*

***

Trig returned several hours later near the end of the lunch service. Another twenty with the maître d' assured he was seated at a table served by the curvy brunette, Maria.

When she returned with his iced tea he placed her broken iPhone on the table.

"I believe this is yours, Ms. Monrovia. We managed to recover a video and some pictures taken with you and my client." He quietly slipped a picture of Lionel on the table. He watched her look at it for a moment, frozen. Then she shook her head.

"I don't know what you are talking about." She glanced back toward the bar.

"One way or another, we're going to get to the bottom of this. I'm a private investigator, not a cop, so if you tell me what you know, then you walk away. Otherwise it gets complicated."

"I don't know." She paused. "You're not a cop?"

"No. I work for Maxine, the lady you telephoned Sunday morning. You must have found her number on Lionel's phone, the one he left in the apartment." He let her absorb that info. "What time are you off work?"

She closed her eyes, exhaling. "At three. But I can't talk here. And no cops."

"Meet me at the Marriot, in the Starbucks. Three-fifteen, okay? We'll talk and that will be it. No cops."

"Can I get my phone back?"

"Not until after our meeting."

"Okay. But then we're done." He'd seen that hopeful but wary look before.

"As long as you are straight with me."

***

Later that afternoon the Marriot lobby was swarming with attendees of the Apple conference across the street at Moscone Center. Trig maneuvered through the noisy throng to find Maria, and then led her through the crowd to the lower level. They snagged a small cushioned settee at the end of a hallway.

"I'm Trig Garcia, by the way."

"Maria. But you know that."

They were sitting side by side. The settee wasn't large, and Trig's broad frame took up most of it. That didn't seem to bother Maria, Trig noticed. She had walked through the crowd with confidence and sat near him without a concern for personal space. But he noticed her eyes kept darting around, as though worried she was being watched.

"I'm an investigator, and I work for Lionel Lane. He's the one who woke up in a bed with you while some guy with a camera tried to bust into the room."

She didn't respond. Her hands gripped her knees.

"Look, you told him to go down that fire escape without you. And that you knew the guy who busted down the door. I'm not the police. I just want to know who has it out for Lionel. No one died. No one got shot. But it was a setup. It looks like you gave him roofies, the date rape drug, right?"

She waved her hands. "This got out of control. I didn't give him any roofies. I was told it was a prank, for a bachelor party, in good fun."

"Who set it up?"

She waited. Two long-haired guys in Apple T-shirts walked past, talking excitedly. She spoke quietly. "His name is Mick. He's the boyfriend of my girlfriend, but she didn't have anything to do with it."

"What happened that night?"

"Mick had the bartender slip the drugs in a drink at the party at the Presidential. The waitress serving Lionel had no idea, she just delivered it. I wasn't working the floor that night. I was in the limo waiting, part of the gag. The idea was to drive somewhere quiet, I'd take my top off, and Mick would take pictures of us. Him guzzling a champagne bottle, smoking a bong and a fake crack pipe, like we were partying. They said they were going to use it as part of a funny video at his bachelor party in a few weeks. He'd be loose and going along with the partying. That's it. And I'd get one thousand dollars. I'm broke. I'm behind on my rent even in that dump. I didn't have a choice."

"You're making decent money as a pole dancer at the HungryLady Club. How do you spend all that?"

She looked over at Trig sharply. "Okay, so you do your homework. Look, it's a long story, but I'm broke. I have obligations, all right?"

"Okay. So what happened?"

"Mick brings him into the limo, but he's staggering, seems really drunk, sits in the back seat, and passes out. Totally gone. So Mick tries driving a while with the back window open, and we put Lionel's head in the breeze, like that will wake him up. It didn't work. Mick calls some guy and says it's not working. Then I knew something was up because they said they overdosed him or something."

"Who was he talking to?"

"Some guy named Ripley. I don't know him."

"What happened next?"

"They wanted to bring him to my place. I said no way. He talked to Ripley and they said for another one thousand dollars they want to bring him to my place, wake him up, and take the pictures. And afterward they'd take him away with them. I said okay."

"Is your place the apartment in Hunters Point, where you both woke up?"

"Yes. We drive to my place, and I gotta help Mick drag him out of the limo to the elevator. Once we've got him upstairs in my bed Mick gets out the bag with the bong and the crack pipes. We strip Lionel and I get naked. He starts taking pictures. Lionel was so passed out his eyes were closed. He seemed exhausted. He couldn't be woken up. The pictures, they weren't working out. Mick tried a video with my iPhone but that was no better—Lionel was like comatose. Turns out they gave him way too much drugs, you know? So Mick calls this guy Ripley again."

"He used your iPhone to call Ripley, the boss of the operation, is that correct?"

"Come to think of it, yeah, because he forgot his in the limo. How'd you know?"

"It doesn't matter." *Perfect,* he thought. *Except that means Ripley is really Blaine Latrell, based on the phone number.* "So then what happened?"

She paused, waiting for more people to pass by in the hallway.

"They decide to leave him there to sleep it off. I said no way. He said there would be another one thousand dollars in it for me, so now we're up to three thousand dollars. They said leave everything alone, we'll get some funny naked shots in the morning when he is awake. Mick put the bag with the pipes in the kitchen and left. It was three in the morning by then. I was exhausted. Next thing I know, it's the next day and Mick's breaking down the door. That's God's truth."

"How did the liquor cabinet get shoved in front of the door?"

Maria closed her eyes, and her head slumped. Then she looked over at Trig. "You can't tell Mick, okay?"

"Okay."

"I couldn't sleep. I didn't like what was going on. So I barricaded the door by pushing over the liquor cabinet. Later on I told them Lionel did it. I didn't want them to come back. I had a shot of vodka to try to get to sleep. Actually a few. And then passed out. Next thing I know, Mick is trying to bust in with the camera."

"You didn't try to run away with Lionel?"

"I knew it was Mick with the camera. But Lionel, it was amazing he had his energy back. But he had no idea what had happened. Like zero. That's when I realized he had been more than drunk. He was like a valiant knight, trying to save me from a bad guy. Real stand up. But I told him, I was with them. I was part of their game, even though they had tricked me into it. So I said to him—go without me. I figured they'd have to pay me anyway, even if he escaped."

"Did they pay you the three thousand dollars?"

"They tried to weasel, and I said, hey, I did my part, and how do you expect me to keep quiet? So they did." She shook her head slowly. Then she looked at Trig, their faces close to each other. "And I thought it was a prank. Pretty stupid, huh?"

"I need to ask. Did you, Mick, or anyone else sexually abuse Lionel during this?"

"What!?" She pulled back, almost sliding off the bench. "You mean . . . well first of all I am a waitress and a dancer, not a whore, okay? Of course not. And no, Mick isn't a pervert. He didn't rape him or anything. Jesus. It wasn't like that."

Trig kept her in his gaze and nodded his head. "Okay. But I do need to get those pictures from Mick. Let him know he can't give those to the guy who hired him, or I will go to the police immediately. And he'll face kidnapping, drug charges, and more."

"Oh, shit." She twisted her hands together.

"But, if he destroys them, I won't involve you or him with the cops."

Then Trig pulled out his cell phone and quickly snapped her picture. "I've recorded this conversation. You can tell that to anyone who wants you to change your story. Although I recommend you keep this confidential."

"There is no one I'm talking to, trust me. Other than telling Mick he's gotta kill those photos."

Trig put his phone back into his coat pocket and retrieved a card, giving it to her.

"If any of these characters tries to bother you, call me. And when this is over, I'm buying you a new phone."

She took the card and looked at it. Then she smiled for the first time.

"Hey, that's real cool. But why would you do that for me?"

"You tried to help Lionel, and I respect that. But the guy who paid for this, that's a different story."

42

MONDAY, MARCH 17TH

Blaine stood at the mirror in the men's room at Axlewright Capital. He examined himself, front and sideways. Damn, he needed to get more exercise. He sucked in his belly and threw back his big rounded shoulders. He adjusted his thick-rimmed glasses, which he fancied gave him an intellectual look. Running his fingers through his hair he was pleased there was plenty still there. *You look smart, successful, a real deal guy. Now, go in there and win this request, damn it!* Picking up his laptop he marched down to John Anderson's office.

"A moment sir?" Blaine asked John, peering in the door.

"Why not? Come on in." He knew John was in a good mood. Two of their portfolio companies were in play, with suitors offering prices that would provide a 10 X return on their investment. It killed Blaine they weren't his deals.

Blaine came in slowly, closed the door carefully, and turned to John. He wanted to appear purposeful and in charge. John waved to a seat, and Blaine centered himself in it.

"I have some decision points on Double Vision, and I'm seeking your advice. I'm sure you'll have some great insight here."

"Sure thing, shoot." *Stroke John's ego early and often,* Blaine thought.

"You wanted results at Double Vision. Well, it appears Lionel Lane is imploding. Quickly."

John sat back and squared his shoulders. "Continue."

"It has come to my attention, through reliable sources, that he has a serious substance-abuse problem. Reportedly large amounts of cocaine are being used at their Telluride office, with his full participation and approval."

"What? Are the police involved or is this just rumor?"

"I have it on very good intelligence their office in Telluride is under police scrutiny. Furthermore, there was some sort of overdose incident with Lionel here in San Francisco, at the BevGlobe conference this past weekend. I'm told it involved passing out in the bathroom of the Presidential Hotel, naked women, excesses in a limo, and an all night party."

"Lionel? How do we know this?"

"It's a very big conference but a small group of well-connected industry players. Believe me, it was all over."

"All over? Jesus—are there pictures on Twitter or Facebook? Was he arrested? Give me a sense of the damage here."

"We were able to contain some pictures that would have gone out. Allow me to keep you at a distance from that. I'm managing the situation."

"I'd love to see Lionel out the door. But damn it, we can't let him wreck our investment in the process. I want to change the pilot, not crash the plane."

"Yes sir."

"What the hell about Maxine—is she using also?"

"No, this is isolated to Lionel."

Anderson grunted. "So Lionel may be out and Maxine takes over. Until he cleans up his act."

"Right. Another consideration is bringing in someone like Sid Shamitz of BodyHamr, through an acquisition. He might be the right one to work with Maxine going forward, maybe reporting to her. And Lionel is eased out permanently, as part of the acquisition strategy."

"Lionel owns a huge chunk of stock. How would you suggest making this permanent?" Blaine heard the challenge in Anderson's voice.

"We know that as CEO, Lionel has moral standards he is expected to meet. A moral turpitude charge would violate his contract, and could unseat him from his CEO role."

"Any CEO would fight that like hell. Especially if he owned a ton of the stock."

"Can you imagine the brand damage to a juice and energy drink company if the CEO is shown to be a crackhead?"

"Nightmare. Hmm. But I assume he'd promise to go to rehab and make a comeback."

"Except for the Big Disrupter. That's only weeks away. If he is faced with killing the company's chance at winning the Big, along with losing the Merry Cola contract, he'd have to leave."

John grabbed a stress ball on his desk and pumped it. "Damn, the Big may be the perfect forcing function. But you're on the edge of something very messy. Make sure you have the facts to support pushing him out, without the details landing on goddamn Twitter."

Now was the time to ask, Blaine decided. "Yes sir. And if I may, I'd like to get your approval to engage our attorneys in acquisition discussions with BodyHamr and to prepare a moral turpitude suit against Lionel."

"Our attorneys? Blaine, first, where are the facts?"

"John, it's like any deal. We're using our intuition here. Instincts. Envision the possible. Like Havermyer does." Blaine immediately regretted his last sentence.

John Anderson's shoulders swelled and he cocked an eye at Blaine. "Look, I'm not going to let you lawyer-up until you bring me some actual facts. This meeting is over."

***

After Blaine left the office John looked out the window, thinking. Then he placed a call to Jacob Havermyer.

"Jacob, this is John Anderson."

"Who?"

"I'm one of the senior partners here at Axlewright Capital and we co-invested with you on Double Vision."

"Do you work for Blaine?"

"He works for me. That is why I am calling. Let me tell you what I heard."

John explained what Blaine had told him about Lionel. Havermyer waited until John concluded before responding.

"That sounds like the biggest bunch of, forgive me, crap I have ever heard. It isn't plausible. No one is perfect, and I am sure Lionel is not, but that isn't his problem. I assure you." There was an uncharacteristic edge in Havermyer's voice.

John knew to segue, in spite of wanting more facts. "Really appreciate that feedback, thank you. If I may, let me broach another topic. What's your opinion of BodyHamr and their CEO Sid Shamitz? Blaine seems to think you are totally onboard with him."

"I'll tell you the same thing I told Blaine. I suggested he learn what the competition was doing that might be advantageous, and to share that with Double Vision management. I never suggested going any further."

There was a pause on the line.

"Hello?" said Jacob.

"I understand. Evidently Blaine has been overzealous. We'll manage it at this end. Thank you, Jacob."

***

That response from Anderson was so typical. He wasn't ever willing to take any risks for me. Blaine slammed his office door.

He called Mick but got voicemail again. Damn, he needed those pictures of Lionel. Especially since that chick Maria lost her cell phone video. Then he tried Jake the Rake, in Telluride. More voicemail. *What a bunch of flakes.* His thoughts were interrupted by a rap on his door.

"I'm busy," he yelled.

The door opened and Anderson's face appeared, with a cold look. "We need to talk." He immediately entered and sat down.

"I spoke with Havermyer."

"What? Why wasn't I on the call?"

"I needed to hear his perspective."

"He's my co-investor, John. If you want to talk to him, that's fine, but our firm has a protocol."

"Not anymore. Havermyer's version of the facts is substantially different from yours. Enough so that effective immediately, you are on probation. You no longer manage the Double Vision relationship or any other clients."

"John, please. This is an overreaction." *This couldn't be happening. He was so close.*

"It's done. I've already talked to HR and IT. They are changing your access rights."

"This might screw up Double Vision's chances for the Big—that's one billion dollars. Any disruption will be considered negative," he pleaded.

"That's the only reason I'm not firing you immediately. After the Big, we'll consider an exit package, if you cooperate. You are here in name only. Take this time to find another career opportunity."

Anderson stood. "Just don't screw anything up, Blaine." He exited with a scowl.

He was fired? Blaine sat stunned. He suddenly felt out of place, out of his body. He couldn't be finished as a VC. He didn't want to be a branch manager back in Des Moines. Double Vision and his plans for Maxine were the most exciting things in his life.

He lost track of time. Eventually he stood, hurried out of his office and punched the elevator button. He descended to the base of the Transamerica Pyramid and entered the fenced redwood grove park. A few smokers hung out at one end. His hands trembled as he pulled out his phone and placed a call.

"Welcher here."

"Hank, it's Blaine over at Axlewright."

"Hello, Blaine. You caught me between meetings, fortunately. What's new?"

"Remember our private conversation in the lobby at Toast? When you said to stay in touch?"

"Sure, sure."

"I'm feeling underappreciated over here at Axlewright."

"How so?"

"First, I practically landed the Merry Cola contract for Double Vision, putting them on the map. Second, I handed Anderson his dream—Lionel Lane on a platter, skewered and roasted. He is about to get yanked for moral turpitude due to hard drug use."

"Hard drug use by Lionel? In a health and energy drink company? That'd be the kiss of death."

"Yet I'm still not getting credit. I'm the one pulling strings over here."

"Interesting. That's impressive. So why call me?"

"Anderson's keeping the credit for himself. Axelwright doesn't deserve me. I was hoping to discuss my building a highly profitable portfolio for you. At Falconvest."

Blaine desperately counted the seconds before Welcher responded. "Blaine, I consider that a compliment, so thank you. But if you want to be my wing man, the single most important thing is to show me you can finish what you started. That's what true producers do. Now is not the time to leave."

"But Hank, they're boxing me in. Limiting my access."

"Then think outside the box. Take it in your own hands and finish it." Welcher's voice rose, vibrating. "Show some balls. Impress me. Then we'll talk turkey."

Blaine pictured Welcher's shiny bald head and grinning front teeth, shaking his clenched fists.

"Show some balls, huh? You want me to man up? Okay, I'm going to do that, Hank."

43

TUESDAY, MARCH 18TH

Lionel hung up the call with Inspector Chang with an emphatic pop on the top of the black speakerphone. He turned to Maxine and Trig.

"You heard the man. Lots of follow-up. Digging deep into all the possibilities. But the reality—no real progress, just a composite picture of that thug I hit with the lamp."

"I feel bad," said Trig, shaking his broad head. "These guys compromised my alarm system, and added bugs after I swept the apartment. They are sophisticated, but still . . . ."

Lionel jumped to his feet and ran his fingers through his hair. "Don't blame yourself. I think we need to be more on offense. Perpetual defense seems impossible." He grabbed a whiteboard marker, pounding it in his fist. "We're going to have to solve this ourselves."

"Can we afford to devote any more of our time to this? I mean with the Big being twelve days away?" asked Maxine.

"I'd like us to be alive for that. Whoever is after us is still out there. And probably more determined than ever to stop us before the Big."

"Then we have no option."

"Trig, talk to me. Ignoring normal policy and procedure, how would you find out who these people are?"

Trig's dark skin hid fatigue well, but with just snatches of sleep the past three days his eyes were red and underscored by dark shadows. Lionel could see he was nearing his limit. "I'm working on something. But it's early."

"What is it?"

"A GPS tracking tool. Something that invades the target's smartphone and beacons their location to us."

"Now we're talking," said Maxine.

"Wait, you've already hacked Igor's laptop," said Lionel.

"But we want to get into his boss's machine and most importantly, identify where they are physically to nail them. That means hacking the GPS in their smartphones."

"How would we possibly do that?"

Trig slid his laptop forward and folded his hands on the table. "The concept is to infiltrate a group via their weakest link, someone we know. Then get them to forward links, spreading the payload, all the way up the chain of command."

"The phones infect each other directly?"

"No, the PCs do, when they sync with the phone. And there is an app on the phone that has to be installed. Once it's working, wherever their phone goes, we go."

"That's incredible."

"I haven't thoroughly tested it yet. Plus it takes tricking them to click on and share an infected link." He rubbed his stubble, staring over at his laptop as he drifted away in thought.

"Sharing what kind of things?" Maxine pressed.

Trig turned back. "We've got the AZ99 mirror software running on Igor's laptop and we've seen his emails to his boss Zebra. Ideally what we would do is get Zebra to click on a link, and on that webpage I'll have a fatal payload, something similar to the Trojan Citadel bug. But in addition to setting up the mirror software, this takes advantage of vulnerabilities in the OS so it invokes the GPS location services on Androids and iPhones. I call it Cyclops."

"The one-eyed giant. Great name."

Trig smiled proudly. "So Cyclops is an app installed in his phone. Plus there is server-side Cyclops code. The phone Apps send continuous updates of their locations to the Cyclops server, which forwards it to the Cyclops app on my smartphone."

"Very clever. Once this is installed, we can track their phones using this Cyclops app on our own phones?" asked Lionel.

"Exactly. We can vector in on them while we're mobile."

"You have some coding and testing to finish, you said. How can we help with the rest?" asked Maxine.

"We need Igor to have a business reason to send a link to his boss Zebra. And Zebra needs to be interested enough to follow through and open it."

"Trig, can't you spoof that with your mirroring software? Or hack into their shared servers, like they hacked into ours?"

"No, I don't have write control. Only the ability to read. And frankly, the place Igor works has a very sophisticated firewall system. I hacked into his apartment building without issues, but his workplace servers are untouchable."

"Ignoring the techie stuff, we have the business problem of getting them to share links, right?" asked Maxine.

"Yes. To share something and click on the link," said Trig.

"Something that either interests them or they fear. Something credible."

"Of all the scenarios we've discussed, at this point, what is the most likely interest our adversaries have?" Trig asked.

Both Maxine and Lionel answered at the same time. "The Big."

"Then we need to offer something relating to that."

"Something about the Big that they want or fear," said Maxine.

"You keep saying fear. Why?" asked Lionel.

"It's primal. Even more powerful than greed," said Maxine.

They sat thinking.

"I've got it," said Lionel. "They have to fear we're going to win."

"At this point?" said Maxine. "We're way behind. Why would someone fear we're going to win?"

"By cheating. By getting to the Schwab and Young judges."

Maxine jerked her head back, frowning.

"That's clever. But how?" Trig asked.

"What if we fake a conversation with the head judge, Jules Longsworth. With me. We have some offer—I don't know, ten million dollars for him if we win. We store that on the server under some stupid filename—like 'confidential.' We know Igor has already hacked into our systems. He discovers it, sends it to his boss all worried, and voilà. When it launches we both mirror his hard disk and start tracking him with Cyclops."

"Why would we have a recording of that conversation?" asked Maxine.

"To protect against Longsworth double-crossing us."

"It's perfect. Except one thing," said Trig. "How do we get Jules Longsworth to go along?"

"No way, never in a million years. Asking him would be ethical suicide," said Maxine.

"If we only had prior recordings of him . . . ." mused Trig.

"Maybe his announcement at the Entrepreneur of the Year awards?" offered Lionel.

"Even if we could wrangle it, the acoustics in that big hall would never sound like a one-on-one conversation," said Trig.

"One-on-one . . ." Maxine repeated. "Oh my God! We do." Maxine jumped to her feet and shook her fists triumphantly.

"We do?"

"Leah Barko. All those interviews she did with Jules Longsworth for her articles on the Big. She certainly recorded them, and there must be at least four."

"And she would give them to us?" Lionel shook his head slowly.

"She loves you. She likes both of us . . . ."

"For a journalist, to give up her sources? No way, even to trap a suspected killer. That is asking way too much."

Maxine dropped into her seat. "Maybe Lionel's right. If we alienate her, or especially Longsworth, it's game over." They sat dejectedly. No one said anything for a while.

Then Trig spoke up. "She doesn't need to give permission. If she followed a link from Lionel, I mirror her machine. Pull down the audio files. We transcribe everything Jules said. And then create a script with Lionel doing most of the talking, and we interlace it with select responses from Jules. We use studio software to sound-equalize the backgrounds, splice, and we have a scratchy but audible recording of the dirty deed."

Maxine stared at Trig, the whites of her eyes bulging.

"That is devilishly good."

"It's also completely illegal. Not only is it inadmissible in court, if we get caught it could be jail time," Trig cautioned.

Lionel slumped forward, shaking his head. "I don't know." Then he looked at Maxine. "What do you think?"

"There are people trying to kill us in the middle of the night. I'm open to doing some hacking to stop them."

The look on Maxine's face was all Lionel needed.

"Screw it. Let's do it, Trig. And fast."

***

Within an hour Lionel had emailed Leah a PDF.

Check out this new study from *BevStrategy*. We pay this research organization a small fortune each year. Does a great job evaluating the energy drink players. Could be very helpful in your next article. Lionel

----

Knowing she was inundated with email, Lionel texted her and mentioned the study. Within minutes, Trig updated Lionel. "She triggered the Citadel-based AZ99 mirroring software. I'll download her audio files pronto."

Maxine plugged in her earbuds and began scanning the audio files, transcribing potential pieces for their script. She taped the transcribed chunks on her whiteboard like a jigsaw puzzle. She ended with multiple versions, each on a wall of her office. An hour later she and Lionel had edited the passages down to one conversation.

Meanwhile, Trig experimented with panels, furniture, and several recorders in Lionel's office to match the sound levels and recording characteristics of Leah's recordings in Jules Longsworth's office. Lionel rushed back to his office with their final script on his laptop, and sat inside the modified office to record his side of his conversation with Jules.

After several takes of each of his passages, Trig did a rough edit. Maxine joined them around Lionel's desk to hear it.

"It'll have a lot of rough transitions, but we'll smooth those later."

"No worries. Let's hear it," Lionel said eagerly.

Trig pressed play, and by the time it was over, Lionel was frowning. He began to worry if this plan was a bust.

"Maxine, in the script, we're missing the most convincing aspect."

"What's that?"

"Jules Longsworth actually saying my name."

"We don't have that in a contiguous segment."

"Can we splice his response? Does he say, 'Lionel,' somewhere else?"

"He does. It's in a totally different context. But Trig said to try to avoid splices within a sentence. That sounds choppy and suspicious."

"That's the other problem. It already does sound choppy. We need to get Jules saying my name, once or twice, to paint a credible story."

"You're right," Trig replied. "We need an audio engineer to create an audio signature to mask all the splicing and smooth it into a single recording. There is someone I can trust, but she won't be cheap. Especially in a hurry."

"How much?"

"Probably ten thousand. But she's the best."

Lionel took a deep breath. Their entire plan counted on this conversation sounding convincing. "Man, I hope she can impress us."

44

WEDNESDAY, MARCH 19ᵀᴴ

The wait stretched on. Helmet snug, goggles clear, bindings cranked. Her poles were pounding as *Dog Days Are Over* created a wall of sound. The entire world was shut out.

The blur of the starter's puffy red coat made her turn. She saw him mouthing words into the radio strapped around his neck. Then he leaned close to her and pointed to his ear.

She turned down her tunes. Florence and the Machine faded away, replaced by wind, flapping banners, and a distant snowmobile whine. An announcer's excited pitch echoed in the background.

The starter yelled above the wind. "Sorry, Reddi. They're clearing that skier off the course. She had to be airlifted out."

She nodded. The word was the super aggressive German girl blew out her knee. Now with an airlift, it might be something worse. There was nothing she could do. The starter cupped his hands near her helmet.

"We may cancel, depending. Once the officials let me know, we'll either call it, or I'll give you sixty seconds to get composed, okay?"

With a shake of her head she turned her tunes back up. Screw it. *On or off, I'm shredding this course. Shake it Out* took over her world. She soared with Florence's soulful voice, her gloves squeezing the grips as she pounded her poles on the snowpack.

The argument earlier that day rose back to the surface. Leaving the pre-competition briefing, Reddi had been hassled by a veteran coach, a nasty witch who called her "double trouble" and the "one hit flame out." She ridiculed Reddi because she had only won one race so far. *So what, it was the X Games!* The coach hated her because she wasn't part of the regular skiing system, paying for all the fancy camps and private lessons. *Screw her, this is about skiing, not some coaching career. It's really hard to win, bitch.* She stamped her feet, pissed off. *Flame out, huh? I'll freaking flame your butt.*

As her eyes stared down the run, the rails, boxes, and mounded jumps went double. Then they became a kaleidoscope. Suddenly she was back home on Telluride's Gold Hill. Skiing the chutes. It was a powder day. Her friends were screaming. Laughing. Puffing along. Wolfie was there too. The lifts had closed, but then it dumped. They snuck a ride up the mountain in a snow cat with a guy working maintenance, and hiked the last part. Wolfie pranced around, and sometimes just the tip of her nose poked above the deep snow. Reddi was wearing a new pair of demo powder skis from Crazy Jack and had a pocketful of treats that Helga had given her for Wolfie. She kicked stairs up the last steep pitch, and then they all stood atop the Rockies breathless. Pyramid-like peaks were sprayed with white in every direction. Trig stood next to her. They were eagles. Then they flew down the mountain together, owning the dream, the secret stash of the universe's best moments.

"Reddi. Reddi. Reddi Christiansen." Her coat tugged.

She looked over, startled from her dream. A giant red sausage of an arm was pinching the edge of her jacket. The starter with the radio was bobbing his head.

"You're up! Course ready." And then faintly she heard the announcer's broadcast.

"On the course now, Reddi Christiansen."

Without hesitation she dropped down the course with every body angle seeking speed. She spun on and off the rails like she was dancing, her feet fast and sure, eager for more. On and off with 270s. Backside, front side, she popped and spun. She went bigger than she planned, but it all felt right, adding extra spins and grabs. The series of three jumps was next.

Her legs felt powerful as she pushed off the first jump, climbing, climbing, and suddenly everything below was tiny and distant. The airtime tricks felt like a slow-motion dream sequence, and then she stuck the landing. The skis were part of her feet, and she danced and floated, anticipating the next jump. She was in the moment, smooth and rhythmic. She launched into her second jump, a huge flat spin 540 bow and arrow. Soaring, she grabbed her skis, around and around. Then nailed the backward switch landing.

Her adrenaline surged as she approached the final ramp. *One more big air.* Then the thought of the German girl flashed. *She'd lost it on this jump.* Suddenly she was on the ramp full speed. *Do this now.* And she was up, spinning and flipping in a double rodeo 900. It was her hardest trick, and as she rotated and flipped going ninety feet in the air she readied for the backward landing. *Focus. Focus.* The drop seemed endless, then the ground rose up and sucked her skis down. Her hips and knees bent deep. In a blur she had landed, and was racing downhill backward. *Yes!* She edged around and suddenly the finish line appeared, and the crowd screamed and rippled like a colorful flag in the wind. She wanted to keep going. It felt perfect. But the snow fence funneled her into the throng, waving and cheering. Her coach Bronco emerged from the noisy swarm, and as he hugged her, it started to sink in. She was at Copper Mountain, and this was the Slopestyle Federation Championship final. And she knew she had stomped it and won today! She couldn't wait to tell Trig.

***

Late that morning, Trig came back to Lionel's office with his laptop. Maxine joined them, and they listened to the revised recording together.

> *Jules, what would it take for us to work together?*
> *Ah, that is difficult to say at this point in time, Lionel.*
> *Would you consider ten million dollars a fair fee?*
> *Well, that certainly sounds worthy . . . worthy of consideration.*
> *Would you be able to guarantee that DV wins the award?*
> *I don't think that would be a problem.*
> *When will this be official then?*

When we announce the award at the end of March. But I can't tell you how important it is to keep this confidential.
Jules, this is absolutely between you and me.
What are your plans for ... ah, reconciling this?
We will deposit ten million in a Cayman Islands numbered account in a series of two-million-dollar transactions, every two months. On our end, it needs to be routed various ways, so it isn't obvious. Is that all right?
That should work fine. I am a patient man, Lionel.

Lionel got the chills. This would fool anyone. At least initially.

"Play it again," asked Maxine.

As they listened to the dialogue, Lionel felt transported into Jules Longsworth's top-floor office. He could almost see the view. What an incredible difference. "Scary good, Trig."

Maxine frowned at Trig. "Don't let anyone else hear this. Lionel and Jules Longsworth would be under immediate criminal investigation, it's that convincing."

"Yes ma'am, other than Igor, of course. I'll store the file on the server in a confidential folder, right where he should find it." He glanced at the bulky watch on his wrist. "I need to finish tweaking and testing the Cyclops app."

"Meanwhile, Lionel and I need to create an email string, cryptically referring to this arrangement with Jules as our new winning strategy?" asked Maxine.

"Right."

"When this works, Trig, what exactly is going to happen?"

"First, we'll be able to mirror Igor's boss's machine to my laptop. Then, if the code works, Cyclops will display blinking dots of our targets on your smartphone GPS maps."

"As they move with their smartphones, they move on our maps?"

"If it works."

"I can't wait to start tracking *them* for a change," said Lionel. He wondered if he should ask Trig for a pistol. But not in front of Maxine, she'd freak.

"It seems strange not including Dasha. She'd be helpful with this," Maxine observed.

Trig's brow creased. "I feel bad about excluding Dasha. But for your safety, until I can validate that Igor doesn't have her in his control, I have to hold off. We'll find out soon, hopefully." He took a deep breath. "If we can get the fish to swallow this bait."

45

THURSDAY, MARCH 20TH

It had been seventy-two hours since Trig had slept in a bed. He had been coding all night in Lionel's office, cramped over three computers, two smartphones, and a string of crushed aluminum DV energy shots. Eventually, he curled up with a sleeping bag on the floor. Just for a few minutes, he promised himself. He was dreaming of Reddi when the noise woke him.

Someone was rapping on the door. They sounded persistent. He staggered to his feet and looked at his watch. He rubbed his eyes trying to read the blurry dial. Six a.m.

"Lionel, good morning. Do you have a minute?" He recognized the voice from beyond the door. It was Dasha.

He scratched his head and rolled his shoulders as he walked, stretching the kinks in his back. He opened the door partway and spoke in Russian.

"Good morning, Dasha."

"Trig." Her bangs were scattered over her forehead, and he saw the helmet under her arm. Her amber eyes seemed to grow larger as she examined him. "Sorry, but what are you doing in Lionel's office?"

"I'm on a project for him."

She pushed the door firmly and leaned in. He held the door from swinging wider, but she peered to the back of the office. *Damn, she'll see the sleeping bag and all my test gear.*

"Were you working here all night?"

"Yes. Big Disrupter stuff."

"Is it some sort of emergency?"

He couldn't tell her the truth, but he also did not want to lie. "Yes. Some things that have to get done. Right away."

"What things?"

Several distinct chirps warbled from his laptop. *It's working.* He was dying to go open the mirror window. What was on the boss's hard drive? Was the GPS tracking working? But first he had to get rid of Dasha.

"Trig, are you keeping secrets from me? Please answer me honestly."

"I am under orders from Lionel and Maxine. Until they authorize me to discuss this further, I can't say. But personally I wish I could."

She frowned. "Does this have something to do with what happened to Maxine and Lionel at her apartment the other night?"

"Dasha. We'll talk about this as soon as I can. Please trust me until then."

She stared at him, her face hardening.

Was she going to try to examine his laptop? He waited as she studied the office behind him, her eyes scanning.

Then she spun and walked down the hallway.

Trig closed the door, took a deep breath, and ran to his laptop.

The trap was working. Igor had forwarded the video package to his boss, code-named Zebra. He had opened it, and the AZ99 mirror software was downloading an exact image of Zebra's hard drive. He examined what he could while the download continued.

Well-organized folders detailed Zebra's real-estate holdings. A country house in Napa, an office on Montgomery Street in the City, high-end apartment buildings on Russian Hill, and a commercial/apartment building in North Beach. He used a Mediterranean villa on Telegraph Hill as his primary residence. His financial folder had his net worth at over one hundred million dollars, and that was the traceable amount. Trig shook his head. One thing was clear, this guy was worth a lot of money. Why was he involved with a hacker like Igor?

Trig saw folders labeled U.S., China, Russia, UK, Germany, and Japan. Each folder had a number of AES 128-bit encrypted files. *No way he'd crack those without a supercomputer and a time machine.*

Then, buried within several folders, Trig found numerous files that had not yet been encrypted. The mother lode! But it would take hours to pore through the details of this criminal operation. He needed to update Lionel.

He dialed Lionel's phone. After four rings it went to voicemail. Damn. But then he saw an incoming call back.

"Sorry, I'm riding my bike to work. It took a while to get to my phone. What's up?"

"It turns out Zebra is located right here in San Francisco. House on Telegraph Hill. Name is Antonio Fanachi."

"Never heard of him."

Trig wasn't surprised. "He owns a lot of commercial real estate. He fronts as a wealthy landlord."

"What about the criminal side?"

"I've only started. But it's clearly cyber crime. Remember the intellectual property we saw Igor collecting on his laptop via his hacking?"

"The info from those Silicon Valley companies—business plans, patent applications and M&A activity?"

"Exactly. Fanachi is selling that information to global corporations, governments, and investors."

"What?! What does that have to do with DV? Is he after our drink formulas and business plans?"

"No offense, but it looks like he has much bigger fish to fry. Like Facebook and Google. Mobile technology companies, chip manufacturers, and Apple."

"Holy shit. That is the big leagues in intellectual property. Why does he want to harm us?"

"I've only seen a glimpse so far. I called hoping you had some ideas."

"Uh, not really." Trig heard a motorcycle's loud pipes blasting past Lionel in traffic, then a cable car bell. "No clue. What about the Cyclops GPS?"

"Waiting for him to download the Audio app on his phone."

"Remind me what that is for?" He heard Lionel breathing harder as he pedaled.

"He needs that to listen to your conversation with Jules. When they try to launch the recording, the dialogue window states it uses a special decoder and they are auto-directed to download the free audio app. That was the first piece I developed and placed on the Apple and Google app stores. It's a Trojan horse, really. When he downloads that, our Cyclops bug gets loaded in their phone and starts beaconing."

"Okay, so that still needs to happen?"

"Right."

"Keep me posted, please."

After hanging up with Lionel, Trig sent an encrypted email.

- - - - - - -

Slurp—Need to know all I can about one Antonio Fanachi, suspected cyber criminal out of San Francisco. Owns properties in Napa and several buildings in the city, addresses below. Targets domestic U.S. businesses to sell their confidential information globally. —Trig

- - - - - - -

He returned to his decryption. Then his phone rang. A blocked number. Hmm. Slurp wouldn't call. He picked it up, wondering.

"Good morning, Trig. It's Inspector Chang of SFPD."

"Good morning, sir. What can I do for you?"

"Normally I'd like to have this conversation in person. But the time frame doesn't allow it."

"Sir?"

"Look, with your background, clearly you are doing some online sleuthing. I get that."

Odd coincidence, Trig thought.

"Anyway, I don't expect or even want you to acknowledge that. But what I do want is for us to cooperate."

"I absolutely believe in that, sir. As soon as I find something useful." The sunrise suddenly pierced the office with yellow shafts, stinging Trig's sore eyes. Why was Chang bothering him now? He had to study those new files he discovered.

"I have my own listening post. Some technology that is outside the normal channels. So don't assume I don't value the importance of cyber and social media info. Right now, I'm sitting at home going through an anonymous server. And I'm on a disposable cell phone."

"I see." Chang, going off road?

"Here is the problem I'm facing. In two hours the FBI is arriving at the precinct. The bigwig panel in charge of the Big Disrupter Award brought them in because of the publicity. Some Jules Longsworth guy, with Schwab and Young."

"I think I've heard of him." *Oh, shit.*

"The FBI will be crawling all over me to understand the deaths of Jan Swenson in Minnesota, Raj Singh here in SF, and the Telluride and SF investigations of Double Vision personnel. Their Critical Incident Response Group, CIRG, has been dispatched."

"You'll never get any work done, sir."

"True. And guess what? You're invited too. And it's not optional. They will be full of questions, and they don't have to be as nice to you since you're unofficial."

Terrible timing. "Sir, can this wait twenty-four hours?"

"I'm afraid the FBI doesn't wait. The official reason for my call is to inform you to show up at the Mission Street precinct at 0900 today. CIRG will be there to suck your time dry. It'll be weeks."

"We don't have that."

"No, we don't. We're sitting on a time bomb."

He had to take a risk with Chang. "You know the park on Valencia near your office?"

"Sure."

"Can we meet there in thirty minutes? I've got some things to run by you."

"Will do."

Trig hung up. Maybe they'd underestimated Chang.

***

The encrypted phone rang. Alpha jumped. Finally. He had been trying to reach Fanachi for the past three days. What the hell went wrong?

"Alpha."

"We have a situation."

"Obviously, Fanachi. Your people screwed up that fiasco at the apartment. Jesus, it's all over the news. Everywhere—TV, press, the web."

"That's not what I'm talking about."

"What do you mean? I told you not to do a double murder, you tried anyway, and now it's become a media zoo."

"There are always operational complications. That can be fixed. This other thing I'm talking about is bigger than that."

Alpha squinted. Shit. The police? FBI? He felt his heart start to race. "What exactly are you talking about?"

"I think it's time for us to meet in person."

"We've discussed this before. It's too compromising for me to be seen with you, given your background."

"The situation has changed."

"I don't like the sound of this."

"I have gone along as your hired muscle long enough. Following orders, taking out people as accidents, no questions asked." Fanachi paused. "Clearly this is all about your winning the Big Disrupter."

"Ridiculous." Alpha regretted he responded so quickly.

"Don't insult my intelligence. The biggest prize ever? One billion dollars. That's real money."

"I have nothing to do with that."

"I see. So you probably aren't interested in the recording I have, then. It's of a secret meeting between Lionel Lane and Jules Longsworth. About how he wins the Big next week."

"What?! Impossible. Double Vision is too far behind."

"Why so surprised? He's cheating. Like you."

"What do you mean?" He felt his face heating up.

"There is a large dollar incentive involved for Longsworth."

"A bribe?" Alpha's mind raced. Then he wondered, "For how much?"

"As I said, I only want to discuss this in person."

"Goddamn it." There was a long pause. *Son-of-a-bitch.* His temples pounded.

"Tell me more first."

"Only in person."

Damn it, he was going to have to risk being seen with him. "This needs to be somewhere very inconspicuous."

"I know a discrete Italian restaurant in North Beach where we can break some bread in a back room, undisturbed. After that I'll take you on a remarkably private ride, from the heights of the City to the depths of our facilities. I think you'll be impressed by the extent and secrecy of our operation."

"Fine. Text me the restaurant address."

"Oh, one more thing. In addition to solving this problem, there is the fee situation."

"More than the four hundred thousand dollars you are getting?"

"Of course the Big Disrupter is one billion dollars. I'm getting a tiny fraction of a percent."

"It's not that simple."

"I agree. But now it is time to have that conversation about intellectual property. I know you work with Google, and Facebook, and multiple chipmakers. We need to discuss specifics so we can help each other."

"I told you that was off limits. I'm only open to cash."

"This is the only currency I want from you going forward. IP. If you hang up now or say no, I can't help you anymore. And you lose the Big."

"This is absolute extortion. I won't have it." He seethed, spitting into the phone.

Fanachi spoke in a calm low voice. "Alpha, you can't go to the police. And there is no muscle that would or could touch me. It's IP or nothing."

A full ten seconds passed.

"Should I text you the address?" Fanachi asked.

Alpha felt pathetic when he heard himself say, "Yes."

46

THURSDAY EVENING, MARCH 20TH

Early that evening Lionel sat alone at a desk in a hotel room, online. Chang had advised him and Maxine to use aliases and stay in different hotels.

Lionel felt on edge. Was it the pressure of the Big? The personal threat to Maxine and himself? He couldn't stop worrying about her.

A text from Maxine came to his laptop via their secure app.

- - - - - - -

See it? The dots?

- - - - - - -

He realized she was talking about Cyclops. It must be live now. He thumbed over to it, saw three dots, and texted her back.

- - - - - - -

Yes. I see three now.
Me too. They go by color. Blue is Igor. And green is Fanachi.
What is this red one?
Don't know. They must have shared the link with someone.
Where's Trig? Can he help?

Still at the frigging precinct with Chang and the FBI. He can't talk—everything is recorded there.
Text?
Yes. But expect delays. Answers during breaks.
Let's check with him at a break.
I'm going to follow these guys. They are at a restaurant somewhere in North Beach.
No way! Too dangerous.
I'll get photos or video. It's a restaurant. I'll be careful.
Wait for Trig. Don't do it.
We've got three of them together at once. This may not happen again. And we'll ID the third mystery guy.
Let me call Chang. Maybe he and Trig can break away.
Whatever. Signing off for now.

- - - - - - -

***

Alone at her hotel, Maxine started to get a very bad feeling. She had to do something. Lionel should not be going near those guys alone.

She heard an odd sound from outside her window. A tingle went up her back. She peeked out between the closed drapes. Reflections lit up like silver daggers under the bright quartz lights in the alley. The shadows looked suspicious. Was it those thugs from her apartment? Her stomach flipped.

The hotel room phone rang. She nearly jumped out of her skin.

"Maxine, it's Inspector Chang."

"Inspector. I'm glad you called." She took an enormous breath. "I need to talk to Trig."

"I'll see if I can get him out of the meeting. The FBI is here. It's been a nonstop debriefing and planning session. Their Critical Incident Response Group, CIRG, sent a dozen people."

"I need to talk to him now." She glanced between the drapes again—then jerked them shut.

"I understand. But first, can I alert you to something? It's why I called."

"Go ahead."

"It's about this guy Fanachi."

"Who?" said Maxine, pretending surprise.

"It's okay. This is a throwaway cell and I'm standing outside the building. Trig and I had a heart-to-heart this morning, when I alerted him to the arrival of the FBI. We've been pooling intel, no questions asked."

"What does this have to do with me?"

"Fanachi is a ruthless character, suspected of drug smuggling, extortion, and gun running. Cyber crime is his new thing, and it is paying off handsomely. He seems like a thug, but in reality is a very clever, extremely dangerous criminal."

"I can't tell you how bad the timing is on this information." *Jesus, Lionel, what are you getting into?*

"Sorry, I got confirmation of this minutes ago through CMap, our criminal data warehouse. It's been hell getting anything done today. The FBI wants to follow their procedures and protocol for everything."

"Inspector." Maxine was thinking through her options quickly. "Tell Trig I am going to be outside the police station in ten minutes in my Mini Cooper. If he doesn't get his ass out of those meetings and join me in that car, I'll be driving by myself to help Lionel take on Fanachi and his gangsters. We're tracking them by GPS right now—don't ask."

She slammed down the phone.

***

Lionel, please pick up. It rang two, three, four times, and then on the fifth ring it went to voicemail.

Maxine's Mini was speeding down Mission Street. She swerved and her tires squealed as she pulled into oncoming traffic to pass. She ran red lights. Honking cars and shaking fists followed her wake.

She snapped her iPhone into her dashboard mount and started the Cyclops application. The dots glowed in the darkness, and she found herself obsessed by them. Suddenly they started moving.

A blaring horn snapped her head up. She had run another red light. The windshield of a bus filled her entire side vision. She could see the driver's startled face. She punched the accelerator. The bus's massive bumper blasted her rear, snapping her head sideways. Spinning lights blurred by as she whirled helplessly.

When she came to a stop, she was perpendicular to oncoming traffic. Brakes squealed, horns sounded, and the sick crunch of collisions followed. Her neck ached. Her hands trembled. But she had to keep going. *Get Trig. Find Lionel.*

She stomped on the gas, veering around the stopped cars. She heard a scraping behind her and saw sparks flying in her rearview mirror. Her bumper was hanging off the back. Damn, that was close.

As she rounded the corner to the police station she saw the bumper spin off in an arc as it scraped and skidded into the gutter.

Trig was running out of the building. He hopped in and slammed the door as she gunned it. He immediately looked at the GPS on the dashboard. Maxine saw Inspector Chang rushing into the parking lot in her rearview mirror.

She felt better having Trig with her. His muscular thighs filled the front seat. He seemed confident, jaw jutting forward, giving the impression this was routine for a Navy SEAL.

She took a deep breath.

A glance at the screen destroyed her moment of calm. It couldn't be. "Trig, the dots are moving. I think they've left the restaurant."

"Yes ma'am." His fingers were flying over his Android.

He finally looked up. "I think they're returning to Fanachi's house. It's on Telegraph Hill. I suggest Powell Street." Her stomach twisted. *Don't follow them there, Lionel.*

She swung around the backed-up traffic, racing through a red light. Trig gripped the roof handle. "Have you talked to Lionel?"

"No, he doesn't pick up. It's frustrating."

"Cyclops and the GPS take over the line, so that probably is the reason. I'll try again." He dialed with his left hand, and gripped with his right, as she swerved around cars. "Still no pickup."

They reached Powell Street, at the base of Nob Hill. A gridlocked ribbon of cars crawled slowly up the hill. She crossed the double yellow line and pulled into oncoming traffic.

A heavy cable car descended directly toward them. The clanging of its bells sounded like Easter Sunday at Grace Cathedral.

"Shit!"

"Ma'am, cable car brakes aren't that effective on steep hills when loaded with tourists."

"Thanks." The Mini's engine screamed. The cable car clattered down, the bells dinging louder and faster. She continued climbing in its path. The cable car conductor was lashing the brass bell. Maxine could see terrified faces of riders in her headlights, grasping in the open air to brace themselves. Then she swerved back into her lane ahead of the final car. The cable car thundered alongside, metal wheels flattening the rails, the windblast from its fifteen tons rocking the Mini.

Moments later the car's nose hopped forward as they crested on California Street, on top of Nob Hill. Around them luxury hotels were ablaze with lights, flags of the world snapping in the wind.

"Ma'am, there may be a future for you in race car driving."

"Driving bores me. It's getting somewhere that interests me."

"That would be straight ahead, toward another hill—Telegraph Hill."

Maxine launched down Powell toward Chinatown, the Mini's wheels chirping as it hopped over cross streets. "Give me an update."

"We have a problem. The dots for Fanachi and the mystery man have disappeared. Igor has branched off. And Lionel's dot has continued on Telegraph Hill, very slowly. But there's no road that way."

"No road!?" She thought for a moment. "Then let's intersect where Lionel will end up."

"Take a right on Broadway and then a left on Sansome. Down closer to the water."

As the Mini raced though the streets of Chinatown, horns blaring and tires squealing, Maxine yelled, "I hope Lionel's not doing something crazy."

***

Lionel searched frantically for a parking spot in North Beach's small winding streets. At last he found a garage with some space and jumped out with the car still running. He sprinted to the restaurant, his chest heaving as he arrived at the entrance. He stared at his iPhone in disbelief. Damn! The dots had moved. He had missed them.

Fanachi and the red accomplice were moving together, with Igor's blue dot following behind. Maybe they were going to a bar or a club? He ran back to his car.

The garage was a nightmare. The valet had parked his car in the rear and a crush of other people had arrived. By the time he was driving he had lost fifteen minutes. He followed the dots up to Telegraph Hill. He passed below Coit Tower, then made a quick left turn along the edge of the cliff.

Threading along a narrow street, Lionel lurched to a stop directly opposite the dots on the GPS.

Across from him was an impressive Mediterranean villa, with huge windows, statues and gardens. An imposing metal front gate and brick wall, ten feet tall, wrapped around. Squeezing the car into a parking place, he considered his next move.

He couldn't let them see him taking their picture. With a shudder, he remembered the huge guy with the silencer pistol invading the apartment.

The reality of the fortress-like protection surrounding the house sunk in. Hunting with Cyclops as a stealth weapon was incredible. *It was a shame the blinking dots didn't contain the power of a drone missile.*

The front gate swung open. A slender man emerged. His blond hair flashed before his hood flipped up.

As he walked by, Lionel noticed the blue dot move.

That had to be Igor. *Should he call the cops? But what proof would they have to search or arrest him?* He heard a car start and race away. Probably that damned Audi.

Then the other dots moved. They seemed to be at the opposite side of the house.

What is going on? He watched the dots as they flickered and then disappeared.

What? They left through the back door? Straight off the cliff?

He got out of his car and ran hunched over, through the shadows. He edged along the tall fence until it ended into a stone terrace. Beyond, through the dim light, he saw a few shrubs and the contours of the cliff. A light flashed. He looked straight out and saw the lighthouse on Alcatraz, the Rock, in the bay. Lights of the Embarcadero piers twinkled two hundred feet below on the water's edge.

Screw it. Fanachi and the mystery guy went this way. He had to follow.

Lionel started climbing down. He grabbed plants, rocks, anything that would hold him. His eyes became better acclimated. Then he reached a drop. It plunged at least one hundred feet down. *How did they do this? And why did the dots disappear?*

He turned and faced the cliff. He had free climbed crazier. Maybe not in the dark. But he had to find these guys. He started down, digging for toeholds, and balancing with his hands. Some of the rock was loose. He moved carefully. He tried to spread his footholds, but then came upon a smooth face with only one option. Just as he placed both feet on a small bump, it gave way. He fell. His clawing hands felt air, then scraped smooth rock, and he twisted wildly.

His fingers caught, then broke, then caught again. Something in his left hand snapped as his body wrenched to a stop. Pain flashed through his forearm and up into his shoulder. He thrust out his other hand and his fingers wrapped around wire. It was chain link. Some sort of barrier to hold back falling rock. He hung in midair, his feet kicking. That was too close.

For the next forty feet he lowered himself down, hand over hand, as the chain link creaked and dropped rock dust, dirt, and small chips on him. His hands burned. He finally reached a small ledge.

He stood, trembling. He suddenly feared Fanachi noticed he was being tracked. Maybe that's why they disappeared. And what if Fanachi was tracking them now? And went after Maxine in the hotel? He hoped she was okay. He'd call her when he got off this insane cliff, but he didn't want to turn off Cyclops.

He had to continue the free climb. It was a crazy situation, but down was the only option. Any slip and . . . . *Don't think about that,* he reminded himself. The Alcatraz light flashed by periodically.

He inched down the next section via a series of cracks. Sparse brambles grew out of the rock, poking his eyes. He wedged his hands in crevices, jammed his arms in larger openings, and balanced on tiny nubs. Several times he followed routes that ended in a sheer drop. He had to climb back up, and try another route down. This route would be crazy on belay, even for an experienced climber. He shook his head. And as an experienced climber he should have known better. He was trembling, totally at his limit. *Too late now.* Face by face he made it down through the dark, the periodic flash from the lighthouse washing the cliff.

His hands cramped into tight balls. His legs vibrated. It seemed endless. *Don't stop.* Then a light flashed on below and stayed lit.

As he dropped closer he could make out some shapes. Immediately below him loops of razor wire twinkled, like sharp teeth atop a high cinderblock wall. The wall protected a compound, butted against the cliff and connected to the back of a warehouse. He studied the inside of the compound. He saw a black Cadillac SUV facing an open garage door that led into the warehouse. The entire building was dark, except for the light shining out the garage door. The compound's gate was closed. The only way inside appeared to be over the wall. He wasn't surprised they hadn't anticipated someone using this cliff route, he thought with grim humor. *This was insane.* Then he jumped.

His leap barely cleared the razor wire. It was higher than he realized. He hung in the air, searching in the darkness for the bottom. Suddenly his knees pounded into his chest, and his wind surged out faster than he could think. He rolled, eventually coming to a stop on his side, flat against concrete, staring at the cliff above. He sucked the vacuum in his chest. Everything below his waist was numb. Grit etched his eyes and he realized his face was caked in dirt and blood. His hands trembled. *Keep going.* When he could breathe again, he crawled on all fours. Then he staggered to a crouch. With a gasp, he limped toward the light shining from the garage. A gleaming Ferrari was parked in one of the bays. *Was this the right place? Check Cyclops.* He fumbled for his iPhone. It glowed brightly.

His phone was flying out of his hand before he realized something had crushed his arm. He felt his head snap back, his neck choked with a gurgle, and realized a huge bicep wrapped him like a child.

A voice growled. "You move, your neck breaks. Understand?" He was like a sloppy grizzly bear, spitting saliva in his ear.

Lionel grunted. The guy was huge.

He was half walked and half dragged by the man-bear into the garage and under the light.

"Oh. You came to me. Very convenient. I have a score to settle."

The giant loosened his grip just enough so Lionel could see a shaved patch in his thick black hair, exposing bruised green-blue flesh. An ugly four-inch row of black sutures looped through his folded scalp.

"Remember me now?" A sick grin flashed a mouth full of metal work.

Lionel's chest tightened. This was the guy he'd smashed with the lamp. God, he wished he had died.

The thug pulled out a large black automatic from a concealed holster. He jammed the barrel against Lionel's temple, squeezing him like a vise.

"Even if your death has to look accidental, it will be very, very painful. I promise."

Lionel heard a door open. A man exited, silhouetted in light. His silver and black hair was combed straight back. As he approached, Lionel could see his bearing matched his expensive tailored clothing. But the planes of his large face were jagged and his mouth cut a hard line. The momentary surprise on his face quickly faded.

"Nice work, Nicco. Looks like Mr. Lane has no respect for private property."

A second man emerged from the door. Short, his shaved head shined pink. Small intense eyes expanded in surprise.

Lionel gasped. "Hank Welcher?!"

Welcher recoiled. "What the hell?! Fanachi, what is Lionel Lane doing here?"

"Trespassing evidently. He just made our job more convenient."

"I can't be seen here." He twisted his hands, looking side to side. "I need to leave. Damn it, I knew this was a bad idea."

Thoughts immediately flooded Lionel's brain. Welcher lowballing him for Double Vision, then funding SocialLending instead. And they were in first place. Welcher spreading nasty rumors about Maxine and Havermyer. Oh, my God, had he killed to win the Big? Welcher was the red dot. The mystery third guy. "It's you, Welcher. You're behind this. I can't believe I didn't figure this out."

"What? I'm strictly an investor." He raised himself taller. "I'm here to consider a real-estate opportunity."

"Don't worry about your story for him. He won't be talking to anyone but angels soon." Fanachi looked at Nicco. "Get the duct tape and put him in the back of the SUV. Make sure he can't move around. Tomas, open the gate now."

"You want to win the Big Disrupter that way? Is Larry Furtig in on this too? You're killing people so SocialLending can win an award meant for social good? What sick psycho does that!?" Lionel was straining against Nicco's grip, screaming in anger.

"I do *not* know what you are talking about. I am a venture capitalist and private investor." Welcher looked away. Lionel twisted. Nicco shoved the gun harder.

"Nicco, wrap him up. Now!"

"Let's go asshole." Nicco shoved him toward the SUV, one paw crushing the back of his neck. Lionel staggered. Tomas returned to the driver's seat.

Then Lionel heard a whine like a chainsaw. A high revving motor echoed off the cliffs as it raced down the street.

Tires screeched through the open gate as a blur of orange and black screamed up, skidding in front of the SUV.

A pistol was pointed outside the passenger window directly at them. Lionel recognized Trig. He wrenched free and dove to the concrete, just as Trig yelled, "Drop the gun!"

Nicco's gun swung to the Mini's windshield, only feet away.

"Drop it now! I've got you in range," Trig yelled.

Welcher let out a moan and raised his hands. "I'm just a visitor. Don't shoot."

Lionel heard another car approaching rapidly. A green sedan skidded out of control directly at the Mini Cooper. *It'll T-bone Maxine.* He raised his hand and cried out "Maxine!" The sedan lurched to a stop inches from her door.

The driver's window was down. A large caliber pistol pointed inside the garage. "Drop the weapons—police!" Lionel recognized Inspector Chang's voice.

Nicco turned his pistol toward Chang.

Three quick flashes blurred out of Trig's pistol, rocking the compound. Lionel saw Nicco stagger backward, then topple like a tree trunk. Trig swung his door open and glided out, pivoting in a crouch with his gun raised.

Suddenly Trig swung toward Chang. He blasted three shots in his direction.

Lionel jumped in alarm. "What the hell!?"

Behind Chang's sedan, outside the black SUV, Tomas collapsed to his knees, three red splotches on his chest. He pitched forward. His right arm splayed out, still gripping an assault rifle.

Lionel spun to see Fanachi reach into his coat and pull out a silver pistol. He pointed at Trig's back. As Lionel shouted, shots rang out.

The explosions from the weapons were deafening, echoing between the garage and cliffs. Lionel jerked with each blast. Gunsmoke filled the air.

Then Fanachi's legs buckled and his knees pounded down. As he fell forward the side of his face slapped the smooth surface, like a fish on a boat deck. His arm bent out awkwardly and the silver gun skidded across the concrete. Smoke was still trailing out of Chang's gun.

Trig ran to the SUV with his gun raised. Chang came forward with his gun trained inside the garage. "Police! Come out with your hands up. Now!"

Lionel stared transfixed as blood seeped from underneath Fanachi, like a growing medallion. It was so quiet he heard the blood.

"Don't shoot. I'm an innocent investor." The whine came from the back corner of the garage. Lionel saw Hank Welcher crouched behind the red Ferrari, both hands gripping his pale head. He sprang up and ran over.

Welcher crawled away, jamming against the wall like a trapped cockroach. "I'm unarmed. I have done nothing."

"You liar. You're the mastermind behind this—you paid to have Jan and Raj killed, you scum." Lionel grabbed him by the throat and smashed his head against the wall.

Welcher's eyes swelled large as Lionel choked him. He lifted him higher, his feet dangling helplessly. Welcher gurgled, his face turning bright red. "Confess you asshole. You tried killing Maxine and me. Right?"

Footsteps came running into the garage. Then Maxine was pulling on his shoulder.

"You might kill him, Lionel. It's not worth it. Let him rot in jail for life." She wrapped herself around Lionel. He felt her fierce grip trembling through him.

Lionel dropped him. He watched as Welcher gasped on the floor, his handprint still impressed on his throat.

Maxine turned Lionel around. They hugged, squeezing so hard Lionel could feel her heartbeats. He suddenly felt her strength was the only thing holding him up. He hung in her arms.

"You rescued me. Again. I didn't plan for it to get this crazy."

"I didn't plan to feel this way either," she answered.

He turned his head and looked at her. She raised her face and he gently kissed her on the lips. She kissed back harder. They eagerly gave in to each other, lost in the moment.

47

THURSDAY NIGHT, MARCH 20TH

The high-pitched wail of police cars was followed by waves of early responders surrounding the warehouse. Trig watched as the darkness transformed into a kaleidoscope of flashing red and blue lights.

This place was going to become a madhouse, thought Trig, once Chang explained who they had here. They'd be searching, flashing cameras and interviewing all night. Trig peered over at the International Trading Company sign. Must be Fanachi's front. He looked up the dark cliff to the twinkling houses several hundred feet above. And Lionel climbed down that? Damn. He wondered how Fanachi and Welcher descended from his villa above. He scanned the cliff and back of the building. Why had they disappeared from Cyclops temporarily? Then he thought of Igor and his neck tensed.

Trig pulled out his smartphone. Cyclops loaded on his GPS, and the blue dot blinked on the other side of San Francisco. The Dogpatch neighborhood. It looked like Igor was back at his apartment.

Two Crime Scene Investigators had been huddling around Inspector Chang. They then moved over to the bodies and began taking pictures. Trig approached and Chang nodded toward his car. He wanted to be out of earshot, Trig realized. They leaned against the doors of his green sedan, in the shadows. An island away from the flashing lights and radio chatter. Chang took out a cigarette. He offered one to Trig, who shook his head. Chang lit it and inhaled deeply. They both watched the commotion.

"Thanks for having my back, Inspector." Then Trig held out a hand.

Chang exhaled and grasped it. "It's Winston, friend. And we're even. I didn't even see the guy with the Uzi coming out of the SUV behind me. Nice work."

His smile had more lines than usual, Trig thought. His job never ended. Then he remembered. "But we're still missing Igor Vasilchenko."

Chang flicked his cigarette and leaned closer. "What does that bloodhound GPS of yours say?" he whispered.

Trig replied softly. "Cyclops says he's back at his apartment."

"Once he gets wind of Fanachi's death, we may never find him." Chang took another drag.

"I agree. And there is someone else. Dasha Romanyuk, the IT person at DV."

Chang looked over.

"I've been worried Igor is blackmailing her. Threatening her family back in Ukraine," Trig explained.

"Interpol indicated the Black Sea gang he was with was wiped out by the Russian Bratva. That eliminates Igor's muscle in Ukraine," Chang said.

"True."

"And now Fanachi can't help Igor here in the States," said Chang, inhaling again.

"Which makes Igor much less of a threat to her. She should be willing to tell me the truth," Trig said.

Chang stepped on his cigarette. "Dasha is your Double Vision internal matter, as far as I'm concerned. Meanwhile, I'm taking some officers to pay a visit to Igor at his place in Dogpatch."

***

There was something about her. A worldly and smart techie with a Cleopatra intrigue. He didn't know if it was good or bad. *Was she on our side or not?* He slid his Double Vision access card. The computer room door opened into the cool dim light.

"Trig," Dasha said, drawing out his name in her Eastern European accent. "Welcome. I didn't expect you."

"Good evening. Can I come in?"

"Yes, of course." She switched to Russian. "Just me and the computers for another late night."

Dasha's heels clicked on the floor as she rounded the desk in her black jeans. Gathering her purse and jacket from the guest chair, Trig noticed the subtle perfume. She stood close to him, clutching her belongings to her tight sweater, studying him.

"It's so good to see you," she said, briefly putting a hand on his shoulder. "Now maybe you can share some of your secrets with me," she added, smiling. The rack of computers flickered amber and green in the low light of the windowless room, coloring her face.

"Please, sit down." She spun like an ice skater on the smooth floor and found a shelf to store her bag and coat. Trig finally sat down.

"You are quiet. What is going on?" she asked, tilting her head. The flickering lights pulsed on the white pattern curving across her sweater. Under her dark bangs her eyes glowed with interest and her lips held an eagerness.

"Right now, it's important you tell me everything you can about Igor Vasilchenko."

"Igor Vasilchenko." She sat down. "Sure, but what does he have to do with anything?" Her dark eyebrows raised, curious.

"How long have you known him?"

"Maybe three or four months," she answered, shrugging her shoulders. "I met him in our parking lot. I was driving my Vespa. He had a motorcycle, a Ducati. He noticed my scooter is painted blue and gold like the Ukrainian flag and we started talking." She reached her hands across the desk. "Did he do something wrong?"

"Are you close?" Trig asked.

"Close?"

"Sorry, part of the investigation. Do you date him?"

"Oh, no. I have a boyfriend. He works at Google."

Trig nodded.

She continued. "Igor is my friend because he needed one. He's lonely. A withdrawn Russian engineer. And far away from home. I was being friendly."

"So you don't see each other often?"

"Often? No. Sometimes online. We're friends on VK. You know, the Russian Facebook. Maybe we've seen each other four or five times coming and going on my Vespa. And we went to lunch once."

"Have you talked to him tonight?"

"No." She shook her head emphatically, her bangs swinging. "Trig, I can tell something is wrong and you aren't telling me."

"Dasha, I need to know everything possible about this guy. He could be dangerous."

She crossed her arms tightly. "Ah, and you think I might be working with him?" She stood up. "You think I am a criminal?" Her eyes looked angry and hurt. Trig could feel their mutual trust disappearing in the cold air of the computer lab.

"Here, read my email. See if I am plotting with him." Her fingers clattered on her keyboard. "There, I am logged in. Come and see."

"I don't need to."

"Why? Have you already hacked that?" she accused, her voice soaring. Her hands searched for something on the table. She found her iPhone and punched in some digits. "Here, read my texts," she shouted, and she threw her phone at him. Trig caught it as it flew by his head. He calmly scrolled through the texts as she stewed. He saw two texts between her and Igor regarding lunch, and no more. He looked up at her as she brushed something out of her eye. She trembled in anger.

"Dasha, please. Let me explain." He motioned with his palms and she slowly sat back down.

"Igor has an entire folder on you and your sister Lilia. He has pictures of her walking to school, your parents, and the outside of their apartment in Dnipropetrovsk. He has a database of all your connections, like your boyfriend at Google. And your other friends at Facebook, Salesforce, and Twitter. Nearly all Ukrainian. And he has audio files. I only listened to one, but it appears he was bugging your apartment."

Her mouth dropped. "He is stalking my family. And me? Why?"

"To threaten and blackmail you into helping him steal intellectual property. He's probably waiting for the perfect moment to strike."

"Intellectual property. From Double Vision?"

"From where your close friends work."

"My friends?"

"It's an impressive list of tech companies."

Trig could hear her swearing quietly. Then she stopped and looked at him.

"Trig . . . wait. How do you know what's on his computer?"

He hesitated. "Because I hacked him. Like he hacked us."

"What?!"

"Log into your IIS server as the admin. I'll show you one of the several places he has compromised the server system. He has been using an exploit to copy all the centrally stored company intellectual property and to track schedules. Lionel's and Maxine's in particular."

Within minutes after she and Trig looked at the hidden code, Trig could see she was furious. At herself and at Igor.

No actress was that good. She was telling the truth.

"What a pig!" She slapped the desk fiercely. "He has been trying to impress me. He said he had a girlfriend in Russia named Lilia, the same as my little sister. He told me he wanted to bring her into this country, once he made a lot of money. He said he could help me do the same for my sister. I worried he was trying to be too nice. Now I know I was right."

"That could explain some things. Anything else?"

She paused for a moment. "He told me he was with some elite unit of the Russian army, and was trained in electronics and explosives. But that his real passion was computers. So I believed he was an honest programmer."

"That's what he said to get his U.S. work visa."

"Trig, I must ask." Her eyes searched his face. "Why did you wait before telling me this? You should have said something. And if I was a crook, put me in jail."

"My concern was that you were being blackmailed. He was in a gang back in Russia and worked for a powerful gangster named Fanachi, here in San Francisco. Now, neither group of criminals is a factor."

She leaned closer. "You thought I would not be able to be honest with you, because of what they would do to my family back in Ukraine?"

Trig nodded.

She sat back, blinking. After a deep breath she said, "Thank you. You have been very kind."

"You deserve it."

"I apologize about throwing the phone."

"It doesn't matter." He stood to go.

"I wish I could do more to help."

"You are working incredibly hard for DV. That's thanks enough." Trig pulled out his phone and glanced at Cyclops.

"Now I know DV's data is safe with you. But I should help out Inspector Chang. The police are about to enter Igor's apartment and capture him." Trig rose and walked to the door. As he opened it, she suddenly spoke.

"His apartment? Trig wait. He said something strange once."

Trig stood holding the door. He had missed a call from Chang and he needed to reply. He didn't want to keep the police waiting. "Yes, what?"

"You know his military background, with electronics and explosives? One time he bragged that no one could ever break into his apartment and steal anything."

"Because of alarms?"

"That's what I asked. Igor laughed and said, 'No. They might get in, but they'd never leave in one piece.' He never said more, but now I'm worried. If Igor is a criminal and his computers are full of hacked data—he might do something dangerous to protect them. You may be walking into a trap."

***

Trig was racing down the stairwell when he got hold of Inspector Chang.

"Winston, it's Trig. Don't go in."

"Why? I borrowed Lionel's phone and Cyclops tells me he's inside. We've got him surrounded."

Trig pulled up, breathing hard. "I spoke with Dasha. His apartment may be booby trapped with explosives."

"But he's inside. He wouldn't have an active trip wire if he is still there." Trig could hear the officers around Chang, asking for permission to proceed.

"Unless he figured out we were tracking him. He might have become suspicious that we caught Fanachi and Welcher together at the same time."

"Why not toss the phone if he suspects it's bugged?"

"Even better, put it in his apartment. We set off the trap, and the explosion takes us out and all traces of his computers disappear."

"Damn." Trig could hear the concern in Chang's voice. "His Audi is sitting outside."

"He has a motorcycle as well. Ducati."

"Okay. Hold on."

Two tense minutes ticked off. Trig made it out of the building and into his car. Chang returned. "We searched the perimeter of the building. Didn't find the Ducati."

"Not good. He must be onto us."

"I'll call the bomb squad. They'll be here ASAP."

"I'm on my way, too."

Trig raced his rental car along the waterfront and through gritty streets fronting industrial buildings. He launched over train tracks and past rows of loading docks. Cyclops led him right to Igor's apartment in Dogpatch. He arrived with tires screeching as the bomb squad pulled up in a heavily armored vehicle. Twenty minutes later, wearing blast suits and a remote control robot, they opened the apartment door.

The C4 explosives rocked the building, blasting out the doors and windows on the entire second floor.

Chang emerged from the outer edges of the smoldering building. White dusk flecked his face.

Trig shook his head as he looked at the ruined building, smoke spewing everywhere, firemen shooting arcing sprays. Searchlights beamed through the smoke and rubble. Residents huddled behind barriers, staring in disbelief. Trig approached Chang, smoking a cigarette next to his car. "I assume everything inside Igor's unit was melted down beyond recognition?"

"His entire apartment was pancaked. The bomb squad was positioned down the hallway, and the pressure of the blast wave still blew them back. Fortunately they're okay."

"Good. But the bad news is the explosion blew out his phone and our Cyclops tracking dot."

"Yeah, along with every other trace of him. We'll put out an APB for his Ducati." Chang looked drawn, but he still managed a smile. He put his hand on Trig's shoulder. "That's the second time today you had my back. The advance warning saved a lot of lives."

"Give that credit to Dasha. Ukrainian smarts over Russian force. She figured it out."

***

The wind gusts whipped down the freeway, adding to the air blasting Igor's chest at seventy miles per hour. His gloves gripped the handlebars tighter and he squinted behind the full visor. He realized now how lucky he had been. Fanachi and Alpha had taken the Rock Elevator, and he had driven around to meet them in the Honeycomb, per instructions. He was glad Fanachi didn't invite him along to tour the remainder of the compound after showing off the Honeycomb. Instead he watched the gunfight in surprise, from the security camera monitor inside. That Navy SEAL and the police inspector must have tracked them via their phones. And then arrived shooting. There was no other explanation. It had been chaos. Then he smiled, remembering how he slipped out and drove right past the flashing police cars as they rushed to the warehouse.

The next freeway exit said Point Richmond, and he took the ramp. He rode toward a corrugated sheet metal building with a sign that declared, "Econo Self-Storage—San Francisco's largest." With a loud rumble, the Ducati rolled to a stop at the iron gate. He pulled out his passkey and swiped it through the lock. The gate clanged and slid aside. He rode into the fenced storage facility and circled to the back, past a long row of identical steel doors. At number 513, he stopped the bike. His key opened the hardened padlock, and he pushed up the roll-up door with a clatter. He rode his bike inside and slammed the door, before removing his helmet and visor. There were cameras everywhere out there. He'd have to hide the Ducati for a while, even though he had swapped its license plate at his apartment. Especially if his trap at the apartment worked. He wondered as he pulled off his gloves.

He took his tablet out of his pack and checked the online news. A picture of a wealthy VC named Hank Welcher popped up. He grunted as he recognized Alpha. That guy was worth over two hundred million dollars? The police would never be able to keep him in jail—all that money, plus important friends. Too bad about Fanachi, Nicco, and Tomas, he thought, as he read about their deaths.

Interesting, there were only three people still alive that knew about the villa's secret Rock Elevator. Welcher, Calabrese, and himself. And only he had all of Fanachi's data sitting in the Cloud on an encrypted server. Now Fanachi was gone. This could be a very profitable business for me, he thought.

He packed a few more items into the van sitting in his storage unit. He pulled on a long brown wig, tinted glasses, and baseball cap.

He checked the news again. A breaking headline reported an explosion in the City's Dogpatch neighborhood. He shook his fist and grinned in victory. *The bomb he had wired to the motion detectors worked!* The tracking device the police had hacked into his phone was a clever NSA trick. But he fooled them by placing it inside the apartment next to his explosives. He would enjoy all the details later. For now, he was glad he had prepared his escape plan so carefully. He drove the van out of the unit and over to the gate. As he swiped his card the LCD displayed, "Thank you Ollie Rasmussen," and he exited.

48

FRIDAY, MARCH 21ST

Lionel stared out the window of the cab. He felt Maxine's warmth leaning against him, pressing close, their fingers intertwined. Kate sat in the front seat, glued to her iPhone. It was good of her to come get them at the police station. He and Maxine had been riding a cyclone. The ordeal with Fanachi and his henchmen had left him thrashed, and the painstaking statements with the detectives and FBI were numbing, especially dancing around the use of Cyclops. Right now he relished this simple downtime, watching the world roll by. Merchants sweeping their sidewalks. The slow motion at the train station. Giants baseball park, the scavenging seagulls the only visitors today. The sun rose across the bay, glowing on his cheek.

"Last chance for you two to head to your hotels for some sleep," Kate offered. "The cabbie can make a quick detour. It's going to be a zoo once you get to the office."

Maxine groaned and sat up, letting go of Lionel. "It's been a long night. But we have work to do." She took a deep breath and clapped her hands together rapidly. Lionel winced.

"It's Friday," she said emphatically. "In exactly one week the final numbers for the Big are submitted. That's it. Finito. The judges make their decision and one company gets to change the world. And damn it, that needs to be DV."

Kate nodded her head in the front seat. "You know it, Maxine."

Lionel remained slumped, forehead pressed against the window. "It sure as hell better not be SocialLending, not after what Hank Welcher did," he muttered.

"The legal system won't settle anything against Welcher in the next week. That takes time," Maxine countered.

The cab thumped and rattled over a pothole. Lionel didn't respond.

"Oh my God. Un-freaking-believable!" Kate leaned back over the front seat, holding out her iPhone. "You guys have *got* to see this."

After last night's chase and shootout, thought Lionel, how could any news surprise Kate? He ignored her.

Kate burst out. "Hank Welcher's PR person just tweeted. He claims Hank was part of a gangster sting operation. And that Hank was instrumental in catching the criminals."

Lionel bolted up. "What! That shiny-headed parasite! I should have finished choking him to oblivion."

Kate's eyes widened in surprise as she drew back. Lionel fumed as he pulled out his smartphone and searched Twitter.

Maxine waited before replying. "Lionel, that part is over. We're safe. No more guns, gangsters, and killing. Let it go. The police are on the case and they'll get Welcher for all his dirty crimes."

Lionel looked out the window.

Maxine's tone softened. "Come back to DV and sell beverages. We have a contest to win. An industry to disrupt. Remember those starving children."

Lionel's temples throbbed. The cab felt claustrophobic. Maxine's words sounded perfectly logical, as always. But Welcher's gall burned him.

"I'm sorry for blurting out," Kate said quietly. "Obviously it's personal. From what you guys have told me, Welcher is guilty as sin. And you two and Trig are the ones who nailed this conspiracy. This is BS Twitter spin."

The cab came to a sudden stop outside their office. Lionel pushed the door open, eager to escape. He gulped the morning air. It tasted salty and invigorating. A seagull flew overhead, cawing. Bicyclists passed by. A traffic light changed and pedestrians crowded the sidewalk as they rushed to work, many with faces glued to smartphones. Suddenly the right response to Welcher became obvious. Lionel froze, mind spinning.

Maxine and Kate walked ahead, crossing the brick plaza toward the elevator.

Lionel stood thinking. They'd have to be really careful, he realized, to protect Trig. They'd skip any description of the hacking, and instead emphasize the dramatic highlights.

Lionel ran and caught up with Maxine, taking her hand and nudging her. "Sorry." She nodded.

"I'm sorry, Kate. I shouldn't shoot the messenger."

Kate looked over. "No problem. You two have been through hell. I get it."

When they reached the far end of the plaza, Lionel stopped. They were away from the stream of pedestrians. He motioned them closer.

"I have a plan. A good plan."

Maxine's eyebrows arched in mock disbelief. "That's a rare privilege."

He smiled. "Funny."

He glanced around the plaza. "Like Maxine said, the justice system will take more time than we have. So let's beat Welcher at his own game. We'll spin this tragedy to accelerate our success. Let's turn Welcher's criminal actions against Jan and Raj, and his attempts against us, to some good. Promoted and spun our way, emphasizing DV's heroics."

Kate and Maxine looked at each other. "Lionel, I'm all for the idea," Kate said, "But do we know what really happened?"

"Look, all the facts haven't come out yet. But at least we know what our people have done."

"I'm ready," said Kate. "What do we have to work with?"

"Trig installed several security measures for us, including dashboard-mounted cameras. Maxine's dash cam was working last night."

"On her Mini?" Kate gasped.

"Yes," he said, grinning. "The camera captured the entire shootout scene at Fanachi's garage, plus Maxine's race through the City with Trig. And they had a wild roller coaster ride, including a near head-on with a cable car loaded with tourists."

"That's a crazy visual. Awesome. I'll get the video team all over this, pronto."

"But skip the kiss part," said Maxine.

"What kiss part?" asked Kate.

"After the shooting stopped, Lionel grabbed Welcher and practically killed him. I pulled him off and we ended up kissing. For a while."

"What?! Especially that kiss part is going online."

"I was afraid you'd say that," groaned Maxine. "I'm not embarrassed. It's annoying that people will talk more about the kiss than our business."

"Everyone loves romance. It's a great lead-in."

"Kate, you've got to see this two-hundred-foot cliff on Telegraph Hill that Lionel climbed down, in the dark. That's how he discovered Fanachi's secret hideout."

"Lionel, you've been holding back. The cliff-climbing CEO of Double Vision, to the rescue? That definitely adds to our extreme image."

Lionel's excitement grew. "A raw, first-release video, then interviews, then follow-on vignettes. It would be huge if multiple versions went viral."

"I want to give Jacob Havermyer a call right away. He should hear this from us, not the press," Maxine said.

"Agreed. He'll be furious with Welcher. I'm sure he'll stir up a serious shit-storm."

"To have a fellow financier arranging murders? Jacob has the ear of reporters from the *New York Times, Wall Street Journal, Huffington Post*—from all his business success and philanthropic work."

Lionel relished the image of Jacob lighting fires under Welcher with righteous indignation. Then he glanced at his watch and frowned. "Guys, we've got to get inside. I promised Leah Barko my first media interview. She deserves to break this story wide open."

In the elevator, Lionel ticked off ideas for social media and TV coverage. "Remember, Kate, include Trig's background as a Navy SEAL."

"Plus his long time relationship with Reddi, in Telluride. She is the face of the company, after all," added Maxine.

Lionel admired the way Maxine now championed Reddi. Then he suddenly remembered Reddi's recent victory. It seemed so long ago. "And she won the Slopestyle Federation Championship this week."

"Oh, the media is going to love this. Navy SEAL rescues CEOs from gangsters, between dates with redheaded ski champion."

"And don't forget Inspector Chang. Emphasize his police work in masterminding the clues and capture. Keep Trig out of that."

Kate looked at Lionel curiously. "Okay. I'm sure you have your reasons. Trig will be the company muscle, then."

"Perfect."

"But where is the dash-cam tape? Do I need to ask the police or DA for a copy? It's part of evidence now, I assume."

"On that, we'll ask forgiveness, not permission. Trig had live streaming set up for the camera, over 3G, directly to his server. Ask him to send you the video, ASAP."

Kate nodded. "With these videos, we're talking about millions of potential views. Online and for TV news."

The elevator stopped abruptly. The doors opened outside Double Vision's office. Lionel took a breath. "It's going to be an insane week."

***

Three hours later Lionel and Maxine were in the middle of a media storm. The DV conference room was so jammed they had to leave the doors open so people could crowd around the doorways. It was hot and stuffy inside. TV crews and reporters shoved recorders and microphones up against Lionel and Maxine, while camera lenses stared from multiple directions. Regional representatives from publications from the U.K., Europe, and Pacific Rim as well as influential bloggers and Twitter stars attended in person or on Skype.

Lionel and Maxine had started with a page of prepared remarks, tempered by advice from their attorneys. Then they played the dashboard-cam video, parts of which had gone online earlier. The video created an enormous stir. Now it was the Q & A session, and Maxine was answering a question.

Lionel's phone vibrated. Someone on his VIP list. Kate would yell at him. But he slipped his phone out and peeked. Garr Gartick of Merry Cola. This was either great news or the end of their relationship. He sucked in a deep breath.

"Excuse me people. Sorry Maxine."

She turned from the microphones and shot him a quick look.

"This is Merry Cola's CEO Garr Gartick. He's calling to either fire or congratulate us, I'm not sure which. But you'll find out soon, so we might as well do this now. I'll put it on speaker."

Lionel saw Kate's look of horror. Maxine crossed her arms. Lionel shrugged and placed the phone in front of him, amongst the microphones.

"Hello Garr, this is Lionel."

"Lionel, I saw the dash-cam footage on TV a moment ago."

"Garr, I have you on speaker."

"Too bad. This question can't wait." His tone was brusque. Garr paused. The reporters quieted, hung in suspense. "How good was that kiss at the end with Maxine?"

The room exploded in laughter. Lionel glanced at Maxine. She was shaking her head, with a resigned smile. *She called that one.*

When it quieted down, Lionel responded, unable to keep the grin off his face. "Sorry Garr, not only are you on speaker, but I'm in a media conference."

Garr chuckled. "You can answer my question another time when we meet in private." Garr then segued smoothly. "Although this is perfect timing, everyone. We have some news the world should hear."

"You have the floor, Garr." Lionel held his breath.

"Merry Cola is proud to be affiliated with a health-conscious, socially responsible beverage company like Double Vision. In fact, my call today was to let Lionel and Maxine know we are placing what will certainly be the largest order they have ever received, for one hundred million dollars."

Lionel turned to Maxine. Their jaws dropped. If he hugged her she'd kill him. He shot both hands up and she slapped them in a high ten. Press cameras clicked furiously, like a crescendo of applause.

As Garr continued, Lionel thought of his clever timing. Garr knew when and how to maximize media coverage. What a smart marketer.

"People love the refreshing energy and taste of Double Vision. Their beautiful aluminum bottles are flying off the shelves and out of refrigerated cases, in convenience and grocery stores nationwide. Imagine the millions of meals this will help provide starving children. And as we are witnessing right now, the founders, Lionel and Maxine, embody the bravery and energy of real heroes."

Lionel looked over at Maxine. The cameras followed. He knew she was wondering the same thing. How much product could they possibly ship this week, to count as revenue toward winning the Big?

***

"Trig, you can talk in here. But I need them back in five minutes—they need to be ready for this prime-time network coverage."

"Yes, ma'am. And thanks for helping me get past security."

Kate nodded a tight smile and closed the door to the small dressing room. *What a pro,* he thought. No drama when he said he absolutely needed a few minutes privately with Lionel and Maxine, on an urgent matter. He was finessed anonymously into the CBS news station in downtown San Francisco. The last thing he needed was some reporter looking into his DOD cyber background right now.

Lionel and Maxine sat on the two swiveling make-up chairs as Trig pulled up a folding chair between them. "I'll get right to the point. I know your time is short."

"What's up, Trig?"

"The drug test came back from the lab. It confirmed positively for roofies. It was a very pure form of flunitrazepam, prescription quality, and a dangerously heavy dose. No wonder you've had total amnesia about that evening."

"I am not at all surprised," Lionel said, shaking his head.

"We know it was a couple of Fanachi's operatives who broke into Maxine's apartment. And we suspect Fanachi had Igor hit Lionel on his bike, and set the avalanche in Telluride. But not the roofie drugging at the BevGlobe Conference."

"What?" Maxine responded. "I thought this was all Welcher and Fanachi."

Trig shifted in his chair. "I'm sorry to tell you this. But I do have a recorded interview and cell phone records. It's awkward."

"Trig, tell us."

"That stunt was arranged by Blaine Latrell of Axlewright."

"Blaine?" Lionel looked over at Maxine. "Holy shit! Why?"

"I was hoping you two would know."

"He is invested in us. Why attack your own investment?" Lionel stood, his arms swinging in the small room. "Why damage the brand and disrupt the team?"

"I was hoping it was Welcher. And that all of this was behind us." Maxine's fingers rolled in circles, massaging her temples. "What the hell is Blaine doing?" she muttered.

"I met with Maria Monrovia. She's the same woman you woke up with, and who called Maxine that morning with the tip about your being in Hunters Point."

Trig proceeded to play highlights of his recorded conversation with Maria, describing the evening. They listened silently, with an occasional curse from Lionel.

"That's not all," Trig said. "That break-in in Telluride that Dasha recorded on video? The guy has been identified as a local small-time scammer named Jake the Rake. He planted cocaine in Lionel's desk."

"That has been confirmed?"

"Affirmative. Twenty grams. That's a felony. Sheriff Masterson and I suspect Blaine is behind this, although Jake hasn't admitted it. But he hinted he'd squeal in exchange for leniency."

Lionel struck the wall with his hand. Trig saw him grimace. "So Blaine wants to systematically destroy my reputation, between roofies, sex, crack pipes, and now coke in Telluride." He looked at Maxine and then Trig, throwing his hands out. "What have I done to this guy? F-ing insane."

Trig shrugged. "Blaine Latrell is a wild card."

"Hold on," said Maxine. "I got a call from Jacob a few weeks ago. Remember, Lionel? It was when he mentioned Blaine and the BodyHamr merger talks. Jacob said these fishing expeditions usually happen when someone wants to replace an executive. Like a CEO."

"Ah. So he's trying to get rid of me. And end up with a bigger piece of the company, and his own puppet in charge. That's why he is doing this." Lionel shook his head. "But these are criminal tactics."

"Blaine is under some serious pressure at work to perform," said Maxine. "Maybe he is being manipulated." She hesitated. "Plus, I'm afraid he has some delusions of romance with me."

Trig saw Lionel look at her sharply. "Romance? With you?" Lionel exclaimed.

"Believe me, I have done everything to discourage him on that front. But I think he dreams of taking over DV, alongside me."

"What a loser. This is so over the line. He's going down." Lionel was pacing.

"Wait. We have unbelievably positive publicity now. We can't do anything to shift the story to one of our own VCs undermining us, or your running down an alley naked. That's suicide."

"He's a criminal. He belongs in jail."

"Lionel, do you want revenge or to win the Big?" she asked.

Trig marveled at Maxine. *That woman does not lose focus no matter what the distractions.*

"We have to do something."

"I agree. Trig, this woman Maria, the one on your recorder describing the roofies setup. Is she credible?"

"I believe her. And we have the photos from her iPhone. But . . . she is a stripper."

"A stripper?" Maxine gave Lionel the look.

"Yes. Not a hooker, but a stripper. For the setup. Long story."

"Lionel, in bed with a stripper . . . that story will come out." The loudest sound in the room was Maxine's exhale of disgust.

"Nothing happened between us," Lionel insisted.

"That's what Maria told me as well," said Trig.

"It doesn't matter. The circumstances will generate loads of negative publicity and derail our winning the Big." Maxine shook her head.

"I'm sure Blaine is counting on our keeping his dirty plan quiet, for that very reason," said Lionel.

"The key is the photos," said Trig. "I'm still negotiating with Mick, the guy with the camera, who broke in on Lionel and Maria that morning. He claims he's not giving the photos to Blaine or us."

"We need to shut Blaine down. Now."

The small studio went quiet. Huddled close together, the surrounding make-up mirrors reflected their worried expressions.

Then Lionel jumped to his feet. "The Telluride break-in. His criminal actions would force the board and his firm to push him out quietly, and crush his credibility."

Maxine grasped Trig's arm. "Trig, can you return to Telluride and get this dealer Jake to talk on the record? Something we could use in an emergency board meeting?"

"Yes ma'am," Trig replied. "But getting a recorded confession from Jake the Rake without a firm deal from the DA won't be easy. This may not work."

A knock at the door interrupted them. Kate poked her head inside. "You're on national TV in five minutes."

49

FRIDAY MORNING, MARCH 28ᵀᴴ— FINAL DAY OF THE BIG DISRUPTER

"Harding, it's Lionel. Sorry to call so early."

"I've been up all night anyway, it's okay."

"Here we are, the final day." Lionel took a breath. "How do the numbers look?"

"Quite surprising, actually. This past week has been unprecedented. Merry Cola orders, large ones, are flowing in from all their regions." Harding's voice rose, uncharacteristically. "We're going to exceed our forecast by fifty percent."

Lionel let out a yell. Then he danced around the stage manager standing in a headset next to him, before returning to the phone and congratulating Harding.

"I knew you'd be excited," Harding said. "We sure are. Is Maxine there? Where are you guys?"

"New York. Backstage. We're about to go on ABC's Good Morning America."

Maxine took the phone. "Harding, this is Maxine. Have you completed the final company submission for the Big?"

"I have it queued up. I waited until the last possible moment in order to have the absolute best numbers."

"And how are operations holding up?"

"Can I get Hugo? I'm sure he'd like to tell you personally."

Maxine put the phone on speaker. Lionel heard Harding call out to Hugo. The sounds of footsteps echoed from the smooth plant floor. Moments later he heard racing breaths. "So, how is the glam couple?" Hugo asked.

"Whoring ourselves magnificently. For the good of the world, of course," Lionel replied.

"Of course. Meanwhile we trolls are bent over double, loading product day and night."

"Are we keeping up with the orders?" Maxine asked.

"We put on extra shifts around the clock. You know those old mine tunnels I told you about, where we have been stockpiling inventory?"

"Yeah, I couldn't believe how much those hold."

"We are backing the trucks in and pulling out tons and tons of beautiful aluminum bottles. It's like the old mining days but instead of silver and gold, it's aluminum and our delightful brew. Between the mine tunnels and our warehouses down in Grand Junction, we're loading Merry Cola trucks 24/7."

"Guys, we could actually win the Big! Awesome work."

"It's the fastest turnaround I've ever seen," said Harding.

"My apologies gents, but Maxine and I are late for another interview."

"Splendid. Keep making it rain you two," added Hugo.

As they hung up Lionel turned to Maxine for a high five.

While the make-up people worked on them, Lionel allowed himself a moment to dream. He thought of the global expansion they would love to do with the sort of funding the Big Disrupter would allow. Europe, India, Australia and New Zealand, Japan . . . and even China. China could be an enormous market for them. Expanding to the world's largest economies. *Within weeks we could be a billion-dollar global corporation taking on the established beverage companies. And changing the world.*

***

Minutes later, across Manhattan, Leah Barko received an anonymous email. Her editor was copied.

The message was short. "Thought you should know."

Attached were a dozen pictures of Lionel. One showed him with a topless woman in a limo holding a bong. In the next photo they were lighting a crack pipe. Lionel looked comatose, his eyes nearly closed.

Lea kept clicking. Lionel was completely naked in each photo. One was of a trashy apartment with Lionel on the floor passed out, surrounded by baggies of suspected drugs and crack pipes. There was a picture looking out the window with Lionel holding a nude woman on a fire escape. The series continued with Lionel climbing down a metal ladder, above a sketchy alley in the middle of the day. The next showed him looking up at the camera with a glazed and guilty expression.

The final photo was a rear shot running naked down an alley alongside razor wire and dumpsters, his face twisted back with a frantic look.

Leah's editor immediately pinged her with one simple word. "Bombshell!"

50

FRIDAY AFTERNOON, MARCH 28TH

Lionel and Maxine floated across Manhattan in the back of a chauffeured Town Car. He loved that the dark glass and driver partition gave them privacy from the world, something they had lacked all week. NBC Nightly News sent the limo to ensure they were on time for the taping. He was hesitant to use it, but Maxine had reasoned it would waste as much energy empty, so the two of them hopped in, laughing.

Lionel rested his hand on Maxine's knee. He leaned over and she tilted her head toward him, meeting his lips. As they kissed he moaned. When she nibbled his ear, he surged. He popped their seatbelts, still kissing. In a moment he was on his knees in front of her, pressing.

Lionel's arms went around her waist pulling her toward him. Her legs parted, the dress riding up her hips. She bit his earlobe as he kissed her neck. He ached for her. He pushed her dress up higher.

Then his phone rang.

They both groaned.

Lionel recognized the ringtone. "It's Kate."

His heart was pounding and he could hear Maxine's breathing in union with his. *Kate can wait,* he thought.

The phone continued to ring.

Then Maxine gave him a light kiss on the forehead and pushed him back. "Just as well. This is crazy. And we've been offline for hours."

He sighed.

"Tell her about SNL. She'll die."

He reluctantly spun around, reaching for the phone.

"Hello, Kate."

"Thank God you finally answered."

"Kate, it's been an absolute madhouse here. Unbelievable."

"Lionel, we need to talk."

"Wait, did you hear Saturday Night Live is doing a skit about us tomorrow? At 30 Rock itself—I can see their building out the window of the limo. We've been invited to be part of the audience and visit the cast afterward. And we're rolling to NBC for the Nightly News right now."

"Great. But we have a problem."

She should be elated, he thought. "Oh, buzz killer. Just when we were finally having fun." He put the phone on speaker. "Maxine's here too. What's up?"

"Leah Barko is in a total panic. Calls. Texts. Finally she insisted they physically pull me out of a meeting. She says she has to talk to you and you've been unreachable."

"Sounds like a deadline problem."

"Leah has a dozen photos of you from an anonymous source, and her editor wants to run them. She refused to tell me the details other than saying they were you, and 'uncharacteristic' and 'very revealing.' Do you know what this is about?"

Lionel froze. Then he looked at Maxine. "Oh no, unbelievable. I'm afraid I might. Let me call her."

"What's up?"

"Honestly, at this point you are better off not knowing."

There was painful silence. He knew Kate hated being out of the loop more than anything.

"Sorry Kate, as soon as I can, I'll fill you in." Lionel hung up. He felt haunted. The guilty pleasure twisted into a guilty nightmare.

***

"Anonymous tip? Not really," replied Lionel. "There is only one person who would send this to you, Leah."

"I can't reveal my sources," she replied tersely.

"And sadly, it's one of my investors, Blaine Latrell."

"I can neither confirm nor deny."

"It's a setup. And you are playing into it. Look, there is an investigation in Telluride by Sheriff Masterson right now. Some small-time dealer named Jake the Rake placed coke in our offices. Inside my freaking desk. We have him on videotape—and we're sure it was Blaine behind it."

"Drug dealers under pressure can be twisted a lot of ways, Lionel. Not exactly reputable sources."

"You don't believe me? Call the Telluride sheriff!"

"That isn't the issue. I've been presented with these pictures of you. They are painfully incriminating. And you admit their authenticity."

"That was the opening night of BevGlobe. I was given a nearly fatal dose of roofies. I can send you a copy of the medical lab results."

"Why wasn't there a criminal investigation? Why haven't we heard of this before?"

"We didn't know who was responsible until recently."

"Then you covered it up."

"We were investigating."

"Lionel, you don't get to use former Navy SEALs like a private police force for your convenience. There are laws and public authorities, you know."

"You're right. And there are journalistic standards, too. Especially during ongoing investigations. Where the hell are those, Leah?" He was shouting.

"Dammit, Lionel," she hurled back. "The *National Times Journal* has the highest standards in the country. Are you calling me a fraud?"

The line was quiet. He knew Leah was a supporter. At least personally.

Lionel exhaled. "Sorry, Leah," he said quietly. "But your boss is blowing it."

Her voice trembled. "Look, I've pushed back a lot on my editor. I argued this was some private issue or vendetta." Lionel sensed her conflict.

"Exactly."

"But he pointed out that you are a very public figure now. You and Maxine published a personal car video a week ago highlighting a shootout at a private warehouse. It's not as though you hold high standards of privacy for yourselves or the people around you. You are a leading trend on Twitter and YouTube. Thank yourself and Google for that."

Shit. She had a point.

"Leah, I'm asking for a little time. This is the last day of the Big—wait until after the announcement next week. I know you care about people. I'm not trying to do image control. I need to stop a bad guy. If I don't, DV loses the Big. Some evil greedy suit wins, and a billion dollars is subverted."

"I have journalistic obligations here, Lionel."

"Leah, please. I'm begging. Can you wait one week?"

The silence lingered. Lionel twisted. He glanced at his phone to see if he had lost the call.

"Twenty-four hours."

"Twenty-four hours? That's impossible! It's Friday afternoon, I need to call a board meeting, we need to present evidence, and get a confession." His voice was panicked.

"Twenty-four hours to positively refute this. Even that may cost me my job. My editor will run the photos whether I work here or not. Twenty-four hours, Lionel."

This time the line did go dead.

51

EARLY SATURDAY MORNING, MARCH 29TH

"Jules, I am sorry for troubling you at home on a weekend."
"Hello, Leah. No need to apologize."

"Thank you." She took a long breath. "I'm worried about something, but I can't go into details. And I'm not positive."

"You certainly were right in your instincts about a plot surrounding the Big Disrupter. I'd say your intuition is quite good."

"First of all, I'm not recording this conversation. This call is an advance warning, about something disturbing that may happen."

"How could your news be any worse than what we've experienced already?"

"I can't tell you any details, but one of the leading contestants may have a series of very inflammatory pictures run in the paper. My paper."

"Is it Hank Welcher? It was shocking to have him revealed as consorting with gangsters. Is it associated with the allegations he contracted for murder?"

"No, it's not about Hank Welcher. I can't say more. I don't want to taint you, since you are a judge of the Big. There may be an explanation—the person involved swears they have been framed. But if these photos are not the result of a setup, the implications will be quite damning."

"Are the police or FBI involved?"

"Not yet. The pictures reflect more on moral character, although there may be illegal drugs involved."

"Criminy, what next? Should we wait until the authorities investigate the situation? I certainly could call them in again. Although," he sighed, "it would mean even more humiliation."

"There isn't enough time. My editor is publishing these pictures in the next twelve hours unless they are refuted. Period. Whether I work at the *National Times Journal* or not."

"In twelve hours? That would be the Sunday morning edition. Your most popular, I take it."

"Exactly."

"It sounds as though you are dealing with an ultimatum from your editor. What are the chances the contestant can exonerate him or herself?"

Leah tried to breathe, but it was like sucking through a tight straw. She hated the situation she was in, and even more, how she felt. "I don't think there is enough time." Then she whispered, "I'm sorry, Jules." And hung up.

52

LATE SATURDAY MORNING, MARCH 29TH

Lionel peered through the conference room blinds. Outside, on the stone terrace, Double Vision board members and advisors were gathering. His bloodshot eyes pulsed painfully, and tight lines pulled across his face. Another sleepless night.

"Has Blaine arrived yet?" asked Maxine, as she leaned over the laptop, tweaking their presentation.

"I don't see him. His boss, John Anderson, just showed up. Jacob's wife, Deborah, is walking him out on the terrace. Man, he looks uptight. Or else he's pissed off about the last-minute notice of a Saturday meeting."

"I got surprisingly little pushback. The board members I spoke with were more concerned about the status of the Big and alarmed about our run in with Fanachi and his henchmen."

He turned. Maxine looked striking, fresh yet understated in a linen pantsuit. How could she appear so composed now?

"Every director was complimentary of us," she continued. "When I said we needed to meet for extraordinary circumstances, they jumped."

He looked back out the window. "The board is curious as hell about the pending legal action against Hank Welcher. Not to mention interested in checking out Havermyer's Pacific Heights mansion."

"Thank God for Jacob. As busy as he is with his philanthropy and businesses, to open his house and send a private jet to pick us up in New York?"

Lionel pulled the blinds farther apart with his fingers. "Finally, Blaine is here. Last one. Figures. Anderson is pulling him aside, to the edge of the balustrade. Jesus, Anderson looks furious. Maybe he'll push Blaine over the edge and save us the trouble."

Just then Jacob walked into the conference room. "How are you holding up, young people?" Animated eyes danced behind his rimless glasses. Jacob's energy was palpable, flowing like his gray ponytail.

"I saw Blaine. We're ready." Lionel glanced at his watch. "But we've only got a few hours to get back to Leah Barko with Blaine's confession."

"You'll have many allies in the room, trust me," Jacob responded.

"Good. There's a lot riding on this meeting." Normally Lionel loved the moments of pressure. But between the exhaustion and anger at Blaine, he felt strangely on edge.

"Now that I know what the hell is going on with Blaine, believe me, he's going to crack and do what we say. His boss will have to choose between his firm's survival or Blaine, and that will be an easy decision." Jacob looked resolute.

"Thanks, Jacob. Hope you're right."

"I'll go bring them in. I'll be sure to walk Blaine right by the glass tank with the hammerhead sharks and manta rays gliding around, so he understands the neighborhood."

***

The group of twelve board members and advisors crowded around the oval table. All except Blaine, the last to enter, who sat fidgeting against the back wall.

Lionel had asked Maxine to speak first. He didn't want his anger to set the tone of the meeting.

Their presentation was stored on the bright green laptop blinking on the table. Maxine walked around as she spoke, working eye contact with everyone except Blaine.

"The information presented today is literally life and company threatening. This was gathered by an independent private investigator.

It reveals an egregious attack on the company and my co-CEO, Lionel Lane. Please keep in mind these actions occurred over time, and only after certain flashpoints were we able to piece together actionable information. If we had presented this earlier to you, it would have been speculative."

As the board murmured, she picked up a silver remote. "This is a video recorded by the investigator. He is interviewing a witness named Jake the Rake, aka Jake Townsend, after he was captured on our video surveillance system trespassing into Double Vision's Telluride office." Maxine squeezed the remote, and the lights lowered and the video started.

The interior of the Telluride office appeared. The walls were covered with DV graphics and event posters. A framed picture showed Reddi standing on the winner's podium at the X Games, next to the windows overlooking Main Street.

The camera focused on a man in his thirties with a lived-in face. The lines suggested many late nights and frequent sun exposure. He pushed his long stringy hair behind one ear, and adjusted the sunglasses perched back on his head.

"Your name please?" Trig's voice asked the question.

"Jake the Rake, everybody knows me as that."

"Full name?"

"Jake Townsend, but if you say that, everybody will be like, who? Everybody knows Jake the Rake."

"Who hired you to break into the Double Vision offices here in Telluride?"

"Yeah, it was, it was this dude Blaine, he was the one who paid me to plant the coke in this office. He told me to make sure it went into the desk drawer of the main guy, Lionel, sort of tucked away like he was hiding it. But findable, ya know?"

"By coke you mean the illegal drug cocaine."

"Yeah. Yeah, of course."

"How much cocaine?"

"Twenty grams. Ya know, more than you'd have as an occasional user, I mean usually. Someone was pissed at Lionel, I guess. But not my problem."

"Is this the person who hired you, and paid for the cocaine?"

A photograph was placed in front of him.

"Yeah, that's the dude. Crazy picture, he looks so formal and uptight there."

The camera zoomed on the picture. "The individual Jake Townsend has identified is Blaine Latrell, a vice president at Axlewright Capital."

Maxine stopped the video. Several directors whispered while others glanced at Blaine and John Andersen. Anderson spoke. "This is the first time I have seen this video. What the hell is going on, Blaine?" He turned toward the back of the room.

Blaine looked miserable, his hair scattered, and mouth downturned. His thick fingers scratched the dark stubble on his cheeks, his eyes glazed behind black rims. Heavy shoulders hunched around his laptop. He reminded Lionel of a big beaten sheepdog. His knee was twitching up and down, jerking without a rhythm, starting and stopping like it had a spasm. He kept switching his gaze between the people in the room and his laptop. Lionel felt no sympathy. He wanted to squeeze the truth out of him and get that to Leah Barko.

Finally Blaine muttered, "That guy is a drug dealer. Don't believe him."

What a liar. Lionel jumped to his feet and took the remote. "Let's listen to the following witness, then. This is a recording of a conversation with a waitress who admits that you, Blaine, ordered me drugged with flunitrazepam, or roofies, the date rape drug, as part of a plan to ruin my credibility and blackmail me into resigning my position."

Lionel played excerpts from the recording Trig made of his conversation with Maria Monrovia, the waitress at the Presidential Hotel.

She described the drugging, Lionel passing out in her apartment, and the call from Mick to Blaine to discuss the operation.

When Lionel stopped the recording several board members erupted. "This is a police matter. Isn't it Axlewright's fault? Is there board liability?"

Lionel managed to quiet everyone down, then asked, "Does Axlewright have a response?"

Anderson frowned and pointed an open hand toward Blaine.

Blaine leaned his chair back, bobbing both of his knees and fluttering his fingers.

"That's an outrageous story." He leaned forward and the chair slammed to the ground. People jumped. Blaine slapped the cover of his laptop closed, pointing at Lionel. "You hired some stripper to lie for you. You're the one who is criminal."

Lionel started to respond, then saw Maxine's hand reach out. He stopped. Blaine said nothing more. He picked up his bag and shoved his laptop inside, fishing around with his hand.

"Don't leave, Blaine. There's more. This is a recording of a telephone conversation our investigator made by eavesdropping on a call between Jake the Rake and Blaine." Lionel pressed the remote.

"Uh, hey Blaine. It's me, Jake the Rake."

"Yes, I know, I have caller ID. What's up?"

"I got real good news. You know that, that thing we set up in the office for Lionel?"

"Keep it general. But yes."

"Well I talked to the sheriff and kinda let something slip. So then he starts putting the heat on me, so I weasel out a story about someone in town with a lot of coke. He doesn't care about pot of course, but coke is different. He seemed real interested in maybe, like making a raid or an investigation or something."

"That's what we want. Soon?"

"I'm not exactly sure when. But I figured you'd be happy to hear that the trap you set up is working, you know?"

"Let's not talk about that here. But great work, do anything you can to move this along."

"Yeah, speaking of which. Any chance you can front me some more cash now?"

"Let me get back to you. Gotta go."

Lionel stopped the audio recording. "There we heard Blaine himself with hard evidence of his guilt. I demand he resign today. We can discuss terms for the return of the Axlewright Capital investment later. If Axlewright proceeds immediately and professionally, I'd consider not pressing charges and sealing this matter with a mutual confidentiality agreement. I have copies of that here." He turned to pick up a box of documents on the floor.

As Lionel stood, Blaine suddenly emerged near him. His bulky shoulders were hunched like a boxer's, one hand clenched in a meaty fist, and the other swinging his black ballistic-nylon computer bag. Blaine grabbed at the remote.

Lionel stepped toward him, still holding the box.

Blaine whirled and swung his computer bag, smashing the box against Lionel's chest. He reeled against the wall.

Out of Blaine's bag came a large silver pistol, shaking in his big hand. He pointed it directly at Lionel. Lionel jerked back. Blaine's face had a sweaty sheen. His teeth were clenched and a desperate gleam came from behind the black rims.

Someone screamed.

A gun? Lionel held the box in front of him. He flashed on Fanachi falling with the two red splotches on his chest.

Blaine swung the barrel from Lionel, past Maxine and stopped at the first board member. He cowered and gasped, "No!" As the gun stopped on the next director, she closed her eyes, trembling and praying out loud. He swung it at Havermyer, who stared motionless. Next to him was Anderson, who raised his hands. Blaine completed the circle to gasps and sobs. The room seemed tiny. Then Blaine pointed the pistol at Lionel's chest and cocked it.

53

SATURDAY NOON, MARCH 29ᵀᴴ

The click of the gun's hammer freaked Lionel. Blaine had gone insane. The gun barrel trembled, making his chest feel hollow.

"I'm in charge now. This is my deal. You screwed up, Lionel. You pissed off the wrong people." Blaine looked to his boss. "Right, John?"

"Blaine." John Anderson kept his hands upward as he spoke. "Please put the gun down."

"Coward!" He lunged at his boss, shaking the gun in his face. "You pushed for this. You can't back down now."

Anderson slunk lower, his hands fluttering like bare branches.

"You set me up and threatened to fire me if I didn't get rid of Lionel."

Anderson turned his head away from the gun barrel, closing his eyes as he trembled. "We miscommunicated. There's been a mistake."

"Don't deny it! I'm not going back home a failure. You are going to make me partner. Understand?" Blaine shouted, spraying spittle on Anderson.

"Of course." Anderson's voice quavered. "Whatever you say."

He turned to Maxine. "You're coming with me. We're going to work out a deal."

Maxine shook her head. "Don't Blaine. This will end badly. Put down the gun and let's talk."

"No," he yelled. "I'm in charge now."

He whipped the gun toward the group. "They will listen to me." He snapped his wrist and the gun exploded.

Lionel's ears rang. He smelled the gunpowder, like salty burning rubber. He dropped the box of papers. Someone screamed.

Across the room, inches above Anderson's head, a dark hole appeared in the wall. Anderson sunk even lower in his chair, his eyes like dull marbles.

"Now do you believe me!?" Blaine yelled.

He turned to the green computer with all the video and audio evidence on it.

"Back away. I'm taking this bullshit evidence." Blaine clamped a hand on the green laptop. He tugged repeatedly but the connector cables held it to the wall.

Lionel watched as Blaine struggled. He hunched his shoulder and ripped the cables from the wall. He spun to a stop, on one knee, near Maxine.

"What are you doing?" Blaine demanded. She looked up blankly from her lap, where her hands where resting.

"Nothing."

"Let me see your hands."

She placed her cell phone on the table.

He dropped the laptop and stepped over. "Oh, a text to your Navy SEAL. He's right outside, huh?" He raised the pistol above his head and smashed the butt down onto the phone.

The table bounced. The crushed phone scattered. Several directors gasped. Another sobbed.

Blaine pointed the gun at Lionel. "You're coming with me, Lionel. Move it. You too, Maxine."

Shoving the gun in Lionel's back, he marched him toward the door. Maxine rose.

"Blaine, let's talk this out." It was Havermyer. His eyes were like black beads behind his glasses, and his hands were held up high. "Let's sit down like smart business people."

"Too late." Blaine kept walking.

"Be reasonable. Let's talk."

Lionel stopped at the door. Blaine poked the gun harder into his back.

Lionel winced and raised his hands. Maxine was close behind.

"I'm serious, Blaine. Let me sit down with you," Havermyer persisted.

"Now you want to talk!" Blaine yelled.

"Put the gun down like a civilized human being!"

"Goddamn you, shut up." Blaine swung the gun back at Havermyer. Suddenly it exploded and Havermyer fell backward. The room erupted in screams.

"Out the door, Lionel. Maxine, try anything and wonder boy here gets it in his back. Just like Havermyer."

Maxine looked back at Jacob, her face twisted. "Help him! Call an ambulance someone."

Blaine shoved Lionel out the door. Maxine started toward Havermyer, and Blaine grabbed her hand. "Follow Lionel or he gets it."

She staggered forward. "Call 911!" Maxine yelled.

Blaine rushed them through the house, room by room. Past the artwork, the shark tank, and the palm trees. Passing across the rotunda, Lionel pushed the heavy front door open.

The daylight streamed down, shimmering off the white marble. Blaine shoved Lionel toward his black Range Rover. "If the SEAL shows up, Lionel is dead."

Lionel scanned the surroundings. He had asked Trig to wait nearby in the event the board wanted to hear more investigation details. As they approached Blaine's Range Rover he saw Trig slump down in his green Ford SUV across the street.

Blaine opened up the Range Rover's rear door and stared at the piles of gear inside.

"Maxine, get that ratchet strap. The one with the hooks and lock on it. Lionel you sit in the back seat, so I can see you. Maxine, wrap that strap around his neck two times, really tight. Make the ends the same length."

Maxine didn't move. "Now!" She turned to the task. Lionel sat in the back seat while Blaine trained the gun on the rear of his head, leaning in from the trunk.

"Give me the ends. Hurry." He looked around anxiously. "I swear if your SEAL shows up, I'm shooting Lionel." He hooked the ends to a metal retaining clip on the floor of the cargo area. The straps buzzed as he cinched them. Then he cranked on the ratchet and Lionel's head jerked back.

"Jesus, you're choking him," Maxine yelled.

"He'll be fine. Get in the front seat." He spun the combination lock mounted on the ratchet, behind Lionel.

Slamming the trunk, he jumped in the driver's seat and started the SUV. He stomped on the accelerator and surged up Broadway Street.

"Where are we going?" Maxine demanded.

"I don't know yet." Lionel saw him scan the horizon, toward the bay.

"Across the bridge. Out of the City."

He twisted the steering wheel hard left and sped over the top lip of Divisadero Street. Even with his neck strapped back, Lionel could see below them, through the windshield. The steep street had flat transitions at each intersection, then immediately dropped toward the next intersection. It looked like a series of ski jumps.

Squeezing the steering wheel in one hand and the gun in the other, Blaine accelerated down the hill.

They hit the first intersection way too fast. The SUV's front end compressed in a deep dip, then went airborne as they popped over the lip. The car hung in the air like a Norwegian ski jumper. Landing in a shower of sparks, the heavy SUV bounced and rolled like a boat in a storm.

Lionel choked. Maxine screamed. Blaine laughed, swinging his head toward them. "Do I have your attention now, hotshots?"

"Watch out!" Maxine yelled, pointing to a car in the intersection. Blaine twisted to the right, broadsiding the Prius's front bumper and sending it spinning. The Range Rover shook with rivet-like shudders as he slammed the brakes. Lionel saw an oncoming truck through the shaking windshield. The truck swerved and they sideswiped it. The SUV's side mirror popped like a champagne cork, showering shattered glass and plastic.

Lionel saw Blaine's black-rimmed eyes bouncing in the rearview mirror, looking back.

"Does the SEAL drive a green SUV?"

"I don't know."

"His car is black," Maxine said. "Jesus, look forward, Blaine!"

"Liars. He's following us."

A red light appeared ahead. Fast-moving traffic crossed the intersection.

"Stop!" yelled Maxine and Lionel simultaneously. Blaine ran the light, leaning into a left turn and screeching rubber. Cars swerved and collided, the thud of pounding metal followed by the high pitch of breaking glass.

He's driving like a runaway Meth addict. Is he cranked up? Lionel wondered. Then in the distance he saw the Golden Gate Bridge.

Blaine looked over at Maxine. "Awesome driving, huh?"

"Insane. We should pull over and talk," she pleaded.

"We'll talk on my terms, when I say so."

"If you take off this combination lock and strap I could breathe better."

"Too bad."

Lionel tapped the back of Maxine's seat four times. She turned her head. He tapped it four more times. "Blaine, this combination lock is strapped too tight."

"Forget it," Blaine responded. He looked in the mirror. "That damn SEAL. He is going to get you killed. Call him Maxine and tell him to back off."

"Who?"

"The SEAL. That stupid Navy SEAL."

"I don't know where he is and I don't have a phone. You smashed it. Besides, I think he is at the police station downtown."

"Nice try. The jerk is following me." He pounded the dashboard with the butt of his pistol.

"Okay, you want to race across the bridge, do you?"

"What?" Maxine said.

"The SEAL. He wants to race. Watch this."

Blaine sped up to seventy-five and quickly came up to the bumper of the car ahead. A pickup truck was in the middle lane and a moving van in the far right. He was boxed in.

He looked in the rearview mirror and frowned.

Suddenly Blaine pulled into the oncoming lane, knocking over the yellow cones in the center divide, scattering them across lanes.

"What are you doing?" Lionel rasped, his throat choked against the ratchet strap. "This is suicide. Pull back into our lane."

"Shut up or I'll shoot," Blaine yelled, waving the gun back at him. The Range Rover pitched dangerously.

They reached ninety, then one hundred miles per hour. Through the windshield Lionel saw oncoming cars frantically moving into the adjacent lane. They blurred past, rocking the SUV.

Maxine put a hand up next to her head and made a zero sign with her fingers. Lionel grunted.

Three cars abreast came at them. The car directly in front of them had nowhere to go, and slammed on his brakes, tires smoking. The Range Rover thundered forward. At the last possible moment Blaine cursed and swung right, blasting through more yellow lane dividers, scattering them like yellow kick-the-can toys. Lionel was flung sideways as the ratchet strap cut into his neck.

Lionel heard sirens behind them. In the mirror he saw two police cars, lights flashing, racing in pursuit.

The Range Rover flew by the north tower of the Golden Gate Bridge at one hundred twenty miles per hour, the metal expansion joints buzzing like zippers under their wheels.

Blaine swerved to the right, tires grabbing and body swaying, narrowly making the Sausalito exit. The police flew past the exit, blocked by a tour bus. The SUV shuddered and skidded on the ramp. They slid through the stop sign, toward the columns supporting the bridge ramp above. They jerked to a stop a few feet from the massive concrete buttress.

Lionel sucked in air like a gasping geriatric. He saw Maxine put a trembling hand on the dashboard toward Blaine. "We'll all die if you continue to drive like this," she said firmly.

He ignored her, turned left and stomped on the gas. They emerged from under the bridge, wheels spinning, and started to climb the cliff road winding up the looming headlands. Unlike the bridge, the road was deserted.

Maxine put three fingers up next to her head. Lionel grunted again.

"What the hell is going on?"

Maxine looked over in alarm. "What?"

"That damn SEAL. Now he has cops with him." Furious, Blaine accelerated, swinging recklessly around the curves.

Maxine clung desperately, signaling quickly. Lionel grunted again. His arms were stretched out behind him, over the seat. He struggled to spin the combination lock, lining up the numbers Maxine was giving him with the center notch. The SUV lurched as they coiled higher up the headlands.

Lionel could see they were well above the top of the towers of the bridge now. The boats below in the Pacific looked tiny. To his right, a sloping rock grade followed the road, carved out of the hillside.

The SUV was racing at sixty miles per hour. The road flattened. They were alongside the top of the ridge, Lionel realized. Just ahead the road bent sharply left to start its descent. *Hurry!*

Maxine flashed five fingers then quickly followed with two. Lionel was confused. There was only one more digit, not two.

"Lionel, what are you doing back there? Put your arms forward." Blaine was staring into the rearview mirror. He pointed the gun backward.

Maxine flashed five fingers then two more, quickly. He got it. *It's a seven.* "Now, Lionel. Arms forward!" *Screw him.* He moved the last combination to seven.

The shock of blasting through the metal gate cracked the windshield. Lionel saw the road blur to their left. *Blaine missed the turn!* The SUV pounded up against the hillside, jamming Lionel backward. The nose shook violently as it climbed. Blaine dropped the gun, struggling with the vibrating steering wheel.

Lionel yanked hard and the lock popped open.

"Seatbelt!" He yanked the strap loops from around his neck. As he threw his right arm over Maxine, she released her belt. The Range Rover tilted dangerously. Lionel dragged Maxine backward over the seat. They fell together against the left rear door. Lionel frantically scraped for the latch. As the SUV rolled sideways, his door popped open, and they launched out backward.

The SUV spun downward, the streamline shape rolling perfectly. A dip in the hillside popped the vehicle up, hanging momentarily.

Then it began cartwheeling like a toy truck end over end. A burnt orange cloud churned up behind. It dove into free fall a hundred feet above the water. Below the SUV a bare rock stack extended upward from the ocean, surrounded by pelicans. The vehicle glided and slowly flipped. With an enormous crash the SUV's roof flattened around the shape of the rock, exploding in fire.

Lionel and Maxine clung to each other on the hillside above, watching.

"How'd you know the combo?" he rasped.

"I guessed. The number 0317 is his birthday. St. Patrick's Day."

He nodded.

Then, with trembling fingers, Lionel dialed his phone.

"Hello, Leah? It's Lionel. Don't run the photos. And you'll want to record this conversation."

54

FRIDAY, APRIL 4TH

Lionel opened his eyes. He was home, in his apartment. Not a hotel. But the bright edge rimming the shades suggested it was much later than normal. Then he smelled her. And felt her warmth next to him, asleep. He turned to see a mass of black hair cascading down the pillow. A bare shoulder peeked from under the white sheets.

Ahh. He didn't want to leave. Lie in bed. Romp around. Eventually shower and get dressed.

Then his stomach tightened. The Schwab and Young banquet was tonight, announcing the Big Disrupter Award.

"We've done everything possible. What can I change now?" Lionel realized he was talking out loud.

"Huh? Are you okay?" she murmured.

He didn't mean to awaken her.

A slender arm reached over, patting his chest. The fingers intertwined in his hand. They rubbed slowly.

He quickly forgot everything except the silky skin under the sheets.

He pulled the sheet down, little by little. She was on her side. He marveled at the smooth shoulder. The curve down to her waist and up her hip. He cupped the softness of her bottom, gently squeezing. Why did this part arouse him so much? He reached around and felt her mound, amazed by the thickness. He plowed his fingers through, exploring and tugging.

"I'm going to get a Brazilian."

"Don't you dare. I love it."

"You don't run your fingers through my other hair like that."

"It's different."

"It tickles," she giggled. She rolled over facing him. "What did you like the most?"

"About . . . the last six months?"

One thick eyebrow arched, with the look. Then Maxine said, "About the last six hours."

"Hmm. The beginning was delightful. Wait, um, the middle was terrific. No, no it would have to be the spectacular conclusion."

He propped another big pillow under his head. He lay facing her on his side. She lay on her back, the sheets covering only their tangled feet.

He lightly rubbed his fingertips down her abdomen. As she teased a hand over his hip, he groaned.

She hummed softly. "Mmm. I want details."

He breathed in jerks. His eyes were closed.

"Maybe I better stop touching."

"No, please, it's good." He spoke in short gasps.

"Then tell me the details."

"Ahh. When we first got reacquainted. The beginning. Head to toe. Licking from your belly button down to the jungle."

"You got pretty lost in the jungle."

"It was the best. I seemed to wake up your tiger."

"You did."

"And a wet tiger it was."

"Well, you had a very wet fountain, yourself."

"Perfect beginning. And then playing cowgirl and bucking bronco."

"When I rode you?"

"Wow. When you threw your shoulders back and shook your hair. And arched until your waving mane stroked my legs."

"You felt that brushing you?"

"Oh yes. And everything else that was on parade."

"You like me on top."

"I do."

"But the finale. Ohh," he groaned, "the finale."

"You didn't know I could do the splits like that?"

"Very erotic."

"Mmm. Wrapping my legs on your shoulders like a jungle gym."

"I couldn't hold back. But it was your eyes that were the best."

"My eyes?"

"When they bulged big and white at the ultimate."

She giggled. "Was I too loud?"

"There is no such thing."

She arched her back. She gasped once, then again, held it, and then let out a long, soft gliding tone, like she was back home after a long trip.

Lionel watched with pleasure. Her fingertips were driving him crazy. So sensitive. It almost hurt.

Maxine eased her hand away and rolled over. She stood, picked up her white terrycloth robe, and pulled it around her nakedness.

"Wait."

She backed up toward the bathroom, blowing kisses at Lionel.

"No," he pleaded. "Come back. Just for a minute."

"Wonderful dessert. Now it's time for a shower."

As she opened the bathroom door, he jumped up. "Then we're having one together."

***

An hour later, as they dressed, Maxine checked her messages.

"Jacob called. Hopefully that's good news."

He saw the worry on her face. The reminder of Jacob being shot by Blaine brought back heavy memories. He sighed. "If he called, he must be feeling better. Let's find out."

She motioned him closer. He saw her hands shaking as she dialed.

"Hello, Maxine." Jacob's voice sounded thin.

"Jacob. It's . . . it's good to hear your voice."

"I'm still here. As irascible as ever, my wife and nurses inform me."

"I'd like to see you. Are you at the hospital, in intensive care?"

"Oh, Lord no. I brought intensive care to my home. The view and food are better."

"I see. Well, when will they allow visitors?"

"Look Maxine, I'm not letting anyone come by now. I don't want to bother people. Or be bothered by some morbid hand-wringing parade. But I do want to talk to you. And Lionel."

"Of course. We feel so guilty."

Jacob's voice grew louder. "For God's sake, the man was a lunatic. Don't blame yourselves. And now he is in the past tense, fortunately." He began coughing. Then he cleared his throat. "No, I want to talk about something else."

"What?" She looked at Lionel curiously.

He wheezed, "When can you come by?"

"When is best for you?"

"I'm obviously not in shape to go to the award banquet tonight."

"Of course not."

"I'll probably be sleeping like a baby by seven p.m." With a gasp he added, "But I'd like to see you beforehand."

"Is thirty minutes from now, okay?"

"I'm not going anywhere."

***

Inspector Chang focused on his computer keyboard, blocking the outbursts from the surrounding desks at the Mission Street police station. His ringing desk phone went unanswered. But when his cell displayed the call from Colorado, he picked up.

"Sheriff Masterson, I've been meaning to call you."

"Good day, Inspector. From what I heard, you've been putting some serious time in the saddle. Do you have a little breathing room now?"

"I do for you. I'd like to compare notes."

"Appreciate that. At this end, I'm afraid I haven't made any progress with Igor Vasilchenko and the avalanche."

"He has been busy out here. He blew out the entire floor of his apartment building with a trap of C4 wired to his computers.

Unfortunately, he is still at large. His boss, Anthony Fanachi, and two of his fellow henchmen, Nicco and Tomas, are dead."

"I got the email you forwarded with the details on the shoot-out and explosion. Looks like you and Trig had some tight ones there."

"Turns out, along with a suspect named Calabrese, Fanachi's operatives were responsible for the deaths of Jan Swenson and Raj Singh, and multiple attempts on Lionel and Maxine."

"What was the motive?"

"We suspect Fanachi was a paid assassin for Hank Welcher. He's a VC who wanted his investment to win the Big. A company called SocialLending. It would provide a huge return for his portfolio, and allow him to raise new funds and generate fees."

"They went to a lot of trouble to make these appear as accidents. Seems like a sophisticated and expensive operation."

Inspector Chang's desk phone started ringing again. He ignored it. "We've seized Fanachi's laptop. Most of it is encrypted, but the files we could access indicate he is into cyber crime. My theory is he was actually doing the hits for Welcher, in order to blackmail him into becoming a cyber crime source. Welcher does a lot of business with high tech companies, and has access to a wealth of intellectual property. Google, Facebook, Apple, and the like. To me, that was Fanachi's end game. They sometimes used code names of Alpha and Zebra for secrecy."

"Do you have Welcher in custody?"

"No. That's the problem I'm working on now. The night Fanachi was shot, Welcher was unarmed, and he has consistently claimed he was visiting Fanachi as an investor. Evidently, Welcher and Fanachi used encrypted phones, so we have no call records. It may get down to getting lucky and finding some financial records on Fanachi's laptop that aren't encrypted."

"Follow the money?" Masterson asked.

"Yes, if we can. Otherwise, the only two Fanachi operators we know of that might incriminate Welcher are Igor and Calabrese. Both at large."

"What a puzzle. We were just one little thread here in Telluride. But what about Blaine Latrell, the guy who hired Jake the Rake, who planted those drugs in Lionel's desk? I read he went off a cliff in an SUV?"

"Wrapped around a rock and burned to a crisp. So far his employer Axelwright Capital won't let us near his business files, citing client confidentiality. But we discovered a detailed personal diary that he kept at home."

"Good find. So did Blaine work for Fanachi?"

"We haven't discovered any evidence of that. The diary swings back and forth emotionally, but I get the sense he was failing at work. There was desperation as his investments floundered, ruining his chances to become a partner and make the big payoff. John Anderson, his boss, confirmed that in my conversation with him. What isn't clear, is if Anderson put him up to this."

"But wouldn't Blaine have done well if DV won the Big?"

"That's what I didn't understand, either. Until I read the end of the diary, and saw him unraveling."

"How so?"

"It turns out Lionel infuriated Hank Welcher by getting a thirty-million-dollar investment from Havermyer and Blaine in twenty-four hours. It was an ego thing, because Welcher expected to get control of Double Vision at ten cents on the dollar when it was near bankruptcy."

"A lot of drama for people making so much money. Don't they make millions and millions?"

"It wasn't enough for Welcher, evidently. His ego seemed to grow in size with the piles of money."

"Yep, I've seen that out here, too."

"Anyway, Welcher hated being outsmarted by Lionel. So he ridiculed Blaine's boss, John Anderson, for investing when Lionel was so close to bankruptcy. Anderson felt duped by Lionel, turned against him, and pressured Blaine. Blaine knew this was his last chance to avoid getting fired. If he could have dumped Lionel and helped his VC firm get a bigger piece of Double Vision while winning the Big, he'd have been a hero."

"So that explains why Blaine had Jake the Rake plant the coke in Lionel's desk in Telluride."

Two heavyset bikers dropped into chairs at the desk next to Chang, complaining loudly. Chang glared at them and drew closer to the phone.

"Yes. And, why Blaine also had him drugged with roofies at the party during the BevGlobe conference. Blaine wanted two incidents where Lionel appeared guilty of moral turpitude, so he could be forced out of his majority stock position."

"Wouldn't that typically involve a time-consuming legal battle?"

"Blaine figured the Big gave him leverage over Lionel. At the end he got desperate and tried to expose Lionel by sending the pictures to the newspaper, hoping he'd resign to save the company's chances of winning the Big."

"So it was all about money?"

"Well, money, and the fear of failure. And Blaine's delusions about a relationship with Maxine."

"Damn. I'm glad Reddi didn't get more involved in this. That scary avalanche and cowardly rape attempt were bad enough."

"Is the rape case proceeding against that BodyHamr guy?"

"Gonzo Sonders? The bites in his butt pretty much marked him at the scene of the crime. It was jealous rage and cruel desire at its worst. He should get locked up for a while."

"I'm sure glad Reddi brought in Trig."

"How'd he figure into this, Inspector?"

"No better partner in a gunfight."

"He struck me as solid. Did any of his spook background help out?"

Chang hesitated a moment. "I don't think we'll ever know, Sheriff. But it sure was good having him on our side."

Masterson chuckled. "Well then, we'll leave it at that. Let me know if I can help as the case against Welcher proceeds. And I'll keep my nose in the air for Igor Vasilchenko. Sure like to pin him."

"Will do, Sheriff. I'll stay in touch."

***

"You weren't kidding about bringing the hospital to you."

"Don't get me started. Every machine in this room, every circuit, connects to a backup diesel generator. All of San Francisco could be dark following an earthquake, but you'd see a glow from my little room here."

Lionel looked at the silver monitors tracking blood pressure, oxygen, heart and respiratory rates. White equipment cabinets stood nearby, laminated labels inventorying the devices and supplies. A stainless steel gurney was rolled against the wall.

On the opposite wall, curtains fluttered, moving with the fresh ocean breeze. He walked closer, drawn by the view of the bay and Golden Gate. Pushing the curtain aside, he could see across to the cliff where it all ended for Blaine. And nearly for them. A chill hit him. And Jacob too, shot here in his own house. Thank God that bullet missed his heart.

An alarm chirped, and Lionel looked back from the window. Next to Jacob's bed was a rolling table with three large LCD monitors, one of which was sounding off. Lionel walked over and noticed news stories, stock prices, currency exchange rates, and other financial data scrolling by. Something blinked in orange.

"These don't look like medical vital signs to me."

"No, you're right. Those are financial vital signs. Just keeping busy. Now come sit down, please."

Maxine and Lionel sat on two chairs and rolled to Jacob's side.

"I want to let you in on a little secret. Totally confidential." His bushy white eyebrows rose with emphasis.

Maxine and Lionel nodded, holding hands. "Of course."

"Although I did not ask, I have been told that Double Vision is winning the award tonight."

Winning. We're winning! Really!? Damn, she's going to break my fingers, thought Lionel.

"Are you positive!?" Maxine asked, leaning closer to Jacob.

"It is a certainty, unless the universe collapses between now and seven p.m."

Maxine and Lionel looked at each other and jumped from their chairs. Lionel let out a yell as Maxine screamed. She dove into his arms. Then they danced around the room.

Eventually they stopped spinning. Lionel looked at Havermyer. He was stroking his beard, looking at them with a smile anchored in the middle of all the white. They sat down, squeezing hands.

"How do you know this?" Maxine pressed, eyes shining large. "Is it because you can't come to the awards?"

"It's a little more than that."

He took a breath and put a hand up. "Now you know I have absolutely nothing to do with selecting the award. That is one hundred percent Jules Longsworth and four other judges from Schwab and Young. There is no 'wink-wink' here. This is a rigorous procedure. I have no part of voting on or influencing the winner."

"We know."

"But, after their final vote today, the judges informed me. In part, because I can't be there tonight. But mostly because my wife Deborah and I are the anonymous donors for the Big."

They dropped their hands and stared at him. "What!? But we always thought it was Melinda and Bill Gates. Or George Soros. Maybe Mark Zuckerberg."

"Sorry to disappoint you. But it was Deborah's idea. She talked me into it."

"Are you kidding me? I am so incredibly proud of you," said Maxine.

She got up and gave him a gentle hug. "Thank you. And thank Deborah. You worked really hard to make that money."

"You're welcome. Now go out and do something amazing in the world. Disrupt your industry—for the better."

He dismissed them with a wave. "I'm pretty tired. And you have a big evening ahead of you. And act surprised, damn it!"

***

Maxine and Lionel walked out of his house arm-in-arm, practically skipping on the front sidewalk.

"Lionel, I'm thinking about a plan."

"You always are. I love it."

"What if we share some of this money with the two companies whose leaders were killed? In memory of them. You know, Jan and Raj of Sweet Boomerang and Step-by-Step?"

"I like where you're going, Maxine."

She kissed him on the cheek impulsively, tugging on his arm.

Then his phone rang, the ringtone familiar. "It's Reddi."

"We can't tell her yet," Maxine warned.

Lionel nodded.

"Reddi, how are you?"

"We're, I mean I'm, great."

"What's up?"

"Trig and I are walking Wolfie right now. We're saying goodbye to her and Telluride for a while."

"Why? What do you mean?"

"We're headed to New Zealand. And Chile. I'm going to ski the endless winter, entering the slopestyle events down there. And Trig's coming. Cool, huh?"

This was her dream. She was doing it. With Trig. "I'm so jealous."

"Yeah. Um, Trig and I are kind of a couple now."

So it was official. She deserved him. "Congratulations. And I meant I was jealous of the skiing. Not Trig. You and he are a great match. Maxine predicted that."

"Yeah, she pretty much figures everything out. How is she?"

"She and I are kind of a couple now too."

"That's no surprise. Duh. About time."

"You too, huh?"

"What do you mean?"

"Hugo had been bugging me about coming out of the closet. At first I thought it was about you and me. But actually, he always meant me and Maxine."

"He's a smart little wizard."

Maxine was listening. She pulled on Lionel's sleeve, smiling.

"So Wolfie is staying with friends?"

"Yep. Kodiak is taking care of her. I'm closing the shop for now. I think I'll get some additional sponsors, for some more cash. But I'll still do tons for DV."

"That's good. But . . . tell you what. Get me your new number when you land in New Zealand. There is going to be a lot to talk about, regarding DV expansion and sponsorship."

"Okay, cool. I'd really like that. Congrats to you and Maxine. And good luck tonight. I've got a great feeling."

"You know it. Best to you and Trig. We're very pumped for you."

Lionel hung up. He took Maxine's hand and they started walking.

Maxine pulled her face close to Lionel's. "I was thinking," she said. "What if we got a wolfdog too?"

The End

CONNECT WITH THE AUTHOR

What do you think? Do you have something to say about your favorite character? Or scene? Or an aspect that drove you nuts!? Maybe a comment about social entrepreneurs, the Big Disrupter Award, or cyber technology? We welcome it all.

We encourage you to visit the website where you purchased the book to comment or review. Goodreads or other reading groups are other ideal interactive feedback venues. Or come visit the author's site or others listed below with your thoughts and comments.

Thanks for joining the journey!
Paul Markun

Website *www.paulmarkun.com*
Twitter *www.twitter.com/pmarkun*
Linkedin *www.linkedin.com/paulmarkun*
Facebook *www.facebook.com/thebigdisrupter*

ABOUT THE AUTHOR

Paul Markun grew up an entrepreneur and dreamer, starting with his first paper route at age nine in the Canal Zone of Panama.

Living in Telluride, Colorado, he started four companies with best friends before he was 24, including Fly By Night Builders, The Illusions Company, High Country Trekkers . . . . You get the idea—great names, cool ideas, not much income.

He moved to Silicon Valley, got more education and tech experience, and started SoftIRON Systems and Fullspeed Networks, and rode the wave of the late 1990s to success, selling both companies to Fortune 500 companies expanding in technology markets.

In the first decade of the 2000s, he joined fellow entrepreneurs to lead marketing for Netcordia, which later IPO'd as Infoblox (NYSE: BLOX). He also ran marketing for Sitecore, a web software company, growing it 10 X from an $8 million fledgling niche provider to an established global corporation. Paul continues to be involved with emerging companies to this day.

Paul met his wife Rachel, an attorney, when he was 18 and she was even younger at the University of Chicago. Their fountains of inspiration are their two sons and a daughter, near the ages of our leading characters in *The Big Disrupter*.

This is his first novel.